WHEN IT
RAINS

Doris
and The community
of Lott
5/27/17

KJ Ten Eyck

KJ TEN EYCK

PAGE PUBLISHING, INC.
New York, NY

First originally published by Page Publishing, Inc. 2017

This is a work of fiction. All the characters, organizations, and events portrayed in this novel are products of the author's imagination or are used fictitiously.

ISBN 978-1-63568-209-0 (Paperback)
ISBN 978-1-63568-210-6 (Digital)

Printed in the United States of America

This book is dedicated to all the wonderful people who have touched my life both now and in the past. I would like to thank my wonderful family for their love and support.
Thanks to RW for your faith in me to begin this new journey and the courage you gave me to continue.

CHAPTER 1

"What do you mean you're leaving?" Those words haunted her, held her, and begged her to return. Return to what?

The wind whipped past her, dragging on the pony tail Steph had made of her long brown hair, as if determined to loosen and set it free. The wind persisted, tugging and pulling until soft, fine trendils came free from the band holding it in place. Steph ignored the wind as she tried to store in her mind the sights and sounds around her, hoping they would drive out the words that haunted her.

Boston had always meant home to Steph, she'd lived here all her life. It had been a fun and exciting city to explore and live in. There was always something new to discover around the corner or down the next street. With its eclectic variety of stores and malls, Steph knew she could shop every day for a year and always find something unique and exciting.

The Boston Harbor, with its bracing sea air, was Steph's favorite place to visit. Bustling with the activity of ships coming and going, it never failed to infuse her with excitement. Steph loved Boston, feeling proud to be a part of it in her own small way and she couldn't imagine living anywhere else, until now.

Change was not something Stephanotis 'Steph' Weatherby handled well. Like a storm, death had swooped in taking the people most dear to her and in its wake, leaving her life in shambles and forever changed.

Steph knew she had to leave as soon as possible once she made her decision or she would lose her nerve. Something was pulling her, driving her to leave Boston and begin again.

A fortnight from the day she'd made her decision, Steph now found herself standing on the wharf of the Boston Harbor, for the last time. She was saying good-bye to her hometown. She fought back tears as she thought back over the past two weeks.

Teaching at a private school in Boston had given Steph security and comfort. She had worked hard and enjoyed the time spent with her students. The dean of the school was surprised then shocked when she told him she was leaving. By the time she had given him her written notice and left the room, she was shaking from the effort it took not to give into his demands that she stay until the end of the school year. After that she spent long hours finalizing the student grades and clearing out her classroom. The school had been her second home, keeping her anchored and focused. Steph found herself in tears every time she thought about leaving the students with a substitute teacher for their last week of class.

As she took in the images of the Harbor one more time, Steph prayed for peace, hope and a fresh start. Turning away at last, saddened and disappointed, she knew in her heart she would not have that here, the memories were too strong and too painful to face. Everywhere she went there were memories of the joy and happiness she had lost.

Steph found herself relieved to leave behind the people she had once believed to be her friends at the school and her church. Steph found their criticism and unkind comments about her abilities to survive outside of the city hurtful and cruel. They were right, she knew nothing about running a farm but she didn't have many choices. It was clear to her that they would never understand but it didn't stop the pain in her heart when she realized they wouldn't make the effort to try. How could she explain to them that everywhere she went she was flooded by painful memories, memories that sprang up taunting her, reminding her that she was now alone?

Once again Steph found herself leaning on the friendship of the handful of people who had remained by her side in the difficulties of the past couple of years. It was their friendship and encouragement that gave her the strength to make her decision and follow it through. This small circle of friends, people like Keri Hall and Betty Brown, had seen their own share of disappointment but they had risen above their circumstances, finding joy in the lives they were leading. Their stories gave Steph the hope that she too would find her way back to the peace and contentment she once felt but for now, she knew she had to take charge of her future and embrace her heritage.

Walking slowly back to where she had parked, Steph promised herself that she would some day return to her beloved Harbor but for now she was headed for a new beginning, searching for the peace she knew she deserved. She had come to terms with the fact that love may never come her way and she almost preferred it that way. After all, love was painful and she'd had enough pain to last her a lifetime. She'd learn to live alone, finding solace in the responsibilities her new life would hold for her.

With determination she brought her thoughts back to the present as she turned on the engine and began the slow process of merging into traffic. Driving along, she began reviewing the route she would take to Ohio, where the farm and her new life awaited her. As Boston faded into the background of her rearview mirrors, Steph found it easier to relax and began to look forward to the unknown that awaited her.

After a natural storm the air is full of sunshine and hope, wiped fresh and clean from the rains that had swept the dirt and filth back to the earth. Steph longed for that hope and sunshine to come once again into her life.

*   *   *

The farm had been in her family for generations, an obscure place Steph had only heard about in stories. Ohio always seemed too far away to be real, just another place she talked about in her classroom, but here she was.

The trip itself had been uneventful with the weather clear until they crossed the state line and entered the "Buckeye State." Coming out of nowhere, the storm had forced her to drive at a slower speed, adding more time to their journey. The rain finally drizzled to a stop a few miles away from her destination. Steph hoped it was a sign that she was on the right path and had made the right decision.

Driving through town, Steph tried to take in the town that would be her new home. She smiled as she drove through the town square. Flowers were planted in the center, brightening up the main green island. Turning the U-Haul onto Capital Boulevard, Steph kept a practiced eye out for traffic as she scanned the buildings they passed.

"There's not much traffic on this street. It seems empty after all the traffic we've been driving through on the main road doesn't it, Misti?" Steph's voice echoed in the silent cab. "Let's see . . . we're on the second block. We should be getting close to the lawyer's office. The letter said it's in the third block . . . on the right. Oh, there it is, 'Wilber and Associates." Steph sighed with relief as she parked the truck in the empty spaces at the front of the building. "We made it, Misti. We're in Ohio."

"Woof."

Steph laughed at Misti's response. The sable colored Shetland sheepdog stood on the seat of the truck cab looking out the passenger window. Opening her own window, Steph checked the temperature outside. It was still cool, thanks to the recent rain. She left the windows open just a few inches to allow in fresh air for Misti. Steph ran a comb through her hair and checked her makeup in the rearview mirror.

Climbing out of the cab, she went around to the passenger door. Carefully opening the door, Steph reached in and picked up the little dog, making sure the leash was secure. "Okay, Misti, we'll stretch your legs before I go in and take care of business." Steph walked Misti up and down the sidewalk since there was no grassy area nearby. Returning to the truck, Steph gave Misti fresh water to drink before putting her back into the cab.

"Good girl, Misti. You're in charge of the truck until I get back. I know I can count on you."

Straightening her T-shirt, Steph squared her shoulders, took a deep breath and turned away. As she took her first step, she looked up at the building for the first time. The fresh white paint around the door and large front window created a sharp contrast to the cold, gray, stone blocks of the three-story structure.

Wow, this place reminds me of the mausoleum in the cemetery where Mom and Dad are buried. Steph grimaced as the thoughts raced through her mind. *I have to stop thinking this way. I have to accept they're gone. I need to let go of the guilt. I need to forget about Fred too, that's in the past. I have to believe I'm doing the right thing. Everything's going to be okay.*

"Let's get this over with." Steph winced as the dread in her voice echoed in her ears. The reality of what she was about to do sliced through her heart, cutting away the last pieces of her past life. There was no going back, she was committed now. Bracing herself Steph began to take a step forward. Her feet felt as if they were chained to the ground. Her legs quivered; her bones were like jelly. With supreme effort, she began taking one step at a time toward the building, spurred on by the embarrassment that someone might see her stumbling along.

By the time she reached the door she was shaking. Her courage and resolve were draining away, leaving her weak and scared. Steph stopped to steady herself as she fought down the impulse to turn and run back to the truck cab.

"Come on Steph, you can do this. You taught a bunch of middle school kids for years. You can do this! All you have to do is sign some papers and then you're on your way." Steph paused as she heard the fear in her voice. Taking a deep breath, she tried to focus on why she was there, then she pulled open the curtained front door.

Pausing in the doorway to allow her eyes time to adjust to the change in light, she noticed the smell of fresh brewed coffee mixed with a hint of lemon polish and floor cleaner. She didn't realize the unique scent of stale fries, wet dog and gasoline was clinging to her until she closed the door. The memory flashed through her mind that it was raining at their last stop when she had bought food and filled up the gas tank. She shrugged her shoulders. *I guess it's too late now to think about changing clothes since I'm here. I just hope it's not too strong.* Crossing her fingers, she stepped further into the front room of the law office.

Steph knew she had to maintain control. Swallowing the bile in her throat, she closed her eyes and took several deep breaths, letting them out slowly. She began to think about her sessions with Dr. Waltzer, willing herself to relax. Determined not to be afraid of the unknown, she slowly opened her eyes and forced herself to look around.

The room was decorated in an old fashioned, masculine decor. Padded, wooden backed chairs stood like soldiers along the left wall. Magazines were fanned out on low wooden tables within easy reach. Across the room was a small desk holding a computer and telephone, obviously the receptionist's desk. A coffee machine sat on a cabinet against the wall behind the receptionist's area. Heavy velvet curtains, their rich burgundy color beginning to fade, draped the front window by the door through which she just entered. Centered in the back wall was an open doorway. Steph could see a hallway she assumed lead to additional offices and storage areas.

A man of medium height, wearing a tailored suit came through the doorway, muttering and shuffling papers. Afraid to move, Steph cleared her throat to get his attention.

*   *   *

Stanley Wilbur, Junior, looked up from his papers to see a tall brunette, wearing a rumpled T-shirt and blue jeans, standing in the waiting area. His eyes took in her slight, curvy figure, but the frustration and fear that was evident in her eyes caused him to pause. Looking her over again, he noticed the weariness in her posture. *Obviously, this isn't the person I'm waiting for. Oh well,* he thought. *I might as well help. It may turn out to be an interesting case. At least I won't be bored waiting for the schoolteacher. I just hope she can afford my fees.*

"Please have a seat. I'll be with you in a moment." Stanley realized his voice sounded harsher than he intended. Making a conscious effort to soften his tone, he spoke again. "Please excuse me, I'll be right back." Briskly he strode back through the hallway to his office, placing the papers to the side on his desk. Taking a survey in the mirror on his office wall, he made a quick check to be sure his hair was neat and his tie was straight.

Plastering a professional smile on his face, he returned to the reception area. Walking briskly toward the woman, he was disturbed to see she had not sat to wait as directed. He was used to having his instructions followed and irritation crept back into his voice as he held out his hand. "I'm Stanley Wilbur. How may I be of assistance?"

"I'm Stephanotis 'Steph' Weatherby. I'm here about my Great-Aunt Hyacinth's farm. I believe you were expecting me." Staying back a step, she shook his outstretched hand hoping he wouldn't notice her unusual cologne.

Stanley stared at Steph.

"You said there was still 'a little business' we needed to go over." Steph tried to keep her own irritation at his brisk behavior out of her voice. Anger replaced her anxiety and caused her to stand up straighter.

Realizing his mistake, Stanley gave a mental shake and forced himself to relax. He had been expecting an older woman, closer to fifty, but here was a woman who couldn't be much more than thirty, if that. Stanley swallowed his irritation. This woman obviously mistook him for his father so she hadn't been told he wouldn't be meeting with her. Once again his father had kept the information to himself, making Stanley look foolish when he met with the client. Fixing his smile in place, he decided to make the best of the situation. "Well, I hope you will forgive me, I was expecting someone older myself when my father said Hyacinth's heir was coming. He said you would be stopping by to sign papers and get the keys. Please, come into my office and we'll go over what my father must have referred to as 'a little business.' " Turning he began walking toward the doorway.

Steph took a deep breath and walked across the soft burgundy carpet covering the center of the dark, wooden floor. She mentally crossed her fingers, hoping she appeared more confident than she felt as she quietly followed him through the hallway to his office.

Passing a mirror just inside the office doorway, she noticed her reflection and gasped. She had checked her makeup before leaving the cab and in the dim light, she felt satisfied with her appearance. Under the bright office lights, the larger mirror showed the dark circles under heavy lidded eyes. She didn't realize her face appeared so thin and pale. Self-consciously she put a hand up to her face. *Okay, I haven't been sleeping well or eating a lot, but wow, that doesn't look like me.* To stop herself from dwelling on her reflection, she moved further into the room and turned to the man at the desk. "What do you need me to sign?"

Stanley paused a moment, something was tickling his nose, a smell he couldn't quite recognize. It struck him as odd that he hadn't noticed it before. To cover his discomfort, Stanley went to a small refrigerator in his office. "Please have a seat." Stanley motioned to the two chairs at the front of his desk. "Would you like a cup of coffee or some cold water?"

"Water would be wonderful, thank you." Steph sat on the nearest chair in front of the desk. She placed her purse on the floor near her feet.

Stanley handed Steph a chilled bottle of water and a glass before opening one for himself. As he sat down at his desk, Stanley made a mental note to check with the cleaning staff on Tuesday morning about their services. Stanley forced himself to forget about the odor and to concentrate on why he was there.

Steph accepted it gratefully hoping it would help settle her churning stomach. The plastic bottle cracked when she gripped it. Embarrassed, she forced herself to relax as she tried to control her nerves. Steph inhaled deeply and released her breath slowly as she sat.

Concentrating, she carefully opened the bottle, poured the water into the glass and took a sip. The cool water quenched her dry throat. Taking another sip, she felt stronger, more refreshed. Intent on the simple task of drinking, she was startled when she realized Stanley was talking to her. She forced herself to focus on what he was saying.

"Please understand it was my father with whom you have been communicating. He is handling Hyacinth's estate but could not be here to meet with you. I hope you will accept his apologies, he and Mother had made plans for this weekend months ago. When we learned you would be arriving today, we made sure everything would be ready for you to sign."

Picking up a thick folder and a pen from the counter behind his desk, Stanley began looking for the papers needing her signature. He spread the papers out between them. "Here's a pen for you to use. If you'll just sign here… here… and here." Using his own pen, he pointed to each place for her to sign. He paused to turn a page. "I can go over all of this with you, but my father said he sent a copy of the papers to your attorney, Mr. Young. I understand Mr. Young was to review them with you. Do you have any questions?"

"No, Mr. Young explained most of this. He also said I would be getting a copy of the papers after I signed them." Steph signed her name as Stanley continued to point out where her signature was needed. She glanced over the pages, trying to remember what Mr. Young told her. There'd been too many meetings with him when her father had died months ago and then after her mother's recent death. She always felt drained after each meeting.

"Here's your copy of the will and title to the land." Stanley carefully handed her a packet of papers. "Father had the house opened up, checked and verified to be habitable. The propane company filled the tank half full, so you should be okay for a while. You may want to check with them yourself once you're settled. Your neighbor, George Landsburg, has been leasing the land to farm and he's been caring for your livestock. His phone number is in the packet. If you wish, we can handle the arrangements to have him continue or if there is someone else you'd like to lease the land to, we can arrange that as well."

Steph sat up a little straighter.

"Is there much livestock to be cared for?"

Stanley paused, unsure of the best way to answer her. He decided to explain what he understood to be the situation and then she could get more information from his father later.

"I'm not sure what the exact count is right now. Landsburg gives us an accounting in the fall, after the crops have been harvested. Father usually handles that personally."

"I think we'll leave that as it is for now. I'll have to think about what I want to do and examine the possibilities."

"With the holiday on Monday, we usually close the office early on Fridays, which is why you're finding me in the office alone today." Stanley leaned back in his chair, relaxing as he smiled at Steph. "Please feel free to call me Stan, Miss Weatherby. It's a pleasure to have you as a client."

Steph cautiously returned the smile. "Thank you, Stan, please call me Steph." Starting to rise, she paused.

"Would it be possible for you to give me directions to the farm? I'm not sure which way it would be from here."

"Since the farm is not far out, just a few miles, I'll be glad to show you the way. I have a couple things to finish up and we can be on our way." Stan began sorting papers on his desk. He moved in and out of the office, keeping up a running conversation about the town and his own plans for the holiday weekend.

Steph couldn't keep the relief from her voice as they began talking about his plans, the town and local events. She was one step further into her new life and hoped she found someone she could count on if she needed help.

Feeling restless, Steph glanced at her watch then realized she and Stanley had been talking for over an hour. "I don't want to keep you any longer. I'm looking forward to seeing the farm, but can we first stop at a grocery store for some supplies? I need to get a few things for Misti and myself ."

Puzzled, Stanley sat down in the nearest chair. "Misti? You mean you left your friend out in the truck? You should have brought her in with you."

Laughing, she shook her head, "Misti's my dog and it's cool outside so she's fine in the truck. She thinks it's her job to guard it and she enjoys it. I just need to get a few staples from the store so we can begin to settle in."

Stanley was caught off guard. Rising to cover his embarrassment, he stood gazing at her. He gave himself a mental shake. "That will be fine." *What a lovely laugh she has. What's wrong with me? I saw a plainly dressed woman walk in and I misjudged her. My instincts were off the mark with this one. When she smiles her eyes shine. There's something about this woman. She's different, intriguing. Too bad I already have plans for the weekend.* "I'll just lock up here and bring my car around. We'll stop by the grocery store on our way."

"Thank you." Anticipation and excitement washed over Steph as she stood up with the deed in her hand. She owned a house! Her future was getting brighter!

Walking to the office door, Stanley gestured for her to lead the way. Following her out, he quickly locked up the office then headed out the back where his car was parked.

Coming around the block in his car, Stanley was relieved to see she was watching for him. Taking his time so she could get her bearings, he headed down the road.

As he drove, Stanley let his mind wander. In its usual meandering way, his mind settled on the strained relationship/partnership with his father.

Stanley Sr. had spent his life working in the thriving law practice that he reluctantly shared with his son. When he began working with his own father, it was a small business in a small town. A great many of his clients had been with the firm for generations like Hyacinth Weatherby and her family. When the big industrial companies began moving into the area, Stanley Sr. cultivated a lucrative relationship with the board of directors for one of the major companies. The business generated from the industrial client had helped the law office grow along with the town. It took a lot of hard work and dedication to keep up with the demand of the largest client while trying to keep in touch with the townspeople who also needed their services. Now the industrial companies were beginning to leave the area, moving to where they could get better tax breaks and pay cheaper wages. Stanley Sr. knew his client would soon follow the others, taking their business away. He had tried to encourage his son to cultivate his own clients and bring in new ones. He believed his son's inexperience and lack of drive would create problems for the firm. The worry it caused him was beginning to affect his health.

Stanley Jr. was well aware of his father's resentment toward his relaxed attitude about coming to work. Stanley Sr. couldn't fault his son's attire or demeanor, but he flaunted his inexperience in his face.

Considering himself a realist, Stanley Jr. did not intend to spend all his time working. He liked the things money could buy but he planned to enjoy his life. He and his father had numerous arguments about the hours Stanley Jr. worked. Stanley Sr., when he came to the office, kept to his routine of being the first to arrive and the last to leave. Stanley Jr. often allowed the staff members to open and close the office, preferring to spend his time on long lunches and late nights with his friends.

Stanley Jr. had brought the office into the technology age, purchasing state of the art computers and software. Stanley Jr. knew his father didn't appreciate his ability to handle business anywhere, even on the golf course. With the new systems and changes, Stanley Jr. tried to explain to his father it was no longer necessary to be in the office all the time. He was available by cellphone or web chat anytime, anywhere. As if to punish Stanley Jr., Stanley Sr. continued to keep track of the bigger clients, often turning them over to another staff attorney when he needed assistance. Stanley Jr. spent most of his time with the less demanding, routine clients. He wrote their wills, handled their traffic cases and assisted with new clients when he was in the office. It was demeaning to have to explain what he did every day at the weekly meetings with his father and the other two lawyers in the firm.

Remembering the last fight he'd had with his father about his retirement, Stanley Jr. was prepared for the worst when his father said he would have to handle today's appointment. His biggest fear was the client would expect him to go over every detail of the family history, something Stanley knew and cared very little about.

Steering the car around a corner, he reviewed in his mind what he learned about their new client. He knew from his father's notes she'd resigned from her teaching position at a private school. Stanley's father said she wanted to make a fresh start because of recent events in her life. Stanley still didn't know what those events were but he was sure his father knew.

Letting go of his first impression of Steph, Stanley had tried to learn more about her. Steph was not very forthcoming with information about herself, keeping her answers to his questions simple and mysterious. He smiled thinking how much fun it would be to get to know more about her.

Logan & Sons Grocery, just off the main road leading to the farm would have everything Steph needed. Once a small grocery store, the building had been expanded over the years. On its shelves could be found anything from canning supplies to gourmet cookware. In the wine section, the store sold imported wines along with wines from the local wineries. The owner stocked specialty foods and spices in an effort to compete with the large specialty stores in the nearby larger cities.

When Stanley turned off the road into the parking lot of a large grocery store, Steph followed slowly, letting her eyes sweep across the area trying to find the most suitable place to park. Out of a habit cultivated over the past few days, she pulled over to the far side of the lot, away from the traffic, but where there were trees for shade. While looking around to get her bearings, she applied hand sanitizer to her hands, hoping to mask more of the odor that clung to her. Checking the main door of the building, she noticed Stanley was standing there waiting for her.

"Be good, Misti. I'm going to buy a few items and then we'll be on our way to our new home." She rolled down the windows again so Misti would have fresh air. Then closing and locking the door on the happy dog, she straightened her shoulders and, feeling more confident than she had in a long time, walked across the lot to join Stanley.

Stanley walked along as Steph guided the shopping cart she had collected into the store. "I thought I'd walk through the store with you. I wasn't comfortable just sitting in the car waiting."

Steph smiled. "That'll be fine. I appreciate your taking the time to let me shop. I'll try not to be too long. I just wanted to pick up a few cleaning supplies and enough food for a couple of days. I'm not sure what I'll find when we get to the farm."

The store was similar to other grocery stores Steph had shopped in. Just inside the entrance was the floral area. Pots of blooming azaleas were arranged in an attractive display. Deciding to indulge herself, she selected a container holding azaleas in a mix of baby pink and rose colored blossoms. The idea of a fresh, bright plant to take with her to her new home filled her with a sense of excitement.

Moving further into the store, they passed an area displaying wines. Steph's parents always kept a bottle of wine in the house to offer to their guests. On impulse, she stopped and selected a bottle of white wine to have in case someone stopped by. *Wow,* she thought. *I just got here. I haven't even seen the farm yet and I'm already worrying about having guests. Oh well! This way I'll have some to enjoy.* Without hesitation, she added a red wine to her cart.

Passing the deli section, she was lured to the case by the selection of salads and sandwich meats available. Catching the clerk's eye, Steph made her choices and they continued on.

As they traveled up and down the aisle in companionable silence, she began to relax. Unbidden, her thoughts wandered toward Fred. Fred hated silence. He talked nonstop as if he was having a love affair with his own voice. After all the noise and distraction of teaching all day, she loved peace and quiet. Fred liked to have loud music blaring out of his car radio when he was driving and the television blasting when he was home. He bragged about being a self-taught gourmet chef and would tell her how to select the right foods, fruits and vegetables. He usually chose fruits too ripe; they would spoil within a day or two if not eaten. One day he decided to teach her the right way to prepare chili, saying it could only be cooked properly by a man. Somehow he added too much of something and they both spent the night throwing up. Remembering made her scowl. Fred never offered to teach her how to cook again. He seemed happy enough to criticize the meals she prepared. At least when she cooked a meal, she knew what contents were going into the food she was going to eat.

Sighing with the knowledge Fred was securely in her past; she moved on to the next aisle.

"Well, you must be getting ready for a big party this weekend Stanley, you have quite a full cart."

Startled, Steph turned and saw a fragile looking woman with blue-gray hair talking to Stanley. She wore a pink sweater draped over her stooped shoulders like a cape. Her slightly faded, red 'Go Buckeyes' T-shirt hung low over the waistline of her brightly colored, floral, capri-style pants. The straps of a large red leather purse dug into the loose skin on her arm. Dainty red sneakers completed her outfit. Briefly Steph wondered if the woman would tip over carrying the large purse without the support of the cart.

"Hello, Mrs. Price. It's nice to see you." Stanley gave Mrs. Price a hug and laughed. "In all reality, I'm not shopping. This isn't my cart." He pointed to the cart Steph had walked away from. "Mrs. Price, may I introduce you to Stephanotis, I mean Steph Weatherby. She just moved to town." Turning, he found Steph watching the conversation.

Steph found herself curious about this older person who stopped to visit with Stanley. Steph reached out and moved her cart over to the side. Forcing a smile, she turned to faced Mrs. Price.

"I do apologize for leaving this in the way. I thought I would get just a few supplies and it looks like it grew to more than just a few items." Steph felt uneasy. She wasn't ready to meet new people but knew she would have to sooner or later. Trying to sound sincere, she continued, "It's a pleasure to meet you, Mrs. Price."

"It's nice to meet you and welcome to our little town. It's a wonderful place to raise kids. Are you driving the big moving truck out in the parking lot?" Mrs. Price glanced around. "Where's your husband?"

"Yes, that's mine, but it's just me and my dog, Misti." Steph felt herself tensing up, uncomfortable with the older woman's questions.

"Misti must be the fierce guard dog barking in the truck. Are you by any chance related to Hyacinth Weatherby?"

Steph forced herself to relax, reminding herself this woman was a stranger and would not know what she'd been through. "She was my great-great aunt."

"I knew Hyacinth well. The first year I began teaching, she invited me to bring my students out to the farm for a day. I took a class out every year in the spring. That is, until the school budget cuts stopped our field trips. You remember going there don't you Stanley?" Mrs. Price looked at Stanley then turned back to Steph not waiting for his response. "It was educational for the kids and a fun day for me. Hyacinth would serve fresh squeezed lemonade and sugar cookies or homemade bread."

"She was always making cookies for some event or other. It was such a joy to know her, she was strong willed with a gentle heart. But of course you already know Hyacinth was the youngest." Mrs. Priced turned toward Stanley as she spoke. "Her sister Lily lived in the next county until her husband passed away. That's when she moved back to the farm to live with Hyacinth. Hyacinth would sometimes talk about her family. She loved her brother, who I believe was your great-grandfather." Mrs. Price turned back to Steph and paused as if waiting for an answer.

Steph felt compelled to nod as Mrs. Price continued. "She felt his loss deeply. She would talk about the times when your father came to the farm. Now that I think about it, she once mentioned her sister Iris and her stepson. He was a terror as a child. When he grew up, he wanted nothing to do with the farm, saying it was nothing but a pile of cheap dirt." Mrs. Price paused to catch her breath. "Hyacinth was hurt deeply. She loved the farm and hoped it would stay in the family somehow." Patting Steph on the arm like an old friend, Mrs. Price collected her cart. "I won't keep you, but welcome to our little town. I hope you're happy here. Hyacinth would be delighted." Dismissing them, Mrs. Price began looking over the items on the shelves.

"Good-bye. It was good to see you. I'll be sure to tell mother I saw you." Stanley smiled, wondering what she would say about seeing him with Steph.

"Thank you. It was wonderful to meet you. I look forward to talking with you again about Hyacinth and the farm." Steph watched the older woman walk away as she tried to absorb what she had heard about the family she herself knew very little about. After a moment, Steph turned to collect her own cart.

"Stanley, I have everything I think I need. I am ready to go whenever you are."

Stanley nodded and began walking toward the front of the store. Walking into an empty checkout line for twenty items or less, Stanley began talking with the clerk.

Steph reflected on Stanley's ease with Mrs. Price and how he was now making the clerk laugh and smile. She couldn't remember the last time she herself had flirted with a man. She moved into a different line to pay for her items. While scanning the groceries, Steph noticed the clerk kept looking over at Stanley talking to her co-worker. She didn't think anyone, including Fred, had ever looked at her that way. She was going to have to do some serious soul-searching later. When did she stop living her life? The question stirred up memories of her sessions with Dr. Waltzer. She decided now was not the time to hash through them. She had to finish her journey. She turned her attention back to the clerk bagging her items and began to mentally review the items she bought.

"Do you need any help stowing these bags in your truck? I can help you by putting them into my car." Steph jumped when Stanley reached out to help her load the packed groceries into the cart. She was so absorbed in her thoughts she hadn't noticed his approach.

"No but thanks." Steph smiled at him before paying for the groceries. She began pushing the cart out the door. "I was planning to put them on the backseat of my car so I won't have to worry about Misti. It will only take me a couple of minutes and then we can be on our way."

"Okay, I'll just get my car." Stanley turned away outside the store.

Steph walked across the parking lot to begin unloading her cart.

Steph lovingly patted the top of her car after loading the groceries. "Don't worry girl, we're close to our new home and we can get you unhitched and set down level." She marveled at how well she had driven the U-Haul with the car towed behind it. This was the first truck she had ever driven. The realization of her accomplishment had her smiling as she walked to the driver's door.

Misti eagerly waited for Steph to get in the cab. Starting the engine, Steph looked over at Stanley in his car and waved to signal she was ready to go. As she followed him, she looked for landmarks and signs so she would be able to find her way to the store in the future.

They drove past the town limits and after a couple of miles, turned off the main road. A few miles down, they turned into a driveway. Steph stopped at the mailbox and saw "Weatherby Farm" in faded lettering on the mailbox.

"Well, Misti, we've arrived. I wonder how much has changed since Dad's last visit. He told me he always felt special here but he never said why he didn't come back." Steph wiped a tear away. "He said his favorite chore was to ride his bicycle down to collect the mail."

She inhaled deeply and then slowly released the air from her lungs. "Okay, here we go. This is the last leg of our journey home. Home… for better or worse, we are home." Taking another deep breath, she turned the nose of the truck down the gravel driveway.

CHAPTER 2

The property revealed itself to Steph as she completed the first curve in the tree-lined drive. This was her new home! With each mild curve and twist of the long driveway she was getting closer to her destination and her new responsibilities. She drove slowly looking around trying to see as much as possible.

Unfamiliar buildings of various sizes and designs were scattered over the landscape. Living in cities and suburbs most of her life, Steph could only guess as to their purpose. A large red barn was visible to one side beyond the house. She recognized two large silos standing straight and tall near the barn. Thick woods ran from the main road along one side of the farm as far as she could see. Clusters of trees dotted the area, breaking up the plainness of the rolling fields. Ancient shade trees populated the front lawn, casting cooling shadows over the grass and the house.

Dad had described it as 'a grand lady' but this is huge! After that thought, Steph's mind went blank as she continued on. Steph would think back on her arrival at a later time and marvel at how she completed the drive. She would only remember watching the house once it came into view.

"Look at it Misti. I can't believe this is mine." Awe struck, Steph sat in the parked truck for a few moments staring at the building, trying to absorb what she was seeing.

Built into a knoll, the 'Grand Lady' faced the driveway greeting its guests. Three of the four floors were visible from the front while an oversized octagonal cupola and widow's walk capped the roof. The wrap around porch, its paint peeling, enclosed the front and sides of the house. The signs of weathering couldn't diminish the charm of the whitewashed porch railings and pillars with their Victorian style trim. Steph's mother always called it 'Gingerbread.'

Mom always wanted a house with gingerbread trim, she thought wistfully. *What a shame Dad never brought Mom here, she would have loved this place. Both of them were too busy with work and caring for me and now they're both gone.*

Getting out of the truck cab, she stopped for a moment, looking up at the top floor. She slowly drew her eye back down. "This place looks like a movie set or one of the places we studied in class for the Underground Railroad. Come on Misti. Let's go check out our new home." Steph placed the Sheltie on the ground to let her run.

Lightly, as if in a dream, Steph walked up the steps to the porch and stopped next to Stanley who was waiting for her with a scowl on his face.

Stanley decided he had been patient enough. He had delivered Miss Weatherby safely to the farm as promised. It surprised him how rundown the place had become. Trying to keep the frustration from his voice, he held out the ring of keys for the property. "Do you want the honor of unlocking the door or do you want me to do it?"

Barking, Misti came running up onto the porch.

"Well, it's reassuring to know one of you is happy." Looking from the dog to the woman standing beside him, he realized she was too quiet. The color was draining from her face. "You on the other hand look terrified." Stanley searched the porch. Picking up a rocking chair he found lying on its side, he carried it over to where she was standing. He guided Steph to sit down, hoping the chair wouldn't collapse under her. Standing over her, he realized the smell from the office was coming from her. He'd smelled it occasionally in the store, but had assumed it was coming from his clothes. Now his indignation helped fuel his anger. "Breathe, damn it." He didn't want to start off his weekend with his new client in the hospital. His father would never let him forget it and he wasn't going to let it happen.

Startled by the anger in his voice, Steph began taking in deep breaths. After a few minutes, she started looking better with color coming back into her face.

"Sorry, I didn't realize I was holding my breath until I almost passed out just then. I didn't mean to scare you. Thanks for understanding." Steph took another deep breath. "I'm usually not like this." *I didn't realize how much of a shock this was going to be. I left my old life to start a new one and the reality of it just hit me.* Steph could feel her face flaming with shame. "I feel better now." She took another deep breath, held it for a moment then released it. Embarrassed by her behavior, Steph was determined to be strong. Slowly standing up, she reached out her hand. "If you don't mind, I'd like to open the door." Taking the key she unlocked the door and stepped inside.

As soon as she walked into the building, she felt a welcome home hug from the house. Mentally she knew it was impossible, but emotionally and on a spiritual level, she knew it happened. *Home! She was home!* Steph stood in the front hallway knowing she was where she belonged.

After taking a moment to calm himself Stanley stepped in behind her and turned on the lights. Relieved when they came on, he heard her quick intake of breath and assumed it was her surprise at the mess they were standing in.

Stacks of mail cascaded from the hall table to the floor. Cardboard boxes of all shapes and sizes were stacked from floor to ceiling along the walls and around the windows. Boxes and containers of all shapes and sizes lined the hallway toward the back of the house, leaving a path only wide enough for a single person to walk through. Sheets of newspapers were strewn on the floor over the rugs. Tucked in and around the boxes were rolled up newspapers, bundled together and tied with string. Every surface was covered with something. Knickknacks fought for space with clocks and empty bottles. As he glanced into other rooms, Stanley could see boxes stacked around on the floor and on furniture. It was obvious to Stanley that Hyacinth had become a "hoarder."

Stanley was not comfortable with clutter. Even as a child he always preferred his room neat with everything in its place. He did not consider himself compulsive about cleanliness but he was feeling uncomfortable in the musty smelling house. Subconsciously moving toward the door, he fought down the feeling of being overwhelmed and closed in.

"Is there anything you need to have done? Would you like me to find you a more suitable place to stay?" Stanley struggled to keep his voice level while his mind raced in a different direction from his words. *If she decides to stay, it's not my problem. I have parties to go to. I deserve time to relax and have fun.*

Steph came out of her trance and looked at him. She had forgotten Stanley was there. Misti was running up and down the hall, then in and out of the open front door. Steph took a moment to collect her thoughts. "No thanks. I'll be okay. I have my guard dog. I need to get the groceries in from the car. I want to start getting settled for the night."

"Will you need any help bringing your belongings in? I can send someone out tomorrow to help you if you want."

"Thank you for your offer. I'm not sure what needs done yet." She walked further into the house looking up the stairway and down the hall. "I think I'm just tired from the trip and overwhelmed by everything. It's hard to believe this is my home now." Steph continued to glance around moving deeper into the house.

"Well, if you change your mind or need anything, you have my card and my cell phone number. Since Monday's Memorial Day, there won't be many stores open. You'll want to get what you need tomorrow. If you like, I can recommend someone to help you clean up this mess."

As she heard the word mess Steph grimaced, glad her back was to him so he wouldn't see how his words were hurting her. Where he saw a mess, her eyes showed her someone who had loved their home. She saw a large house and yes, many rooms that will need to be cleaned and organized. Work that would give her a focus and help heal her wounded spirit.

Keeping her thoughts to herself, she turned to face him with a smile. She walked slowly and deliberately toward the front door. She decided not to let his careless comments upset her.

She began talking as she walked. "Thank you for everything. I wouldn't have found this place without your guidance. It was considerate of you to show me." She watched as Stanley stood a little taller and puffed out his chest enjoying the praise. She continued as they walked to his car. "You have done so much already to help me. You mentioned you have plans for the weekend and I feel guilty taking you away from them. I need to carry my groceries in and get ready for the night. I'd better get started, thanks again." With an air of determination, she turned, walking toward the Impala. Misti trailed in her wake. She lifted her head in time to see him drive away without a backward glance.

"Okay Misti, we're on our own again."

Misti barked and ran about in response. Laughing at the antics of her companion, Steph began the task of unloading the car.

Laden with groceries, Steph was tempted to stop and explore the wonder that was hers. The house gave the impression it was growing larger as she walked down the hall looking for the kitchen. She knew part of the illusion was the newness and lack of familiarity with her surroundings.

When she walked into the kitchen, she headed straight to the large refrigerator. Plugging it in, she made a mental note to watch it to be sure it would cool down. She brought in a cooler she had in the trunk of her car to keep her perishable items cold until they could go into the refrigerator. After bringing in all of her groceries, she fixed herself a snack.

Finding a bedroom on the main floor, Steph decided to give it and the small adjoining bathroom a thorough cleaning so she could use it for the next few days as she explored the house. The exercise helped work some of the kinks out of her back and shoulders. She knew she would have sore muscles tomorrow but was proud of all she completed since she arrived.

Steph located the clothes washer and started a load of linens to wash. Then she made preparations for the night.

Steph went outside and unhooked the Impala from the back of the U-Haul moving it up beside the truck. She began carrying some of the smaller items into the house. As the sky was getting dark, she set up her coffeepot and treated herself to a 'good' cup of coffee. She had sampled various coffees on her trip, but found she preferred her own brew. She didn't understand why people bought expensive cups of coffee when she enjoyed what she could make at home.

Steph felt tired but restless. Carrying her coffee and a treat for Misti, she went out the back door to enjoy the evening before the sun set.

*   *   *

As he drove home, Stanley felt guilty about the way he had behaved and about leaving Steph alone. He didn't have to put himself out but he decided he should do something. Delegating was a talent Stanley had been cultivating his entire life. Realizing it was the best thing to do under the circumstances and it would leave him free to do as he pleased for the weekend, he called her neighbors, the Landburgs.

"Hello, Jenny? This is Stanley Wilbur. I wanted to let you know your new landlady is in town. I just dropped her off at the farm."

Stanley waited only a moment before rushing on. "I called to see if George would check on her tonight. Okay? Thanks. Oh and by the way, she may need some help unloading her U-Haul. Gotta go."

Jenny Landsburg slowly moved the telephone from her ear and looked at the instrument. She had barely said "Hello," before Stanley was issuing orders and hanging up. She started to redial the phone when she realized what he had said. Shaking as she tried to contain her excitement, she dialed George's phone number.

*   *   *

"What do I look like, some kind of baby-sitter?"

George complained to Jenny when she called on his cell phone to tell him the news. He was working on the tractor in the north field. He had repaired it twice earlier in the spring. This was the third time he was attempting to get it to run. *I'm glad Hank's helping*, he thought, as he glanced over to where his friend started up the tractor.

The tractor was standing in a puddle of water, evidence of the morning rain. Both men were wet and greasy from working on the open engine. Hank seemed to know instinctively more about machinery than George could learn from reading a repair manual. George could fix the engine, but Hank could make it run like new. George's relief was evident on his face as he waived at Hank to cut the motor.

Bringing his mind back to Jenny who was still on the phone George continued. "We're just about finished here. I have to feed the livestock and check on the new colt. Hank and I will go over after dinner." George's voice softened. "Are you okay?" George spent much of his time worrying about Jenny. She was beginning the ninth month of her first pregnancy. It was not an easy pregnancy for either of them. No longer able to stand on her feet for long periods of time, Jenny quit her job in town. Jenny still helped with chores around the farm but the money she brought home had helped ease some of the financial burden. George knew he wouldn't be able to manage without Jenny's help. He couldn't afford to hire anyone and now with her pregnancy, he was more than relieved to have Hank here.

"I'm fine. You just do what you have to do. I'll have dinner waiting for you when you're ready. Stanley just wanted you to go over and introduce yourself in case she needed something done. I told him you would go over later. I'll let you get back to work. Remember I love you George." Jenny hung up before George could respond any further, hoping she wouldn't have to admit she didn't really agree it was just that Stanley hadn't given her a chance to disagree.

"Hank, we're going to have to speed up a little bit. Are you up for a ride on the ATV's? We can take them out after dinner."

"Sounds like fun. It's been a long time since we took them out." Hank carefully climbed down from the tractor seat.

"Let's go get the livestock fed and then we'll get some dinner. I have to go check on the new landlady. Jenny called to tell me she arrived and Stanley Jr. wants us to make sure she's okay."

George picked up the tools they were finished using and put them away in his truck.

"Thanks for fixing the tractor." George stood by the truck door. "I'm glad you were well enough to come and help me. I don't know what I'd do without it."

George climbed into the driver's seat and waited to continue the conversation as Hank joined him in the truck.

"When I saw you in the hospital that first time, I was really worried about you."

"I don't even want to think about it." Hank grimaced as he subconsciously opened and closed his hand. "I'm still not back to full use of my hand as you saw today, but it's stronger now. After all the surgeries and the physical therapy, I still find it hard to hold things for long. I know I should be glad the bastard was arrested and convicted. Some days it's not enough. I thought I would never get out of the hospital."

Hank looked down at his hand. *If I have this much trouble handling a screwdriver and wrench, how will I ever be able to shoot a gun? I have to get past this. I want to be a cop again.*

Hank raised his eyes to stare out the windshield. "I know it's been a long time since I worked on an engine. It just frustrates me." Hank swallowed a sigh. "It shouldn't have taken me as long as it did but it's running now."

Hank grinned at George. "I just hope you can handle driving it."

George laughed in response.

The men rode back to the barnyard in companionable silence.

After George turned off the ignition, he turned to Hank. "If you'll take care of the horses in the barn, I can get started outside. I'll meet you in the house when you're done. After dinner, we'll go check on the new landlady."

"Okay."

Hank left the truck and went into the barn. After he fed and watered the horses in the barn, he went to see how George was doing. George was finishing the last of his chores so Hank headed for the house.

Jenny Landsburg was putting the final touches on their dinner when Hank walked in the back door.

"Jenny, it's me. I'll go wash up for dinner. Are you okay?"

"I'm okay. I'm running late with dinner so take your time."

As Hank was coming back downstairs, George came into the kitchen.

"Jenny, do I have time to clean up a little?"

Jenny walked over toward George to keep him from coming farther into the kitchen with his dirty clothes.

"I need ten more minutes so you have time for a quick shower."

George gave Jenny a quick kiss and hurried upstairs.

Jenny watched George leave then turned to Hank.

"It's times like this when I'm glad you're here."

Jenny studied the face of the man standing in front of her. He was a little taller than George with an athletic build. His face was ruggedly handsome where George had a round pleasing face. Hank had narrow shoulders. George had broad shoulders and a broad chest. Both men had long legs and narrow waists. Jenny preferred George's smiling hazel eyes to Hank's piercing blue ones.

"Sit down and I'll get the table set. We'll eat as soon as George comes down."

Jenny moved about the kitchen putting plates and glasses on the table. She started to hum a tune as she began spooning food into serving dishes to place on the table.

Hank sat quietly watching her trying to keep his envy from showing on his face. *If I could just find someone as wonderful as Jenny to love me, I would be the happiest man on earth.* Hank looked at his hand, seeing again the scars left from the surgeries that restored its use. Determination was clear on his face. *I may not be as strong as I once was, but I'm going to do my best and try to be. Maybe someday I'll find someone who won't mind the other scars either.* Mentally he sighed. *Who am I kidding? I'll go back to the force where I belong. I was once a damn good officer. I know I can be again.*

Hank heard George coming down the stairs and grinned.

"Jenny. Why don't you divorce George and marry me? I know you don't love him. We'll run away to Las Vegas or California. No, I know, just divorce George and we'll live in sin."

31

Jenny laughed. "I'm still training George and am not ready to take on another full-grown man. I'll start the next one as a baby and train him as he grows up. That way I'll have him trained by the time I have George trained."

"Some men can't be trained," Hank chuckled. "I think you're wasting your time on George. Run away with me and we'll live in sin. That way Ole George can foot the bill."

"Are you trying to steal my wife again?"

George walked into the kitchen and sat down at the table.

"I'd let you have her, but I just got her trained to have dinner ready for me on time. I don't think I could train another one this well."

Jenny walked behind George as she set the dishes of food on the table.

"I think I'd change the subject if I were you. Soon it will be your turn to cook for yourselves. I don't think you want to rush it."

Hank laughed.

Grinning, George reached for the dish in front of him. "I guess we'd both better behave. Let's eat. I'm starving."

As they ate their dinner, they discussed the tractor and the land-lady. When they were finished, George rose from the table.

"We've got to get going so we don't catch her sleeping. Jenny, we're going to take the ATVs."

"Are you sure Hank will be okay on the ATV?" Jenny noticed Hank began to look tired as the meal progressed.

"Yah, I'll be okay." Hank grinned. "It'll be fun." Nodding to George, he left before Jenny could protest any more.

"Promise me you'll take it easy. I don't want either of you hurt. It'll be dark soon, please be careful."

"We'll be fine." George kissed Jenny good-bye.

*   *   *

Hank was looking forward to riding the ATV. Prior to his injury, Hank spent many happy hours riding around the farm on an ATV.

"I'll lead the way. I want to see what this baby can do."

Hank sped off.

It wasn't long before Hank regretted his decision to ride off-road. He didn't realize the bouncing and jarring he used to enjoy could bring so much pain. He remembered feeling free and happy when he rode. Now he felt as if every part of his body jiggled independently. He went faster hoping to finish the ride sooner and end the torture. When he realized the speed only made the bouncing and jarring worse, he slowed down. His body protested with every turn of the wheels.

Hank struggled to control his impulse to stop and get off. He worried that if he did stop, his legs wouldn't work. He knew George couldn't hear him over the noise of the engines but he shouted anyway.

"I've got to get off this torture device." Hank saw the lights of the neighbor's farmhouse coming into view. *Hold on Hank. You can do this! Use the lights as a guide and go for it. They're getting closer.*

Hank was concentrating on the lights of the house and didn't see the woman walking around until he was almost upon her. He turned in a wide arc to avoid her and her little dog. As he was circling around he saw her turn and fall. He pulled up and removed his helmet. He sat looking at the woman lying on the ground while he waited for George.

*   *   *

Steph was watching the sun set when she heard what sounded like a motorcycle. At first it was just a noise in the background. As it became louder and more noticeable, she realized it was coming from the woods. Steph always lived in residential areas with neighbors close by, not alone as she was here. It was quiet and peaceful until the noise disturbed the night. Now the noise was getting louder and nearer. Steph worried about the images the sound invoked in her mind. Seeing a single light coming toward her, she started to back up slowly toward the safety of her house. She realized she'd wandered further away than she originally thought, having misjudged the distance in the unfamiliar area.

What was once beautiful and tranquil all around her was becoming dark and scary. Steph found herself wishing the yard was better lit. The weak mercury light hanging on the barn cast a feeble beam, creating more shadows than light.

Steph jumped when Misti began to bark. She couldn't see what made the noise but it was getting louder. Suddenly there was another light coming from a different angle. Could this be a motorcycle gang coming to scare her? Her frightened brain kept conjuring up images of wild men on motorcycles wanting to kill or rape her. She was alone and only Stanley Jr. knew she was there. Would he care if something happened to her? Her heartbeat was pounding in her ears as loud as the machines. She imagined more of them coming from all directions, cutting her off from the house where her cell phone laid on the table.

Turning to run back to the house, hoping they hadn't seen her yet, she tripped on a stone and fell, landing with a thud. Terrified, she stayed where she'd fallen.

Misti stopped her frantic running in circles and raced over to Steph. Growling and barking, the little dog stood between Steph and the intruders.

George parked his ATV a short distance from Hank. He was still moving when he saw the woman fall. As he dismounted, he saw the dog turn toward him growling and showing off sharp white teeth. George removed his helmet and slowly walked forward as he kept his eye on the dog. He stopped when he was a few feet away.

"Are you okay lady? I'm George Landsburg from next door and this is my friend Hank Dawn. If you'll call your guard dog off, we'll be glad to help you up."

CHAPTER 3

Steph remained still on the ground unsure of what to do next. Her already sore muscles were jarred by the impact. Every pebble and small jagged rock in the gravel driveway felt like a boulder to her stiff back and sore buttocks. In reality, they were small stones, but they were plentiful. She was grateful the ground was only slightly damp, not wet from the morning rain.

Her evening began silently and soothingly. Then the peace exploded with the noise from the machines. Now they were turned off and quiet, no longer resembling motorcycles but off-road machines. It was Misti who now tore at the silence with her growls and barks.

Trying to maintain a blank expression, Steph raised a hand to check for tenderness on the back of her head. Reassured there was no head injury, she continued to take stock of what injury she might have incurred. Struggling to sit up, she became aware of a throbbing pain in her ankle.

Steph's nose burned with every breath. She could barely distinguish between the exhaust fumes from the machines and the other odors assaulting her senses. Some of the scents seemed familiar and others were foreign. There was the scent of sweaty males mixed with something that smelled like grease.

The ground released a damp fragrance of its own but it was overpowered by the odor of animals. A mental picture of a tractor near a barn flashed through her mind. Steph realized that these men were not a motorcycle gang, but farmers. *This must be the man who rents the land on the farm. Boy, what a way to make an impression.*

Hopefully, I can stand up and keep my dignity intact. Her racing heart was beginning to slow down.

Bravely Misti stood her ground not letting the men near. She dashed from one side of Steph to the other trying to appear as threatening as she could. Unfortunately in her excitement, Misti jumped on Steph's sore ankle more than once.

"Ow! Misti stop it. Be quiet! Oh Misti! Sit!" Obediently the dog sat but she still tried to bark while sitting at the same time. Misti was good at sitting and growling, but barking was a behavior she only could do standing up. She raised her tail end slightly off the ground to get some balance. Letting out a bark she fell back into a sit.

Steph was torn between being proud of her small dog and laughing aloud at her antics. It was obvious Misti was frustrated. Steph remained seated watching her. Misti's behavior was changing from being protective to impatient. She became quieter, as if encouraging the men to help.

"Lady, are you hurt? Should we come help you up?" *This woman might be hurt. She's just sitting there watching the dog. Maybe she hit her head.* George tried again.

"Lady? Can you hear me?"

George stood in the growing dark waiting for an answer. Stanley Sr. said the woman coming to live on the farm was a schoolteacher. He, Jenny and Hank spent many evenings trying to decide how old she would be. He was sure she was old but the impression he had before she fell was of a younger person. What if she was a young looking older person? Or perhaps he was mistaken and she was old. If she was old, then she might have broken something in her fall. Jenny would not be happy if he caused the landlady to break a hip or have a concussion.

Steph put a reassuring hand on Misti. "I'm okay I think. Just give me a minute to check my leg. It's a bit sore."

She tried to move her right foot. "Ow!" Inhaling from the pain that spiked up her leg, she gingerly set it back on the ground. "I don't think it's broken, but it's painful. I guess you'll have to help me up."

Hank had been setting on the ATV sideways trying to bribe his body to let him ride the monster back to George's. Thinking about his own pain he watched the Sheltie's antics. The loud, little dog was small, but he knew from experience that it could do damage if it decided they were a real threat. Those teeth weren't just for show. It was funny seeing it trying to bark and sit at the same time, like the kickback from a gun being fired.

Hank heard the concern in his friend's voice and knew that if this was the dreaded "landlady," it could mean trouble for George if she was injured.

Hank knew George didn't have a current contract with the estate but had planted his crops anyway. George was tending the Weatherby stock and boarded the horses at his farm. For years George cared for the land and stock as if it were his own property. George planted his crop hoping the agreement would be approved by all parties.

As he walked toward Steph, George gestured for Hank to take one side of Steph while he moved toward the other. They moved slowly but for different reasons. George was watching the dog. Hank was disguising his pain. Leaning down together, they each grabbed an arm.

"Okay Hank, on the count of three we'll lift her up. One…two…three. Up!"

"Humph! Thanks for the lift. Let me see if I can stand on it. Ow! Ow!" Clenching her jaw tightly, Steph leaned heavily on to George. "Maybe you better help me into the house. I don't think I can walk."

With Steph hopping on one foot supported by George, Hank went ahead, climbing slowly up the steps to the back door. When George and Steph managed to hobble up the steps, he held the door open for them.

George tried to hide his obvious relief that this was not an older person he was helping to hop-walk. Once they got into the kitchen, George eased Steph into a chair.

"Hank, get some ice or something for her ankle. Use that fancy first aid training of yours."

Glancing over at his friend, George saw Hank moving slowly and deliberately, as if each movement was causing him great pain.

"Never mind, come sit over here and keep the lady company while I find something to put on her ankle."

Grateful for George's quiet way of letting him rest, Hank sat down. He searched his mind trying to think of something to say.

"So, where is the retired teacher who inherited the farm?"

George was searching the near empty freezer for some ice. Wincing when he heard his friend's tactless question, he quickly grabbed the half frozen tray of ice from the freezer and closed the door.

"Umm, maybe I should introduce myself again."

Walking back to the table with the tray in his hand, he offered his empty hand to Steph.

"I'm George Landsburg and this is my friend Henry Dawn, but we call him Hank." George gave Hank a look he hoped would advise his friend to use more tack when he spoke.

Steph laughed and shook George's hand.

"I'm Steph. Stephanotis Weatherby, the 'teacher' you were expecting." Steph noticed Hank was beginning to squirm.

"It's nice to meet you George, Henry- Hank." Steph nodded at each man. "You must be the neighbor attorney Wilbur told me about. He explained that you plant and harvest the land and then a percentage goes to the farm. He advised me this is something we will need to discuss. For now I think it can wait a little longer."

Dragging an empty chair closer, Steph raised her foot up to rest on the seat. She turned and looked at George who was still standing with the dripping tray of ice in his hand.

"There's ice in the cooler on the floor over there. If you'd put some of that ice into one of those plastic zip-lock bags on the counter, I'd be grateful."

George relaxed and did as directed.

Hank began to feel better as he rested in the chair. Looking around, he noticed what George was doing.

"Hey buddy, better use two bags so it won't leak."

George put the ice into the bags and carried them over to Steph, carefully placing the ice bag on her ankle.

Steph gestured at an empty chair for him to sit down as she reached down to adjust the ice bag.

"Since I'm mildly hindered, I do apologize for not getting up to get you gentlemen a drink. There's coffee or water if you would be willing to help yourselves. I have wine, but my corkscrew is out in the truck. I don't know if there's a corkscrew here in the kitchen."

"Coffee's fine. I'll get it." George rose and walked to the coffee-maker. "This sure smells good." Pouring coffee into two of the mugs set out on the counter, he carried them to the table. "Can I get you some?"

"No thanks, I've had my limit for the day." Steph was trying to remember if the mug broke when she fell. She made a mental note to rescue it in the morning. "If you'll just bring me a bottle of water from the refrigerator and that bottle of aspirin on the counter by the sink, I'll be fine."

When George returned with the water and aspirin bottle, he sat down across from Hank. Trying to think of something to say, he drank from his mug.

"This is good coffee. I wish my Jenny could make coffee this good."

Realizing he just criticized his wife's coffee to a stranger, he glanced at Hank.

Hank took the hint, nodding to let George know he understood. Drinking deeply from the cup and trying not to envy Steph the aspirin she just took, Hank let his eyes wander around the room.

"George said the woman who lived here died. She must have been old. Seems like a big house. Needs some work."

Hank paused embarrassed; he didn't usually have this much trouble talking to women but tonight he was struggling. To cover up, he spoke quickly.

"You make good coffee."

Steph forced a smile but didn't answer as she hoped the aspirin would quickly take effect.

The men stared at their cups not knowing what to say. It was quiet in the kitchen except for the purring noise from the refrigerator compressor, until George's cell phone rang. They were all startled, the ringing sounded magnified in the silence.

Misti was lying in the corner of the room where she could see them and barked when the cell phone rang.

George glanced at the screen.

"This is my wife. I'd better take it."

Walking across the room away from the others for more privacy, George answered his cell phone.

"Hello Jen. Yes, she's here... Yes, we introduced ourselves... No, she's alone. I don't know, I haven't asked her." Looking slightly embarrassed, he turned away. "I can't tell you that right now. She's here in the room. I'll explain everything when I get home. Okay... Okay... Bye, I love you. We'll be home soon. Bye."

Putting the phone back into his pocket, George resumed his seat and finished drinking the coffee in his cup.

"That was an enjoyable cup of coffee, but we have to go."

George jerked his head towards the door as he started to rise. He was hoping Hank would take the hint so they could be on their way.

Hank was trying not to think about the unbearable ride back, looking past it to a long hot shower, then a soft bed. Absorbed in his own thoughts, he missed George's subtle hint. It was Steph's moan of pain that pulled him back to the present.

Steph stood up to show the men out the back door, hoping the ice bag had eased some of the soreness from her ankle. Unfortunately for her ego, she couldn't hold back a moan from the pain when she tried to stand on her leg. The searing pain wrenched the sound from her clenched lips.

Once she shifted her weight by leaning on the table, she could manage the pain. Her pride gave her the courage to hobble across the floor with them to the kitchen door. She knew she wouldn't make it across the interior of the attached porch to lock the far door.

Earlier in the evening she prepared her bed, putting clean sheets and pillows on it. She told herself she would just show the men to the door lock up and then hobble off to bed. Knowing she could soon get off her sore leg gave her the strength to continue.

"I'll let you see yourselves out. Thanks for taking the time to stop by."

Gritting her teeth, she watched from inside as they walked across the yard to where they left their machines. She noticed Hank was walking slowly and deliberately as if each step was jarring his body. She filed the observation away for a later time.

Hobbling to the bedroom, she started getting ready for bed. She slowly began to relax as she settled down, the ice bag draped over her swollen ankle.

Hoping she would be able to walk by morning, she drifted off to sleep.

*   *   *

Hank forced himself to ride the monster home. They drove slower on the way back but it was still a jarring ride. Hank imagined a few times his ATV deliberately sought out and hit every bump or hole in the ground it may have missed on the way to the neighboring farmhouse. Hank almost cried as he got off the ATV at the farm. Lifting the helmet off his head caused pain to shoot down between his shoulders. He clamped his mouth shut on a moan of pain. He was recuperating, but he knew he'd reached his limit. He prayed he would be able to move tomorrow.

George saw Hank straining to walk. He rushed ahead to the door of the house, hoping to head Jenny off so she wouldn't see how Hank was walking. Hank was proud of his recovery progress. George knew Jenny would fuss and worry if she saw he was in pain. George enjoyed having Hank around and appreciated his help but George felt pulled in different directions. He needed Hank's help on the farm but not at the cost of his friend's health.

As George opened the door, Jenny was standing just inside, waiting for them, an anxious expression on her face.

"I'm so glad you're home."

The sound of fear in Jenny's voice brought George up short.

"We're home safe. Are you okay?"

Worry about Jenny and the baby pushed all thoughts of Hank from George's mind.

Jenny put her hands around her baby-swollen belly and smiled.

"We're fine. We were just waiting for you." Jenny hung her head. "I know it's silly but I was starting to get worried about you."

George gave Jenny a hug and then a long, lingering kiss. Hearing a noise, he looked up over Jenny's head and saw Hank opening the door. George drew Jenny into the house away from where Hank was slowing walking in.

Letting his concern seep into his voice, he began asking Jenny about what she'd been doing and how she was feeling. He reached over and touched her belly. It always amazed him that she was carrying his child. He knew he was blessed having her for his wife, but this was so precious. Together they were creating a baby. Caught up in his love for Jenny and the wonder of his baby, George once again forgot about Hank.

Jenny always loved the soft look that appeared on George's face when he asked her about the baby. She was humbled by the depth of his love for her and their unborn child. She forgot about Hank, until she heard the water running in the shower. With a jolt she remembered where George and Hank were all evening.

Stepping back from George, Jenny searched his face for any sign that his distraction was deliberate. She was curious about the new neighbor but concerned about Hank. She walked away creating a space between George and herself. She paused for a moment then turned back determined to get answers. Hank was more important.

"How did Hank handle riding the ATV? Was it too much for him after all he did today? Did you keep your promise and keep it slow? I was afraid the bouncing around would be too much for him."

George just shook his head and sat down. They had been standing in the front room, just a few feet from his comfortable old chair. If he was going to have to be interrogated, he was going to relax.

"Okay, I'll answer your questions if you'll just sit down and rest."

George mentally sighed as he sat, knowing she was not going to be distracted again. He took his time getting comfortable, enjoying the tension on Jenny's face as she tried patiently to wait for him to begin.

"First of all, Hank handled the ATV well. He led the way over. He took it pretty slow at first, but he kept speeding up and I sped up to keep track of him. So, do I think he handled it okay? Yes, I do. Did I keep my promise that I would take it slow? I led the way home and kept it slow and steady. Was the bouncing and working too much for him? Yes, I think it was and that's why he's in the shower, probably trying to relax some sore muscles. Now do you have any more questions about Hank, or do you want to hear about our new neighbor?"

While George was talking, Jenny relaxed, leaning back on the sofa. Now she struggled to sit up.

"I'm sitting here like a beached whale, and you ask me stupid questions. Of course I want to hear about our new neighbor! What makes you think I wouldn't? Someone new has moved into the Weatherby house, I want to know everything."

Working the footrest, George put his feet up and began telling Jenny about their adventure. He told her about Steph falling when they arrived. How he was heroic and caring, helping her into the house and putting ice on her ankle. Satisfied with his tale of the evening, he began talking about the new colt and the livestock he was thinking of selling. When he began talking about what he planned to do the next day, Jenny interrupted.

"But how old is she?"

"Who?"

"The landlady!"

"I guess she's our age. I don't know. I didn't ask her."

"What does she look like? What was she wearing?"

"She looks like a woman with brown hair. She's about your height and was wearing clothes."

"Has she started moving in?"

"Yeah, she's got boxes of stuff sitting on the counters. Seems like more clutter's in the kitchen than there was when I went to check on the pipes and turn on the water."

"Is she staying in the house tonight or going to a motel for a few days."

"She's staying the night and settling in. She offered us drinks, coffee and water. She said she had wine but didn't know if there was a corkscrew. We drank some coffee. It was good."

"What else?"

"What do you mean what else?"

"She means she wants details and impressions. Does she seem smart? Is she well put together? How she was dressed? Those are the 'what else' your wife is asking you about."

Hank was wearing a pair of comfortable sweats and a t-shirt. He had gone into the kitchen for some water to take his pain pills and heard the conversation. Realizing Jenny would want to make sure he was okay with her own eyes, he meandered into the room. Her voice made it clear she was frustrated with George so he decided to join them for a few minutes. After all details were an important part of his job and he had always been exceptional at noticing details.

Sitting down on an empty chair, Hank leaned back and relaxed. Jenny and George were two of his favorite people and he always enjoyed their company. Taking a deep breath he wondered where to start. Judging by the impatience he saw in Jenny's eyes, he decided to begin with the basics.

"She's a little taller than you, brown hair, brown eyes. I would judge her to be roughly thirty years old. She wore her hair pulled back into a ponytail and the ends were curling. She's good-looking, slim, a little under fed but nicely put together. George here helped her hobble into the kitchen. As I said, she is nicely put together."

Hank grinned but wiped it off quickly when he saw the frustration on Jenny's face. Hank thought for a moment before continuing.

"She was wearing a t-shirt, shorts and sneakers. She's cleaned up some of the kitchen. She unpacked a few boxes, the most important of which contained the coffeepot. She makes great coffee. There was a slight smell of bathroom cleaner about her so I would say she cleaned up a bit. Also, there was a slight hint of fabric softener in the air over the mustiness, so I'd say she washed some clothes."

"She's eating mostly sandwiches and cereal. Her companion is a noisy dog who is also brave of heart. I thought it was going to tear

George here into pieces." Hank started laughing at the memory of George carefully watching the little dog.

He continued to chuckle as he went on. "She fell when we came ripping into the yard and that little dog stood barking and growling at us. I've had my share of experiences with growling dogs. I wasn't getting close until it was called off. Here was Hero George, moving in to help a fallen lady and the brave little dog trying to keep him away. It was a sight."

Hank stood up. "That ends my report chief. I am off to bed."

He waved a backhanded good-bye as he left the room.

"Well, that is more like it. Details. I needed more details. I feel better." Struggling to stand up, Jenny started giggling.

"What's so funny?" George put in a long day and was feeling drowsy. He got to his feet to help Jenny up, but she was already standing and walking toward him. Giving him a kiss, she turned and started walking away before answering.

"What if Hank falls for the neighbor? Then he'd be a farmer too! Hank the police officer a farmer! Isn't that a hoot? Good night George, I love you."

Laughing to herself, she went to bed.

Sitting back down with a flop, George decided he'd have to think about that too. Since he was sitting down, he decided to watch the news. He needed to know what the weather was going to be so he could finish his work plans for the next few days.

Miss Weatherby sold most of the stock as she grew older but she kept a palomino stallion whose bloodline ran back to the days when her grandfather bought the farmland. George had a contract first with her and now with her estate lawyer for the stallion, Sun Dancer, to be boarded at George's farm.

Sun Dancer had always been well-behaved and loved to be ridden. Jenny was an experienced rider and before she became pregnant, she would ride Sun Dancer to exercise him. George thought he was the most beautiful horse he'd ever seen. Seeing his Jenny astride Sun Dancer always took George's breath away.

As part of the contract, George was given the right to breed Sun Dancer to his private stock under certain conditions, and one condition was all colts born were to be gelded. George bred the stallion occasionally to mares he would buy and sell, keeping a few to raise. The buying and selling of animals was part of their livelihood, but for sentimental reasons George kept the firstborn filly for Jenny.

George was proud of the care he had given the old boy and knew he would miss having Sun Dancer in his barn. George sighed as he thought about it. The new colt was starting to develop the confirmation Jenny always said was important in a good show horse. She was the one who knew about horses in their family. He always admired them but knew more about raising crops and cattle than horses. He still found it amazing Jenny would prefer riding a horse to an ATV. He hated being perched up on a horse with no brakes to use.

Jenny would tell him about the horse shows she went to. She said people are always willing to pay top dollar for a good show horse but George knew they needed more care and attention than his cattle. George didn't have much free time now to spend with Jenny, he wasn't sure he wanted to give that up to tend show horses.

Jenny's best friend growing up owned horses and Jenny had been allowed to ride with her beginning at a young age. Jenny worked hard, becoming an exceptional rider. Many of her weekends were spent at horse shows with her friend until she went to college, where she met George and they fell in love.

Thinking of Jenny and horse shows reminded George of his father's friend, Chris Huckabee. Chris showed horses in his younger days, and then trained them for a number of years. He called it a hobby and his first love.

Chris took George to visit the stables when he was visiting for the weekend. George was awed by Chris's quiet manner and how the horses would react to his voice. They would know Chris was there and seemed happy to see him. Of course, George always suspected it was the sugar cubes they got excited about that Chris carried in his shirt pocket. It'd been a while since George had heard from Chris. He made a mental note to ask his father about him when they next spoke.

With all of these thoughts swimming in his mind, George found he had to concentrate to understand the weather information on the television. Turning on the closed caption feature, he set the volume to mute so he would not disturb Jenny. Watching the weather map flipping on the screen from one set of temperatures to another, he quickly fell asleep.

*   *   *

As Jenny progressed further into her pregnancy, she found it difficult to sleep all-night. More and more, she would have to get up and relieve the extra pressure on her bladder. Often she would joke with George about the baby using it for a soccer ball. When she got up that night, she noticed George had not come to bed. It was two a.m. and he was still downstairs. Jenny decided to check on him. Hearing his soft snoring, she stopped in the doorway to the living room to watch him for a few minutes. He was sprawled out in his easy chair with the floor lamp glaring in his face. One foot was up on the footrest, the other draped over the edge. His shoes were scattered on the floor near the chair.

She moved the shoes over, and then lifted his foot to a more comfortable position. Trying not to disturb him, she covered him with the quilt from the back of the sofa. Taking a small pillow, she tucked it under his head hoping he wouldn't have a stiff neck when he woke. As Jenny turned to walk away, something flickered, catching her eye. She noticed the television set was still on. Rummaging around, she finally found the remote control and turned it off. Smiling, she switched off the light and went back to bed.

CHAPTER 4

Steph woke up in a strange room, tired and disoriented. Sitting up she realized she was at the Weatherby Farm. She started to stand up but flopped back down remembering her ankle. Misti was awake, jumping around and barking. Steph understood Misti needed to go outside. Carefully she stood again and gently shifted her weight to test her ankle. It was stiff but not as painful.

"Okay, I can walk. Let's go Misti."

Steph let Misti out the back door and watched her for a few minutes to be sure she would be okay. Blocking the doors open for the little dog to come in on her own and to let the fresh morning air into the house, she went to get dressed. Slipping into a pair of jeans and a T-shirt, she went to the kitchen to start fresh coffee.

While the coffee brewed, she leaned against the counter with a thoughtful expression on her face. There was work to do. She couldn't decide where to begin and found this disconcerting. Being an organized person, she felt at loose ends. Deciding to start with her normal routine, she fed Misti. The little dog was enjoying herself, running around the kitchen and out the back door. Smiling at her dog's antics, she sat at the kitchen table with her cup of coffee and the list on the tablet in front of her.

Checking off the last items on the list which included getting safely to the farm, she realized she forgot something important. In her anger and grief, she only planned to get here. She didn't know what to do now. She didn't know anything about farm life, how was she going to run a farm? What was she going to do with this place?

She turned the page on her tablet and began making notes. Jotting down any idea that came to mind, she let her mind wander, hoping to find a solution.

There was a time when she was a strong and confident woman, happy and content with her life. Then her world changed and nothing would ever be the same again. It began in the form of her father's cancer.

She had been coming to terms with her father's death. He had suffered so much with the cancer eating away at his body and spirit. When the drunk driver had gone through the stoplight and killed her mother just a few short months later, it was almost unbearable.

Steph thought she could depend upon Fred. They'd been dating almost a year when she moved in with him. After a few weeks, she realized the mistake she'd made and spent months trying to make it work, hoping she was wrong. It had taken everything in her to find the strength to end it.

They'd been seeing so much of each other it seemed natural to take the next step. Looking back, it was clear he had manipulated and planned even that.

Steph thought back to when she first met Fred shortly after her father had died. She and a friend were at a Community Theatre play. His seat was on the end of the row and they had both noticed when he changed seats with an older gentleman who was having trouble walking through the chairs to his seat. Steph and her friend had each assumed the gesture was from kindness. Later Fred told her he had exchanged seats because he wanted to meet her friend, but he changed his mind. After spending time with them both, he decided it was Steph who he was attacted to.

From that first night on, she began to notice him other places. She saw him at the grocery store, the local deli and he seemed to frequent the diner she enjoyed. Steph remembered how he always seemed friendly and interested in what she was doing.

Fred began joining Steph and her friends when he would see them. Then soon they were dating. Fred started going with her on her visits to see her mother just before ...

Wrestling with her thoughts, Steph looked over to where Misti laid asleep by the doorway. It was Christmas when her parents came to her apartment with the small puppy. They wanted to give her a special friend to help break the news. She remembered the puppy looked so tiny in her father's strong and capable hands. Her parents laughed when she said she would call the puppy Mistletoe, Misti for short.

Over the next few months Steph tried to ignore how ill her father was becoming. Pretending to herself that he was getting better when she knew in her heart he wasn't, she spent as much time with him as possible. He held on for over a year before the cancer defeated him.

Steph slowly shook her head and then took a sip from the cup in her hand. She should have known things with Fred were too good to be true. She had believed him when he said he was allergic to Misti, using the allergy as an excuse to force her to give the dog away. Steph sighed. If Keri Hall hadn't offered to take her for a while, Steph wondered if she would have given Misti away.

She tried to push those terrible thoughts away. Of course she wouldn't.

Steph quietly stood up and moved to close the doors she had left open earlier. Her thoughts continued on as if they had a will of their own.

She had felt so humbled by Fred's attention that she didn't realize he was manipulating her. She was mortified when she learned Fred didn't have allergies. He merely refused to pay the pet deposit for the apartment.

Steph closed the inner door hard enough to cause Misti to wake with a start. She quietly returned to the table taking another sip from her cup. Her thoughts refused to be shifted from the path they were following. It was humiliating to remember how easily she had trusted him.

Keri hadn't liked Fred the first time she met him. She had tried to warn Steph but Steph hadn't listened.

Steph later noticed that her other friends no longer called to invite her out and she felt as if they were turning away. After her mother's funeral only a few friends stayed to talk with her. Many merely murmured condolences then left as soon as the service was over.

When Fred asked for payment 'for services rendered for estate planning', Steph realized she'd made a mistake. The day she walked into Mr. Young's office crying, terrified about what she was going to do, would always be imprinted in her memory. Mr. Young had been a good friend to her father and Steph knew he was a good attorney. Mr. Young made inquiries about Fred. Steph was devastated when she learned about Fred's disreputable past and how he had lied about his involvement with planning her mother's estate.

Mr. Young had also discovered that Fred had effectively alienated Steph from her friends by spreading rumors and telling outright lies.

For Steph's protection, Mr. Young filed a restraining order against Fred. He encouraged her to move in with Keri Hall while her mother's estate went through probate.

Steph experienced depression after her father died. Losing her mother and trying to get over Fred's betrayal had eroded her self-confidence and the depression returned. Having been one to trust in the goodness of people, she learned how painful it could be to have that trust abused.

Because of the depression, Steph began seeing a psychologist, Dr. Waltzer, soon after her father died. She stopped her sessions when she began dating Fred, hoping to avoid the embarrassment of telling him she needed help.

Steph thought about the day Mr. Young had told her about the farm. Prior to her father's illness her parents had sold their home and moved to an apartment so they could travel and begin to enjoy their golden years. Because of the change of address, the notification of Hyacinth's death and her will had been delayed, arriving while her father was ill. Steph found the letter with other correspondence after her mother died. Steph felt as if she was carrying all the burdens of the world on her back including the responsibility of the farm.

Steph had been finding it hard to get through each day. She would force herself to go to school, pushing through one hour at a time trying not to lose her patience with the children. When she'd go home, she chided herself for not being the teacher she knew she could be. Worry kept her awake at night as she wondered which student had been overlooked that day and who would pay the price for her lack of attention. She was touchy and moody, often spending her breaks crying in the teacher's restroom.

Mr. Young had encouraged her to seek help so she resumed her sessions with Dr. Waltzer. With his support, she was able to realize inheriting the farm was an opportunity. He had encouraged her to take a few days off, drive over to the farm, check it out and see what she had inherited.

Deciding to follow his advice and get away from everything that made her feel like a failure, she packed up her belongings and came hoping her life would be better. She was alone anyway, what did it matter where she lived?

Steph sighed as she fought back the tears that threatened to fall. *Okay, I'm here, now what am I going to do? I know nothing about running a farm, caring for animals or growing crops. I expected a small, cozy farmhouse, not this large building. I understood the house came with some property but…* Steph shook her head. *I'm not even sure how large an acre is. From what I saw as I drove in, the farm is huge! I signed papers yesterday accepting responsibility for hundreds of acres with buildings and various livestock, including horses. How am I supposed take care of all of that by myself?*

"Good grief Misti. What am I going to do?" Steph stared at the cup in her hand as if excepting to see the solution in the dark liquid. She nearly fell out of her chair when the doorbell rang. Steph looked out the back window to decide which door to answer. Since no one was there, she walked stiffly and slowly to the double front doors.

Misti tore through the house like a bullet barking and running up and down the hall.

Steph reached the front door hoping it was not Stanley Wilber. *I don't think I can handle him on an empty stomach. I'll just see what he wants and if necessary, I'll tell him I'll come to his office next week to handle it. I don't want him asking me any questions I'm not ready to answer for myself. I won't be rude, just stern and send him on his way so I can get back to solving my own problems.*

As she unlocked the door and swung it open, she began, "Stanley, it was not necessary for you to come out here."

Steph tried to hide her shock when she realized it wasn't Stanley standing on the porch but a woman. Laughter twinkled in soft, hazel eyes. Her jet-black hair was pulled back into a long ponytail, giving her a youthful appearance. Wonderful odors were coming from the container she was holding in front of her protruding stomach.

"Good thing I'm not Stanley. You don't seem too happy to see him."

Jenny smiled. She instantly knew she was going to like her new neighbor. Despite Hank's description, she had been expecting someone wearing fancy clothes and lots of make-up. Here was just a regular person in jeans and a T-shirt. Jenny instinctively knew they would be good friends.

"Can I help you?" Steph quickly recovered herself, remembering her manners. "Please, let me help you." She reached for the container expecting it to be heavy, surprised when it was light and warm. Stepping back she held the door open with her body.

"Please come in."

Jenny walked into the house heading to the kitchen. She always felt welcomed during the short visits she had with Miss Weatherby. When Jenny stopped by, Hyacinth would always invite her into the kitchen for a drink while they talked.

This person was alone and appeared to know her way around so Steph followed her to the kitchen. Setting the container on the table, she watched as the other woman eased herself into a chair at the table.

"It's been a while since I was last here. George comes over and checks the place out once in a while. I always enjoyed coming here. I think the last time was when I helped move Hyacinth to the nursing home. I cleaned out her refrigerator and freezer for her." Jenny paused and looked around.

"It seems funny not seeing Hyacinth fussing around the kitchen. I hear you made quite an impression last night."

Steph was uncomfortable wondering who this strange person was. Her earlier mood was hanging over her head like a depressing cloud and now this stranger was making herself right at home. Steph remained quiet trying to decide what to do but as she listened, everything began to make sense. Steph tried to keep the relief from her voice.

"You must be Jenny, George's wife. He said his wife was pregnant and took the call from Attorney Wilbur about my needing to be checked on. May I get you a cup of coffee?"

Smiling at Steph, Jenny absentmindedly rubbed her protruding belly.

"No thanks, I have to watch my caffeine intake with this little guy. I wouldn't say no to a cup of tea though." Jenny's expression turned sheepish. "I guess I should've introduced myself." Jenny grinned again. "I was just too excited to wait any longer to come and meet you. I know you're going to love it here."

Returning the smile, Steph began preparing Jenny's tea. Her mother always loved a good cup of tea and even though Steph preferred coffee, she knew how to brew a decent cup. She was grateful one of the boxes she'd already brought in contained her mother's favorite teapot and strainer.

Steph was keenly aware she had not eaten breakfast and the fragrance from the container on the table was making her stomach grumble. Not wanting to appear too eager, she turned from the counter and suggested the container with a nod of her head.

"Whatever you brought sure smells wonderful."

"It's just a coffee cake I made this morning. I've been making some dishes ahead to freeze so Hank and George won't starve when I have the baby. I'm trying to plan ahead but it's not easy. If you have some plates and forks, we can have some now. It always tastes better when it's still warm from the oven."

Setting plates and forks on the table, Steph turned back to finish the tea.

Glancing out the window, Steph saw someone entering the barn. Stanley didn't say anything about a farmhand. She knew George was caring for the livestock and horses. She didn't know if any animals were in the barn, but instinct told her this person was not an employee of hers.

"Someone just went into my barn. Should I call 911 or the police? No, I'll dial 911 since I don't know the phone number for the police."

Panic made Steph's voice sound higher than normal. Turning to reach for her cell phone on the table, Steph saw Jenny laughing.

"I forgot to mention I brought Hank with me. George doesn't like my driving now that I'm so far along. Hank overdid himself yesterday so he needs to take it easy. He forgets he's still healing and is as much of an invalid as I am. He was a member of the Columbus Police force. An arrest went bad and he was injured. He's getting better but some days are better than others. George wanted to get some fieldwork done since the tractor is fixed so it's just us. Hank said he'd look around while we women became acquainted. I think he's afraid he might be outnumbered."

Jenny stood up pulling her cell phone out of her pocket. "Hank promised George he'd stay in the barnyard. I'll give him a ring to have him come and join us for some coffee and cake. That'll keep him out of trouble."

Jenny chuckled as she walked out the back door to the deck and called Hank. When he appeared at the door, she waved and returned to the kitchen.

*　*　*

Hank reluctantly went to join the women. He had found some interesting items in the barn he wanted to study. Stiff and sore from the previous day's activities, he decided to indulge Jenny and go in. Thinking about the coffee cake Jenny brought made his mouth water. He fervently hoped he would not be as tongue-tied as he was last night. Usually he was confident and in control when he was around women. He could not understand his blundering tongue. Something about this woman turned him into a mindless fool. He decided he would just keep his mouth shut.

The doctors told him he would experience times when his confidence would be lacking. They warned he might suffer anxiety attacks. He had only experienced minor attacks of anxiety so far, but he had no wish to experience a major one. The minor ones were upsetting enough, causing him to sweat and shake. This was not a time for one to happen.

Walking into the kitchen, Hank heard the women's voices. He smiled when he saw Steph sitting at the table talking with Jenny. *How pretty she looks this morning. Coffee and cake with two lovely ladies, the day is looking up.*

"What do you mean you didn't know your family? Why haven't you looked around?" Jenny was doing her best to stay seated.

"If it was my house, I'd be looking around and checking out all the rooms. I've only been in a few rooms on the main floor. Hyacinth said when she was growing up her father would tell her stories of strange happenings in this house. She said he talked about railroad people, conductors of some kind, coming to visit. He heard the stories when he was young and repeated them to her. If your Great-granddad lived-in this house, I bet some of his belongings are still even here."

"I used to sit in this kitchen and imagine what it was like when they would have large parties here."

Jenny's eyes took on a faraway look as she continued.

"The original Mr. Weatherby built this house and then remodeled it for his wife, Primrose. Hyacinth said the kitchen was on the lowest level originally. Primrose had some elaborate ideas about how the house should be built and wanted it to be as modern as possible. His wedding gift to her was to have the whole house remodeled and updated while they were on their honeymoon. They had lots of servants and used to hold grand parties here." Jenny sighed.

"I bet the parties were wonderful." Jenny perked up, and then went on.

"They owned a ranch out west too. Hyacinth said she never knew what happened to it. Her father said they owned this land and it was important for their family to tend it well. When Hyacinth was a little girl, there were still servants who worked here. She said when times became hard; her father let some of them go because he couldn't pay their wages. Since he needed the men to work the farm, it was the house staff he fired. They changed this room into a kitchen and Hyacinth said her mother learned to make-do with one servant when there were at least six to help before. When they were old enough to help, the three sisters picked the chores they were willing to do. Of course being the son, your Great Granddad worked on the farm." Jenny paused and drank from her cup before continuing. She was beginning to wonder how much more she should say. Shrugging her shoulders she went on.

"Hyacinth said she learned to help cook. Iris was older and didn't like helping around the house. She would pretend to clean. When their mother would punish her for the poor job she was doing, Iris had temper tantrums." Jenny paused again before rushing on.

"Hyacinth would cry when she talked about Iris so I tried to avoid the subject. Over the years Hyacinth closed up most of the house, living more and more downstairs as you can tell."

Jenny slowed down to get her breath back, exhausted from telling her story.

Steph felt her excitement about exploring the house build as Jenny spoke. Steph didn't know why but she trusted these people. She just met them yet something about Jenny made Steph feel as if they had been friends for years.

Hank was another story. Steph didn't understand why, but with Hank, she felt safe. This was a different feeling then she ever had with Fred.

Steph decided to take a leap of faith.

"When we finish our coffee cake and drinks, we can all go looking around the house together. I'll be glad for the company."

Steph cut the coffee cake and served each one a plate. Hank had not said a word since he sat down. Steph poured him a cup of coffee and set it on the table. He stared at the full cup with a glazed expression on his face.

"I can get you tea if you don't want coffee." Steph's voice cut through Hank's thoughts.

"No, coffee is fine. I was just wondering how many floors there are." Hank was recovering from a sudden vision of his morning being spent wandering around the large house. He was already worn out but didn't want to spoil Jenny's fun. He realized it was up to him to watch her and if she became tired, they would have to leave.

"Three levels above the ground and one below according to Hyacinth." Jenny replied sipping her tea.

"What is your secret to brewing tea? This is delicious."

Smiling Steph answered. "The secret is having a mother who enjoyed a good cup of tea. She said the best way to brew it is the old fashioned way. You must be sure the water is at the right temperature when you steep the tea. I grew up learning to brew it the way she liked it best. I used to get so upset when she would tell me it was 'just passable.' Now I wish I could make her a cup of tea just to hear her say that again. Since she's been gone, I haven't had anyone to make it for." Trying to shake the grief that suddenly struck her, Steph told herself to be grateful. She'd learned a great deal about her family history sitting at this table with Jenny. She could grieve when she was alone.

Jenny started wiggling around in her chair, bringing Steph back from her own thoughts.

"Are you okay? You seem uncomfortable."

Jenny grimaced and stood up. "Being pregnant is fun, but when the kid kicks your bladder and kidneys, you can't hold out long. Please excuse me."

Getting up from her own chair, Steph escorted Jenny to the small room she slept in the night before. The bed was not made but Steph hoped Jenny would overlook that lack of housekeeping since the bathroom was clean. Assured that Jenny would be okay, she quickly made the bed and wandered back to the kitchen.

Glancing around after the women left, Hank saw the writing tablet lying on the table. Checking the doorway to be sure no one was looking; he pulled it over and picked it up so he could read it. The title intrigued him. '*THINGS POSSIBLE*'.

Hank lifted an eyebrow as he continued to read: "One, run the farm; two, write a book; three, open the house up as a B & B; four, rent rooms like a boarding house; five, get married and have a large family; six . . ."

"Ahem!" Steph cleared her throat. Her anger was clearly written on her face.

Hank jumped and nearly dropped the tablet.

"Sorry, I didn't realize I was reading this out loud." Hank did his best to sound apologetic.

Alone and bored, he had allowed himself to be tempted by curiosity. He knew he should feel guilty but he felt some of his old humor coming back. *After all it was lying there for anyone to read. Why not me?* He grinned. *I'm going to have a little fun with this.*

"So this is a list of goals to accomplish with your life. Hmm, at the top it says '*Things possible.*' Do you think you can possibly run this farm? No, wait, I know, you are going to hook some unsuspecting fellow into marrying you. You'll have a large family and fill the house with kids. That way you won't need to rent out rooms. You'll be so busy popping out kids; you won't have time to write your book."

Warming up to the subject he began to elaborate. "You could open a day care and then have a doggie day care on the side."

Reaching for the pen lying on the table, he started to write his ideas down. "How about boarding horses? If you're going to be boarding people, you can set the barn up to handle their horses."

Watching the play of emotions crossing Steph's face, he was starting to feel a twinge of guilt. It was none of his business. After all, who was he to say anything? He didn't have a place to call his own. He was forced to live with his parents after the assault and now he was living with George and Jenny.

"Those are all great ideas, Hank. I hope you're writing them down. This is a big place for one person. If it were mine, I'd want to do something with it." Hank jumped as Jenny walked back into the room. He forgot she was around. George told Hank he was to watch her so she wouldn't overdo and here he was paying so much attention to Steph, he forgot about Jenny. Hank loved Jenny as if she was his sister and felt she brightened up any room with her bubbly personality. He hadn't understood that expression until he met her. Now he felt her brightness slightly dimmed next to the pretty brunette Steph.

Steph took a calming breath. "Since you're holding the pen and tablet, I am dubbing you the official mapmaker."

Turning to walk past Jenny, Steph tried to dampen down the anger she was beginning to feel toward Hank. It was too soon and her pain was too raw. He wouldn't know he was being hurtful. She was willing to admit she found him handsome and attractive in a rugged way. She was not willing to admit that when he smiled and started teasing her, she found it hard to breathe and her heart began to race. They'd just met and she was already attracted to the man. She was going to have to be careful. Once again the pain of Fred's deceit and controlling behavior threatened to overwhelm her. She forced herself to straighten her spine and walk away.

CHAPTER 5

Steph led the way down the hall.

"I think the best place to start is at the front door. Shall we start this way and work our way around the ground floor to see what's here? Later we can tackle the other floors."

Steph stopped to look at the others, watching for their reactions. She was hoping they would agree to her suggestion. Her ankle was starting to limber up, but she didn't want to sprain it again.

Hank bowed and held out his arm to signal she should continue to lead the way. He was relieved by this strategy but found his back muscles protesting to his low bow. He tried to hide the pain from his voice as he straightened up.

"I think slow and steady would be best for Jenny. She shouldn't be marching up and down stair steps after all the baking she did this morning. George made her promise to be home for lunch so she can rest this afternoon." He bowed slightly again to take the sting out of his words.

"Lead on."

Steph followed Misti through the maze of boxes and past the curving steps that flowed gracefully upward toward the mysterious upper levels.

The Sheltie abruptly halted and was sniffing at the baseboard of a paneled wall. Embarrassed, Steph turned to her companions.

"I guess we have to go back."

"No, I'm sure that Hyacinth mentioned there should be a door around here somewhere. She said it was near the stairway." Jenny started running her hands on the wood searching for a door.

"I know there's a room on the other side of this wall."

Steph stared at what she thought was a solid wall. "How can there be a door here?"

Jenny stopped what she was doing and gave Steph an exasperated look.

"I don't know where it is exactly, I just know it's around here."

"Okay, then I guess we keep looking."

Not wanting to disappoint Jenny, Steph ran her hands over the wall until she located notches that appeared to be out of place. When she inspected the wall further, she realized it was not a wall but closed floor-to-ceiling pocket doors. Holding her breath, hoping it wasn't somehow locked, she pulled one door to the side revealing an elaborately decorated stained glass door. Opening the door, a flood of light caused temporary blindness. She heard Jenny gasp and when her own eyes adjusted, she knew why. The sunlit room was a conservatory.

Misti dashed into the room and immediately began to explore. She ran across the floor stopping to wag her tail and sniff the floor or the empty pottery scattered about. Once satisfied, she quickly moved on to another spot racing back and forth around the room. Finally, she laid down waiting for the humans.

Slowly Steph, Jenny and Hank, wandered into the large room. Its emptiness was a sharp contrast to the other rooms they'd walked past. Unlike the little dog, they moved as if they were afraid of disturbing the room. They had watched her from the door together, but once inside, they separated and moved about as if each was searching for something.

Jenny found herself drawn to the rounded area of the room facing the front of the house. She had passed this room from the outside many times but never dared to venture in. She turned around looking for the others.

"Hyacinth said her father closed down parts of the house when her mother died."

Jenny was surprised at how well her voice carried. She meant to speak in her normal voice, but what she heard sounded as if she shouted. While covering her mouth with her hand to hide a giggle, she shrugged embarrassed at her behavior. She tried to speak a little quieter.

"Sorry, I didn't mean to be so loud. Hyacinth's mother loved plants. Hyacinth said this would be full of exotic orchids, ferns and a variety of other plants. It must have seemed like a jungle to a small child."

Grinning, she began to explore the area.

Large, heavy curtains hung across the front windows and down the side of the long room, effectively blocking the outside world. Jenny looked up and admired the ceiling created from curved iron and glass. Windows were hidden in the artistic design to allow for ventilation as needed. Unfiltered sunlight flowed into the room, reflecting off surfaces while sending rainbows of light across the floor. Looking across the room from her vantage point, Jenny could see a faint path worn in the thick tile floor. Continuing to gaze around, she noticed two large, old-fashioned plant urns standing to one side waiting patiently for new plants to hold. Occasionally glancing at Hank, she studied the room.

Steph forgot about the others as she moved across the tile floor. She closed her eyes, drifting to the center of the room, an unknown force drawing her there. She reveled in the sunlight that penetrated the darkness of the room from the ceiling high above. Slowly she turned in a small circle, allowing her mind to fill with pictures of how this area must have looked at one time. In her mind's eye, she saw vining plants hanging from the walls, green and trailing from containers suspended in the air. She saw towering exotic plants blooming and growing, their limbs reaching for the sky. She knew this room was once filled with life. *How wonderful this place is.* Steph spread out her arms and turned once more feeling herself transported to another time her thoughts reeling. *I can smell the roses and lilies as they open and mix their fragrances with rosemary and jasmine. I promise to fill this with life again.* Steph knew in her heart this was a promise she would find joy in keeping.

Hank leaned against the far wall watching Jenny and Steph. He felt the emptiness of the room as a weight on his chest. He knew it wasn't possible but he felt the emotion as if it were his own. Ashamed, he turned away. Shaking off the loneliness it caused, he turned back to face the center of the room. What greeted him took his breath away.

Steph was standing in the middle of the room oblivious to her surroundings. Hank found his heart stirring with feelings for this stranger. Now he understood the expression "she was a vision". Steph stood with her eyes shut, her face turned up to greet the morning sun. *How beautiful she looks. The sun brings out the chestnut color of her hair. She belongs here. It's as if the house was built just for her.* He watched the slight rise and fall of her breasts that proved she was alive. As if in a trance she started to turn.

Afraid to break the spell, he simply stood and stared, trying to memorize the serene look on Steph's face; knowing it was a moment he wanted to remember forever. There was something about this innocent, trusting woman who let complete strangers into her house. He wasn't sure why, but knew he wanted to get to know her better.

Jenny searched the room for a chair or a place to sit down. It was hard for her to stand for long periods and she sat much of the time at home. She felt the heavy weight in her womb pulling on the muscles of her back. She began baking early this morning so she wouldn't feel guilty about coming to meet Steph. Jenny saw Hank watching Steph as if mesmerized by what he was seeing. She regretted what she was about to do. She took a deep breath and released it slowly.

"Hey Hank, are you getting all this down? What did you put down for the name of this room Mr. Mapmaker?"

Hank jumped with guilt at the mention of his name. Leave it to eagle eye Jenny to see what was happening. He was grateful that she said no more, but she did have bad timing. He enjoyed watching Steph but now the spell was broken and he was back to reality.

"Umm, I put this down as the conservatory. I'll sketch it." Bending down to his task, he hoped Steph didn't know he was watching her.

64

Steph too jumped when Jenny spoke. She was enjoying the moment. *If this is the first room, what other wonders are in this house of mine? How long have I been standing here? I feel as if I have always been here.* She tried to keep her voice even as she spoke.

"Let's move on. I see a door over there by you Hank. Would you like to open it for us?"

Steph waited until Jenny walked over beside her. The women walked slowly across the room as if they were reluctant to leave.

As Jenny and Steph walked into the next room, Steph noticed the overflowing bookcases. Broken only by doorways, windows and a fireplace, the bookcases lined three of the four walls. Boxes of all sizes and shapes were stacked haphazardly around the room. Some were open, spilling books and office supplies from their bulging tops. The doorway through which they had just entered was semiblocked by a stack of books on the right. Two oak filing cabinets stood side by side along the wall to their left. A single wooden chair, placed beside the filing cabinets was the only other adornment on the otherwise blank wall. Steph wondered briefly if the closed door across the room was a closet or a door leading to the next room. Hank was sitting at the desk reading a letter when the women came into the room.

Steph quickly dismissed the impression there was something special about the room, shrugging it off as nerves. She wandered around examining the fireplace behind the desk.

Jenny walked over to a wing-backed chair nestled in one corner of the room. With a heavy sigh, she settled down, ignoring the faint cloud of dust that rose around her from the cushioned seat.

Steph opened her mouth, intending to ask Jenny how she was feeling. Her worry about Jenny fled when she glanced over Hank's shoulder and saw him reading a letter typed on business stationary. Frustrated by his rude boldness, she made a mental note to come back and go through the other papers on the desk. There may be something important about the farm she would need to know. She reminded herself she had invited them to look around with her as her guests.

"Where are the keys to the desk?"

Hank had finished the letter and was trying to open the desk drawers. He tugged on each drawer handle finding them locked.

"I don't have the keys. They must be somewhere in the house. Attorney Wilbur only gave me keys to the house and an outbuilding he said was padlocked." Steph tried to keep her voice even, not wanting to share her frustration. *If I don't find the keys, I'll have a locksmith come out and open it.* Making a mental note about the keys, Steph tried to mask her own curiosity by looking at the books on the shelves near Jenny. The desk and its contents were quickly forgotten as she looked at the leather bound volumes.

Steph's attention was drawn back to Jenny when she heard her give a small sigh.

"Are you okay? You seem a little flushed."

"I'm okay. The baby pulls on my back. It's nice to sit down. This must have been the study. Hyacinth said her father spent most of his time in here. I'll just sit here and relax while you and Hank scope out the room. This is a comfortable chair. I don't think I'll move for a few minutes if you don't mind."

Hank had left the desk and was walking around the room checking in corners, moving books around and opening boxes. Restless, he moved on into the next room then returned shaking his head.

"Someone's been sleeping in that room."

Steph looked through the doorway. It was the room she used the night before. She was sure there were no doors in the room except to a closet and the bathroom. She walked into the room and closed the door. The paneling was cut to allow the door to 'disappear' when it was closed. Now that she knew where to look, she could clearly see the outline of the door and the delicate handle. Steph ran a hand over the wood admiring the handiwork.

"It took someone with skill and patience to camouflage the door this way. I've never seen anything like it. This is the small bedroom I'm using."

Steph opened the door again to allow Hank and Jenny to enter the room.

"I found it set up as a bedroom so I cleaned it up to use. It seemed a perfect place to sleep at the time."

"This was the library. Hyacinth turned it into a bedroom when Lily died. She said the steps were getting too much for her. She was living alone and wanted everything on the main floor. The bookshelves were dismantled and moved to another part of the house."

Jenny kept walking on out into the hall.

"I'm going to sit in the parlor while you keep looking. Have fun!" She smiled as she moved away.

Steph and Hank continued to search the main floor of the house. They walked through glass French doors into the dining room. The etched glass panels of the doors gave the room an airy appearance. Solid wooden doors were set into the wall between the parlor and the dining room, allowing easy access in and out.

Steph felt drawn to the intricately carved wooden mantel of the fireplace that dominated the outside dining room wall. A matching pair of crystal candelabras glistened on the mantel. Steph tentatively reached up to touch the crystals causing them to swing and catch the light sending rainbows of color around the room.

"It must have been wonderful to host large dinner parties in here."

She walked the length of the room, carefully avoiding the items scattered about the room. Absently she moved her hand over the dark, smooth wood of the long dining table, ignoring the stacks of items piled on the table.

"I can't believe this is mine. Just think. Generations of my family actually ate at this table."

She pulled out a chair and sat down, looking around in disbelief.

"I think I'll sit here for a few minutes. If you want to go on Hank I'll check on Jenny before I join you. I just want to absorb this."

Hank didn't reply as he left the room. A sense of unease was growing with each room they walked through. Unwilling to spoil Jenny's fun, he kept his thoughts to himself.

Jenny was sitting on the sofa with her eyes shut as he entered the parlor. Hank knew she wasn't asleep, just feeling the baby move, something she'd done since the first time she felt the baby kick. Getting past his own embarrassment at first, he now enjoyed watching her face when she closed her eyes to feel the baby move. At his approach, she looked up at him.

"Are you doing okay? Do you need anything? Will you be alright sitting here?" Hank was relieved to see that she was sitting on a sheet covered sofa that was completely devoid of clutter. "Is it safe for you to sit there?"

Jenny smiled as she nodded her head and closed her eyes again. "Hyacinth always sat here, she was careful about keeping the clutter off the stuffed furniture." Jenny sighed.

Taking his time, Hank looked around the parlor but couldn't sit down. He felt as if he was being pulled to look further. When he opened the pocket doors from the parlor and walked into the next room, he found what he was looking for.

Like the conservatory on the other side of the house, the rounded front section and long sidewall of this room were also covered by curtains. The heavy black material had been faded by the sun over the years to a charcoal gray. Unlike its twin, the closed curtains made this room spooky. Molded plaster tiles covered the ceiling of the room and were reflected in the high gloss shine of the wooden floor. Searching for a way to open the curtains, Hank moved from window to window until he found the cording to work them. Gently and slowly, as if the slightest disturbance would alter the room, he invited the sun to brighten and cleanse the room of its darkness.

Jenny and Steph joined him as he marveled at the size of the room. French doors of heavy leaded glass opened out onto the covered outside porch. Discarded furniture was scattered about the room. Some of the furniture was stacked up neatly. Other pieces held stacks of newspapers and other items as if waiting to be used. The clutter seemed contained to one end of the room.

"Ah! The music room!"

Jenny moved to sit on an empty chair she'd spotted when she walked in.

"Hyacinth told stories about the Sunday afternoon recitals they used to have. She and her sisters took private dance lessons and they all learned to play the piano. There should be mirrors behind the curtains on this inside wall."

Jenny turned and pointed but didn't rise from her chair. "Hyacinth said her mother didn't want the mirrors ruined by the sunlight so they covered them with curtains."

Jenny watched Hank and Steph explore the mysteries the room had to offer. There was a baby grand piano in the far corner covered with heavily padded material. It took both of them to remove the coverings. Gingerly Steph tried a few experimental scales. She was rewarded by a rich, if slightly off-key sound.

Steph and Hank continued to discover what they could about the room. They peeked under the curtains and found the mirrors intact. Conversation flowed freely between the women as they talked and speculated about the parties held there.

Hank's stomach was telling him it was getting close to lunch time. Jenny was enjoying herself but she was beginning to show the strain of the morning. He checked his watch before interrupting the conversation.

"Jenny, I promised George I'd get you home by noon. We'd better be going. It's been fun Steph."

Taking Jenny by the arm, Hank gently steered her back through the parlor and out the front door.

Steph followed them outside.

"Be sure to come back anytime Jenny and you too, Hank. I enjoyed meeting you and appreciated having both of you here. Thanks again for the coffee cake."

Steph waved good-bye, watching as they drove away. When she turned back toward the house, she realized she hadn't seen Misti for a while. She went back through the rooms looking for her and found her curled up on the bed. When Steph entered the room, Misti merely opened one eye and then went back to sleep.

What a good idea. I could use a little rest too. Steph stretched out beside the sleeping dog and went to sleep thinking about lavish formal dinner parties and afternoon recitals.

* * *

Steph woke with a start. She was disoriented and tired. She remained still, thinking of what she had seen of the house already. It had been fun having Jenny and Hank around, their conversation filling the empty silence of the house. It would be different looking around alone. She knew she should get up and start cleaning, but it was too overwhelming to think about right now. The question nagging at her was *where to begin?* She heard a noise and realized her cell phone was ringing.

Searching for the sound, she finally located it on the kitchen table where she had left it.

"Hello?"

"Hello Steph, it's Keri Hall. I was calling to check up on you. I wanted to be sure you arrived safely. How's Ohio?"

Steph settled down in a chair to talk with Keri.

"It was a nice drive but long. Misti traveled well and made herself right at home. I met the man who rents my land. He and a friend stopped by last night. I was out in the yard when they pulled up on some kind of vehicles. Wouldn't you know? I fell and sprained my ankle so they helped me into the house. You would have been proud of Misti. She growled and barked like a real guard dog. She was being protective until she jumped on my sore ankle." Steph giggled. "I told her to sit down and she found it hard to bark and sit at the same time." Steph laughed at her own description.

Keri chuckled.

"I imagine she was frustrated. She's a good dog but doesn't realize she's not a big guard dog. She can make noise when she wants to." Keri paused, attempting to sound serious.

"That's a unique way to make your guests feel welcome. Do you always fall for strangers?" Keri began laughing at her own joke.

"Ha, Ha. I was so embarrassed. It was nice for Misti to 'break the ice' so to speak. George is the neighbor. His wife Jenny is expecting and she came over today with Hank. She knew Aunt Hyacinth and told me about her. I hope to spend more time with her and find out what else she knows. She was very nice."

"Who's Hank?" Keri didn't miss the change in Steph's voice when she said his name.

"Hank's living with George and Jenny. Jenny said he's a friend of George's and he is helping out with the farm work. Jenny said he spends most of his time driving her around when he's not helping George."

"It's nice to know you're making friends. I was worried about you. I know you're a capable person, but it's a long way from here and you're all alone."

"I appreciate your concern. It's been hard for me but for now I'm okay. I have next-door neighbors I can call and if George can't come, I know Hank will. Everything is fine."

Touched by Keri's concern, Steph felt tears threatening to close her throat so she decided to change the subject.

"Let me tell you about the house. It's really big. It has a conservatory on one side and a music room on the other. I'll have to send pictures for you. You won't believe it! I've only been on the main floor so far. There's a lot of work to do. It's awfully big for one person. I have some ideas what to do with it but for now they are just ideas. I'll tell you more after I've given them some thought."

CHAPTER 6

Steph was sitting at the kitchen table staring at the open notepad in front of her but not seeing it. *Today is Monday. It's hard to believe its Memorial Day. It feels like any other day. I should be getting something done but I don't know where to start in here.* She let her thoughts wander back over the past two days.

Jenny had returned Saturday afternoon bringing Hank and George along to help Steph unload the UHaul. The furniture and boxes were now stacked neatly in the music room. Steph planned to hire someone to unload the truck but Jenny insisted the men were willing to help. Working together, they unloaded most of the items on Saturday and returned on Sunday afternoon to unload the remaining items.

When they were done, Jenny had invited Steph to a barbecue at their home Monday, saying it was an annual event for their friends and family.

Steph looked around the room, torn between cleaning out the cabinets in the kitchen and going to the party. *If I start right away, I bet I could get a few cabinets cleaned out by lunchtime.* She reached for her cellphone to call Jenny and cancel when it rang.

"Hello?"

"Hi, It's Keri. I'm home from the cemetery. I sent you a picture on my cell phone of the flowers I put on your parents' graves. I wanted to be sure you received it."

"Oh Keri! It's so good to hear your voice. Thank you for doing this for me. Let me check my phone, just a minute." Steph looked for the picture while Keri waited. As soon as the picture came up, she had to fight back tears to see. Steph was surprised by the emotions welling up within her. "Oh, they are so beautiful!" Her throat choked with guilt. She forgot to order flowers before she left and at the last minute asked Keri to take flowers to the graves for her. Now as she looked at them, she felt the sharp pain of her parents' loss again.

With tears running down her cheeks, she sat and stared at the picture, forgetting her friend was on the phone line.

"Hello? .... Hello Steph? ... Stephanotis, are you there?"

Hearing the faint voice of her friend, Steph tried to pull herself to together. *I can cry later,* she promised herself.

"I'm sorry. I'm here." Steph wiped the tears away.

"Thank you for getting the flowers for me. They're lovely. Mom would have loved them. I'm sorry I had to ask you to do this for me. I still can't believe I forgot."

"It was no problem. I always put flowers on my husband's grave so I was going anyway." Keri paused. "I was afraid there for a minute you were disappointed. I'm glad you like them." Keri cleared her throat. "So Steph, tell me what are you doing today? I hope you have plans that don't include packing or unpacking."

Steph laughed. Keri always knew how to make her feel better. "Jenny invited me to a barbecue but I'm not sure I'll go. Jenny said it's mostly family and a few friends. I'm not sure I'm ready for the social scene just yet. I'd like to start cleaning here in the kitchen. I'm tired of using paper plates."

"Steph, you're too young not to take the day off and enjoy it. It bothers me to think of your slaving away in that house all by yourself. If you go to the party, maybe you'll meet someone special. Dress yourself up and go. You deserve a little fun. You can start cleaning and working again tomorrow. I know Dr. Waltzer would tell you the same thing."

"I don't know." Steph could hear the whine in her own voice. She took a deep breath, releasing it slowly before going on. "I was sitting here thinking of all the work that needs done. I feel guilty thinking about going."

"Okay, look at it this way. Didn't you tell me George rents land from you and he's taking care of your animals?"

"Yes."

"Well, as the landlord you have certain duties. If your tenant invites you over, you should go. This would be a great opportunity to see the horses and other animals without prying."

"I hadn't thought of that. I guess when you put it that way, I should go." Steph bit her lower lip to keep the trembling from her voice. She wanted to ease into her new life nice and slow now that she was here. She didn't want to jump in hoping she was up to the challenge and find out she wasn't.

"Good! That's settled. Now go get ready and have fun. I'll talk with you later; I want to hear all about it. Good-bye for now."

"Good-bye." Steph sat staring at her phone after she hung up. Keri was right. She didn't have to start today but she wasn't in a party mood. Now what was she going to do? Keri wouldn't let Steph forget it if she didn't go to the party; which meant Steph would go.

Steph thought back over her sessions with Dr. Waltzer and how the Dr. encouraged her to trust herself. Steph had been an emotional wreck when her father died. Losing her mother almost put her over the edge. She felt alone, unloved and miserable. Dr. Waltzer helped her to see she was not the cause of what had happened but a victim. Somehow, with his help, she had found the strength to leave Fred and then move here.

Steph admired people like Keri and Betty Brown. They didn't let their circumstances stop them. They kept on going, enjoying what they could in life. Steph sighed. She had promised herself to be more like that. After all, she had no one to please but herself now. Keri was right. She deserved some fun. Steph smiled slightly as she walked to her room to decide what she should wear. Most of her clothes were still in boxes. It was going to take some time to get ready for the party.

*   *   *

Steph stood by the front door waiting for Hank and Jenny to come by. They were going with her to take the U-Haul to the local dealer. As she waited, she smiled, thinking of the direction her life was now taking.

She was the owner of a farm and was fast becoming good friends with Jenny, and of course, George and Hank. She attended a holiday barbecue, met George and Jenny's family and friends and had a wonderful time.

Looking at Misti sitting on the floor beside her, Steph thought about her horses still in George's care. Jenny had told her about Sun Dancer and Steph wondered if Jenny exaggerated until she saw him for herself.

Sun Dancer was impressive. Jenny described him as magnificent and Steph could not think of a better adjective to use. He let her pet him and even took part of an apple out of her hand. His muzzle was so soft. It felt like a warm cloud of air blowing on her hand. His lips barely brushed her open palm when she held the apple up for him.

Now as she looked at Misti, her heart was full of joy. She had a brave and true companion in Misti and she owned a marvelous horse, correction, she owned horses. What more could a girl want? She would have to learn to ride.

Steph's thoughts were interrupted by the honking of a car horn as Hank and Jenny arrived. Steph gathered her purse and sunglasses. "Be good Misti. I'm taking the truck on one last ride. Hank and Jenny are bringing me home. Stay here and I'll be back soon." Steph checked the lock on the door as she closed it behind her.

Hank yelled from the window of Jenny's SUV. "Follow us. We'll lead the way." He preferred driving his own truck, but Jenny insisted on going with him to pick Steph up. It was easier for her to get in and out of the SUV.

"Don't forget, we're going shopping before we come back. Steph needs a few things and I promised to help her pick them out." Jenny was sitting in the backseat where she had more room.

"I don't know how you talk me into these things." Hank complained as he drove into town. "I agreed to pick Steph up and the next thing I know, I'm taking you two shopping. The least you could do is shop in a store I wouldn't be embarrassed going into."

"We're going to stores with curtains and kitchen supplies. It's not as if we're asking you to take us to a lingerie store."

"Well, at least that I might enjoy." Hank glanced at Jenny in the rearview mirror.

"Hank!" Jenny pretended to be shocked. "I'm keeping my eye on you mister."

*   *   *

"So that's what that is, a doughnut cutter. I couldn't figure it out. I'm so glad you knew." Steph was sitting at the table in the kitchen talking on her cell phone with Betty Brown, a friend from her old apartment building. Her laptop computer was open on the table in front of her. "I still can't believe I'm almost finished cleaning out the kitchen. The cabinets held a lot more than I realized."

"It's been fun helping you like this but someday I'll have to come to visit so I can show you how to use a few of these kitchen gadgets. I know you'll use them when you learn to cook." Betty tried to keep from laughing. She had given Steph lessons and knew Steph just needed more practice at it.

"I can boil water and make a decent stew. If push comes to shove, I'm not a bad cook. I just haven't had much reason to cook." Steph looked around at the open boxes sitting on the floor. "I'm going to put your name on these boxes so when you come visit, I'll know which boxes contain all this stuff. I tried to keep all the pieces together but I still have a box of unknown items."

Betty sighed trying not to sound too wistful. "It was hard to know what some of the pieces were without being there. Some gadgets are easy to remember but some of the items I haven't seen in years. Those digital pictures you sent were nice and clear."

"Well, it was great to get this room done. The new shelf paper brightened up the cabinets. I still can't believe I let Jenny talk me into getting everything that matched. It was extravagant but worth it." Steph looked around again as if seeing the room for the first time.

"I feel as if I'm in someone else's kitchen. I don't think I've ever had a tablecloth that matched the curtains. It's fun being coordinated!"

Betty laughed.

"It makes cooking and baking more fun when you're comfortable in the kitchen. It sounds as if you're settling in."

"It's made it a lot easier to clean out the cabinets knowing I have the new shelf paper. I have it organized the way I like it. I'll finish the last cabinet today and then I can start on another room."

"I must say I'm impressed you're keeping a record as you clear out the cabinets. At first I thought you were causing yourself more work, but the pictures you've been sending do show the cupboards were stuffed full. It's hard to imagine so many dishes could fit into one cupboard. What inspired you to take the pictures?"

"Well, it started out as an idea to keep Jenny busy. She said she's bored sitting at home and George approves. I think he likes knowing he's just down the road if she needs him. She can't do too much since she's so large with her pregnancy. She needs to sit and rest most of the time. Writing down what I find in the cabinets was something that came to me the first day. She felt as if she was helping. When I opened a cabinet and saw it so full I didn't know where to begin. I was actually fooling around when I took pictures of how it looked before I started. Now as I go back over the lists, it amazes me what we found. It's been fun to look at the pictures and compare them to the written list. The dishes and items were stuck wherever they would fit; there was no organization in the kitchen. I wouldn't have known the grinder should have more than one blade without your help. It was quite a discovery to learn those funny shaped metal pans were actually pie plates."

"Well, years ago you didn't have foil pie plates. You baked a pie in glass or metal pie plates and if you gave it to someone, you hoped you would get the plate back. Now there are many nice inexpensive throw-away food containers. It sometimes makes me wonder if that's better or worse."

"I guess you could argue either way. Jenny's coming again tomorrow. I want to move into a bedroom upstairs. I need to start unpacking some of my clothes. I'm wearing the same ones almost every day. I'll call you later this week and tell you if we find anything interesting."

"I'll look forward to your call. Be careful Steph. Bye."

"I will. You too! Good-bye."

Steph began clearing out the last wall cabinet in the kitchen. The cabinet contained home-canned foods, empty containers and dishes. As she stood up on a small stepladder to clear off the top-shelf, she found herself missing Jenny's company. Jenny could not help physically, but her cheerful comments and observations about the items Steph found in the cabinets made the work easier and more fun.

Now the house seemed too quiet. Steph set down the glass bowl she was holding and went to get her MP three player and speakers. She decided music would be good company right now.

*   *   *

"I'm going to start in here." Steph showed Jenny the largest bedroom on the second floor. "I plan to redecorate and use it as my room. Come over here, I want to show you something." Steph signaled for Jenny to follow her. They walked over to the window where the floor-length curtains hung closed. "Look." Steph drew the curtains open and revealed a glass door leading to a deck area over the covered back porch. "See, I have my own patio upstairs. I can sit out here at night and relax before going to bed. Isn't it wonderful?"

"What a great feature! Hyacinth never mentioned anything like this and I didn't notice it before. Of course this may have been her parent's room and she didn't use it." Jenny opened the door but didn't walk out. "You should have someone check the deck before walking on it." She closed the door, turning back into the room. "It's a wonderful room with several possibilities for decorating."

"I know. I just loved it when I found it. I've taken digital pictures of the closet, the bathroom and the bedroom. I've been think-ing it would be smart to take pictures of the drawers and closets before clearing them out. I wondered if you'd keep an inventory of what we find. I'm hoping we'll find some toys or personal items that belonged to my great-grandfather. I'd like to be able to show them to my children."

"Sure, I'll just need a comfy chair and I'll be all set. Hank can carry the boxes downstairs for us. You're going to leave some furniture aren't you?"

Steph sat down on the bed. "I think it would be foolish to move the furniture around until I have a place to put it. I was just going to strip the rooms of the smaller pieces that I can carry myself. I'll wash the curtains and put them back up. I want to get the drawers and closets cleaned out."

Jenny sat down on the stool at the dressing table. "Are you sure you want to do all that work?"

"I don't think I have much choice. The cleaning fairy isn't going to come in and do it for me. I could probably pay someone to do it, but I'd be uncomfortable with that. I think it's best if I just do it." Steph paused. "That is if you feel up to helping me."

Jenny grinned. "I'm fine and to tell you the truth, I'd have been disappointed if you wanted to do it without me. I like going through strange closets. You never know what treasures you might find."

"Okay, then let's find you a chair and get started in here." She hopped off the bed to search for a comfortable chair for Jenny.

*   *   *

Other than daily chores on the farm, there was not much work for Hank to do. He'd fixed both of George's tractors and had tuned up the combine. Since Hank drove Jenny to Steph's farm almost daily, he spent the time exploring Steph's barn, outbuildings and the farm. He made friends with Misti, too. He always wanted a dog but his work schedule would have been unfair to a pet. He was away from home for long hours every day. A few good friends were officers in the K-9 unit and he often wondered if he should give it a try. He watched them train a few times and learned it was almost as physically challenging for the handler as it was for the dog. Hank wasn't sure he would ever be that fit again. For now, he would just take it one day at a time and play with Misti.

Hank knew Jenny and Steph were on the second floor today. They told him they were going to explore and wanted him handy in case they needed something moved. He was glad for the excuse to be around Steph. Lately, he spent most of his time thinking about her. She deserved better than an unemployed former police officer. He kept pushing thoughts of her from his mind telling himself that she deserved someone who could take care of her and she could be proud of.

"Come on, Misti, let's go play ball in the conservatory." Picking up Misti's favorite ball, Hank headed to the long, open room to play with the Sheltie.

CHAPTER 7

"Wow. This looks bigger now that it's empty." Jenny stood in the doorway of the room she and Steph finished cleaning out.

"I find it eerie the way the rooms echo when we've finished. I'll get the curtains washed and hung back up. That cuts down on the noise." Steph was holding a bag containing the curtains among other items from the room.

"It's hard to believe we've finished another room. The cleaning is going faster than I thought it would."

"I couldn't have done this without you. It seemed weird at first going through other people's stuff, as if I were violating their trust." Steph laughed. "That was until I found that ten dollar bill in the pocket of a jacket. Then it became more like a scavenger hunt."

Jenny giggled. "The look on your face! I thought you were going to tell me it was another receipt." She grabbed her swollen belly as she started laughing harder. "You looked so shocked. It was so funny. At first I thought it was one hundred dollars the way you were carrying on."

"Hey, any tips are welcome." Steph grinned.

"Then you ran downstairs and brought back another empty jar to collect money in." Jenny was still laughing.

"We have two and a half jars filled with the coins we've found. I'll have to count the money one of these days, meanwhile, we'll keep adding to it. When we finish on this floor, we can start upstairs."

Jenny sighed. "I don't know if I could take another set of stairs."

"Don't worry about it. I don't want you trying to climb those stairs. I think coming up here today was enough strain on you. Let's head back downstairs." Steph led the way down the main stairway to the parlor.

"Sit down for a while and rest. I'll bring you a cup of tea." Steph made sure Jenny was comfortable before going to the kitchen to make Jenny's tea.

When she returned, she found Jenny asleep on the sofa. As she tried to gently put a pillow under her friend's head, Jenny woke up with a start.

"I did it again, didn't I? I am so sorry, Steph. I can't seem to help it. If I'm not standing up, I fall asleep. The doctor said it's nothing to worry about; my body's resting up for the childbirth. I don't know. This kid is due soon. I hope I don't sleep through the birth." Jenny sat up to drink her tea.

"I don't think that will happen. I'm sure you'll be fine." Steph tried to think of what to say to reassure her friend. She searched for a different topic to discuss.

"I hope the locksmith doesn't call and change his appointment again. He's changed it three times now because of emergencies. I would like to know where the keys are. The large ring of keys we found in my bedroom didn't have any keys to fit the desk drawers in the study. They didn't fit the filing cabinets either. I just don't understand where the keys could be." Steph leaned back against the cushion of her chair. "I feel sometimes as if I'm not supposed to open it yet."

"Don't worry. He'll come. I just know it. Let's talk about something else. Have you heard from your friend Keri? You said she was the one who gave you the idea for the burgundy curtains in your bedroom."

"Yes, she found them in a catalog and sent it to me. I just love them. She has wonderful taste. It was hard to find wallpaper to match but I really like the wallpaper I found. The soft rose tones look great with the rich burgundy of the curtains."

"Too girly if you ask me." Hank joined the women in the parlor, sitting down beside Jenny.

"Where have you been?" Jenny was tired. Her short nap was not restful.

"I was up on the top floor looking around. All the rooms are full of boxes and stuff. Why?" Hank suddenly realized how tired Jenny was looking. "Are you ready to go home?"

Jenny set down her teacup. "Yes, if you don't mind. I don't feel well."

"Sure Jenny. Let's go." Hank helped her up. "See you later Steph. I'll let you know if anything develops." Hank winked at Steph as he helped Jenny stand up.

"Be careful with her. She's going to be a mom soon."

"Let's hope it's not until I get her home to Dad." Hank winked at Steph again. He was trying not to laugh at Jenny's discomfort.

"I'll call you tomorrow Steph. Thanks for the tea." Jenny let Hank lead her out to the car.

* * *

"It was another false alarm. I felt guilty getting George up in the middle of the night. By the time he was dressed and ready to go the contractions stopped. It was only indigestion." Jenny was shifting pillows around as she sat on the sofa in her living room. "I'm sorry if I sound whiny but I can't help it. I can't seem to get comfortable anywhere."

Steph came to visit Jenny who was under doctor's orders to stay home and rest. "I know you're due anytime now. Is that normal?"

"The doctor said I would have false alarms but that I would know when it was time. I hope he's right. Anyway, I feel much better. For a few days I felt as if I were stretched tight like a balloon and I worried about bursting. Then I realized women have babies every day. I'm sure everyone feels that way." Jenny sighed and leaned back against the cushions. She looked around her living room. "I know the baby will come when he's ready, but I'm getting tired of these four walls. Hank's been working out in the barn so he's nearby, but I worry sometimes I won't know what to do when the time comes."

"You'll be fine. You're a levelheaded responsible person. You'll do what every levelheaded responsible person does, you'll panic." Steph chuckled. She had been trying to lighten up her friend's spirits but Jenny still looked miserable.

After a few moments Jenny laughed too. "You're probably right." Jenny rubbed her swollen belly. "I'm so ready to hold this little bundle and see what he looks like. I want to hug him and tell him that I love him so much." Jenny started to cry. "I'm sorry, it's just hormones. I've scared Hank more than once when he's come in and found me crying. He's uncomfortable with it. I have to be careful when George is around too. He panics and thinks I'm in labor. He's so good with his animals, but he just goes overboard when it comes to me." Jenny sighed. "Just wait, it'll be your turn and you won't think it is so funny."

Steph was still giggling. "I have this mental picture of Hank and George taking off for the hospital and leaving you behind."

Jenny joined in the laughter. "That would be something wouldn't it? I'd have to call you for a ride."

Steph rose. "I'd better be getting home, you need your rest." She put out her hand to stop Jenny as she struggled to stand up. "Don't get up, stay put. If you need anything, just let me know. If you get too bored, have Hank bring you over to my house and we'll just relax. I'll see you soon."

"Thanks for coming over. I'll let you know if anything happens." Jenny sighed and leaned back on the sofa as she watched her friend leave the room. She closed her eyes and was soon asleep.

*   *   *

Keri Hall decided she wasn't doing anything fulfilling with her life, just sitting around her small apartment feeling less and less needed. A couple years ago, Keri found herself forced into an early retirement. The company she worked for was bought out by another company. They called it a business merger and to Keri it was a travesty. She loved her job but the new company management gave her a settlement she couldn't financially turn down. Widowed, she enjoyed volunteering her time at the hospital and nursing home, but felt restless and useless. When Steph moved into her apartment building a few years ago, they became acquainted in the laundry room. Over time they developed a close friendship.

Keri tried her best to support Steph when her father died. She and Betty Brown became acquainted through Steph. Their acquaintance grew and they all three became good friends. They had many interests in common and enjoyed spending time together. Keri gambled with their friendship when she told Steph what she thought of the man Steph moved in with. She felt guilty and responsible when Steph left him after her mom was killed. Keri loved Steph as if she were her own daughter.

Steph and Misti brought joy to Keri's heart and she missed them both. Keri realized she was becoming more and more depressed after Steph's calls.

Keri wanted to help Steph but she was too far away, so one day she made up her mind she was going to go to Ohio. She called her family and friends to tell them where she was going and why. Then she packed her bags, got into her car and left.

Since she didn't have a schedule planned out for her trip, Keri was free to stop anywhere she wanted to shop or tour along the way. Taking her time, she enjoyed herself but she was excited to see Steph's new home.

*   *   *

Jenny's baby was past due and Jenny was feeling bloated and uncomfortable. "I hope I'm not an imposition. I just didn't want to stay home again today. Hank would have suffered quietly being cooped up in the house all day again but I had to get out. He's been a good sport, but I'm sure he's bored just sitting around watching the TV and me. George is out working in the field. He has some work to get done before the rain comes tomorrow."

Steph smiled at her friend. "I don't mind at all. The locksmith rescheduled to come today and I really didn't want to be upstairs working if he came. I don't think I could hear the doorbell way up there. With you here I can take the day off and not feel guilty, so you're doing me a favor."

Steph helped Jenny settle onto one of the sofas in the parlor putting her feet up on an ottoman. "I think we deserve the day off to watch someone else work for a change. I don't think the locksmith will take a long time. He said it usually takes about five to ten minutes to open a lock. He's going to take imprints to make me keys."

Steph settled down on the chair across from Jenny. Misti walked over to lie down at her feet.

"I don't want to be any bother. I just feel funny. I always get restless when it rains, but the weather forecaster said it wouldn't rain until tomorrow night. I just have this feeling something is going to happen." Jenny wiggled around trying to get more comfortable.

Steph rose, careful of the sleeping dog. "Jenny, you just sit there and rest. I'm going to go make us some tea. I have some fresh baked cookies. I think we deserve a treat."

Steph was returning to the parlor when she noticed a car coming down the driveway. Thinking it was the locksmith, Steph went to the front door to let him in. Misti went dashing into the vestibule, jumping at the front door.

Funny, that looks like Keri Hall's car. "Come here Misti." Steph was trying to get Misti's attention but the little dog was running around back and forth. Finally she stooped down and picked up the little dog that was now trembling with excitement. Steph started to open the door for the locksmith but was shocked at what she saw. Letting out a scream of delight, she put Misti down and then raced the excited little dog to the newcomer. Keri Hall came to Ohio! Steph could hardly believe it. She gave her a hug, leaned back to look at her face and then gave her another hug as she fought the tears threatening to fall.

*   *   *

Jenny was trying to decide if the pains she felt were real or if they were Braxton Hicks again. She timed them and they were still thirty minutes apart. She was trying to convince herself they weren't very strong and they were going to stop. She didn't want to tell Steph about them until she was sure they would continue. Jenny heard Steph's squeal. Assuming her friend had fallen down the porch steps and was hurt, she lumbered to her feet.

As Jenny stepped outside the front door, she saw Steph hugging the driver of the car. When Steph stepped back, Jenny saw it was an older woman, about five feet tall. Touches of gray were beginning to show in her blond hair. The woman was laughing and holding Misti. The thought, *this must be a friend from Boston* flashed through Jenny's mind.

Jenny started to step further out onto the porch, when something warm and wet gushed down her leg. Her water broke! She was so astonished that she just stood there looking down at the wet puddle at her feet. Jenny gasped aloud when she realized what was happening. She was in labor! She was stunned!

*   *   *

Keri blinked back tears of joy as she gave Steph a hug and then reached down to pick up the happy little dog at her feet. Her throat was too tight with emotion for her to do anything but grin and hug the happy dog.

Jenny's gasp of surprise caused Steph and Keri to look up at her. Jenny smiled at them throwing her hands up in surprise. "I guess I'm going to have a baby." She was torn between embarrassment and joy.

Steph rushed up the stairs while Keri, still carrying Misti, followed moving a little slower. Gently Steph helped Jenny inside. Then she started calling for Hank.

Hank knew Steph was waiting for the locksmith to come. He assumed the car that pulled into the drive was the locksmith so he turned his mind back to what he was doing. He was in one of the front rooms on the top floor. He'd wandered in there a few times before, but only to look around. Today, he decided to open a few of the boxes. His search proved fruitful when he found an old trunk among the stacks that filled the room. The trunk was locked and Hank thought the locksmith might be able to open it. Pulling it to the top of the stairs, he was trying to figure out the best way to get it down by himself when he heard Steph calling his name. At first he was going to ignore her, but something about the tone of her voice nagged at his conscience. He moved the trunk to the side and headed down the stairs.

Hank met Steph coming up as he was going down. She was extremely agitated. Wondering what caused her to be so excited, he waited for her to come up to the landing where he stopped to catch his breath. He was eager to tell her about the locked trunk. Steph stopped climbing the stairs and glared up at Hank.

"What is the matter with you? I've been calling for you. Jenny's water broke. We have to get her to the hospital." Turning and racing back down the stairs, she left him standing on the landing trying to absorb what she said.

Hank started to follow Steph then her words registered in his mind. Realizing what was happening, he continued down as fast as he could go calling out to her.

"Did you call George? Is she standing or sitting? Let's go. Get out to the truck. No, wait, we'll have to take your car." He was talking and trying to think at the same time. As he reached the last step, he saw a strange older woman standing beside Jenny coaching her through a contraction. She was holding Jenny's hand and talking to her in soft tones.

Steph dialed her cell phone. "Darn this thing. I keep hitting the wrong buttons." Steph was trying in vain to call George. Out of frustration, she stopped pushing buttons and shook the cell phone, hoping it would dial itself.

"Here, let me. I have George on speed dial." Pulling out his cell phone, Hank called George. "Hey Dad, meet us at the hospital. We're taking your bride for delivery." Hank started laughing and disconnected the call. "He's on his way. As fast as he drives, he'll probably beat us there. Let's go."

Steph ran to grab her purse and keys. Pausing for a moment, Steph dashed off a note for the locksmith to put on the front door then ran to her car. Keri and Hank helped Jenny down the porch steps to Steph's car.

As Jenny was struggling to get into the backseat of the car, Hank noticed her sharp intake of breath. "Is it another contraction?"

Jenny merely nodded her head as she paused to wait for the contraction to end.

"How far apart are they now?"

Keri spoke up, unsure if Jenny was timing the contractions. "I've been timing them for her. They're still about fifteen minutes apart but that could change quickly."

Hank nodded his thanks to Keri. Making sure Jenny was in the car, he turned to Steph.

"Better let me drive, I know the way. We did a couple test runs earlier this month." Hank held out his hand for the keys. Steph knew he was right and gave them to him. His calm manner helped her to get a firm grip on her own fears. She was close to panic a few minutes before but was much calmer now.

Keri was with Jenny in the backseat trying to help her get comfortable.

"Are you going to be able to ride that way or do you need to lean on me?"

"If I can lean on you I would appreciate it. It's more comfortable." Jenny looked into Keri's blue eyes and saw compassion. As she leaned on the older woman, she was reminded of her own caring grandmother.

"Don't you worry now. We'll take care of you. You just relax and we'll have you to the hospital in no time." Keri patted Jenny on the hand. "It'll be over before you know it. Then you'll have a tiny baby to take care of."

"How's it going back there?" Hank was finding it hard to concentrate on driving. He could see Jenny's face in the rearview mirror.

"I'll be okay. I just hope George makes it." Jenny was suddenly afraid George wouldn't make it to the hospital in time. She worried the baby was coming too fast, but not fast enough and she was frightened. She needed George's calm, strong support.

When they arrived at the hospital, George drove into the emergency lane behind them. Jenny was having contractions five minutes apart. She held tightly to Keri's hand during each contraction, turning it bright red. As Hank stopped the car, Steph got out and ran into the hospital for a wheelchair.

George jumped out of his truck, leaving the engine running. He raced over to the car to help. Jerking open the car door, he leaned in. "Jenny, are you okay?" George was out of breath, finding it hard to breathe until he saw her. The site of his wife in labor shook George up. He was calm when one of his livestock went into labor, but this was different. George froze in front of the open car door.

While Jenny struggled with another contraction Hank took charge again. "George, move your big rear away from the car. Let me get your wife out of there before she has the baby in the car." Shoving George aside, Hank helped Jenny as she wiggled out of the car to sit in the wheelchair. George was still in a trance like state. Hank pushed Jenny's wheelchair into the hospital with the speechless George following. Keri and Steph were left standing by the car.

"I guess we get to be valets," said Keri with a laugh. "Do you want the truck or the car?"

Steph had been feeling left out and forgotten in all the excitement. Hearing Keri's laugh, she remembered her friend arrived when all the excitement started. Always grateful for Keri's sense of humor, Steph turned toward her to give her a hug, and realized they were blocking the entrance to the Emergency Room. "I'll take the truck if you'll park the car."

Parking the vehicles, they made their way up to the maternity waiting room by way of the cafeteria, bringing snacks and drinks for the men.

"This could be a long wait. Babies come when they're ready." Keri sighed.

"If we can find Hank, he'll know what's happening. We'll just take the elevator up and see if we can find him. He's been calm and reliable so far. He'll tell us how she's doing."

Walking down the hall from the elevators, they found Hank talking aloud to himself while pacing nervously in the waiting area.

"I thought I was done with hospitals. I was never coming back to one. I don't like the smell. I don't think it's safe for her to have the baby here! I'm going to go get George and have him take Jenny home to have this baby. This is the wrong place for her to be!" Hank turned and saw Steph looking at him with a surprised look on her face. He was ashamed to be caught ranting. With a sheepish expression, he looked at the stranger with her. He had almost forgotten about the kind woman who helped Jenny. Hank noticed the wrinkles beginning to form around bright blue eyes. This was a woman who smiled quickly and often, he decided. Her round face was thin, but it glowed when she smiled. He found himself grinning back.

Realizing Hank and Keri were not introduced in the rush, Steph handed Hank a cup of coffee. "Keri, this is Hank. He's staying with Jenny and George. That was George the husband, who I hope is with Jenny. Hank, this is Keri Hall, a good friend of mine. She'd just arrived when Jenny went into labor."

"It's nice to meet you Hank. Is it always this exciting around here?" Keri asked as she sat down. She was feeling tired from the long day and all the excitement. "Oh, my! What a wonderful event to have happening! Do we have a name picked out?" Keri felt as if she belonged with these young people. She instantly liked Jenny and was delighted to be here for the birth of the baby. She was sure she was going to love being here. From her vantage point, she decided to study this new man in Steph's life. Steph would mention Hank on the phone and tell her about how helpful he was but that was all she would say. Keri knew she trusted him in the short time she knew him, but decided to wait see how Steph felt about him.

"Jenny has four names picked out but won't tell me what they are. She said she would know the right name when she sees him." Steph sat down beside Keri. "They know it's a boy so it was easier to settle on names." She turned to Hank. "Why don't you sit down and relax? Jenny's going to be fine. You were so calm before. Why are you so uptight now?"

I must've looked like a fool ranting when they came in. Hank tried to keep his thoughts from showing on his face. "I spent a lot of time in hospitals and they have a lot of sick people here." He walked over and sat down near Steph, glad she was there with him. It was important to him for her to understand his behavior but he couldn't explain right now. He shrugged to cover his embarrassment. "I wouldn't want her or the baby to catch some deadly disease. I just don't think it's healthy for her."

"She'll be fine. George is with her and he'll make sure she's okay."

Steph's heart went out to Hank. It was clear he was struggling with an inner turmoil.

"If I may suggest, when I gave birth to my daughter, I wish I had a picture of the first time her daddy saw her and held her. I never saw that expression on his face ever again. If they'll let you go in near the time, it would be a picture they will always cherish." Keri sighed.

"I don't have a camera." Hank pulled out his cell phone. "I guess I could take it with my camera phone. It takes some nice pictures."

"I know they'll appreciate it." Keri smiled encouragingly.

"Mr. Dawn?" A nurse stood just inside the waiting room.

Hank stood up. "Yes? I'm Henry Dawn."

"Mr. Dawn, Mr. Landsburg asked me to tell you everything is going well."

"Would it be possible for me to be in the room when she delivers? I'd like to take some pictures for them." Hank looked over at Keri. He was having second thoughts but decided to at least ask.

"I don't think it would be a problem since Mr. Landsburg said you are family. I'll come and get you in time to scrub and you can stand to the side if you wish."

"That would be great. Thanks." Hank sank back down into his chair to collect his courage while he waited. He loved Jenny and George and reminded himself he was doing this for them.

*   *   *

Keri and Steph brought dinner every night since Jenny came home with the baby six days ago. Steph would clean up the kitchen and do the dishes while Keri washed laundry. With Jenny, they would sit in the kitchen folding clothes while they talked. Hank and George would either go out to the barn or sit in the living room and talk about the farm.

"I'd forgotten how nice it is to have a little one to care for." Keri was coming down the stairs from the nursery on the second floor. She had carried the baby to bed for Jenny. "It's hard to believe little George Henry is so big already." She joined Jenny and Steph in the kitchen.

"I know. It's still hard for me to believe he was inside me." Jenny rubbed her deflated stomach. "I know I need to think about losing weight, but I'm still hungry all the time."

"The baby needs you to take care of yourself. Once he's a little older you can worry about losing weight. For now you have your hands full just taking care of the two of you." Keri sat down beside Jenny at the table. "Has Steph told you what we did today?"

Steph walked away from the sink and joined the other women. "We have the servant's rooms almost all cleaned out. We found two complete sets of maid costumes. They must be from different years because they're very different styles. I want to do some research on the Internet later to see if we can date them. There were a few nice aprons and more coins lying around. When the locksmith was here to open the desk today, I asked him to open the locked trunk Hank found too. One of these days I'll start going through the papers, but not tonight." Steph sighed with the thought of the loose papers she had been collecting into boxes. "Stanley's secretary called and said he would like to see me later this week. There are probably more papers to be signed for probate. I need to remember to ask him about the old papers I found on the top of the desk too."

"That's enough talk." Keri stood up. "I think we need to let Jenny get some sleep while the baby's napping." She grinned at Jenny as if reading her thoughts. "Don't worry, it won't be long and he'll be sleeping all night. Let's just hope he's not an early riser like his daddy."

Keri and Steph went in to the living room to say good-bye to George and Hank before they left.

CHAPTER 8

Steph experienced a restless night. She woke up early feeling as if the world had shifted and something was wrong. She decided to get up and start the day.

As she sat at the kitchen table enjoying her coffee, she kept thinking about what to wear to the law office. She thought about wearing shorts or something casual. Remembering it was a business meeting she began thinking about the clothes she should wear to give the impression she was taking this meeting seriously. Stanley's secretary had said it was an important meeting.

When Keri finally joined her for breakfast, Steph had considered and eliminated most of her wardrobe. Steph was becoming more and more frustrated and began to consider calling to postpone the meeting until she had time to shop for a more suitable outfit.

"My, you have a serious look on your face. If you keep carrying all that weight around you're going to have stooped shoulders before you're thirty one." Keri sat across the table from Steph and noticed the frustration as it crossed Steph's face.

"I have the appointment with Stanley Wilbur the attorney this morning. I know it's probably to just sign some papers, but I want to look nice. Remember I told you I went to his office the first day I arrived. I made a total fool of myself when we came out to the house."

"Oh, he's probably forgotten all about that. After all, you'd just driven into town and saw the house for the first time. This is a big house and everyone is entitled to a case of nerves." Keri realized as she spoke, Steph was more upset than Keri first thought.

"I have to wear something that says I'm here for business and I'm a serious person."

"Well, we have that black suit you found in a closet. With a few nips and tucks I think we could get it to fit okay. There's a nice selection of ties and we could probably find a white shirt to go with it." Keri stopped and thought for a second trying to keep a serious look on her face. "I think your black pumps would set it off just right." Keri tried hard to keep her face neutral as she watched the emotions play across Steph's face. Finally she couldn't contain her laughter any longer.

Between bouts of laughing Keri tried to talk. "I wish you could see your face! I was kidding, but you thought about it for a minute."

Steph too was laughing now. "I did. As soon as you said I could wear my pumps, I had this picture flash through my mind. I could see me in that man's suit trying not to trip over the long pant legs."

Keri started to calm down and looked at Steph. "Now seriously, you have some very nice outfits you wore to school. How about the teal blazer outfit? That is serious but fun."

"I think it's too hot to wear a blazer. I thought of that too. I was thinking about my beige cotton pants with a long shirt."

"I'll tell you what. After we finish eating, we'll go up and take a look."

"Okay, thanks." Steph breathed out a sigh of relief and turned her thoughts to other issues.

*   *   *

Steph had finally settled on wearing a soft cotton dress with hues of mauve and pink. It was a princess style design with a scoop neckline and short puffy sleeves. Steph loved the way the dress made her feel classy and confident.

At Keri's suggestion, she was wearing low heels and rose quartz earrings. A long sleek necklace set off the outfit and gave Steph an extra boost of confidence.

Steph left early enough to take care of some errands before going to the law office. She wanted to get in some grocery shopping later while she was in town and the comfortable shoes would make it easier. She enjoyed helping Keri cook for Jenny and George. Steph was growing to love Jenny, George, the baby and even Hank more every day. Jenny was feeling strong enough now to do the cooking and Steph and Keri would be on their own for the night.

As she drove away, Steph thought how wonderful it was having Keri around. Keri with her wonderful sense of fun was so helpful. She had helped soothe Steph's anxiety this morning, and she made the work fun. With all the cleaning in the house to be done, having some fun made it go faster and easier. Keri also shared great ideas about how to turn the place into a Bed and Breakfast. Keri would bring home magazines when she went to the store for groceries so she could show Steph her latest idea for decorating.

Steph went to the dry cleaners to pick up her dry cleaning. As she waited for her clothes, she found herself getting nervous about going to the law office. She tried to tell herself Stanley only wanted her to sign some papers; she knew it was not rational to be afraid. Still, she found her heart pounding with fear. Thanking the clerk as she paid for her dry cleaning, she hoped she did not appear as nervous as she felt.

Steph stopped at the bookstore and bought books on remodeling homes and decorating. Steph found herself warming up to the B & B ideas for the house. It would be fun to have the old house filled with people. While she was buying the books, she looked for books about running a B & B and began to relax. She could just be open during part of the year, which would give her time to travel if she wanted. If she cut off part of the house, she would still have privacy.

Steph was in high spirits as she drove to the law office, suddenly looking forward to seeing Stanley.

Steph wanted to make a good impression so she arrived a few minutes early at the Wilburs' law office. Delighted she remembered where it was, she parked her car in the same place she parked the U-Haul the day she arrived. Unlike that day, the street was lined with cars.

When she entered, she was aware again of the masculinity of the room. The cheerful, blonde receptionist seemed out of place in the dark room. Steph walked over and introduced herself.

"I have an appointment with Stanley Wilbur Jr. I'm Stephanotis Weatherby."

With a well-practiced smile, the receptionist replied, "Please take a seat and I'll tell him you're here." Without waiting for Steph to respond, she rose from her desk and went toward the doorway Steph knew led to the offices.

Steph started to turn and walk across the room toward the chairs. An older gentleman, who was standing to the side of the desk, approached her. "I'm Stanley Wilbur Sr. I believe we have spoken but have never met. I wanted to introduce myself to you. Will you please come to my office so we can speak?" Turning, he led the way to his office. Once they reached the office door, he stopped and gestured for Steph to enter first. "Please have a seat."

Steph looked around the room before sitting in the chair he offered. She wasn't sure what to think. The secretary she talked to on the phone told her it was Stanley Jr. who wanted to talk with her. Here she was sitting in Stanley Sr.'s office.

Steph took a moment to collect her thoughts. This office was so much different in appearance from how she remembered Stanley's office. Two antique wooden filing cabinets stood like regal soldiers along one wall. Standing next to them were glass-covered bookcases filled with books. Stacks of papers and file folders sat on the tops of the filing cabinets and bookcases. The book shelves behind Stanley Sr.'s desk held books of all sizes. Some of the bindings were faded from age.

The desk itself was larger than Stanley Jr.'s and didn't have a computer monitor on it. Open books were stacked haphazardly on top of the desk. Loose papers lay scattered carelessly over the open books, as if a strong wind blew through the room.

The windows were covered with the same heavy curtain material used for the front windows. Even the air in the room seemed heavy and still. Steph found her mind straying, thinking about all the legal cases that must have been handled in this room over the years.

She was sitting here with someone who actually knew Hyacinth and may have some interesting stories about her.

Sitting behind his desk Stanley Sr. began, "I thought it would be best if you and I had a little chat before you spoke with Stanley. There are some events I think you should know about." *What a pretty woman she is,* he thought. *Stanley said she was nice looking, but he didn't seem too interested when I asked about her. She was always a delight to talk with on the phone.* Mentally shrugging about his son's taste in women, he went on. "There are some issues about Hyacinth's estate that need to be further dealt with."

"Father, I thought we agreed I should talk with Miss Weatherby." Stanley Jr. strolled into the room. As usual he was dressed in a fresh suit, matching shirt and tie. This was a large contrast to his father who was wearing an open necked polo shirt and casual slacks. Though vastly different from one another in many ways, both men struck Steph as being strong and powerful. The air was crackling with energy.

Steph glanced from one to the other. *Stanley is a younger version of his father, but with more stuffiness and starch.* Steph felt the knot in her stomach tighten. Now both men wanted something from her. She took a deep breath to keep from bolting from the room. *What is wrong? Why do they both want to talk with me?* She felt trapped between the two men.

"Well, come on in and we'll both speak with her." Stanley Sr. emphasized the invitation to his son by waving at an empty chair.

Understanding his father held the upper hand for now Stanley Jr. shut the door and took a seat beside Steph. While doing so, he reminded himself this was not a competition with his father. They each would play a part in dealing with what was to come.

Forcing himself to relax, Stanley Jr. looked at the woman sitting there. How different she looked today from the woman he first met. She looked better rested and had a healthier glow about her. He noticed how nicely the color of her dress set off her eyes. The dark circles were gone and she seemed younger than when he last saw her. The cut of her simple dress flowed flatteringly along her soft curves. He appreciated the light touches of jewelry she wore. Steph had swept her hair up with a clip to hold it off her shoulders. Stanley Jr. wanted to reach over and release it. He felt a strong urge to run his fingers through its velvety softness. Reminding himself she was his client, he turned his attention to his father and why she was here today.

"Miss Weatherby," began Stanley Sr. as he closely watched his son. "It is with deep regret that I must advise you there has been a challenge to Hyacinth's estate. We have received papers from an attorney for a Mr. Rodchester Wilgood. He is contesting the estate and your inheritance of the farm."

Steph felt as if she was on a whirl-around ride at the amusement park. The room was spinning and she couldn't breathe. She felt dizzy and light-headed. Fighting the fainting feeling and trying to keep her head from swaying she stuttered out a reply. "I don't understand. I thought I was the sole heir to my great aunt's estate. How can this be?" Gripping the seat of the chair to keep from falling off, she tried to follow what she was being told.

Stanley Sr. began to explain. "Years ago, Rodchester Wilgood tried to get your aunt committed so he could take over as power of attorney for the farm. She came to my office and wrote a new will. I had power of attorney if needed and your father was to inherit the farm. When your aunt became ill and was placed into the nursing home, I took over her affairs per the power of attorney. I knew your aunt's wishes and I followed them to the letter. I contacted your father and he advised me to continue as if Hyacinth were still in charge. He directed me to contact Mr. Young, his attorney, and we handled things per his wishes until he could come and see the farm for himself. I learned about his illness through Mr. Young. When he died, your mother became the heir to the farm. Your mother was planning to come here and decide what to do when she was killed. Since you are the heir to your father's estate through your mother, you are the heir cited in Hyacinth's will." Stanley Sr. paused to let Steph absorb this information.

Watching her closely, he went on. "Rodchester was informed of the contents of her will when Hyacinth became too ill to live on the farm. Hyacinth's will stipulated he was not considered an heir to the farm or her estate. I met with his attorney, acting in her best interest. Hyacinth and her father both mentioned on numerous occasions that prior to her marriage Iris willingly signed a document giving up any ties to the farm." Shaking his head as if he did not understand such behavior, he continued. "She did not care about the farm. Being the oldest, she was raised with servants and when they were let go, it must have been a blow to her adolescent pride. Hyacinth worked hard to make the farm profitable again. She was determined to keep it in the family."

Stepping in when his father paused again, Stanley Jr. took control of the discussion. "Two days ago, I, that is, we, received a letter from Wilgood's attorney. He states on behalf of his client he is filing an injunction and they are contesting the will. He is filing on the grounds his client is also a living relative to Hyacinth. They state he should inherit half of the estate, which includes the farm and its contents. I'm sure we can settle this. I have reviewed all the documents father has in his possession. It may end up in court but I know we can win." Stanley paused to gauge Steph's reaction before he continued. "It would be helpful if you could locate the document Iris signed."

Steph looked from one to the other. She felt as if she was watching a tennis match and had lost track of who was next up to serve. She suddenly felt a lot of sympathy for the net strung between the players. Their words were hitting her stomach as hard as any ball ever could.

The words "*it would be helpful if you could locate the document Iris signed*" finally took root and gave her some air to breathe. This was something she could do! She would find the missing document and end this nightmare. Drawing strength from this knowledge, she turned to Stanley Sr.

"Do I understand that if I can find the document, it will end this lawsuit?"

"Well, it could be a factor in determining if this lawsuit would even go to court." Stanley Sr. hesitated a little. He was trying to decide if now was the time to let her know the rest of the bad news. He sincerely hoped Stan would let him finish before he interrupted again. Making up his mind, he explained, "I need to elaborate on this a little more. You see, the original lawsuit was filed by Rodchester Wilgood, the grandfather of the man who has filed the lawsuit recently. The elder Mr. Wilgood became angry about Hyacinth's refusal. He died within a few weeks of learning she went into the nursing home and he was not in the will.

"That is why the original lawsuit was dropped. The younger Rodchester Wilgood has added a few zingers to the lawsuit. He is suing you for the untimely death of his grandfather. The elder Mr. Wilgood died as the result of a heart attack. The lawsuit states the elder Wilgood had been in excellent health until the '*inhumane and cruel treatment received by the executor and power of attorney for Hyacinth Weatherby.*' This will be a separate wrongful death suit against you and the law firm. I thought the matter was over with and did not follow up as is my habit, to make sure any legal loose ends are tied up."

"Father, you couldn't have known that Mr. Wilgood would have a heart attack and die. You are capable of many things, but being God is not one of them."

Stanley Jr. came to his father's defense. It hurt him when they received the documents about the lawsuit. It wasn't just the estate that was at stake, but his father's reputation and good name. A scandal could destroy all the goodwill and hard work that had made the law firm a valuable asset to the community.

"I don't understand." Steph felt the thin thread of hope sliding through her fingers. "Do you mean there was something you could have done back then and I would not have this to deal with this now?" She was trying to understand. She was fighting down panic but heard fear in her own voice. Sitting back against the support of the chair, she let out a sigh. "Am I going to lose the farm?" She had fallen in love with her new home and was becoming choked by the fear of losing it.

Seeing the emotional struggle in the woman sitting next to him, Stanley Jr. knew it was up to him to comfort Steph the best he could. Under his father's watchful eye, he could not give in to his desire to pull her onto his lap and kiss her until she forgot about her troubles. He simply placed his hand on hers and gave it a squeeze. "We're going to do all we can to keep it from coming to that." He tried to sound warm and reassuring. He was surprised he was developing feelings for this woman.

Stanley Sr. was watching Steph also. She could either forgive an old man or she could rant and rave. He wouldn't blame her if she did. He didn't know whether to allow himself to feel relief at her reaction or put more blame and guilt on himself. At the time, he thought he performed his duties to their full extent. Looking back, he was now acutely aware of what he left unfinished. Researching why the first lawsuit was dropped should've been a priority. It was too late now. He needed to concentrate on fixing what he had left undone. His lack of professionalism could possibly cost this young woman her home. Before he could answer Stanley Jr. spoke up.

"Don't you worry, Stephanotis. You have the best legal minds in the city on your side. When father and I take on a client, we do our best to win." *Atta boy Stan, now you're on a roll,* he thought. *Keep going, you're good at this. You've got her attention now.* Stanley Jr. was feeling better as he spoke. "Everyone makes mistakes. We wouldn't be in this business if they didn't. Do you have any idea where the document could be? Have you seen any legal papers in the house?"

Steph forced herself to calm down and think. They found several papers in different rooms as they were cleaning and put them together in the library with all the other papers. "I had a locksmith come out to unlock the desk in the study. I was going to go through the desk and clean it out when I got back today. He unlocked the two filing cabinets as well. I put off going through the papers I've been finding until I had all the rooms cleaned out."

Struck by what he thought was a brilliant idea, Stanley Jr. said, "Don't open the desk or the cabinets until I get there. I'll come by tonight and we can look through them together. That way, I can help you sort through the legal documents and the common household papers." His mind began looking for ways to turn this to his advantage. *Way to go, Stan. It would be just you and her in that big empty house. You could really comfort her then. You can show her you know how to take care of your women.* Giving himself a pep talk was making him feel even better about working after hours with this woman. He began to make plans, forgetting his father was still there.

"Why don't you come for dinner? We'd love to have a guest. That way you and I can get started right away." Steph was starting to feel guilty. It was nice of him to spend his evening working for her. She was not sure what the document would look like. Steph began to worry she might overlook it when sorting through the papers.

Stanley Jr. let the "we" in her invitation slide. He was sure she meant herself and her dog. *The dog should be no trouble. Toss it a few scraps and it should be happy. Then I can concentrate on making us happy. It was convenient of her to play into my plans like that. Dad will never suspect a thing. And then nature can take its course.* Not wanting to seem too excited about working that night, Stanley Jr. said out loud, "Are you sure it wouldn't be any trouble? I can bring a pizza or something if you'd like."

"Oh, no! We like cooking for company. We'll be glad to have you come."

Steph didn't want to appear too relieved by his offer to help. After all, dinner was a small repayment for having him come out to the house.

Feeling better, Steph left the office with the reassurance that she wouldn't have to handle this alone. Trying to show more confidence than she felt, Steph thanked them for explaining everything and assured Stanley he would be pleased with what she was doing with the house.

Driving home, Steph tried not to think about what might happen. When she left that morning to go to town, she was full of hope and joy. Now it seemed as if her world was crashing down around her and she was helpless to stop it. She started thinking of her dad and mom and how she lost them both. She worried she was letting them down.

Steph knew the sun was shining but it felt cold and hostile to her. She didn't want to upset Keri with her problems, and definitely didn't want to tell Jenny. She forgot to ask about George's farming the land and caring for the animals. She hoped George would be willing to manage everything for a little longer. She would try to remember to talk with Stanley about it tonight.

With her emotions tearing at her heart, she was having a hard time concentrating on her driving. Tears kept welling up in her eyes and she finally let them fall. She pulled the car over to the side, off the road, when she was halfway home; she was crying so hard she couldn't see. After she was more in control of her emotions, she drove on home.

Letting herself in the back door, Steph heard excited voices in the parlor. *It must be Jenny bringing George Henry to visit. I'll just quietly run up the back stairway and freshen up before I go into see them. Funny I didn't notice a car.* Unfortunately for Steph, the guard dog was on duty. Misti heard Steph's car pull up and came running to the back door to greet her. Keri came to the back of the house to see why Misti was so excited.

"I'm so glad you're home, Steph. I have a wonderful surprise for you. I'll just put away the groceries while you go see who is in the parlor to see you." Seeing no groceries on the table or counter, Keri was a little puzzled. "Didn't you bring in the groceries? No matter, I'll go out to the car and bring them in."

Steph realized she was so upset, wanting to just get home, she forgot to stop at the store. "Oh Keri, I forgot to go to the store! I knew I was doing everything wrong. That's why this is happening! It's my entire fault! First Dad! Then Mom! Then Fred! Now this! I just can't seem to do anything right." Sobbing, Steph ran up the stairs to her room with Misti on her heels. She left a disturbed Keri standing openmouthed in the kitchen.

*   *   *

Hank liked working at the Weatherby farm for Steph. He could work at his own pace and help George whenever he was needed. Hank could feel his body getting stronger each day. The old farm had buildings and equipment that had not been repaired in years. There was a lot of work he could do if he took his time. Hank was glad to be useful. George told him he seemed more settled. Hank knew he was sleeping much better. It was a month since his last nightmare and he was no longer afraid to go to sleep.

Keri began mothering Hank the day she met him. She would ask him to do small jobs and then make him take breaks, bringing him drinks and snacks. She seemed to know instinctively when he was getting tired. His thoughts often wandered from the farm to the city and what brought him here. Hank admired Steph and her conviction to clean up and repair the house. He knew she wanted to settle down and have a life on the farm. He was proud that he could help her, and help heal himself at the same time.

With Steph's permission, Hank set up solar floodlights in the yard. He installed motion detectors with floodlights attached in the dark corners of the wrap around porch. Pole lights in the yard lit up the area at the back of the house. Hank placed fixtures for outside lighting both above and below the back deck. He enjoyed seeing the results of his labor lighting up the dark nights.

Some days he worked on the security system he was installing. Various pieces of furniture blocked access to some of the windows. Hank could not move the furniture alone, so he was forced to wait until George could come and help.

Hank installed new locks and dead bolts on all the front and back doors. Any weak locks on the windows were also being replaced as he worked. He was doing his best to make sure the women were safe.

The previous week he spent time trying to fix the old lawn tractor he found in the shed. After two days of hard work, he was forced to admit even he could not revive the dead. And that rusty old mower was truly dead!

Hank was pleased with the new lawn tractor Steph bought. He could mow the lawn and not be stiff and sore. It rode smoothly over the ruts and the wide deck cut a wide path with each sweep. He volunteered to keep the lawn mowed just to ride the lawn tractor.

Hank was mowing the lawn when he saw Steph drive her car into the backyard. He watched her slam the car door then run into the house. Realizing something was wrong, Hank climbed off the lawn tractor and headed for the house. Hank walked into the kitchen during Steph's outburst and watched her run up the stairs leaving Keri standing in her wake.

Fresh mown grass clung to his shoes. Because he planted flowers in the flowerbeds earlier, there was dirt on his jeans as well. Mindful of the clean floor, Hank stood quietly and waited to see if he could help.

Keri smelled Hank before she realized he was there. The strong smell of dirt, freshly cut grass and male sweat blended in the kitchen air. Hank always moved quietly and could usually walk up behind her before Keri knew he was there. Today, it was different. Turning to face him, she saw the look of concern on his face. "She'll be alright. Sometimes she feels she has the whole world on her shoulders with no family to help." Walking over to him, she gently patted him on the arm. "She'll tell us in her own time. Now, you need to get your dirty shoes out of my clean kitchen." Keri turned Hank around and gently nudged him out the door.

Hank was baffled. He knew Steph was going to the lawyer's office. Maybe this had something to do with Jenny and George. He decided to hunt up George and find out what he knew.

*   *   *

Keri went back to the parlor and sat heavily in a chair. "Well, that was dramatic. We'll give her a few minutes then go up and find out what's going on. I'm so happy you came. We can use your help."

"I'm glad it worked out for me to come. I have to admit I was feeling jealous of your being here and I was stuck at home." Sitting on the sofa and talking with Keri was a tall, thin woman. Short, curly red hair framed a pale, oval face. Betty Brown put down her cup of tea and stood up. She crossed the room and looked at the carved detail in the wooden mantel of the fireplace. Turning back to Keri, she spoke quietly. "My nephew's wedding was so beautiful. The bride was just lovely. We had such a good time. It was delightful to see my family. It was special to be able to enjoy it with them but I'm here now and I want to know what is going on. You know I love Steph too and want to help."

Keri tried to think of the best way to answer her friend. She was not aware of any reason for Steph to behave in this manner. "Well," she began as she searched her mind for answers. "Steph's trying to decide what to do about this place. It's too big for one person so she's toying with the idea of turning it into a B & B or a boardinghouse. Right now, she is leaning toward the B & B idea. I've started putting together some ideas for redecorating. I would like your advice about what to do in the kitchen. After all, you're more at home in there than I am."

Keri paused, a thoughtful expression on her face. "Jenny, that's our girl with the new baby. She told us the kitchen area was once a sitting room and the kitchen was down in the cellar. We haven't gotten that far. Steph thought it best to just get the bedrooms cleared out and to sort through those items first. I hate to admit this, but it has been a lot of work. We've found a few interesting items and have quite a collection to finish sorting. I went through some of the old clothes and have a large pile I'd like to make quilts out of. Of course, that's a later project. Right now, we have to finish getting things cleared out. There's a storage area on the top floor we've just begun to go through. It's filled with trunks and boxes. There are some old Christmas decorations too. We'll need a man to help. Steph's idea to use tables in the conservatory was a good one. It gave us a place to sort through the smaller items. Knickknacks, pictures, whatever we find we've set out on the tables and the floor. We may want to use some of the items in the redecorating so we kept them all."

"Hank," Keri continued, "you saw him riding the tractor when you drove up, he's been a big help. We get George to help him when something's too heavy for him to move alone. It's nice to have a man around again. Since Jenny had the baby, we have been taking them dinner every so often. You know, to lighten her load a bit."

"Oh, I know. That must be a great excuse to get to help with the baby." Betty laughed at her friend, her brown eyes twinkling. "I think we've given Steph long enough to pull herself together. Let's go see check on her." Betty started out of the parlor and paused to let Keri catch up with her. "I know she's had it rough, but we're both here for her now, so let's go take care of our girl." They walked up the curving front stairway together to Steph's room.

CHAPTER 9

Hank finally found George standing at the fence watching the young colt romping in a field. He was surprised at how big the young creature had grown.

"I almost didn't recognize him. He's really growing." Hank walked up beside George.

"Yeah, I keep wondering what Steph's going to want to do with him. Sun Dancer sure has some fine looking offspring." George was enjoying the antics of the young colt. It was racing around playing with the other young horses.

"I don't know, but something sure has her upset. She came back from her appointment with the lawyer and she went running into the house. I could see by the way her face was all puffy and red that she'd been crying." Hank shook his head at the memory, surprised at the anger he felt.

"I followed her into the house and heard her tell Keri she was sorry she didn't get to the store. She said she was doing everything wrong and it was all her fault. She was blaming herself for her parents and someone named Fred. Then she started crying again and ran up the stairs. I figured it had to do with the lawyer and the farm so I came to tell you. I know it's none of my business, but it might be yours." Hank watched the colt wishing he could be free to play and run.

"I guess I'd better call Stanley Jr., find out what happened. I wonder if they told her something about the contract I have for the land. That may be what upset her. I'll go call him." George left Hank standing by the fence and headed off to the house.

Hank stood there for a while trying to figure out why Steph's behavior tore at his heart so badly. Sure he was attracted to her. She was kind and caring. She was not what he would call a beautiful woman, but she was attractive in her own way. It was her smile that captivated him. It warmed his heart and made him feel alive again.

Hank was trying to help her get her new venture started, whatever that was. He promised himself that whatever the problem was, he was going to do his best to help her resolve it. Hank reminded himself he did not have anything to offer Steph but his help. He was a man with no job, no current future. He had a broken body that was still healing and a tired soul. He began again to wonder if he would ever have someone love him the way Jenny loved George.

Hank shoved his self-pity aside and walked to the house. He was determined to help and needed to know what George was finding out.

*   *   *

Keri and Betty stood outside Steph's room. They looked at each other waiting for the other one to knock. Suddenly, Steph opened the door. She saw Betty and with a squeal of delight, she threw her arms around her giving her a big hug.

Steph just finished giving herself a stern scolding for letting her emotions control her. She now sported a headache from crying and an upset stomach from not having eaten lunch. She decided to go get a bite to eat and to take some aspirin when she opened her door and found Betty standing there. She was so surprised and delighted to see her friend she forgot all about her headache.

"Betty, what are you doing here? It's so great to see you. Please excuse my manners. Have you eaten lunch? Did someone bring you or are you alone?"

Steph kept asking questions as they walked down to the main level. Betty waited for her friend to pause and take a breath before she answered her questions.

Betty explained about her nephew's wedding. How she drove by herself to be with her family for his wedding. Afterward, she came on down to the farm. She told Steph how she missed her friends and decided to join them.

As they were talking, Keri went on to the kitchen and made Steph a sandwich. Steph and Betty moved into the parlor where Keri joined them. The three friends spent some time catching up.

When the clock in the parlor chimed three o'clock, Steph jumped with a start. "Is that really the time? Oh dear. I have a guest coming for dinner."

Steph had explained about the problems with the lawsuit. She mentioned Stanley's offer to come and help sort the papers.

"I forgot to tell you, Stanley's coming to dinner. He wanted me to wait to go through the desk until he was here. I don't know what the document may look like so I'm glad he'll be here to help find it. We can eat dinner together then get started right away." Realizing she didn't get to the store, she started to rise. "I'll just run into town and get the things I forgot this morning. Do we need anything else that's not on the list?"

Keri shook her head. "No, but are you sure you want to go? I can run into town while you take a break."

"No thanks, I need to get a new camera so we can take pictures of the items in the drawers before we work on them. Mine just isn't working right."

As Steph was leaving, Betty turned to Keri. "Why does she need a new camera? The pictures I've seen were just fine."

"Steph has a nice camera but it doesn't zoom in really close. She probably wants to photograph and log any important documents as she finds them."

"Did I tell you I bought a computer program that allows us to use scanned pictures of the rooms? Using this software we can decorate the rooms in different ways on the computer and see the results before buying the paint, carpet and curtains. It's been fun to take a room and see how many different ways it can be decorated. It gives us the freedom to redecorate without the work and expense. Jenny has the program right now. She was feeling left out so we're letting her select some decorating styles for a few of the rooms. Of course Steph will have the last say in everything." Keri stood up. "We'd better go see what there is in the kitchen to make for dinner. Once we decide what to have, we can call Steph and tell her if there is anything else we need."

Keri began clearing up the dishes still in the parlor. She paused and looked at Betty. "It'll be nice having you here to help with the cooking. I don't mind cleaning up, but I am not the best cook. Steph has been cooking most of the time and I'm sure she will enjoy having some help."

Keri and Betty went into the kitchen. "Steph has a couple of boxes with your name on them in the music room. She said they're filled with some of the kitchen gadgets she didn't know how to use. Later, we can get them for you to see what's there."

"That sounds like a fine idea." Betty opened the refrigerator door. "Let's see what possibilities we have in here."

*   *   *

George was still talking with Stanley Jr. on the phone when Hank walked into the house. George was trying not to talk loud enough for Jenny to hear him up in the nursery. Hank could tell George was losing his battle to remain calm.

"What do you mean you can't tell me! I just told you that if it involves the farm, it involves ME... My future is at stake and you say it is none of my business... No, I won't calm down! I have the right to know what is going on with that farm. Steph is my landlady and my friend. I should be included so I can help her. Don't tell me to wait it out! I can't wait. Wait a minute, wait for what... What court date? Does Steph know about a court date?. . . Oh, she does. Okay, I'm listening. Uh huh... uh huh... oh... Umm... Okay, if you think that's best then I'll wait.... Yeah, I know. You've taken care of things so far. Okay... Okay, but you'd better let me know... I know, okay... Goodbye."

Hank tried to follow the conversation but gave up. He knew George would tell him all about it when he was ready. Hank was enjoying a cold drink while sitting at the table to wait for George.

"Let's take this outside." Defeated, George headed out the back door with Hank close behind.

When they were in the barn, George sat down on an old stool while Hank perched on a tack box. The air was heavy with the scent of horses and hay.

"Okay, before I tell you, you have to promise to keep this from Jenny. She doesn't need to be upset by all of this."

"All of what?" Hank felt as if his nerves were being pulled and stretched like a batch of taffy in a machine. It was all he could do to just sit there and wait for George to tell him what was happening.

"As you said, Steph went to see the lawyer Stanley Wilbur Jr. today. Well, it seems some relative of Hyacinth's is causing trouble. Her sister Iris had a step-great grandson who is trying to sue the estate and Stanley Wilbur Sr. for wrongful death of Rodchester Wilgood. That was Iris's stepson. The great grandson is trying to sue saying Hyacinth's refusal to allow him to be her power of attorney caused him severe stress. The result of the stress caused him to die an early death."

"Oh, don't be ridiculous. How could a refusal kill a man? I've seen enough violence and I don't believe that." Hank could no longer stop himself. He started pacing up and down the length of the barn. As a police officer in a large city, he saw different kinds of death. Gang drive-bys, whores shot by their pimps, overdoses on drugs, traffic accidents or sometimes people just gave up on life. It was hard for him to believe refusing something to someone would cause them to die.

Sun Dancer was stabled at the far end of the barn. There was access for him to walk to an outside corral through an outer door. When the door was open, the Palomino could move in and out as he pleased. Currently the door was open and as if mirroring Hank's movements, Sun Dancer was pacing in and out. He would period-ically stomp his foot, shake his head and snort, as if agreeing with what was being said. The more Hank ranted, the more agitated the horse became.

Hank stopped and watched the golden stallion for a moment. Turning back to George, "Okay, what's the rest of it?"

"They're contesting Hyacinth's will because Rodchester is also a relative and should inherit a portion of the estate. Since he was technically Hyacinth's nephew thru Iris's marriage, he felt entitled to a share of the estate. Now his heirs feel they have a right to half of the estate. If they win, Steph will have to sell everything and split it down the middle."

George stopped and took a deep breath before continuing. "Stanley Jr. is going to help Steph go through the papers in the study. If they can find the document Iris signed giving up her inheritance to the farm, then they have a good chance having this stopped." George felt suddenly tired. Just when he was getting on his feet financially, everything was going wrong again.

"If Steph has to sell, will you be able to buy any of the land? Will this affect you and Jenny?" Hank saw George sag on the stool and realized how much Steph's problems were adding to George's.

"It would depend on how they sell it. If they sell the farm as a whole farm then no. I might be able to buy a few acres if they sell it by lots. However, I don't have money to invest right now." George felt the anger building as he talked. "My money is setting on the land in the crops. That's why we have to keep this from Jenny. She is so happy right now and I want to keep her that way. She'll feel pressured to go back to work. We would have more money but I enjoy having her around the house. I would miss her." George could not hold back a sigh. He straightened up and looked squarely at Hank. "It's nice not having her so stressed out from working all day then coming home to work more." George suddenly realized he had been holding back his resentment of Steph for a long time. *I'm so glad Jenny has the baby to keep her home now. I was so tired of hearing about 'Steph this and Steph that'. I didn't realize how much it bothered me that Jenny was spending so much time with Stephanotis and not at home.* George grimaced when he realized how resentful he had become. *I know I*

113

should be glad Jenny has a friend who lives so close. She did seem to have a lot of fun helping Steph out.

Hank stopped pacing and stood in front of George. "I'll clean up and go tell Steph and Keri not to tell Jenny until you do. They talk about everything. I get the impression they're afraid they'll miss knowing something. Can't women keep things to themselves and learn to mind their own business?"

George laughed, grateful for his friend's sense of humor. It helped him to get control of his own emotions. "You'll learn some-day women want to know everything they can about everyone. Then they have to tell someone what they know to make room in their heads so they can learn more. I figure it's a girl thing and try not to get involved."

Grinning at George's theory, Hank went back to the house. He found Jenny standing in the kitchen looking in the open door of the freezer. She was shaking her head and muttering to herself.

"How's it going beautiful? Did you lose something?" Jenny jumped when Hank spoke. She was concentrating on what she could make for dinner. Jenny had felt guilty letting Steph and Keri bring meals over every night. She found she enjoyed being spoiled but knew it would have to end. She told them she was feeling up to han-dling everything now and tonight she was cooking herself.

Keri and Steph made her promise to call for help if she needed them. Unfortunately, Jenny didn't realize how much time it takes to care for the baby. She still had to do the laundry, which seemed to double in size each day and cook for two men with healthy appetites. Getting one of the casseroles out of the freezer, she closed the door and turned to look at Hank. Seeing him in his grass and soil covered clothes she sighed. "What a mess! I hope you plan to clean up before you touch anything!"

Chagrined, Hank removed his shoes and slowly made his way to his room trying not to drip any dirt on Jenny's clean floor. He planned to take his shower and go talk with Steph. If he timed it right, he'd have plenty of time to be back before Jenny had dinner on the table.

*   *   *

Steph phoned home several times while she was at the grocery store. She kept thinking of what she wanted done before Stanley arrived. With each call, however, her shopping cart grew fuller. Betty was going through the kitchen checking out the supplies and staples, adding suggestions to Steph's list. Steph couldn't decide on the wine they should have with dinner, so she bought three different bottles. Selecting flowers for the table, she impulsively picked out a plant to add to their collection in the conservatory. Finally she moved into a line to check out.

Standing in front of her was Mrs. Price. Steph was uncertain if Mrs. Price would remember her but she wanted to be friendly. Smiling, Steph moved closer.

"Hello Mrs. Price. It's nice to see you again"

Mrs. Price stared at Steph as if trying to decide whether to talk to her or not. When she responded, her voice was cold, not the warm and friendly voice Steph had remembered. "Hello. How are you doing out at the Weatherby Farm? Are things going well?"

"Yes, I am getting settled in and we're getting things cleaned up nicely. It's such a lovely home. It needs some repair work though. I'm trying to get as much done as possible before winter."

"I hear you're starting a business up out there. I'm sure Hyacinth wouldn't approve of what you are doing. She was a good Christian woman after all." Mrs. Price turned to pay for her groceries. When she turned back to Steph, her disappointment was clear on her face. "You know, I thought you seemed like a good person when you were here with Stanley Jr. Obviously first impressions are deceiving. I thought maybe you and he might hit it off. But now that I know what sort of person you are, I hope he looks for a wife elsewhere." Mrs. Price abruptly turned and walked away, pushing her loaded grocery cart in front of her.

I don't understand. What did Mrs. Price mean? I'd only met her once. Thinking back over everything that had taken place since she came to town Steph turned to the checkout clerk. Absently she smiled at the girl. "Hello"

"Did I understand Mrs. Price? Do you work out at the Weatherby Farm? I hear they're setting up a strip club out there. Someone said they're remodeling the upper floors of the house into all bedrooms so they can rent them out by the hour. One woman said she heard they were putting a bar in the old music room and a hot tub in the conservatory. Do you suppose they'll have male strippers or just women? If you work there, do you think you could tell me?" The clerk didn't notice the shell-shocked look on Steph's face as Steph swiped her credit card.

Packing the groceries, the clerk continued talking unaware of the effect her words were having on Steph. "I know it supposed to be a secret but it's so exciting. Well, that's it. Thanks for shopping with us. Let me know if they get any male strippers out there. That's a show I would love to see." Turning to the next customer, the checkout clerk changed subjects and started a new conversation.

In shock, as if it were a bad dream, Steph walked out of the grocery store. She didn't remember loading the groceries into the car until she reached into the shopping cart and it was empty. *I don't understand. Where are people getting that idea? I'm glad Stanley is coming to dinner. I can ask him about this.*

While Steph was driving back to the farm, she tried to think about the people she'd met since she'd moved in. Did she mention anything to anyone that would help start such a rumor? She was concentrating so much she was surprised when she realized suddenly she had arrived home. Keri and Betty came out of the house when Steph drove up. They helped her carry the groceries into the house.

As Keri was putting the items away, she noticed Steph was quiet and withdrawn. "Steph, are you okay? You're not still upset are you? You seem awfully distracted."

"I'm okay, I just had another shock. Keri, did you mention to anyone in town my idea of opening a B & B or a boardinghouse?" Flopping down into a chair at the table, Steph decided to tell her friends about the vicious rumor. "I just found out at the grocery store that we are opening a strip club, putting the bar in the music room and a large hot tub in the conservatory."

"Hey, that's a good idea! You really could put a hot tub in the conservatory." Hank entered the room while Steph was explaining what she heard. "I bet it would be great to lean back and look at the stars through the glass roof. You could use it year-round! We could even have a wet t-shirt contest! Hey, Keri, did you bring your t-shirt?"

Knowing Hank was teasing, Keri played along. She strutted across the floor as if she was walking down a stage runway. "I would beat them all!" Keri threw her arms up with a flourish.

Hank applauded and gave her a deep bow. Taking one of the flowers from the bouquet Steph bought, he handed it to Keri, pulled her into his arms and waltzed with her across the floor.

Betty and Steph burst out laughing at their antics.

"It feels good to laugh," grinned Steph. She felt her spirits lifting. She laughed so hard tears formed in her eyes. "I am glad to have you for my friends. What would I do without you?"

"Set up a strip club," laughed Betty. "I bet Hank here would make a great stripper!"

"Whoa, ladies! Just because a good-looking guy like me comes into your midst, it doesn't mean you can have your way with me. At least not until you feed me some of whatever smells so good!" Hank inhaled deeply. The kitchen was filled with delicious aromas. He wasn't looking forward to dinner with Jenny and George, secretly hoping the women would invite him to stay. He didn't like to hide things from Jenny.

"What brought you over? I thought you finished mowing for today?"

Keri dipped some fresh baked apple crisp into a bowl for Hank. "Would you like some Ice cream with this?"

"Oh, yes!" Hank was already drooling from the wonderful aroma of the apple crisp. "I came over to talk to Steph. Can we talk in private?" He reached for the bowl with a mischevious look on his face. "I'll just take this with me." With a wink at Keri, he headed out of the kitchen.

Hank tried to think of the right words to use and waited until they were alone in the Study. He decided a direct approach was his best option. "You were upset when I was here earlier. I didn't want to intrude so I left. I mentioned it to George. We knew you were going to see the lawyer Wilbur today. George was worried and called Stanley Jr. He told George to wait and see how things turned out. George panicked and started yelling at Stanley. Finally Stanley told him about the challenge to the will. George doesn't want Jenny to know. He's afraid she'll feel she has to go back to her old job. She's so happy being home with the baby and working on the farm as needed. George likes having her around the farm. I know it is upsetting to you, but will you please not mention it to Jenny?"

Hank watched her face and waited as he ate. Finally Steph said, "I'll do my best to keep it from her, but George has to realize that someone in town may tell her. They talk about the farm as if they know what is going on out here. I was at the grocery store and found out that I'm going to turn this house into a strip club."

"I heard part of your conversation when I was coming in. You were talking about a hot tub in the conservatory and a bar in the music room. Actually, I like those ideas. That would be something funny Jenny would like to hear about. Can I tell her and George at dinner tonight?" Hank was relieved to have a safe topic to discuss.

"Of course you can tell her. She knows the truth and she may get a kick out of it." Steph stood up from the desk, unsure if she should be relieved or angry that he cared enough to encourage George. "Now, I have a guest coming for dinner, so if you'll excuse me, I have to go freshen up." She left the room and went up the stairs, trying to keep her emotions under control until she knew he was gone.

Hank returned to the kitchen, putting his bowl into the sink. "So, who's coming to dinner?" Hank asked, unsure if he really wanted to know the answer.

"Stanley Wilbur Jr., the lawyer is coming. He told Steph if she can find the document Iris signed stating she gave up her inheritance of the farm, it would be helpful to getting the matter settled faster." Keri was getting plates out of the cupboard to set the table. Turning back to look at Hank, she continued. "He didn't want her to go through the desk until he was here as her legal representative. He said she might not know what to look for." Seeing Hank's expression, she rushed on to add, "Don't worry. She's stronger than you think. She's got all of us helping her." Keri left the room hoping she hadn't said too much.

"Don't worry Hank. We'll be here with them." Betty grinned as she checked the meat in the oven.

"I don't know what you're talking about!" Frustrated because she saw through him, Hank turned and strode out of the room. Betty chuckled and started working on the salad they were having with dinner.

CHAPTER 10

Stanley Jr. finished the last of the work he needed to do at the office. He was looking forward to having dinner with Stephanotis.

Stanley spent most of his personal time with the same group of friends. His last serious relationship ended two months before. They had been together for eight months when she started to take him for granted. She would make plans and forget to ask him if he was busy. With his profession, there were times when he needed to work evenings and weekends. She wanted him to arrange his schedule around her plans. Once they were living together, her favorite way to begin a sentence was "If you really cared for me you would …" and it was usually followed by something Stanley knew he wouldn't like. Stanley thought they were compatible enough most of the time and he enjoyed their physical relationship. He broke it off when his mother called the office one day extremely excited. She told him she was going shopping for wedding dresses with his fiancée. He was careful not to let his mother become friendly with any of the women he dated. He was determined not to let her assume he intended to marry. He was not ready to settle down and share his life with just one person yet. He had plans for his future. He was still young enough to enjoy himself before being chained to a family. His plan was to start enjoying himself now.

* * *

Stanley Jr. left the office early to go home to shower and change for dinner. He wanted to wear something more casual for the evening. He chose a burgundy colored cotton shirt that buttoned down the front and tan slacks. Stanley stopped for a moment in front of his full-length mirror, admiring his attire; confident it gave him a more athletic look since the color of the shirt set off his tan.

Satisfied he was ready for an evening of relaxation, he went to the kitchen to select a bottle of wine from his collection. A good wine was necessary for setting the mood. Sure he intended to help Steph, but they didn't have to sort papers all night. How many could there be? He was confident he would find the document in one evening. Besides what was wrong with having a little fun too?

Stanley was surprised when he turned onto the driveway to the Weatherby farmhouse. The mailbox was brightly painted and easy to read. Large, light catching reflectors were placed strategically along the drive where it met the road. As he drove closer to the house, he noticed other changes. He saw flowers were planted in the flowerbeds and lights lined the walkway around the house. The lawn was freshly mowed and the shrubbery looked neat and trimmed. Walking up onto the porch, he noticed the furniture had been set up and cleaned.

As he neared the entryway, he noticed a new light fixture highlighted the double front doors. Entering the vestibule to ring the doorbell, he was amazed to see new curtains and cushions flanking the windows. He admitted to himself he was impressed with the way Steph was turning the old house into a home.

*   *   *

Steph paced nervously in the kitchen while Betty put the final touches on dinner. "I feel so guilty letting you both do all the work. I should've cooked dinner, but it wouldn't have turned out this well. I can't believe this is happening. He'll be here soon. I hope I have everything set up okay. I hope he finds the document tonight so this will be over."

"Will you settle down!" urged Keri. "You're getting all worked up again and you'll have an upset stomach. What will happen, will happen! Right now you need to concentrate on what you can do. Let the rest of it go."

"She's right." Betty was slicing the warm pot roast, putting it on the platter. She stopped working and looked at Steph, nodding her head in agreement with Keri. "If the document is here, we'll find it. Did you get the batteries charged on the cameras?" She nodded again not waiting for Steph to answer. "Good. That's a pretty dress you're wearing. You look very nice. Now stop fidgeting." Betty turned her attention back to the meat.

When the doorbell rang, Steph quickly left the kitchen, yelling back, "I'll get it," on her way. She pretended to race Misti to the door. When she reached her destination, she paused to take a deep, calming breath. As her heart started calming down, she opened the front door and smiled. "Welcome to the Weatherby Farm. I think you'll find it a lot different from when you were last here."

"Thank you. This is for you. It's a nice little wine from a local winery. I think you'll enjoy it." Stanley handed Steph the bottle of wine as he entered the house. Misti was barking and running back and forth. "Well, hello to you too." Stanley leaned over to pet the Sheltie as he chuckled at the dog's antics.

"Misti, settle down." The little dog stopped barking and stood looking at them. Motioning for Stanley to join her, Steph walked into the parlor. "Dinner is almost ready. Please have a seat and I'll go open the wine for dinner. I'll be right back." Leaving the room, Steph hurried to the kitchen.

Stanley walked around the room noticing how different it was. The ticking of the old fashioned clock on the mantel filled the quiet room. Appetizing odors were coming from the kitchen and Stanley realized he was getting hungry. He had only a quick lunch and that seemed a long time ago.

On his last visit, Stanley had been overwhelmed with the clutter. Scowling, he remembered the mantel was once covered with figurines and pictures. Relaxing, he realized he liked the room the way it was now. The tables were cleared and the throws and blankets had been removed. Plump pillows were scattered around as if inviting you to sit and lean on them. A feathery Boston fern placed on a plant stand by the window added a touch of life and grace to the room. Looking around, it never occurred to him to wonder where the clutter had gone.

After giving Steph a few minutes to finish whatever she may be doing, he decided to go look for her. He thought he should offer to give her a hand in the kitchen. It would be a nice romantic beginning to the evening. He was surprised to meet her coming down the hall.

Steph smiled at seeing Stanley coming toward the kitchen. *Typical male, thinking with his stomach first and can't wait to eat.* Steph paused to take a calming breath. "I was just coming to get you. Dinner is ready. We're eating in the formal dining room. I thought it would be fun. We usually just eat in the kitchen."

Stanley was stunned when he walked into the dining room. A soft, cream-colored tablecloth covered a portion of the long formal table. Candles and a low, sweeping arrangement of mixed fresh flowers graced the table. Four place settings were arranged with two on each side of the table. Stanley counted twice to be sure he saw four places.

He quickly controlled his surprise. "I see we are not dining alone this evening. Who else is joining us?"

Stanley felt an explanation was in order. Secure in the knowledge he and Steph were dining alone, he was looking forward to a quiet, romantic evening. *I'll be nice for a while, but they better leave soon after dessert.* He thought quickly. *I'll explain I came to work and hurry them along.*

Steph didn't miss the changes of expression on Stanley's face. She saw the determined set of his jaw as he came to a decision. Betty and Keri were coming into the room behind Stanley through the open door. She pushed her worry aside and smiled.

"Stanley, I would like you to meet my friends from Boston. This is Keri Hall and Betty Brown. Betty and Keri made dinner for us. Keri and Betty, this is Stanley Wilbur, Jr. He is the lawyer who is going to help me find the document Iris signed." Taking a deep breath, Steph waved her hand over the table, suggesting a chair on the opposite side. "Stanley, please sit down over there and we'll be right back with the rest of the dinner."

Steph left the room, followed closely by Keri and Betty who had placed their dishes of food on the table. Silently they collected the rest of the meal and carried it into the dining room.

Steph turned to Stanley after everyone was seated. "I know you came to help me look for the document tonight, and I appreciate it but there's something else you need to know."

Keri, who thought the strip club rumor was a great joke, spoke up first. She always enjoyed a good laugh and found even greater pleasure in sharing the joke. Without any more thought she blurted out, "Steph's turning this house into a strip club."

Stanley started to choke. He was drinking wine when Keri made her announcement and the shock made him choke. Coughing and sputtering, he finally got himself under control. "What do you mean you're turning this place into a strip club?" With flashing eyes, Stanley turned to Steph but saw she was laughing. Thinking she was laughing at him, he continued, "Don't you know what that sort of scandal would do to our lawsuit? It would make the lawsuit stronger on the side of the Wilgoods. We can't afford even a hint of that to get out." His temper was beginning to flare and the more he thought about it, the angrier he was getting.

Betty was trying so hard to keep a straight face. She held her napkin up to hide her smile while she kept her eyes downcast. She missed the shock on Stanley's face.

Between fits of laughter Steph managed to get enough breath to speak.

"Calm down Stanley. Keri is only repeating a rumor I heard at the grocery store today. I stopped in to buy groceries and saw Mrs. Price. Remember you introduced us the first day when we were at the grocery store. I said hello to her not sure if she would remember who I was. Well, she certainly remembered me. She told me Hyacinth would disapprove of what I was doing out here and that I should be ashamed. I didn't understand but was in the checkout line at the time. The clerk knew all about it and filled me in. She said she heard we were turning the upper floors into bedrooms to rent by the hour. Also we're putting a bar in the music room and a hot tub in the conservatory."

"Don't forget the male and female strippers." Keri couldn't help but add that part. She enjoyed her waltz with Hank and their antics that afternoon. Keri began laughing so hard, she was getting hiccups.

"Since we know it's not true, it is funny," laughed Betty looking over at Steph. "It would sure shake things up more than your idea of a B & B."

"B & B? What's a B & B?" Stunned, Stanley wasn't sure if that was also part of the joke. He couldn't decide if this was funny or not. How could such a vicious rumor get started? He knew Mrs. Price liked to gossip, but so did all the women he knew. He would have to call Mrs. Price and get to the bottom of where this got started. Meanwhile, he was going to have to learn more about what Steph was planning. Forcing himself to relax, he waited for Steph to explain.

Steph took a deep breath. "A B & B is a Bed and Breakfast. Oh, you know! It's like a hotel, but homier, more like an inn. There are a lot of them in Boston. People stay at B & B's for romantic week-end getaways, shopping trips, vacations, and other reasons. We have several ideas on how it could be done. There's lots of room and this would be a great place for one." Steph wanted Stanley to understand how special the farm was becoming to her.

"Steph could have a little landscaping done and she'd have a wonderful place for outdoor weddings. My nephew was recently married in an outdoor setting and it was wonderful."

Keri spoke up not wanting to be left out. "She could rent out stalls in the barn and clear a place for trail rides. Jenny said in some towns the local horse clubs are always looking for places to trail ride. We could set up bird feeders and birdhouses; then clear walking paths in the woods for hiking."

Stanley relaxed getting into the spirit of the discussion. He thought it sounded like a workable business venture. He wasn't sure what permits would be needed, but a call to the county courthouse would settle that. A secure business plan would show Hyacinth was not remiss in making Steph her heir. He relaxed and joined in the discussion. "You could have wine tasting parties with wines from the local wineries. The Chamber of Commerce is always looking for a place to hold meetings and events. This would be a nice backdrop for one of their events. I know when we have our annual festival; the local hotels are always sold out months in advance. I think the area could use another good inn."

Eating her desert, Keri choked. "Wow, so you agree it's a good idea?"

"Yes Keri, I agree that it would be a good idea. I'll have my secretary start checking for permits to get you started." Stanley pushed his chair back from the table. Even though it wasn't the romantic evening he planned, he had enjoyed an excellent meal with three charming companions. He felt encouraged to pursue Steph if just to come and enjoy the excellent cuisine. "Steph, before the evening gets any later, we should probably take a look at the papers you have for me."

Feeling a little nervous, Steph rose and led Stanley to the library. She had dismantled the bed in the library and removed it to give them more room. Any papers, receipts, notes she found were put into boxes in the library to be sorted.

"As you can see, we have a few boxes of papers. While we're cleaning, we're collecting any papers we find and putting them in here. I wanted to take my time when I sort through them. I hate to think we might throw something important out and not know it." Steph couldn't keep the pride from her voice knowing her efforts might save her home.

Stanley was astounded. There were five boxes of papers in this room alone. "Where did you say these came from?" Amazement mixed with dread could be heard in his voice.

Steph saw the shock reflected in his eyes. Carefully measuring her words out of the fear that Stanley would be overwhelmed with the sheer amount of letters and papers they had complied, Steph decided to stay positive. After all the work they had done collecting the papers, she was certain it wouldn't be that large of a task to sort them. "The papers in these boxes were found in the servant's quarters on the third floor and throughout the bedrooms. The larger bedrooms had smaller desks with papers crammed inside. When we took the drawers out to clean them, we even found papers wedged behind and under where the drawers slide. We took all the drawers out of any furniture and made sure to check for anything in cracks and crevices. I've tried to keep track of where they were found."

Stanley was speechless. Unwillingly he found he had to admire the work Steph was doing. This was a large house and now he could see that this was a larger task than he thought.

Steph moved on into the study. She walked around turning on the lights. "The locksmith unlocked the drawers on the desk, this trunk and those file cabinets."

Following her, Stanley saw Steph was pointing out a large, old-fashioned trunk and two large oak filing cabinets similar to those in his father's office. Remembering why he was here, he decided to make the best of the opportunity. Hoping to appear eager and willing, he moved to the desk. "This is a lot of paper to go through. The best way to do this is to just begin."

Steph nodded her head. "I tried to think of the best way to sort this mess out. I have some boxes labeled for trash, receipts and so on. I tried to think of any way that would make it easier. The papers I need to keep, I can file later. Since our objective is to find the signed document, I wondered if you wanted to start at the desk first. I took a couple of pictures of the top of the desk. The papers that were there are here in this folder." Steph handed Stanley a thick folder filled with papers. "I wanted to clean the top off to give you a place to work. I thought I would go through this trunk while you worked on the desk papers."

Stanley settled down on the chair at the desk. He opened the stack. The first paper he saw was the copy of the original lawsuit. He took a deep breath and started sorting papers.

Before Stanley arrived, Steph took pictures of the top of the desk, and the desk drawers opened showing their contents. She photographed the open file drawers with their tabs and labels. Now she was going to make a photographic record of what was in the trunk.

At first, Stanley was so absorbed in what he was doing he didn't realize Steph was taking pictures. After a while, the flash of the camera began to disturb him. He sat a few minutes and simply watched what she was doing. Then he sneezed.

Opening the lid and making it secure, Steph began photographing the contents. It was full of small bound books and pictures. Placing the items on a table, she began to sort them as she removed them from the trunk. Steph photographed each layer prior to moving them to the table. She was working her way to the bottom of the trunk and had forgotten Stanley was there. She stood up quickly feeling slightly embarrassed when she heard him sneeze.

Stanley enjoyed watching Steph absorbed as she was in bending over and taking her pictures. Stanley knew his face had reddened with embarrassment. He felt like a little boy caught doing something he knew he wasn't supposed to be doing. He was willing to admit he had enjoyed as any healthy male would, the peeks up her skirt as she moved. Each time she bent over to either take a picture or to retrieve an item, he saw a hint of what she was wearing underneath. He knew it was an image that would keep him awake nights if he dwelt on it. He had been trying to guess the depth she was working at by the way the skirt of her dress was hiking up in back. He was hoping to be rewarded with more than a peek when she found the bottom.

Reminding himself she was a client, and determined not to cause Steph any embarrassment, Stanley didn't mention what he was thinking. Since Steph was now aware he was watching her, he decided it best to pretend his interest was for the objects she found, not the back view of her skirt. Stanley rose from his chair and walked over to the table Steph was standing beside. He picked up a few of the pictures and then the bound books. Stanley moved slowly and deliberately, selecting an item, looking it over and then replacing it.

"These look like pictures of the house and the farm. I wonder what years they were taken." After showing Steph a black and white picture, Stanley carefully laid it back where Steph placed it with a collection of other pictures. Stanley then picked up a bound book and flipped through it.

Steph had forgotten Stanley was in the room and that she was wearing a dress. Absorbed at the time in the contents of the trunk, she wondered if she had revealed more than she knew. *I can be a mature adult about this too, since he's not embarrassed, I won't be either,* she decided. Taking a deep breath she looked at Stanley. "The trunk is filled with pictures and journals. I think it was used to store records over several years. I took pictures of each level so I have a journal of how things were packed in the trunk."

Warming up to her subject, she continued. "I had a wonderful anthropology professor in college. I don't remember everything I learned but I was impressed with the way the anthropologists document their digs. When we started cleaning, it made sense to document the items with pictures and lists. First Jenny and then Keri helped me. Each room has its own inventory sheet and set of pictures. I can get distracted by what I find sometimes. It's reassuring to have the information so I know where I found it."

"It looks like some of these books were hand bound." Stanley was holding a book with a soft suede binding and long uneven stitches. He opened the book and glanced at random pages. The small neat handwriting was easy to read. In a clear voice he read:

"I am so excited. Paw said I was to go to Cousin John's Farm...

Paw said I must apply myself and learn the ways of a large farm and then come back and teach him...

Cousin John grows tobacco and cotton. He has a fine herd of cattle but Paw says he is more interested in raising fast horses than running his farm...

Paw says that if Cousin John spent as much energy bragging about his farm as he does about his horses, he would be able to keep Aunt Lula happy...

Paw always tries to keep Maw happy he says."...

Carefully Stanley closed the book and placed it on the table. He was impressed by what he'd read. "This book is someone's diary. I didn't expect to find that. I thought they might be farm records or journals with boring information about crops and livestock. That's a fabulous find. I wonder if Hyacinth's father kept a journal. If he did, and we can find it, it would good evidence on our side. I'm impressed with the way you're documenting everything. It would prove authenticity of anything you find."

Steph found her mind suddenly muddled. She felt as if she trespassed into a sacred place. She believed a person's diary was something precious and no one else should read it. It was full of personal and private thoughts. She wondered about the person who wrote those words Stanley read. Obviously it was a male. Was he really young or near her age? She felt her mind clear as she speculated about the author of the journals.

Bored, Stanley went back to the desk. "I'm almost finished with these papers. I've organized the stacks, putting a note on top recommending what you can do with the stack. I'll leave them here for you to handle. I haven't found any documents similar to what I expected to find. I'll finish with the desk tonight and try to come back tomorrow night to start on the files in the filing cabinets."

Steph turned back to finish the trunk and this time she was careful to stoop when removing the items. When she finished, the emotional turmoil of the day returned. She was suddenly feeling drained of energy. She sat down and looked at her watch. They'd been working for two hours. No wonder she was tired. It had been a long day. She glanced over at Stanley. He was bent down looking through the bottom drawer.

"I've gotten all the papers out I can find. I left the items in the drawers for you to sort." He stifled a yawn and stood up stretching. "I'm going to have to be going. I have a lot to do tomorrow. I'll check my schedule and let you know if I can come back out tomorrow night. If it takes as long as this, I may have to schedule you in for a full day on Saturday. I'd like to say good-bye to Keri and Betty before I go and thank them for the wonderful meal."

Steph stood up and led Stanley into the kitchen where Keri and Betty were sitting and talking. They had opened one of the boxes from the music room for Betty to sort. Various kitchen tools and utensils were set out on the table and on the countertop.

Stanley tried to ignore the clutter. "Keri, Betty, I'd like to be able to tell you the search is over, but it isn't. I will tell you I have enjoyed this evening. The meal and company were superior and I look forward to doing this again. I'll let Steph know if I can return tomorrow night. Have a pleasant evening, ladies. I look forward to seeing you another time."

Steph walked Stanley out to the covered porch. "It's a nice night," she said looking around before turning to face Stanley. "Thank you for coming out to help me. I'm scared about all of this but I feel better knowing you're helping me." Steph gave Stanley a kiss on the cheek and a smile. "Thank you seems inadequate for the peace you're giving me."

Stanley was touched. He put a hand on each of her arms and pulled her to him. He kissed her gently and softly. "I'm glad to be able to help. It was an enjoyable evening and one I won't soon forget." Realizing now was not the time to push his advantage he felt it best to leave her wanting him more. Releasing her, he turned, walking down the stairs to his car. He turned and waved before getting in.

Steph stood on the porch and watched Stanley drive away. She kissed him on the cheek impulsively to thank him for helping her. His kiss, while warm and inviting, was also possessive and somewhat disturbing. Confused by her feelings, she went back in to the house to check on Keri and Betty before going to bed.

Steph found them in the kitchen still discussing the kitchen items.

Betty explained what they had found. "It's no wonder we didn't know what some of these are. The food processor was in pieces. I've put it together and we were trying to see if there were any more parts to it. There should be different sizes of blades." Picking up a cone shaped sieve and a wire stand, Betty continued. "This is for canning juice. I always used one for making tomato juice. You put the hot, cooked tomatoes into the sieve. It sets in the wire stand and the whole thing sets in a pot to catch the juice. There should be a wooden cone shaped item, like a cone shaped rolling pin. You use it to smash the tomatoes and the juice squishes out of the sieve. Making your own juice takes several tomatoes and much work, but it is well worth it."

Keri was packing some of the items back into the box. "We'll have to put these back until we can decide where to put them in the cabinets. Since we may not be canning this year, we'll just put this in storage to use later. I don't know about you ladies, but I am ready to get some sleep."

Covering a yawn with her hand, Betty nodded. She'd put in a long day beginning with a long drive. Clearing off the table, they turned off the lights and locked up.

Steph was glad to have her friends with her. She knew everything was going to be okay. Letting Misti wander around, Steph went to bed and quickly fell asleep.

Steph woke up in the night feeling something was wrong. For a few minutes, she remained still, disoriented. She got up out of bed and walked to her door, listening to see if she could hear any noise. When she was satisfied there was nothing to hear, she returned to her bed. It was a long time before she fell back to sleep.

*   *   *

The man parked his car just inside the woods in the place he made for it. He memorized the way to the barn so he could avoid any obstacles without the aid of a flashlight. He was eager to see what his cameras had to show him tonight. From previous visits, he noticed the people in the house had a definite pattern of behavior. That was going to make it easy for him. He had a job to do and he was going to earn his money. But, oh he was going to enjoy himself tonight! They would know someone meant business. They had better be willing to do what his employer wanted them to do. He'd been doing subtle convincing for years and was good at it. This employer only wanted to scare them, but there are many ways to scare people. The man knew all of them. Walking quietly across the lawn out of the woods, he began planning his next move. They would know tomorrow he was here.

CHAPTER 11

George liked to get an early start every day. When it was summer, he tried to finish as much work as possible before the day became too hot. This didn't happen often. Some days he would work in one of the buildings or under a tree in the shade. This summer he was trying to spend time in the house with Jenny and the baby.

George loved his son and enjoyed helping Jenny care for the baby when he could. The baby was adjusting to the routine of the household. He woke up when George did, so George learned to change his diaper and feed him, giving Jenny the freedom to sleep a little longer if she wanted to. He knew it was vain, but he was proud of himself for helping Jenny. After feeding and changing the baby, George would put him back to bed then make his own breakfast.

Hank woke early today to eat breakfast and talk with George. He told George and Jenny last night about the rumor that Steph was starting a strip club. He even told them about waltzing around the kitchen with Keri. Hank thought all night about it and wanted to ask George what he thought was going on.

As Hank came downstairs he could hear George talking in the kitchen. Assuming Jenny was up as well, Hank walked into the kitchen. He stopped in amazement. Here was his friend trying to change a wiggling baby while it was lying on the kitchen table. From the smell, he also had a diaper filled with poo somewhere. Now as Hank looked closer, there was poo, but not just in the diaper. George was wearing poo on his shirtsleeve and it was smeared on the table. Hank could see some had fallen to the floor. The diaper George was hanging on to with his free hand also had a few smears on it. Hank couldn't decide whether to laugh or run. Thinking it best to beat a hasty retreat, he started backing up to leave the room. Then he had an idea.

George looked up just in time for Hank to snap a picture on his camera phone. Hank started laughing at the look of dismay on George's face.

George was trying his best, but all he was doing was smearing poo on everything he touched. Here was his best friend taking pictures as he failed to diaper his own son. The baby was wiggling as if trying to get away. George was breaking into a sweat trying to hold on and get him cleaned up.

The flash from the camera startled George Henry who was already tired of being on the hard table, waiting while his dad changed his diaper. He decided to just let it all go. First he peed on his dad and then he let out a wail. George Henry didn't want to wait any longer for breakfast.

Hank was still holding the camera phone and took another picture as George Henry whizzed on his dad. Hank was laughing so hard he nearly wet himself. He was holding onto the back of the chair, trying not to fall down. George Henry's wail sobered him up as quickly as it calmed down the upset George.

"Hank, make yourself useful. Go get another diaper. Don't bother running upstairs, just grab one from the diaper bag." Hank dashed off to do as he was told. He was as worried as George about waking up Jenny.

George pulled on the baby wipe sticking out of the baby wipes container, yanking the top off. He was trying to hold George Henry, talk soothingly to him and wipe up poo at the same time. George was muttering as he worked. "I should get the Father of the Year award for this. Where is Hank with that clean diaper anyway?"

Hank brought George the diaper but held it out at arm's length. "Don't just stand there man. Get a wipe and start wiping."

"Wipe what?" Hank slowly backed out of the kitchen. He hit something solid in the doorway and stopped. Turning around, he met Jenny.

After watching Hank get the diaper and take it to the kitchen, Jenny followed. She had heard the baby crying and was worried. Now she stood in the doorway and took it all in. Here was her husband, smearing poo all over with a giant wad of wipes. Hank, his best friend was trying to sneak away. It took her a couple of minutes to realize why she was seeing wet areas on George's face and shirt.

Hank started laughing again watching Jenny's face as she took the scene in.

Jenny started laughing too and went to help George by taking charge. "Hank, get the bottle ready for me. George, go upstairs and change. Then bring that shirt back down for me to launder. Hank! Where is the clean diaper you gave George?" Each man did as he was told. George hurried upstairs to change. Hank handed Jenny first the diaper and then the bottle. Quickly Jenny cleaned up George Henry. After putting on his diaper and a clean outfit, she turned to Hank. "If you'll sit down and feed him, I'll finish cleaning up this mess."

Hank was so relieved Jenny didn't expect him to clean up he was willing to feed the baby. "I can do this. I'm getting the hang of it."

Jenny watched him as he mimicked the way she held George Henry, supporting his head and holding the bottle. Just as Jenny finished wiping down the table with disinfectant, George came down the stairs.

George hurried so Jenny would still be busy. He didn't want her to be mad at him. Seeing Jenny wiping the table and Hank feeding the baby, he felt a tug of jealousy in his stomach. He pushed the feeling aside as he walked on into the room.

"Hey Dad, you sure know how to start the day." Hank knew he would have to wait until later to talk with George but he was enjoying the day so far. It was pleasant to hold George Henry and feed him. Hank had been afraid he would drop him the first few times he held him. He was more confident and willing now, as long as the baby didn't wiggle around too much.

George sat down beside Hank in an empty chair. He couldn't stop grinning as he remembered what was happening when Hank walked in. "I'll take over here." George reached over and took the baby from Hank's arms. George looked so content. Hank took another picture.

Jenny began to cook breakfast. She had bacon frying in one pan and was scrambling eggs in another skillet.

George Henry finished his bottle and was yawning in his dad's arms. Placing the baby on his shoulder to burb, George gave a contented sigh.

"Yeah, Dad, I think you've earned this." Jenny walked over to George and gave him a heartfelt kiss.

Hank snapped another picture and was flipping through the pictures of the morning when Jenny walked behind him to see what he was doing. She knew she needed to get back to the stove and the food she was cooking there, but couldn't resist checking to see what Hank was doing.

George was curious; he wanted to see the pictures too.

Jenny started laughing. "Hank, don't forget to send me a copy of those. I'll put them with the others you've sent me."

"Others, what, there are other pictures?" George shifted the now sleeping baby to cradle him. "What are you doing over there, Hank? What does Jenny mean by others?"

"I'm sending copies of this morning's pictures to my mom. She thinks I'm in the way around here and should go home. I figured as long as I keep sending her baby pictures, she'll leave me alone. She really loved the pictures I took at the hospital. I've been sending them to Jenny through her email so she has copies of what I take, too."

"He sent some wonderful pictures from the hospital. I will always cherish the picture of you holding the baby right after his birth. I just loved the look on your face Daddy. I cry every time I look at it."

"What do you mean you have a picture of that? Hank, how did you get a picture of that? You weren't even in there." George tried to remember if he saw Hank come into the delivery room.

"Sure I was. The nurse told me when Jenny was moved to the delivery room so I could be present. She had me put on scrubs and I was in the room. I took pictures for Jenny. I knew she'd like it. I tried to be sneaky about it and not distract anyone. Keri told me what pictures to take. She said she always wished she had a picture of the first time her husband saw his child. She made me promise to take it. We were going to frame it for you for Father's Day. I figured you could hang it in the barn." Hank started laughing. "I've changed my mind. I think I'll put the picture of you covered in poo on the Internet. Jenny do you have a social page?"

Jenny set plates of food down in front of Hank and George. "No, I wouldn't want that picture on the Internet. It would be more fun to save and show it at family parties. How about George's birthday party? We could have it blown up like a poster and put it out in the yard so the neighbors could all see it too." Jenny was laughing so hard she had to sit down.

After a moment, George realized they were teasing and joined in. "That picture would make a good portrait to hang over a fireplace mantel at Steph's strip club. Think we could talk her into it?"

"We'll have to show them to the ladies and see what they have to say. Betty can't wait to meet both of you and see the baby. She'll probably come over today."

After finishing his breakfast, George stood up and handed the sleeping baby to Jenny. "Here you go. I have to get to work. I'll see you both later. I've got livestock to feed." Kissing Jenny good-bye, George left the house.

"Is there anything I can help you with before I go? Would you like me to take you to see Steph today?" Hank was secretly pleased the girls were becoming good friends.

"I'll just take this little tyke and put him back to bed. Then I'll clean up. I'm not dressed to go anywhere yet. I have some things I want to get done while the baby sleeps. I may go over later though. Go have fun and don't work too hard."

"Okay, but call me if you need me." Hank went out to the barnyard. He was going to search for George. He knew George had a set pattern for feeding the various animals around the farm. Hank would often help him out, but some days, George said, he liked to do it himself. It gave him the chance to check every animal to be sure they were okay. Hank was beginning to understand what he meant sometimes you have to see for yourself.

* * *

Stanley went to the office early. He wanted to clear more of his schedule over the next couple of weeks. He decided in the night that he was going to spend more time with Stephanotis Weatherby. He enjoyed his evening with Steph and the good-bye kiss. He smiled remembering the softness of her lips.

"Good morning. I thought I'd find you here." Stanley Sr. joined his son in his office. "So, how was your evening? That smile on your face tells me you had a good time." Sitting down in the chair across from Stanley Jr.'s desk, Stanley Sr. studied his son's face. "I don't mind if you had a good time. I just hope it wasn't a great time. We can't afford to alienate our client and co-defendant. She's a nice young woman and seems to be happy we're handling this for her. I want it to remain that way." He paused for his words to sink in. Raising an eyebrow to emphasize he meant business, he continued, "Do you understand me?"

Stanley Jr. gave up trying to please his father years ago. He considered himself a better man because he pleased himself first. Doing what he thought was right, not what his father thought was right. He decided to take control of the conversation.

"I was just thinking of a rumor Mrs. Price told Steph. According to this rumor, Steph is turning the farmhouse into a striptease club." Stanley paused to watch his Father's reaction.

"A what? Did you just say Mrs. Price used the words striptease club?"

Stanley Sr.'s face looked as if he'd just eaten something extremely bitter.

"Affirmative." Stanley was enjoying his father's discomfort. "I introduced Steph to Mrs. Price the first day Steph arrived. She wanted to stop at the grocery store before going to the house. I took her to the closest store on the way to the farm. You know, the newer one, on Coggan's Road. Anyway, Steph said she shopped for groceries yesterday and Mrs. Price was upset about what she was doing at the farm. Steph even got details about a bar in the music room and a hot tub going into the conservatory. I know gossip travels fast in this town, but there are two older women now living with Steph out there. I met them both last evening. I can't imagine either one of them giving cause for this type of rumor."

"I told Steph I would look into it. By the way Father, Steph is thinking of turning the place into a Bed & Breakfast for people to come and stay. I told her I would look into what permits would be needed for her. Do you still have that friend who works at the Health Department?" Stanley Jr. paused, pleased to be the one asking the questions.

"Oh, you mean Harry Hopkins? I think he's still there. He may have retired by now, but you can call and find out. It's nice of you to take an interest in Stephanotis. That is as long as it is a legitimate interest. Don't do anything to jeopardize the firm." Stanley Sr. rose from the chair. He wanted to give the appearance he was satisfied with the conversation. He had an uneasy feeling Stanley was keeping something from him but he was relieved to know there were other people at dinner last night.

"They've amassed a large amount of papers to be sorted through. I'll be going out to the Weatherby Farm often until I find the document. I just wanted to let you know." Stanley Jr. knew he didn't need his father's permission, but wanted to give the impression he was doing this for the good of a client.

Stanley Sr. refrained from comment. He waved at Stanley as he left the room. His mind was already reviewing all the implications of what he'd just learned. Weighing the pros and the cons of what could happen.

Congratulating himself for successfully dealing with his father, Stanley went back to rearranging his schedule. He wrote down a list for the secretary to handle including asking her to call City Hall to check on any building permits Steph might need. He would call the Health Department later in the day to speak to the superintendent himself. As he prepared for the day ahead, he realized he was glad the meeting with his father went so smoothly. He remembered past times when talking with his father had been difficult for him. He penciled in a call to Mrs. Price for later in the day and called the secretary into his office. He wanted to get started right away.

*　　*　　*

Steph woke up exhausted. She had fallen into a deep sleep when she finally slept. She was not sure what it was that had disturbed her enough to wake her up. She lingered in the shower hoping the hot water would chase the cobwebs from her mind.

When Steph went down to the kitchen for breakfast, Keri and Betty were sitting at the table talking about the various sizes of the cast iron skillets found thoughout the house. The skillets were rusty and Keri thought they should be painted and hung up as decorations on the back porch. Betty was explaining they could be cleaned and would look nice hanging on the brick of the boarded up fireplace in the kitchen. That would keep them handy for use. Steph let them continue their discussion as she headed for the coffeepot.

"It's not as tasty as you make it, but it'll wipe that sour look off your face." Keri walked up beside Steph to refill her cup and Betty's. "We've been spoiled having you make the coffee. When we came down and saw it wasn't on to brew, we decided Betty should make it. You look in need of a cup yourself."

Steph turned to face Betty, who was seated at the table. She gave her a weak smile of apology. "I was really shaken up when something woke me up. It took me a couple of hours to fall back asleep. Then I slept so hard I just couldn't get going this morning."

"Did it have anything to do with that kiss last night?" Keri had returned to her seat and hid a grin behind the rim of her coffee cup. Watching Steph, Keri took a deep drink then smiled. "We thought you were already in the house and went to lock the door. We saw Stanley kiss you." Setting down her cup, Keri leaned toward Steph so she would not miss a word. "Now we want details. Are you going to date the lawyer?"

Betty started to choke on her own coffee. She forgot how blunt Keri could be sometimes. When Betty was in control of herself again, she rose from the table. "Since it is already hot in here, I'm going to start breakfast." She went to the stove and began to prepare breakfast, keeping an ear open for anything Steph may say.

Leaning on the counter, Steph sipped at her coffee and remained quiet. She sensed by the way they acted when she came in they already knew about the kiss. It was not something to get excited about. A man kissed her on her front porch. Big deal! She walked across the room and sat in a chair at the table across from Keri. Realizing they were waiting for her to say something, she took a deep breath. "Okay, so you saw a good-looking man kissing me. It's not like I haven't been kissed before. He is my lawyer and wants to help me. I would say the kiss was to make me feel better. It was just a good night kiss, nothing more. Now, I don't want to talk about it anymore."

Keri reached across the table and put her hand on Steph's arm holding the coffee cup. "So did it make you feel better?" She said it softly, knowing Steph was still hurting in many ways.

Steph nodded. "Yeah, it made me feel better. Actually, it was nice." Leaning back in her chair, Steph decided to give them a little more. "Okay, it was a nice kiss." She grinned and leaned forward again. "Now when's breakfast? I have a lot to get done today."

*　*　*

When Hank arrived at the farm, he felt something was wrong. He wasn't sure what it was, but something was not as it should be. Since he didn't know what it was, he shrugged if off and went on into the barn.

He had been working off and on cleaning out a stall to house the lawn tractor. Together, George, Steph and he had walked around the barn one day the previous week. They decided the best place to put it would be in the end stall farthest from the front door. When Steph was ready for animals in the barn, she planned to put the lawn tractor in a toolshed. The toolshed was missing part of its roof currently and would need to be repaired before the tractor could be stored there. It would be less work and expense for now to have it in the barn.

Hank removed most of the items out of the stall earlier in the week. It contained bales of straw, old grain sacks, some empty barrels and various tools. Hank was sure he left the wheelbarrow by the stall.

141

When he entered the barn today it was by the front barn door. He turned it around and wheeled it to the back. As he walked, he looked around wondering what it must have been like when the barn was first built.

The barn was built on multiple levels. A sloping mound of packed dirt embraced the front of the building and tapered down on the sides toward the back. This provided an easy access to the upper or main level of the barn. Toward the back and underneath the main level, was an open area for animal pens. Pigs, sheep and/or cattle could be housed there. The warm body heat from the animals below would rise to the main level. The box stalls on the main level were for horses. There were some narrower stalls too. George said the working horses might have been kept in the smaller stalls. They would be working all day and just need a stall in which to be fed and for sleeping. The original barn had sections added to it on the sides. George suggested the tack room was an addition, not part of the original barn. Hank didn't know much about barns, but it was a large building and seemed well built.

George had gone down into the lower level to check the floor supports while he was there. He wanted to make sure they would hold the weight of the lawn tractor. Using a ladder, he climbed up and checked it over carefully. George declared it secure, so Hank knew it would be strong enough to support the weight.

Mowing the large lawn and planting flowers for Keri had taken up most of his time on the previous day. He left the lawn tractor out, but knew Steph and the ladies wouldn't mind. He parked it near the barn so he could finish clearing out the stall and then put it inside.

Hank had left a couple bales of straw to move out completely for last. They were brittle and dry. He didn't want to worry about breaking them apart until he was ready to move them. Once they were moved, Hank could put the lawn tractor away, driving it into the stall. As Hank walked up to the stall, he noticed the floor he swept two days before was covered with straw. One of the bales had broken and the straw was all over the floor. Hank was mildly surprised. The bales were held together by old baling twine. It could have broken after Hank moved the bales toward the front of the stall. He was sure he swept the rest of the stall clean. After getting the old broom from the tack room, he started to sweep the floor. As he stepped to the middle of the stall, there was a loud crack and a section of the floor started to break under his foot. It had sounded so much like a gunshot, Hank instinctively moved backwards from the sound and toward the bales of straw still stacked in the stall.

As his rapidly beating heart started to slow down, he sat on the supporting straw. The fast rush of adrenaline left him weak and tired. When he felt his strength return, he stood up and looked around. Where he was standing moments before, there was now a hole. Carefully he walked over to the edge and looked down. The wood flooring that had broken off under his step was shattered on the ground ten feet below. He would have been badly injured if a larger area had broken and he would have fallen through.

Hank looked to be sure no one from the house heard the noise and was coming to check it out. He blocked the barn door partly shut with a bale of hay so he would hear anyone coming in. He went back to the stall and began to examine the 'scene of the crime.' He was not pleased with what he found. *Someone cut the floor with a saw. That must have been why the bale was broken. It was to cover up the cut floorboards. They must have cut the boards within the last two days. Lucky for me, they misjudged my weight and I had time to jump away before more than one of the planks fell.* Hank shook his head as he looked around, the sound of his own voice giving him little comfort as his mind raced. "If I were driving the lawn tractor, I don't think I'd be walking away."

Hank took pictures to show George and the police. Then he carefully stacked bales of straw over the opening. As he was working, he realized it was the way the lawn tractor was sitting that bothered him when he drove up. When he finished making sure the hole was completely covered, he went to check on the lawn tractor.

He decided while he was working not tell Steph or the ladies about the hole in the barn floor. When he saw the damage to the new lawn tractor, he knew he would have to tell Steph. Someone slashed the tires on the side facing away from the house. A sharp object was used to scratch the paint on large areas of the body. The seat had a strong smell of gasoline and the steering wheel was bent. Visible wires and tubes were cut into pieces and Hank was sure there was more damage not clearly visible. Someone had been here in the night and wrecked this on purpose. Hank called George.

"Hey buddy, we've got some trouble over here." Hank fought to keep his voice calm.

"So now I'm supposed to stop what I'm doing and run over there to babysit you and the women?" George was catching up on some work he'd been putting off. He was getting tired of setting aside his own work to go help Steph. He knew she and Keri had been a great help to Jenny, but he needed to get his work done. His family's livelihood depended on the farm being productive. He was beginning to hate every interruption more and more.

"Listen, someone tore up that new Lawn tractor I was telling you about. They completely destroyed it."

George had been on the verge of telling Hank he'd check it out in a week or two when something in the tone of Hank's voice made him stop.

"I'm sure you're going to want to see this for yourself. _I_ need you to see this." Hoping he was doing the right thing, Hank headed toward the house as he listened to George.

"Ummm, ok. Let me finish up here and I'll be over." George understood something bad had happened and Hank needed him. Hank wasn't one to ask for help so George finished up as quickly as he could then went into the house looking for Jenny. While working, he'd come to the decision that he needed to be the one to tell Jenny everything. If it was as serious as Hank seemed to think it was George needed to stop hiding the bad news from Jenny.

"Jenny, something's happened and I need to talk to you." George called out as he entered the kitchen. "I need to tell you something important."

Jenny was surprised to hear George calling her. She went into the kitchen.

"Shh, George, you'll wake the baby." The serious look on his face caused her to sit down, the sleeping baby temporarily forgotten.

"What is it George? Has something happened to Hank? To Steph? To one of the animals?" Jenny tried to stop the tears that threatened to flow.

"No, not exactly. There are some things I've been trying to keep from you, but now I need to tell you." George sat beside Jenny and reached for her hand.

"You know Steph had a meeting with Stanley Wilbur. It seems that Iris had a stepson whose grandson is trying to get a portion of Hyacinth's estate. He's also suing Stanley Sr. too. If this goes to court and Steph loses, she'll have to sell the farm."

"Oh George! How can that be? What can we do?" Jenny tried to keep her fears under control as she waited for George to explain more.

"Stanley Jr. came out to the farm last night to help Steph find a document Iris signed. If they can find the piece of paper saying she agreed to give up her right of inheritance to the farm, then it should be okay. If the grandson can prove Iris was cheated out of her inheritance, then he has a solid claim on Hyacinth's estate and the farm." George watched Jenny's face to see how she was going to react.

"Does this mean we will lose money too?" Jenny stared at the table top, unwilling to see the expression on George's face.

"It means that I won't be able to rent the land if they sell it. I might be able to buy some of it, but we can't afford to pay a high price for it. If we sell some livestock, we'll be fine. It would mean losing the extra money for boarding the horses and they'd have to sell Sun Dancer and the others."

Jenny sat very still for a few moments. She took a deep breath as she blinked back the tears that had begun to fall. Her eyes full of love, she looked up.

"George, we'll be okay. We'll work it out somehow. At least we have each other. We still have our own farm and livestock. If Steph has to sell, it would be harder for her. We have to remember how lucky we are. I know I'm very lucky. I have you and a healthy baby. We have a roof over our heads and food on the table."

He was so proud of her he thought his heart would burst. "Jenny, I was afraid you wouldn't understand. I'm so proud of you.

I love you so much." George went to Jenny and gathered her up in his arms.

"I love you too. I know we'll get through this. Did you tell me Stanley was at the farm for dinner last night?"

"Yes, he wants to help look for the document so they can get this settled as quickly as possible. Why?" George gave Jenny a startled look.

"Don't you see? Steph had a date! Give me some time to pack and get ready." Jenny gave George a quick kiss and then pulled away from him. Jenny hurried around packing baby items and food. She packed an extra diaper bag and the baby monitor. By the time she finished, George was pacing the floor. Jenny quickly changed the baby and sent George to start loading the truck.

CHAPTER 12

As Betty straightened up after putting a casserole into the oven for lunch, Hank came into the kitchen. Thinking he was there for some coffee, she smiled and walked over to greet him. Noting his behavior, she realized at once something was wrong.

"Where's Steph?" Hank wanted to speak with her alone. It was after all, her barn and lawn tractor.

"She's in the storage area on the top floor. She and Keri are looking for more papers or journals. Shall I go get her?" Betty tried to hide her concern about the young man's gruff behavior.

"No. But thanks. I'll go on up. I know the way." Hank went up the backstairs. He tried to think through all the alternatives. He knew Steph was going to have to call the sheriff's office. This deliberate vandalism to an expensive piece of equipment needed to be reported. He felt a sick knot forming in his stomach. He didn't know what he was going to say or how he was going to say it. He found Steph and Keri coming out of the storage area. They were carrying an antique travel trunk between them.

"Need a hand?" Hank walked up and relieved Keri of her load. He helped Steph carry it over to the top of the stairs. "Let's leave this here for now. George is coming over with Jenny. We'll carry it downstairs for you later. I came up because I needed to talk with Steph alone. Let's go down to the study." Knowing he sounded much harsher than he meant to, Hank decided not to say anymore. Turning away, he went down the steps.

Steph was astonished; she simply started walking behind Hank. Going down the long stairway, she found herself getting nervous. *Why is Hank being so brisk? What right did he have to treat me this way? What happened to cause him to behave like this? Did he know Stanley kissed me last night? Well, so what if he did. I don't owe him an explanation!* When Steph reached the bottom of the front stairway, she found she was becoming angry. She followed Hank into the study and watched him close the doors. She decided to let him rant and then she would cut him off and tell him to mind his own business.

It took Steph a few minutes to realize Hank was fighting an internal battle of his own. She sat down at the desk and decided to wait him out.

Hank was having a hard time trying to find the right words to use. He didn't want to frighten Steph, Keri or Betty, but he needed to tell them about the damage to the lawn tractor. Hank found to his own embarrassment that he was still slightly shaken up himself. Taking a steady calming breath, he decided it was best just to tell her. "Steph, I have some bad news to tell you. Someone deliberately wrecked your lawn tractor last night. I need to know if any of you heard anything strange or if you saw anything out of place in the night. I called George and he's coming over. I want you to call the sheriff's office and have a deputy file a report. I am sorry, but it's beyond repair." Hank wasn't sure how Steph was going to react so he watched her closely.

Steph just stared at him. She was prepared in her mind to defend a simple little kiss. But this was not about the kiss. It was about the lawn tractor. "What do you mean someone wrecked the lawn tractor? I don't understand." She almost choked on her own disbelief.

"When the sheriff's deputy gets here, we'll go out and I'll show you. Meanwhile, we need to know if anyone heard or saw anything. I want you to call your insurance agent after you call the sheriff's office. They'll need to send out an adjuster. I need to use your camera. Where is it?"

"It's in the library. I moved my computer in there and both cameras are on the table. The newer camera has a better zoom. I put a new memory card in yesterday. Please, take it." Steph took a deep breath. She slowly released it. "I'll have to call Stanley. With the estate still in probate, they've been paying the farm insurance from the estate accounts. I don't even know who the insurance agent is." Steph paused trying to collect her thoughts. "Do I need to get the receipts? Stanley was going to have the lawn tractor put on the insurance right away. As riding equipment, we decided to list it on the insurance as farm equipment. I'll get the receipt just in case. Is there anything else I should do?" Steph was glad Hank was there. His calm attitude helped her maintain her own composure.

"Make the calls first and then get the receipts. It would be a good idea to bring the owner's manual. The deputy can use it to check some of the damage done." Hank walked over and put his hand on her shoulder. He gave it a reassuring squeeze. "Will you be okay? I'll go talk with Keri and Betty. I need you to make those calls now. I'll be back to check on you. I want it to be on record that you called in the damage. I'll talk with the deputy when he gets here. Just remind yourself no one was hurt. Take a deep breath and make the call. Okay?"

Steph covered Hank's hand with her own. She tried to give him a smile. "I'm okay. It is just upsetting that someone would cause damage to something of mine intentionally. At least they're not trying to actually hurt someone."

Hank grimaced inwardly. If he hadn't jumped when he did, he would have been injured. He hoped he would be able to talk to the deputy privately.

"I'll be back as soon as I can. George is on his way with Jenny and the baby. I didn't want Jenny left alone." Giving her shoulder one more squeeze, Hank left Steph to make the necessary calls. He went looking for Keri and Betty.

*   *   *

Keri and Betty were in the kitchen having coffee and discussing their individual ideas about what upset Hank. He walked in as Keri was talking.

"I don't think a little kiss is what this is all about. She's an adult and a little romance is what she needs. I, for one hope she has a little fun."

"I don't mind her having some fun, I just hope she doesn't …" Betty saw Hank in the doorway. "Hank, what's happening? Is something wrong? What can we do to help?"

Betty started to get up from her chair.

"Sit down and relax. I'm going to ask a few questions to get your answers and then I'll tell you what you want to know. Did either of you notice anything out of the ordinary last night? Did you hear anything in the night?" Hank wanted to give them time to think before they answered. He walked over to the coffeepot and helped himself to a cup of coffee before joining them at the table.

Keri put her own cup down on the table. "I don't remember hearing anything other than Misti. She was growling throughout the night. She seemed restless when we went to bed. I don't usually leave my door open, but while I was getting ready for bed, she was wandering in and out. She acted like she was trying to find something. I just left my door open for her to come and go. She was pacing around and would try to look out the window. I woke up once when she jumped on my bed. She kept looking out the window, but I didn't see anything so I went back to sleep. I remember thinking she must have been watching a cat. She didn't bark, she just growled and paced."

"I remember now. She did behave odd last night." Betty tried to concentrate. "My room faces the front of the house. I'm across the hall from Keri and Steph. Misti only came in a couple of times then I didn't see her the rest of the night. I remember waking up once and thinking I heard a car door, but when I didn't hear any other noise, I went back to sleep."

"Do either of you know what time those things happened? George is bringing Jenny and the baby over. I don't want any of you ladies to be alone for a while. Steph is calling the sheriff's office. Someone has damaged the lawn tractor. This means someone was on the farm last night after I left. It was fine when I was here before dinner. There's no need to worry, no one was hurt."

"Oh! Dear! Can it be repaired? How did Steph take the news?" Keri was close to tears.

"Steph is strong. She'll be okay. It's an object Keri. I'm sure the insurance will take care of it. As Hank said, at least no one was hurt." Betty reached over and patted her friend on the hand. "I'll go check on Steph. Since Jenny and the baby are coming, why don't you go and make sure we have the baby area ready?" Betty rose and went to see if she could help Steph.

"That's true. We want to be sure we're ready for our little guest." Sniffling, Keri got up and left Hank sitting there shaking his head. He decided he'd better get his pictures before the deputy came. He picked up the camera on his way through the library. He was hoping to get some good pictures.

*   *   *

Hank went back to the barn. He carefully walked around outside taking pictures of anything that could be a possible clue. He took several pictures at the back of the barn and then zoomed in to take pictures of the ground. The packed ground was covered with debris blown in over the years by the wind. Hank worked his way under the area where the hole was in the upper floor. He zoomed in and took pictures from different angles of the hole. He also took pictures of the section of the floor lying shattered at his feet.

Hearing a motor in the yard, he left as swiftly but carefully as possible. When he made his way back to the front of the barn, George was in the house with Jenny and the baby.

Hank knew George would be out to find him as soon as he could. Hank walked over to the area around the lawn tractor and began taking more pictures.

When Hank was satisfied he had taken enough pictures from different angles and views, he decided he needed to check on Steph. He couldn't understand what was taking the deputy so long to come.

*   *   *

Steph was sitting at the desk staring at her cell phone. She couldn't believe the dispatcher told her someone might be out later this afternoon or tomorrow morning. Hank told her she needed to have a deputy come right away. The dispatcher said a vandalized lawn tractor was not an emergency.

Steph was trying not to cry when Betty came into the room. "Oh Betty, did Hank tell you? He said someone ruined my new lawn tractor. I just can't imagine why anyone would do something like that."

"Yes dear, Hank told us. It's upsetting that something like this could happen. Would you like a cup of coffee or anything?"

Steph gave Betty a weak smile. It was a comfort knowing Betty worried about her. "Yes, that would be wonderful. I'll come and get one when I'm finished. I called the sheriff's office. They are sending someone out either this afternoon or tomorrow morning. I guess I'd better get Stanley called. Hank said I should inform the insurance company."

Steph dialed the phone when Betty left the room. "May I speak with Stanley please? I would prefer to speak with Stanley Jr. but I can speak with Stanley Sr. if he's there."

Steph waited a few minutes and then a familiar voice came on the line.

"Hello, Miss Weatherby. This is Stanley Wilbur, Sr. How may I be of assistance?"

Steph tried not to let her fear into her voice. "Mr. Wilbur. I have to report something to the insurance company. Someone was here at the farm last night and vandalized my new lawn tractor. It's ruined."

"Oh dear. Have you called the sheriff to report this?"

"I tried. The dispatcher said they would be sending someone out later this afternoon or tomorrow morning. I'm worried. I don't understand why anyone would do something like this."

"Don't worry. It must have been some kids out having some fun. I'll take care of the insurance company. I'll call them myself and let them know you'll be filing a claim."

"Will you tell Stanley? He was here last night. Maybe he saw something when he left."

"I'll be sure to let him know. He's out of the office right now. Do you want me to call the sheriff and have things sped up a bit?"

"Thank you. I would really appreciate it. I'll feel better after the deputy has been here. Thanks for your help."

"That's what I'm here for. Keep us posted. We want to help if we can."

"I will. Thanks again." Steph was reassured when she hung up. She was relieved knowing Stanley Sr. would take care of handling the insurance.

*   *   *

Steph was walking into the kitchen when Jenny came in the back door. She was carrying a sleeping baby, a diaper bag and a canvas bag. George came in behind her carrying an armload of other baby needs.

"I didn't know how long we were going to be here, so I brought a few supplies along. I have baby bottles I need to refrigerate. I also brought some food just in case."

After Betty was introduced, she and Keri helped George carry the sleeping baby and bags to the parlor. Since Jenny and the baby were frequent visitors, a playpen was set up for the baby there.

Steph and Jenny stayed in the kitchen to put the food and bottles in the refrigerator. Jenny realized it was now or never. "So how was your date last night? Is he a good kisser?"

Steph had forgotten about the previous evening. She was too shaken up about the lawn tractor and the dispatcher. It took her a few moments to realize what Jenny was asking about.

Steph smiled. "We had a lovely evening. We didn't find the document so Stanley is coming back." Surprised that Jenny would guess she had kissed Stanley and knowing Keri would talk about it, she decided to clear the air. "Yes, he kissed me and yes he is a good kisser."

Jenny laughed. "I knew it! I knew he would kiss you! He's coming to visit again!"

Delighted her friend had a little romance in her life, Jenny momentarily forgot why she was there.

Betty heard them laughing as she came back into the kitchen for the baby monitor. "We put the car seat in the Parlor if we need it. George is going out to help Hank. Jenny, has anyone told you what's going on around here?" Betty tried to keep her confusion to herself but she was glad to see Steph was more relaxed.

Hank walked into the kitchen and looked at the three women standing there. Turning to Steph and trying to contain his frustration, he asked, "Did you call the sheriff's office? Are they sending someone over?"

Steph felt like a small child being chastised for being bad. She drew herself up, straightening her spine, and took a deep, calming breath. "Yes, I called the sheriff's office. The dispatcher said they would be sending someone over this afternoon sometime or tomorrow morning. I also called and spoke with Stanley Wilbur, Sr. He said he would call the insurance agency. He was also going to check with the sheriff's office."

"Good. That was smart to let him know. Maybe he can light a fire under the local law. Where's George?" Hank was getting anxious and wanted to show George what he'd found. He also wondered why the sheriff's dispatcher didn't think this was important enough to send someone right out.

"Right here!" George walked in the door from the front of the house. Keri was behind him carrying the baby.

"Someone woke up so we brought him along." Keri was walking around and lightly bouncing the baby in her arms. George Henry was happy and content.

"George, I need to show this to you. Please come outside." Hank looked over at Steph. "If you need anything, we're out back. If you don't see us, give us a call." Hank pulled his cell phone out of his back pocket and waved it over his shoulder as he walked away.

Hank led the way out the back of the house. When they were far enough from the house, Hank stopped and showed George the pictures on his cell phone. "These are only some of what I took on my camera. I have other pictures I took on Steph's camera. I want you to see this." They walked over to the lawn tractor.

154

"Son of a bitch! I hated the thought that I was leaving work for nothing but this isn't nothing."

George was taken aback by the damage. He and Hank were careful not to step too close. The fluids draining out from the lawn tractor made the ground soft in places.

"There's more I need to show you. I'm not sure if the two incidents are related but I know someone is trying to give Steph a message. I hate to admit, it's talking loud and clear." Hank led George into the barn and showed him the hole in the stall floor.

George turned pale and felt faint when he realized how close Hank had been to being hurt. They went to the front of the barn taking a couple of bales of straw to sit on while they waited for the sheriff deputy.

After another hour with no sign of a deputy, Hank asked George to call Stanley Wilbur, Jr. so he could talk to Stanley himself. George quickly agreed. He had been sitting there thinking of all the work he wasn't getting done but he hated to leave his friend alone to handle things in case the women panicked.

George dialed the number on his cell phone.

"This is George Landsburg, I need to speak with Stan, it's very important." George tried to remain patient while he waited for Stan to come to the phone. As quickly as he could, George told Stan why he was calling and why he should listen to what Hank had to say. Nodding his head, George handed Hank his phone.

"Mr. Wilbur, as George explained, I'm a good friend of his. I've been helping Steph out here at the farm and found the lawn tractor has been destroyed. Steph called the sheriff's office over two hours ago. They told her someone would be out this afternoon or tomorrow morning. I'm hoping you can get someone out here a little sooner. This was an expensive piece of equipment; some evidence may be corrupted by then."

"I understand my father has called the sheriff himself. I'll call again to see if I can find out why no one has been out. I'll let you know what I find out. Is Miss Weatherby okay? How is she holding up?" Stanley tried to keep his tone both concerned and professional. He was having trouble understanding why a friend of George Landsburg's would be calling him about Stephanotis Weatherby.

"She's strong. She'll be okay. She said you're going to let the insurance company know about this."

"Yes, my father has already spoken with them. An adjuster will be out tomorrow. They want to give the sheriff's office time to write up their report. I was sorry not to have been here to take Miss Weatherby's call. I was conducting business. Let me call the sheriff's office and I'll call you back."

"Fine." Hank frowned as he handed the phone back to George. "Well, George, I guess we sit and wait some more."

George nodded and leaned back on the straw hoping it would support his weight as he tried to get comfortable while they waited.

*   *   *

Stanley closed his eyes for few minutes mulling over the conversation he'd just had. He could understand George Landsburg's concern about the equipment. A vandal who destroyed thousands of dollars worth of equipment needed to be stopped before more farms were hit. Stanley's frustration came from hearing the obvious care and frustration coming from this stranger, Mr. Dawn. Steph hadn't mentioned him when he was with her the previous night. Multiple reasons quickly came to mind as to why. If they were lovers she certainly would have mentioned him. Stanley slowly shook his head, deciding that wasn't the reason. He slowly began to smile as he remembered the repair work he knew had been done. The man mentioned he had been helping out on the farm. Of course, he was a hired hand doing the manual labor the women couldn't do. That would explain his concern for the equipment. It also explained why he was the one to find it. He was paid labor. Steph didn't mention him because one doesn't talk about their hired help at dinner.

Relieved to have figured the situation out, Stanley picked up his phone to call the sheriff and get some answers.

*   *   *

While Stanley Jr. was talking with Hank, Stanley Wilbur Sr. called the sheriff's department and spoke with the sheriff himself.

The sheriff was an older gentleman, more of a politician than a sheriff. He had a natural tendency toward having a potbelly but until the last few years, he had been able to camouflauge it with his six foot two inch frame. Sitting at his desk all-day with little exercise had increased his stomach. As he grew older, he became sway backed and now wore his belt up over his prominent stomach. His body was aging but his mind and his wit were still sharp and agile.

The sheriff found it difficult to believe what Stanley Wilbur Sr. had told him. His staff was small but efficient. Walking out of his office, he heard the dispatcher talking with a caller.

"Yes Sir. I understand there has been property damage. Yes, I have logged the call. When a deputy is free, I will send someone to look into it." The dispatcher leaned back in her chair.

"No Sir. I am not stalling. I have to follow procedure. I will advise the next free deputy to stop by." Leaning forward the dispatcher picked up her coffee mug and took a quick swallow.

"Yes Sir. That is the best I can do at this time." Rolling her eyes, the dispatcher took another quick swallow.

"I understand Sir. Yes, it is an expensive piece of equipment. Yes, we will have to write up a report." Shaking her head, the dispatcher sat her mug down trying not to sound as annoyed as she felt.

"I cannot give you a specific time. Someone will be there as soon as we have someone free to send. I will log the report. Thank you for calling." The dispatcher huffed out a sigh as she released the call.

The sheriff walked over to see what was written in the log. "Problems?"

"What?" The startled dispatcher turned to see the sheriff standing beside her desk.

"I asked if there were any problems." The sheriff tried to keep his disappointment hidden.

The dispatcher worked for the sheriff for years. She was always competent, handling emergencies calmly and expertly. He was proud of the job she did, until today.

"Why don't we step into my office and have a chat?" The sheriff started to walk back toward his office.

"But sir, what if a call comes in?" The dispatcher looked helplessly from the sheriff back to her computer monitor.

"Don't worry. This shouldn't take long. Someone else can answer it for a few minutes." The sheriff waved at one of the deputies to take over the phone before returning to his office.

The dispatcher walked timidly into his office, looking nervously around. Stopping just inside the door, she remained silent.

"Please shut the door and have a seat." The sheriff sat, waiting patiently for his instructions to be followed.

The sheriff looked over his desk at the person sitting there. "I've known you for many years Judith. You've always been calm and cool in emergencies. You were a reliable and dependable part of this staff." The sheriff paused for effect, "until today." He waited to see how she would react.

Looking down at the floor, Judith spoke in a soft voice. "I've tried very hard to be good at my job."

"And you were. Today is one of the few times I've ever questioned your competence. To be frank, today I find it lacking." He watched as she squirmed in her chair.

"Since we both have better things to do, why don't we cut to the chase. What is all this about?"

"I don't know what you're talking about, Sir." Judith looked up over the desk but still did not look at the sheriff.

"Okay then. Have it your way. I want copies of your call log for today. Unless we have an emergency that I'm not aware of, I would like to know where all the deputies are. It seems to me we should have someone free to answer that call you just took."

Reassured that she now understood what he was talking about and assuming he would understand Judith smiled. "Oh that. It's just some damage done to a lawn mower out at the Weatherby Farm. They think we should drop what we are doing and come out to write up a report." Judith leaned back in her chair, relaxing for the first time since she entered the office.

"So let me get this straight. Someone called in a report of vandalism and we aren't going to investigate?"

"It's the Weatherby Farm, Sir. I'm sure it's nothing important."

The sheriff looked at her, watching her reaction in disbelief. "How can you be so sure of that?"

"They're turning it into a striptease club, Sir. We don't want to encourage that sort of thing. If we start running out the first time they have trouble with one of their patrons, we won't have any peace."

"How can you be so sure this was done by a patron?"

Judith smiled, sure of herself. "Who else would do it Sir?"

If the sheriff had not just spoken with Stanley Sr., he would have believed what his dispatcher was telling him. "How do you know what they're doing there?"

"The men were talking about hearing it in a bar, Sir. They stopped by for a few drinks after shift and some guy at the bar was telling the bartender about it. He said they were going to have rooms to rent by the hour and strippers. The guys were a little upset. The married deputies made me promise not to send them out there unless it was a real emergency. They don't want trouble with their wives."

"I see. So, we run the sheriff's department based on the gossip heard at a bar and by the whims of the deputies. It's a wonder we still have a department."

Finding it difficult to control his anger, he decided action was better. Standing up to underline his authority, he leaned onto his desk. "I am going to say this only once. I am the sheriff and we do things my way around here. I want your call logs. I want to know how many times someone has called about that vandalism. I want to know when we received the first call and I want to know now!"

Jumping up from her chair, Judith mumbled "Yes, Sir!" as she raced from the room.

Satisfied with the results, the sheriff sat back down to review the information being sent to his computer terminal.

CHAPTER 13

The sheriff decided it would be best if he went to the Weatherby Farm himself. He had not been to the farm for years and wondered how the place was holding up. As he drove around the last curve in the driveway where the house would come into full view, he was pleasantly surprised by what he saw. The lawn was mowed and the shrubbery was neatly trimmed. There were flowers in the flower beds and in large pots under the trees. Colorful baskets of trailing flowers and green vines were hanging from the eaves of the covered porch.

After parking at the front of the house, the sheriff went up the steps. Looking around, he noticed pillows decorated the rockers and the porch swing. The bright colors of the pillows made the porch look warm and inviting. *Hyacinth would be so happy someone loves this place,* he thought.

The sheriff pushed the button for the doorbell then stepped into the vestibule. Almost at once someone answered the bell.

Steph was jumpy waiting for a deputy to arrive. She ran down the hall from the kitchen to answer the door as soon as Misti barked. "Thank you for coming out. We were getting worried when no one came. Please come in and I'll take you outside to where the damage has been done."

Steph was trying to hide her disappointment as she picked up the barking dog. She wasn't sure this older gentleman would be of much help.

The sheriff followed her through the house, noting the baby items in the parlor and the cleanliness of the other areas as he passed through. Other cars were visible as they walked out onto the back deck. He was beginning to wonder about the people living in Hyacinth's house. He decided to contain his curiosity until he found out more about why he was here.

Seeing Steph come out of the house with a man in uniform, Hank and George walked over to the stairway of the back deck. As he was coming down the stairs, the sheriff recognized George standing at the bottom. *This explains the baby things in the front room,* he thought with relief.

"Hello George. I hear congratulations are in order." The two men shook hands.

"Thanks, Sheriff. I'd like to introduce you to Officer Henry Dawn on leave from the Columbus Police Department. Hank's visiting me and helping Steph out around here."

The sheriff looked Hank over glad he had come in person to handle the situation.

Steph was nervous watching the men. They no longer seemed to notice her. As she put the wiggling dog down, she heard the introductions and was glad she didn't express her disappointment to the sheriff. She was impressed and relieved the sheriff had come himself. After a few minutes Steph realized no one was going to introduce her so she gathered her courage, took a deep breath and decided she needed to take charge. After all it was her home and lawn tractor.

"Sheriff, I'm so glad you came. I'm Stephanotis Weatherby by the way. I own this farm now." Steph had been carrying the receipt and the owner's manual around for the last thirty minutes afraid if she laid them down she would forget where she put them. She held them out relieved to hand them over to someone else. "Here are the receipts, warranty and the owner's manual for the lawn tractor. As you can see, it was a recent purchase."

"Thank you." The sheriff glanced through the documents. "This is a top of the line model. I bet it's a dream to drive."

"Not anymore. It's over here." Hank began walking toward the damaged lawn tractor. "I used it yesterday and left it out over here. I was planning to put it in the barn this morning but found it like this."

The sheriff looked at the damaged lawn tractor and then looked again at the manual in his hand. He checked the date of the receipt. "Excuse me." He walked away from the others so they wouldn't hear his conversation with the dispatcher.

"Judith, this is the sheriff."

"Yes, sheriff."

"I want two deputies out to the Weatherby Farm pronto. Who's close by?"

"Austin and Thompson are in the area."

"Send them right away. We have a situation here."

Satisfied his instructions would be carried out, the sheriff returned to the others.

"Miss Weatherby, I want to apologize for the lack of response on the behalf of my staff. I can assure you we will take this matter seriously."

"I understand sheriff. I appreciate you're taking the time to come out yourself. When the dispatcher told me it may be tomorrow before someone could come out, I admit I was upset. I had the distinct impression she was just putting me off and I didn't understand why." Steph was talking to the sheriff but staring at the damaged lawn tractor. Seeing the cut hoses and wires, the scars on the side and smelling the gasoline, she tried not to cry. She was not aware of the tear slowly making its way down her face. Over and over again she repeated to herself: *No one was hurt. No one was hurt.*

Hank felt twisted inside as he watched Steph tear up. His instinct was to rush over and hold her. He expected her to break down and sob. He was impressed when she let only the single tear escape. Captivated, he watched its progress down her face. He wanted to kiss away her fears and tears. He wanted to sweep her into his arms, tell her it was all a bad dream and she could wake up now. He knew it was real. He was fooling himself if he tried to think otherwise.

"Sheriff, Hank took some pictures for you. He also has some pictures of the ground before the oil and transmission fluid leaked out completely." George was uncomfortable seeing Steph's emotional struggle.

Hearing George say his name, Hank became aware of how he had let his mind wander. "Yes, here let me show them to you." He was carrying Steph's digital camera. "It's a little bright out here. Why don't we go into the barn?"

Hank nodded at George as he and the sheriff walked toward the barn.

*   *   *

George wanted to be with Hank when he showed the sheriff the damage in the barn. He and Hank planned how they would handle the situation while they were waiting on the sheriff to arrive. They had argued back and forth about whether Steph should see the hole. Finally they came to the conclusion it would upset her more.

Now George was glad they weren't telling her about the damage. He could see she was fighting to stay in control. As she began to shake, he walked over to her and put his arm around her. As if leading a child, he guided her back to the house.

Keri, Betty and Jenny were standing on the deck when he brought Steph to the bottom of the stairway.

Jenny rushed down the stairs. Sliding her arm in Steph's she began to direct her up the stairs. Jenny spared a glance for George and gave him an encouraging smile. She knew he was uncomfortable and was proud of him for caring enough to bring Steph to them. She hoped it showed on her face.

Keri called for Misti to come in as well. She knew the little dog would get in the way if left outside. Watching Misti coming up the stairs, Keri said a prayer of thanksgiving that no one had been injured and they were all safe.

*   *   *

Hank was explaining what he had found to the sheriff as George walked into the barn.

"I was stupid and assumed the baling twine had broken on its own. I was sweeping the floor when I heard a crack and I jumped to the bales of straw." Hank was moving the bales he had set over the hole as he talked. "Here's the hole."

The sheriff stared at the floor. He stooped down and inspected the remaining floorboards. "Looks like he weakened them, here, here and here. You're lucky it was just a small hole, it could have been bigger." The sheriff pointed out other marks on the adjoining boards. He looked around as he stood up. "He may have been counting on you not sweeping, just bringing in the tractor. If so, why damage it? He had to know you couldn't drive it in the condition it was in."

"George and I talked about that. I removed most of the stuff from the stall a couple of days ago. I intended to put it in the stall when I finished mowing yesterday, but something happened and I just left it out." Hank looked at George as if deciding how much he should tell.

"When I finished up, Steph was coming home from her law-yer's. She seemed pretty upset. I parked the lawn tractor and left it to go check on her. I forgot all about it until this morning. I was tired enough yesterday, if I would have brought it in, I would have just parked it on the scattered straw."

"Lucky for you, you didn't. The person or persons responsible must've damaged the lawn tractor out of frustration when their plan didn't succeed." The sheriff turned and spoke into his radio. "Judith, this is the sheriff."

"Go ahead, sheriff."

"I want a forensic team out to the Weatherby Farm pronto. Send all available deputies out. We have a serious situation brewing."

"Copy that."

The sheriff turned back to face Hank and George, talking over the static noise of his radio as his instructions were being carried out. "I deeply regret the actions of my staff. However, I believe we will be able to show you that we will take this seriously and investigate to the best of our abilities. May I take a look at those pictures again?"

"Sure." Hank handed the sheriff the camera.

The sheriff walked away from the stall, toward the center of the barn before looking at the pictures again. When he was finished, he began to look around the interior of the barn.

"This is a large barn. What made you decide to put the lawn tractor all the way back there when there are other stalls closer to the front?" The sheriff continued looking as he waited for an answer.

"George, Steph and I walked around looking for a good place to put it. There is a shed with a wide door, but the roof has to be repaired. Since the barn was empty for now, Steph thought it would be easier to put it in here. George and I checked the structure. We looked at all the stalls. The others all need some repair work done on the walls or doors. This stall seemed to be in the best condition so it made sense to use it. I just can't figure out how they knew what we were going to use this stall for. I was clearing out two of the others too."

Hank paused watching the sheriff's reaction as the sheriff started to look into other stalls. "I've already looked. Nothing has been disturbed in any of the other stalls. Remember the pictures I showed you? I took pictures of the floors under each stall when I was on the lower level. They only worked on this stall." Hank took a deep breath before continuing.

"I also want to tell you, sheriff, why I'm currently on leave. I was injured during an arrest and am still recuperating. You can contact my Captain if you want to check me out. I'll do anything to help. I didn't get much out of Steph, but she or one of the others may have heard something last night. I know you'll want to ask them about it."

"Okay thanks. You've done well. Let's leave this for my men."

The sheriff turned toward the doorway watching a car pull up outside. "If you'll come outside with me, I'll start putting my people to work."

As they walked from the barn, a second patrol car was parking behind the first. They walked over to the deputy getting out of the first car.

"Austin, I want you and Thompson to take lead. We have two areas of damage to investigate. These men are Officer Henry Dawn and George Landsburg. George here owns the neighboring farm and rents some of this property. He's also a volunteer firefighter and Dawn here is a fellow officer, I want both men kept in the loop. They'll show you the areas of vandalism. I also want a search for any cameras that might be hidden on the property. Someone knows what's going on around here and I don't like that. These men will show you. Officer Dawn here has some pictures we'll need. I'm going to go talk with Miss Weatherby. Have someone set up interviews with her and the two women living with her for later. According to Officer Dawn, they may have heard something and not know it." The sheriff started to walk away and then turned back. He held out the lawn tractor receipts and owner's manual. "Here, you'll need this for your report."

*   *   *

The sheriff walked up the stairway to the back deck. He walked into the enclosed back porch. Looking around, he noticed a small group of chairs clustered together on one side. At the opposite end, boxes sat on the floor and on the odd pieces of furniture pushed together. It looked as if a whirlwind had blown everything together.

He walked up to the door leading into the house and rang the doorbell, waiting patiently for someone besides the barking dog to answer the door.

Keri answered the door. "Sheriff, please come on in. We were hoping someone would come in and talk with us."

The sheriff removed his hat this time as he entered the house, keeping an eye on the small dog. "I'd like to speak with Miss Weatherby if you don't mind."

"Sure, we're in the kitchen having a cup of coffee. Please come in and join us." Picking up Misti, Keri led the way.

"Thank you. I would appreciate it."

As they entered the kitchen, the sheriff noted Steph looked better, more in control of herself. He worried for a few minutes as he walked up the stairs if he would find her still crying.

He walked toward her as she stood up. "Miss Weatherby. I want to apologize again for the behavior of my staff. I deeply regret their actions but I can assure you it will not happen again."

"I sincerely hope we will not have to bother you again. I appreciate your apology and the effort you made to come yourself. It is reassuring to know you understood the gravity of the situation." Steph was feeling better and remembered her manners. "May I introduce Mrs. Keri Hall holding Misti, Mrs. Betty Brown and Jenny Landsburg with George Henry? Can we get you something to drink? We have coffee, tea and lemonade."

"No, thank you. It's nice to meet you. Congratulations, Mrs. Landsburg, on your new baby." The sheriff nodded to each woman before turning back to Steph.

"Miss Weatherby I wanted to let you know I'm ordering a unit to drive by during the night. With the house and buildings partially obscured by trees from the road, they may not see much. Just having them drive by though might make the rascals think twice before doing something else. I have to return to the office and start the reports on this for your insurance. It's been a pleasure to meet all of you." The sheriff went out the front of the house to his patrol car. As he was driving out to the road, he turned over everything in his mind. He was hoping his deputies would find something. He knew this was deliberate damage, not something the local teenagers would do.

*   *   *

As soon as the sheriff returned to his office, he called the Wilbur law office. Stanley Jr. was with a client, so he spoke with Stanley Sr. He explained in detail the damage to the lawn tractor. After Stanley Sr. expressed his shock and outrage trying to blame the area teenagers, the sheriff explained about the hole in the floor of the barn. "I don't think we can blame the local kids for something like that. It takes a devious mind to plan to hurt someone like that." The sheriff didn't want the attorney to start placing any blame without evidence.

"Well, Sheriff, I have to agree with you. Quite frankly, I now wonder if it has anything to do with a malicious rumor being deliberately spread around town about the Weatherby farm." Stanley Sr. went on to tell the sheriff about what Stanley Jr. learned from Mrs. Price. A newcomer to town was in the beauty parlor and deliberately told the beautician the Weatherby Farm was being turned into a strip club.

"Do you mean to tell me a bunch of women sitting in the local beauty parlor believed some stranger? They thought this stranger knew more about what was going on out at the farm than they did?" The sheriff was surprised by what he was being told until he remembered his own men believed what a stranger in a bar told them.

"It seems she was convincing and told the women she called her priest to see if the church could get involved in having the strip club closed. By the time Mrs. Price left, she not only believed the story, but called a few of her friends to tell them. From there it was a ripple effect." Stanley Sr. laughed. "Maybe we could send our wives in before the next election and you could save yourself the cost of running again. It would only cost you a new hairdo for the girls. They'd get a kick out of it too!"

Picturing his wife sitting in the beauty parlor trying to get him votes, the sheriff chuckled. Then he became serious again. "Do you have any idea why someone wants to scare Miss Weatherby from the farm? When I went out there today, I was impressed with the work she's doing to fix up the place. It's starting to look homey. She seemed like a nice person too."

Stanley Sr. thought it over for a moment. "I guess I'd better tell you the estate is being sued by another family member. His name is Rodchester Wilgood. He is the grandson of Hyacinth's nephew by marriage. He wants half of the estate. I'm not sure he would cause harm to something he wants half of. The tractor is not part of the estate. Stephanie just bought it a few days ago. The barn is part of the estate and if Mr. Dawn was injured, he would have good cause for a lawsuit. That would lessen the value of the estate. I'll call the insurance agent again. The insurance was increased when we learned about the lawsuit. I added Steph's lawn tractor under the insurance as farm equipment. We decided that any damage or injury to the person driving it needed to be covered. She has someone who has been helping around the farm. Stan would know more about all that. Have you spoken with George Landsburg? He rents the land and we have an agreement for him to tend the livestock until the estate business is handled."

"I spoke with George today and met Officer Henry Dawn, a friend of George's. Henry is the one who was almost took the dive in the barn. He said he's on leave from the Columbus Police Department. He was running the show when I got there. He followed procedure and stayed away until we arrived. He seems to be very capable. He and I had a nice little chat. He said he'd keep an eye on things and I trust him."

"Is he on retirement leave?" Stanley Sr. couldn't keep the curiosity out of his voice. Stanley Jr hadn't mentioned the man.

"I'm not at liberty to say. I'm going to call his supervisor and check him out. He gave me the name and the phone number to call. Said he wanted me to know he would let me handle the case." The sheriff chuckled again. "That is, he said I could handle it until I messed it up. He seemed pretty steamed at our lack of response. He settled right down when he found out I was concerned enough to come myself. He said he worries about his 'girls'. I met two other women with Miss Weatherby and Landburg's wife. They seemed a little old for being girls, but if he wants to watch out for them, I'll feel better."

"Thanks for calling me. I'll fill Stan in on what you've found. He was out there last night and ate dinner with Steph and the women. He told me about them. He plans to go back out tonight. He'll be glad to know you're taking this seriously. I am too. I hope you'll keep me informed during your investigation. If we can find out who did this, I'm sure we'll want to prosecute." Stanley Sr. finished his conversation with the sheriff as Stan came into the room.

Stopping at the door to be sure it was securely closed, Stan walked over to the empty chair farthest from the door. "Okay Father, what have you learned?" Stanley Sr. began to tell his son about the details he learned from the sheriff.

CHAPTER 14

Hank worked on the security wiring inside the house while the deputies were working on the crime scenes outside. He wanted to get the system connected and working so the women would be safe. This was something tangible he could do to protect them.

Hank finished wiring the upstairs windows and doors, which were accessible from the second floor porch at the front of the building. He had wired the basement windows and door the week before. After he finished with the upstairs, there were two more windows on the main level to connect and then he could test it out. Moving across the hall, he began wiring the windows accessible from the back porch roof. Finishing the window in Keri's room, Hank glanced out to see how the deputies were doing. He saw them standing around in a cluster looking at an object. After checking his work on the last window, he gathered his tools and equipment then headed down the stairs.

"Keri, Betty, Steph, where are you?" Hank went looking for them when he realized they were not in the kitchen or parlor. He noticed the baby things were gone from the parlor. "Hey, where is everybody?" Calling and looking into the other rooms, he found them in the study going through some leather and fabric bound books. "Betty, do we have anything I can take out for the hard workers in the barnyard? I bet they would appreciate something to drink."

"Why, of course, we have a bag of lemons. I'll go make some fresh lemonade. I could go for a drink myself." Betty started to walk through the library, pausing she turned back. "Keri, I could use some help squeezing lemons."

"I'm coming." Keri was reading a book with fabric binding. "I'd love to finish reading this. I'll help then come back to read some more. If we each take a few journals, we could get through them faster." Keri laid the book back down on the table. Sighing she gave it a fond pat. "I'll be back and read more of you later. Don't go away." Smiling with mischief at Hank, "I was just reading about how the author had fallen in love. It was just getting juicy too!"

Not waiting for Hank's reaction, Keri quickly left the room.

Steph was laughing at Keri. She never grew tired of Keri's upbeat attitude toward life. "I just love how she makes even boring tasks fun. She was reading some of it aloud and there was nothing juicy about it. The words the man used were long and hard to follow. We're going to go through these to see if there's any mention of the document we need to find." Steph was sitting at the desk. Rising, she walked across the room to the wall opposite the desk. "Each time I sit here at this desk, when I look up at the wall, it seems to be off a little." She ran her hand over the wall. "I'm sure it's nothing. I must be imagining things." Walking back to the desk, she reached for a journal. "I cleaned out the trunk you brought down from upstairs. After Jenny and the baby left, Keri and Betty got restless. We went back up to see if we could find any more boxes of papers. We didn't find any boxes marked papers or books. We looked but didn't find any more trunks. There are suitcases up there and holiday decorations. We left them for another day, I didn't feel like being up there very long today. Stanley is coming back tonight. He'll help us sort more of these papers. Until then, we're going to read journals." Steph sat down in the wing chair and laid the journal in her lap.

Hank worried about Steph. He was afraid she was more upset than she seemed. He searched her face for any signs she was just pretending to be okay. Since he couldn't tell if she was still upset, he decided the best thing to do was just ask her. Walking over to stand in front of her he asked gently, "How are you holding up?"

"I was upset earlier but now I'm angry. I was worried it was someone's way of scaring me and when I kept thinking about it, it made me mad. I've decided mad is the way to go right now. I refuse to be scared. This is my home and the lowlife that ruined the lawn tractor just ruined a bunch of metal and wires. As you said no one was hurt and that's most important."

Steph paused and smiled. "You used it and for now the lawn looks great. I appreciate how well you're handling this. You've been very supportive and I want you to know I am very grateful."

"How grateful?" Hank couldn't resist teasing her. He placed his hand on her chin and lifted her face up to meet his. Following an impulse he bent down and kissed her.

"That'll do as a down payment. Now I'd better get going. I need to see if Betty has the lemonade made. I want to finish getting the security system up and running before I leave. I also want to see if they found anything." Kissing her again, he turned and moved swiftly out of the room, leaving Steph sitting there speechless.

Flustered, Steph flopped back into the chair. She wasn't sure what to think. In fact, it was hard for her to think of anything but his kiss. *What brought that on? Wow! Stanley's kiss was nice, but... Wow! What am I going to do?*

Steph sat for a while deep in thought. Suddenly she realized how quiet the room was. Worried, Steph went to find Keri and Betty.

Steph found them watching Hank from the back door. He was talking with some of the deputies. It looked to Steph as if even more deputies had arrived. There were several uniformed people walking around. Hank led the way and a few deputies followed. "We decided it would be easier to have them come in here and get a drink rather than for us to carry everything down the stairs and outside. Hank is inviting them for us." Betty was organizing the furniture on the porch. She placed a tray of cookies on the table. She had moved the chairs around for their guests to have more room. As the deputies came onto the back porch, Hank introduced Keri and Betty but left Steph for last. They all shook hands. Keri and Betty hovered, checking to be sure everyone was given lemonade and cookies. The air was thick with tension and no one spoke.

Steph wondered if they still thought she was going to open a strip club or if they suffered from a guilty conscience. Searching around in her mind for something to say, Steph grabbed the most obvious choice. Tossing it out to get the conversation started she asked, "So have you found any clues?"

"Yes Ma'am. But we're not to discuss it. The sheriff said we're not to tell anyone except Officer Dawn until he said it was okay." The taller deputy, Austin, who was speaking turned to Hank. "We need to show you some things before we leave. We're almost done. Leave the tape up until the sheriff says otherwise."

"I'd like to see anything you may have found. I was going to ask after you enjoyed some refreshments." Hank knew they earned their drinks. He was glad to just sit and relax a few minutes. Thinking about the two last windows he had to connect, he began to form a plan.

"Is there a good electronics store around here? I want to get some equipment for George and Jenny to set up so they can tape the baby. He's growing so fast and Jenny talks nonstop about the cute things he does. I think George feels left out and it would be nice to have a recording device going. Jenny could send copies to the Grandmas too." Hank knew what equipment he wanted but he needed to know where he could get it.

"You might try a teddy bear camera. You can go to Lodge's in the next town over. They have a large variety of video recorders. They come small enough to put into a teddy bear." The first deputy, Austin, was finishing his lemonade and answering the question.

"They even have smaller cameras now. They can be put in all kinds of things. My sister has three children and she feels more secure with the cameras around. She has one in a wall clock, a tissue box and a couple stuffed animals. They're called Nanny Cams. She can set them to record when the babysitter is there and she can see what's happening while she's gone. She uses SD cards and DVRs. She even has one she can access from her work computer to check in during the day." The female deputy, Morris, joined the conversation.

Hank had one more question to ask. He was hoping to make things more relaxed, so he could get more cooperation from the deputies on a couple of ideas he was mulling over. He was carefully thinking how to best phrase it.

Keri, frustrated with the tension, didn't understand what the fuss was about. She decided to stop what she thought of as foolishness. "So, what do you think of Steph's strip club?" She blurted it out so fast a couple of the deputies choked on the lemonade they were drinking. Keri started laughing. "That's what Steph thought of it too when she heard about it at the grocery store. Some woman in the checkout line and the clerk told her. We had no idea this was that kind of town. Is it common for farmers to turn their homes into strip clubs?"

Keri stood still searching the faces of all the people who were staring at her. One by one, the deputies began to look ashamed and dropped their eyes to the floor. Hank sat there glaring at her. He started to speak before she made things worse. Keri knew she needed to finish what she started so she cut Hank off.

"When I came here to help Steph, I thought this was a nice town. I still think so. I haven't met anyone, including all of you, who would cause me to change my mind. Of course, I like to make up my own mind."

Careful not to look at Steph, Keri went on. "I'm honored to have met each of you and hope you feel the same about us. We all make mistakes and make assumptions we learn later are wrong. I know since you've met Steph, and of course Betty and I, you realize this will not be turned into a club of any kind. Steph is fond of this house but didn't get to meet Hyacinth Weatherby. If any of you have any stories about her to share, she would like to hear them." Keri could no longer contain her natural optimism. She started giggling and then laughing. "I wish you could see your faces. Steph running a strip club!" Shaking her head in disbelief, she continued to laugh. Some of the others laughed with her too.

Hank didn't know whether to be amazed or amused. Keri handled the situation better than he could have. He admired the way she settled the issue in her own way and no one was hurt or angered by it.

When Keri started talking, Steph was worried her friend would anger some of the deputies. Steph decided to lay down an olive branch. Rising from her chair, she sat down her empty glass. "Would any of you like a tour of the house? I didn't know if you would need to check the view from any of the windows. I'd be glad to show you."

Austin, who was in charge, spoke up. "I think that's a good suggestion. I'm sure you don't want all of us going through but I'd like to have a couple of the men check out the view from upstairs. Jackson, Turner, Morris, you three go with Miss Weatherby. Danbridge, you get drinks for the others who are still outside. I'm going to have a chat with Officer Dawn." He looked at Hank and nodded toward the door. Hank gave a slight nod back and rose to lead the way out.

"I'll help Deputy Danbridge with the drinks while you and Keri take the others on their tour." Betty was relieved everyone was getting along. She didn't like the tension but was unable to come up with a solution herself.

Steph led her little group into the house, showing them the main floor. Keri was following along talking quietly to Deputy Morris. "I am so glad you're getting to see the house. I fell in love with it when I got here. I can't imagine thinking this grand house should be turned into a sinful place. Of course, we have it in a mess right now, but we've been cleaning and sorting through all the rooms. We plan to redecorate." Keri kept up her conversation as they went up the main staircase talking about the ideas they have for each room and listened to the deputy's suggestions.

When they reached the second level, the deputies split up and each went into a bedroom. They took pictures from the windows of the rooms along the backside of the house. Returning to the hallway, they glanced through the other rooms.

Walking out onto the second level porch, Morris took a few more pictures for the sheriff to see. When she was satisfied, Deputy Morris returned to the others. "May we see what is on the next level?" Steph led them up to the top floor.

As the other deputies glanced through the rooms, Deputy Morris went on up the spiral staircase to the octagonal area, which was the fourth floor of the house. Steph followed her up. "This is quite a view," the deputy's voice was filled with awe. "This area looked smaller from the ground." She walked over to one of the walls. The bottom half of the walls were solid wood but the upper half was constructed completely of framed glass. "You can see for miles around."

"We haven't gotten up here yet to clean." Embarrassed by the grime and dirt on the many windows and the litter on the open floor area, Steph began picking up pieces of clothing. "We decided to leave it until we had most of the other areas taken care of. We started on the main floor and worked our way up. The plan is to start up here when we get the storage area finished.

Deputy Morris had been walking around, taking pictures from the various views. She paused as if thinking and then lowered her camera. Turning to face Steph for the first time since they were introduced, she drew a deep breath. "I want you to know I am ashamed of myself. I was willing to believe the worst. Working with men, you pick up their habits and you trust what they say is the truth. I'm sure they're as ashamed as I am, but they won't admit it. I would be upset if anyone thought this wonderful building could be turned into something sinful. Mrs. Hall was right. It was wrong of us to believe in rumors. I'm wondering though, isn't this an awful large place for just the three of you?"

Warming up to the deputy and hoping to be making a new friend, Steph decided to confide in her. "I'm trying to figure that out. My inheritance of the estate is being contested, but I'm sure that it'll be resolved. Meanwhile, I'm thinking of turning the house into a Bed and Breakfast. We keep kicking around different ideas. I'm still thinking about all my options."

"Wow! That would be a great idea! You could even have wedding receptions out here. The music room would be a great place for a small reception or party." Her delight showed on her face as Deputy Morris considered the idea.

"It's still in the planning stages but attorney, Stanley Wilbur Jr. is helping out. He's researching what it would take for me to get started." Steph led the way back down to the others.

"We'd better head back out and tell Austin what we've found. He'll be wondering where we are." Deputy Morris, followed by the other deputies, headed on down to the main level and out the back door.

"Well. I think that was successful. They seemed nice." Keri's eyes twinkled with delight. She enjoyed chatting with Deputy Morris. She was wondering about Deputies Jackson and Turner. They were still a little stiff and formal.

*   *   *

While Steph and Keri were giving the tour of the house, Hank talked with Deputy Austin. "So what did you find?"

"We found this." Austin handed Hank a small cylinder shape with a short piece of metal attached at a right angle. "What do you think it is?"

"I think it is the way someone has been watching the place. Where did you find the camera?" Hank was turning the small wireless camera over, looking at it carefully.

"We found it mounted on the outside of the barn. It was on the right hand side, but in shadow so it wasn't noticeable. There were no footprints on the ground in the area. We don't know how long it has been there. It has an SD card, so whoever put it there has been replacing the card." Austin cleared his throat before continuing.

"We found another one mounted inside the barn. That one has a DVR and appears to be motion sensitive. This SD card is new. I don't have the equipment to read it here. We're going to take it to the sheriff. I left the other camera alone since the DVR can be rewound. There may be another camera, but we haven't found it yet. I'll make a report to the sheriff. He'll have to decide if we keep looking or not." Deputy Austin stood there for a few more minutes as if unsure what to say next.

Hank recognized the signs of someone fighting an inner struggle, so he kept looking the camera over as if he was trying to memorize the design. With a heavy sigh, as if he might regret what he was about to say, Deputy Austin began, "I knew Miss Hyacinth Weatherby when I was young. She would let our school bring kids out for a day to see how a farm works. I was impressed an old woman still lived on a farm. She set up a butter churn and let us each try churning it to make butter. She probably worked on it most of the day, because after the last one in line tried; we were given a sample of the butter on homemade bread."

"We took turns trying to milk a cow and she had one of the farmhands take the class for a ride in a wagon pulled by the tractor. It was my first hayride and I'll never forget how much fun it was. She went to a lot of trouble for us to come and visit. We were a bunch of noisy kids. I'm sure we weren't easy to be around. Some of the kids raced around the yard, yelling and screaming most of the time. For an older person, she didn't seem to mind the noise." Austin paused for a moment before going on.

"When I was a new deputy, there was a call from the farm. One of the farmhands caught a local teenager hunting on the farm. Miss Weatherby didn't approve of hunting on her land and posted new 'NO HUNTING' signs every year. She was always afraid someone would get hurt or one of the livestock would be shot by mistake. There used to be some beautiful horses and fancy cattle raised here." Austin's voice had gained a wistful quality.

"Anyway," Austin cleared his throat. "I took the call to check out the problem. I'll never forget Miss Weatherby asking me to have a stern talk with the boy. She was sure I could make him understand how wrong it was to hunt unless you needed the food. She said she didn't mind his being there on the property; it was the gun she objected to.

"I had a talk with the boy. He said he was bored and thought it would be fun to go hunting." Austin stopped and chuckled with the memory. "I asked him what he was going to do with the carcass. I knew he was too young for a license. I planned to take him in but was curious if he was hunting for food or sport. Miss Weatherby was standing there waiting to hear what the boy said. He looked at me and then looked at her and said, 'I've never shot anything before, what do you do with the carcass?' Well, Miss Weatherby started telling him right away that when you shoot something, you have to field dress it. She was telling him if he shot a rabbit, he would have to hang it up and let the blood pour out. Then he would have to skin it. I caught on to what she was doing when I saw him starting to look a little sick. I joined in and added a few grisly details of my own. When we were done, he was almost green. You could see his Adam's apple moving up and down as he swallowed fast to keep his last meal down."

Austin snorted and shook his head. "Miss Weatherby must have decided he learned his lesson. She asked him if he had ever ridden a horse. When he said no, she put her arm around his shoulder and started to walk him up the stairs to the house. She stopped, turned around and thanked me for coming and helping with the little problem. Then she turned and led him into the house. That boy was never a problem since. I don't know where he is now. When I would drive by different times, I would see him walking around the yard leading one of the horses. She was a good person for helping people. It made me mad to think someone might turn her home into a den of whores."

Austin paused as if embarrassed. "Now that I've been here, I know that man was lying. They said he was telling the bartender and some of the patrons at the bar the other night about the new Madam who was setting up at the Weatherby farm. He said she was from another state and brought some of her 'ladies' with her to sell their wares for entertainment. Some of the others were there and heard him talking. They told the rest of us about it the next day. A couple of the deputies have jealous wives and were worried about having to deal with the prostitutes." He paused as if ashamed and changed the subject. "These cameras still look new. I don't think they've been up for long. I can't help wondering if the cameras are connected to the man starting the rumors."

Hank handed the camera back to Deputy Austin. "I've been wondering that myself. I'm sure the person who assaulted the lawn tractor is the same person who put up the cameras. I have to finish hooking up the security system and then test it. If you'll show me how to rewind the DVR on the camera you're leaving, I'll rewind it to where I showed George the hole. That way they'll know we found it. I plan to make a trip tomorrow to get a couple cameras of my own." Hank followed Deputy Austin to the barn.

* * *

Stanley Wilbur Jr. was finding it hard to concentrate. He kept wondering what the sheriff found out. Looking at the clock on his desk for the third time, he caught himself before he sighed aloud. Deciding he needed to do something more productive, he placed the call to the building inspector's office himself. He had promised to find out what permits Steph would need before she could begin any remodeling. The person answering the telephone was filling in for the Inspector's secretary. It was obvious they were clueless about the answers to his questions, but they were trying to find out. He didn't mind being patient because the person was new at the job. What irritated him was the person was eating while talking. He could hear the sound of chewing coming over the telephone line. Trying to be patient, he was currently holding on while they were searching the computer.

"Okay, I finally found it. (*Crunch, crunch*) It says they have to have building permit number 4552 if it is to add an addition to the current building. Permit number 6573 is for (*swallowing sound*) remodeling an existing structure. There are additional schedules on the permit (*slurp, gulp*) depending on the cost of the remodeling. Permit 8549 is for electrical construction, 9224 is for gas lines, 9235 is for water lines. Do you know when you will be coming by? (*Crunch, Crunch*) I can print off the forms and have them waiting for you if you want. Are you getting married or something that you want to remodel?"

Stanley was reaching the end of his patience with this person. "NO! Err I mean no, I'm not getting married. This information is for a client. Thank you for the assistance. I'll let the client know they should call before coming in. Thanks for the help."

Stanley hung up frustrated from the call and frustrated with himself. He was proud to know his staff wouldn't behave like that on the telephone. He looked at the clock one last time. He knew he wasn't being productive, so he decided to leave early and go out to the Weatherby Farm. He might be needed there.

CHAPTER 15

Hank was working in the conservatory trying to finish the wiring for the security system. The last window to be done was in the formal dining room. The control boxes by the front and back doors were already in place so he just had to run some wire and he would be ready to test the system. He began congratulating himself on being so close to finished. "There, that takes care of this room."

Picking up the wire and tools, he moved into the formal dining room. A large buffet had recently stood in front of the window. Keri and Betty removed the dishes from the buffet and stacked them on the dining table. Hank shook his head in disbelief at the numerous dishes now on display. Before he left, George had helped Hank move the furniture so Hank had access to the window. "Okay, this is the last one, and then I can run the wires and start testing." Hank was getting tired. It had been a long day with all the excitement. He was sore from his morning surprise. Wiring the windows and doors meant twisting and stretching. "I'm going to get this done so I can go take a long hot shower." Setting his tools down, he began to work.

*   *   *

Keri heard someone talking and walked in while Hank was working. Concentrating on what he was doing, Hank didn't know Keri was watching him. He felt the hairs on the back of his neck stand up and knew something was different in the room. *What if there's a camera in this room? If it's watching me, maybe I can catch it on.*

Turning around slowly, he jumped when he saw it was Keri standing in the room. "Keri, you startled me! Did you want something?"

Keri too was startled, and embarrassed at being caught watching him. "No. I heard you talking and wondered who was in here. Then I wanted to see what you were doing. Will we be able to open the windows? Steph said you wired our bedroom windows too."

Catching his breath, Hank took a moment to think. "Yes, you can open your windows before you turn the alarm on and if you close them it will just register they've been closed. I can set the system to recognize the windows should be closed. It will go off if you open them again. It registers changes after its set. You need to check the doors before setting the alarm because they need to be closed. If they open, it will go off. I just have this window to finish." Hank picked up a screwdriver. "Then I can run the wires up from the basement to connect them. Jenny said there is a dumbwaiter around here somewhere and I think I can use the shaft to connect these two floors. Do you know where it is?"

Keri thought for a moment. "I don't know exactly where it is but Jenny said there used to be a kitchen in the basement. I wonder if there's a dumbwaiter in this closet area. We haven't gotten there yet. It's full so we decided to leave it until after the storage area. Steph thought some of it may have to go up there." Walking over to the door of what she thought was a storage closet; she opened the door and stood looking into the room. "I wonder if this was a butler's pantry. If so, then the dumbwaiter would be in here. There should be a work area of some type too. I'll see what I can find." Keri started moving items out of the closet, stacking them around the room.

By the time Keri cleared an area in the butler's pantry, Hank had finished wiring the window. He followed Keri into the pantry looking around. "This is a large area in here. What am I looking for?"

Turning to look at the outside wall, Keri started moving more boxes out of the way. "It'll be a door or panel and will probably be in the outside wall. I thought the mudroom seemed off center from the porch. Disguising a dumbwaiter would explain why. The wall has to be thick enough for a small elevator to move up and down. That is what a dumbwaiter is you know. You put the food on a platform.

Using a rope or some device, you move the platform from one level to the next. Usually there's a pulley system."

Satisfied with what she found, she pushed on a piece of wood on the wall. It moved sideways and revealed an open area.

Once Hank looked at it, he realized it was different from the other wood on the wall. "So that's a dumbwaiter. Huh." Shaking his head he leaned into the opening and examined the wide shaft. Turning he saw a series of ropes. "Keri, can you get my flashlight from the dining room? It's on the end of the table with my gear." Hank was examining how the dumbwaiter was disguised in wall of the house. Pleased the door to the dumbwaiter slid sideways into the wall and not up, he felt more secure leaning into the shaft.

"Careful, Hank. Here's your flashlight. This is so exciting." Keri beamed. She watched Hank lean in then turn to look up. "Don't fall"

Absorbed in his exploration, Hank ignored the concern in Keri's voice. "Keri, there's a bunch of pulleys and gadgets. This looks like it could hold a lot of weight. The rope is good and thick but old. Don't use it until I've checked it out. I'll get George to come sometime and we can thread it with new rope for you." Hank leaned down and looked into the basement. He was trying to see how he was going to find the shaft in the basement. Hank chuckled when he felt Keri grab his belt. Standing up, he reached for his spool of wire. "I'm going to tie an end of my wire to one of these pulleys and drop the end down into the shaft. I"ll connect it down there first."

There was a loud bang when the spool landed. "Let's go see if we can find the matching dumbwaiter in the basement."

He started out and Keri followed him. As they were going through the kitchen to use the stairway to the cellar, Hank started counting. "Twelve, thirteen, fourteen…"

"What are you doing?"

Holding up a hand for Keri to wait, he continued to count until he was at the top of the stairway door. "I was counting so we would know how many steps from the stairway it will be, just in case it's covered up." Turning, he led the way down.

Keri paused at the top of the stairs thinking how useful that tip was. She'd never tried using her strides to check for spaces in a wall. She went down the steps quickly to catch up with Hank.

She found him staring at a blank space on the wall. "Do you think they might have blocked it up?" Hank turned toward her.

"No, that would have been too much work. Something's not right. Let me look around."

Keri looked at the old stove sitting by the wall. She looked at the table stacked with assorted items and boxes. She turned and looked at the shelves stocked with glass jars of canned foods. She saw metal cans of food. Slowly she turned trying to imagine what it would have been like when this was a kitchen area. She closed her eyes and tried to imagine where it could be. "Wow!" She opened her eyes and moved to a different area of the room.

Keri stood looking at a section of the wall with a large, antique fabric calendar hanging on it. She reached up and took it down.

Hank saw Keri was trembling so he rushed over to help. Under the large calendar was a door identical to the door they'd found earlier for the dumbwaiter. Astonished Hank turned to look at Keri. "How did you know it was there?"

Keri just shook her head. "I don't know. It's fun to try to stand in a room and try to imagine how it would look different ways. I've only used my own imagination before. This time it was as if I was actually there. I had a clear picture in my head of what this was like when it was a working kitchen. I actually saw someone putting a large platter on the platform to go up to be served. There's a tube along here somewhere they would talk into. They could communicate between floors without shouting."

Keri slowly shook her head in awe. "I saw that too. I have to sit down. This is too much."

Hank helped Keri over to an empty, but dusty chair. "Will you be okay?"

Nodding her head, she gave him a weak smile. "Steph would tell us about how real her dreams are. She thinks the house is talking to her, but I just thought it was the girl's imagination. I believe her now. You go do what you have to do." Waving Hank away, Keri continued to sit and marvel. "I think the house knows you're trying to protect it and us."

Hank slowly moved the door. He had to test it to see if it moved sideways or up. He was relieved when it moved sideways into the wall. Looking in he saw his spool of wire on the center of the platform. Taking it out, he connected it to the wires already on the windows and door. Hank placed another control box by the outside door in the basement. When he was finished running his wiring, he tested it to be sure the control box was working properly.

Keri was feeling stronger and decided to look around while Hank was working. This was her first time in the cellar. Walking around, she made a mental list of the work to be done in this area of the house. Along one wall, she found two doors. Opening the farthest one first, she found a storage area. Piles of boxes and furniture filled the room. Near the door she found what looked like an odd snow shovel. It had a wide scoop that was too deep to move heavy snow. Keri realized the handle was too short for a snow shovel. Not sure what it was used for, she wondered if Hank might be able to use it outside when he was working. Keri picked it up to show him and closed the door.

Moving to the other door, Keri entered the larger of the two rooms and stopped. She knew the house was heated in the winter because she cleaned her share of radiators and vents on the upper floors, but she hadn't given much thought to what was used to heat the house. She found herself staring at the mouth of a large furnace. Keri knew the furnace was not lit and would be cold to the touch, but on another level, she was sure she could feel the heat of the fire that would burn in its belly. Giving herself a mental shake, she stayed where she was and looked around. The room was larger than she originally thought. She moved to the far side of the room and picked up a large black rock. There was a slight shine on the pitted surface. Putting it back on the floor, she realized this was once a coal furnace. Looking closer, she found the end of the coal chute and the trapdoor. Now it made sense, she was carrying an old coal shovel. She set the shovel down and leaned it against the wall.

She looked around again. *I wonder if Hank knows about the coal chute. It would be an easy place to get in and out without being seen.* She stepped out of the room as Hank was closing the door to the dumbwaiter. "Hank, did you know there's a coal chute? It's right in here." Not waiting for Hank, Keri returned to the room she just left.

"What?" Hank turned around and didn't see Keri. He saw the door open and walked into the furnace room. He knew about this room but knew there were no windows in there. He had counted the windows from the outside and knew he wired all the windows. Walking over to stand beside Keri, he had trouble understanding what she was talking about. The light from the single bulb fixture dangling from a fabric-coated wire was casting more shadow than light. He looked up to see what she was looking at.

The sun shining brightly outside was barely visible around the dark shape of the trapdoor. "What is that Keri?" Hank was shining his flashlight around trying to understand what he was seeing there.

"It's a coal chute." Keri pointed to the black rocks along the wall. "See the coal? This used to be a coal furnace and I'll bet the chute can still be opened from the outside. Since we can see the sunlight, it's not completely covered up outside."

"I don't remember seeing a coal chute when I was mowing the grass. I don't know how I would have missed it. I'd better wire it up too." Hank went out to bring back his tools and wire. As he was working, Hank realized he couldn't reach the back part of the coal chute while he was standing on just a chair. It was as if the wall was constructed at an angle at the top and the trapdoor was over part of the angle. The wall was built out at the bottom and leaned in at the top. When he finished, Hank promised himself he would come back to check out the wall another time. He was curious about why the wall was made that way, as if it was built over something. Hank checked the rest of the cellar for any missed openings. When he was satisfied there were no other possible ways to enter, he and Keri went back to the main floor of the house.

* * *

Stanley Jr. was feeling pleased with himself as he drove along the driveway toward the Weatherby house. He had learned some useful information for Steph about the zoning codes for a Bed and Breakfast. He smiled; sure she would be properly appreciative. Parking the car at the front of the house, he stopped for a minute to look up at the octagonal widow's walk at the top of the house. It was a unique feature for a farmhouse. His thoughts wandered to the old journals Steph found and he wondered if she found any more. It might be interesting to find out why the widow's walk was built. He reminded himself to ask Steph about it later.

With a light heart he began to climb the front steps to the covered porch. As his foot touched the top step, an alarm sounded from inside the house. Stanley wasn't aware a security system had been installed. He was so surprised he stumbled and caught himself by grabbing the iron railing before he fell. As quickly as the alarm sounded, it became quiet.

As he walked on up to the door, he tried to regain his normal cool manner. Stanley stepped into the vestibule to ring the doorbell when the front door opened a crack and the alarm sounded again. The door was shut and the alarm was silenced. He walked up and knocked on the door.

Steph opened it quickly. "Oh Stanley, you scared me. Please come in. Hank was showing me how the new alarm system is going to work. We're all learning the codes and how to turn it on and off."

Standing behind Steph was a scruffy looking man. He had the dirty and disheveled appearance of someone who worked outside. Stanley didn't think of himself as a snob, after all, many of his clients were hardworking laborers, but something about this man told him he would need to be careful. He had an air of protectiveness toward Steph that Stanley didn't like.

"Steph, I talked with the insurance agent about the lawn tractor. When you're finished with your alarm systems technician, I'll be glad to talk with you about it. It's nice to know you are taking steps to be safe out here in the country. Meanwhile, I can go on into the study and get started." Stanley started to walk away.

Steph realized Hank and Stanley didn't know one another. "Wait, Stanley, I want you to meet Hank. He's the one who found the lawn tractor and talked with the sheriff. He's been helping me with the farm and he just finished installing an alarm system. If there is something I need to know about the lawn tractor, he should be told too."

Stanley turned and quickly reassessed his opinion about Hank. He remembered their conversation on the phone earlier in the day. Now he understood there may be some competition for Steph's affection.

Hank had been watching Stanley since he walked into the house. Instinctively he didn't like him, but thought it was just because he was a lawyer. He worked with a couple shady lawyers before going on his medical leave. The experience left a tainted impression. Hank was thinking the man appeared too much at home here. But if the lawyer was going to help, he wasn't in a position to turn down any help.

Reaching out his hand toward Stanley, Hank said, "I believe we spoke on the phone earlier today. Thank you for getting the sheriff out here. He said he was a friend of your dad's."

Stanley shook Hank's hand mentally reviewing the conversation. At the time he was grateful someone was handling the situation. Now he wondered if Hank was more involved with Steph than he first thought.

Steph was watching the men size each other up. It was like watching two dogs getting ready to square off before a fight. She was trying to decide how to stop them when Keri came into the hall.

Keri was trying to keep Misti calm. The little dog was shaking with excitement. When Hank tried the alarm earlier in the day it scared Misti. He made each of them practice using the boxes by the front and the back doors. Hank watched as they first set the alarm and then turned it off. He would open the door to make the alarm sound. Misti became braver each time the alarm went off until they were forced to hold her to keep her from running up and down the hall barking.

Keri heard Steph let Stanley into the house. She knew both men liked Steph, each in his own way. She also knew right now, Steph needed both of them. So, Keri came to help.

"Why, Stanley, you're early." Keri decided it would be best to distract Stanley and let Hank finish what he was doing. Putting Misti down, she walked over and gave him a hug. "Let me show you what was in the trunk we found today." She linked her arm in his. "Please excuse us. I want to go tell Stanley my idea." Keri winked at Hank as she led a surprised Stanley away.

"What's with Keri?" Hank turned to look at Steph.

"The trunk you and George brought down and put in the conservatory is full of livestock certificates and registration papers. There are pictures and show ribbons. Keri has an idea about decorating the enclosed area of the porch out back in a western theme. She thinks if we frame the pictures of the animals known to have been raised here, it would be a nice touch." They were walking into the music room as she talked. Misti raced ahead of them.

"Stanley made us each promise to have him check any papers we found, so she's been waiting to show him." Steph stopped and turned toward Hank.

Taking a deep breath to steady herself, Steph continued. "I want to thank you for everything you've done for me, especially being here today to handle things. You're a good friend. I want you to know we feel safer having the security system working. I'll admit I was scared for a while. I know the lawn tractor was a sign." She paused looking thoughtful. "I wonder how they knew about it and if it has anything to do with the estate lawsuit." Giving herself a mental shake, she gave Hank a determined look. "I want to let you know that this is my home and I'm not leaving. I know Jenny is expecting you for dinner, but you're welcome to stay if you'd like to."

Embarrased at her outburst, Steph bent down to pick up Misti.

Hank was touched by what she said. He knew they'd be okay tonight. Besides, Stanley was there and Hank was too tired to handle him. "I'd better go. I need to get an early start tomorrow. I have to run some errands. Don't forget to set the alarm after he leaves." Hank nodded his head in the direction Stanley and Keri had gone.

Impulsively, he gave her a quick kiss. "Call me if you need me. Call the sheriff's office if Misti behaves tonight like she did last night. See you tomorrow." Hank stopped by the kitchen on his way out the door.

"See you tomorrow Betty. Tell Keri I said 'bye!' Don't forget to make sure someone sets the alarm before you go to bed. Do it as soon as Stanley leaves okay?"

Betty was putting the finishing touches on their dinner. "Can you take these baby bottles with you? Jenny forgot them and I'm sure she'll need them." Betty walked over to the counter and picked up a bag for Hank. She looked at him and sighed. "Take a long hot shower and go to bed. You've earned some rest. We'll be okay. I found a baseball bat on the third floor and have it in my bedroom. Anybody who gets past the alarm and the guard dog will have to deal with me." She gave him a quick hug and went back to work.

*　*　*

Steph walked into the conservatory while Keri was showing Stanley the table of treasures found in the latest trunk. Earlier they'd removed most of the items and placed them on a long table from the butler's pantry. Keri was telling Stanley her idea for using them to decorate. "We've laid them out with the pictures so you can see which picture goes with which certificate. We'll only use the pictures of the horses and their certificates to begin with. If there is room, I might frame some of the livestock certificates. I think it would make an interesting display on the walls of the back porch. A western theme would be a natural atmosphere, a comfortable place to relax and look out into the barnyard."

Stanley was politely listening to Keri and wondering what was taking Steph so long. He was going to go looking for her if she didn't show up in the next couple of minutes. Stanley was relieved to see her coming around the corner. He relaxed and listened to Keri more closely for an end to their conversation. Realizing she was waiting on a response, he searched for something to say that would impress

Steph. "As I am going through the papers, shall I bring all the live-stock papers out here to add to your collection?"

Keri was delighted. He had been listening! She knew he would have preferred being with Steph but she also knew Steph needed time to thank Hank. After all, Hank had worked hard today. "Oh Stanley, I would be so pleased. Thank you for looking at these for me. I'll let you and Steph get to work now and won't bother you until dinner is ready." Giving Stanley a quick hug, she swept out of the room.

Smiling Steph walked over. "You've made her happy. She was delighted with the pictures she found. I showed you the family pictures we have in the library. I was thinking of inviting a few people over some time and we can go through the pictures. I've been scanning them into the computer so we can do it like a slide show. I plan to invite people like your father who knew the family. I want to document the names of the people in the pictures. Any pictures of someone they don't know, I can try to identify later." They were walking into the study. "I worked in here a little bit today. I found a stack of warranty books and receipts in the bottom drawer of a filing cabinet. I sorted them into stacks and will file the ones matching the appliances we still have. I took the drawer out and found a bunch of papers smashed behind it. I straightened them out and they're under the stack of books. I was hoping they would be easier for you to read after they're flattened out a little bit."

Stanley sat at the desk and started sorting papers. He went through a great many of the papers quickly. A few papers had faded print and it was harder to read them. He finished sorting through the top drawer of one of the filing cabinets when Betty announced dinner was ready.

Walking with Steph into the dining room, he was surprised at the change from the previous night. Rows of dishes were stacked on the end of the table near the window. The large buffet was sitting away from the window and the door to the closet was wide open. It looked like a storm blew through.

Betty saw the look on Stanley's face and quickly explained. "We're sorry about the mess. We had to empty the buffet so it could be moved. Hank needed to wire the window for the security system.

Keri moved some items from the butler's pantry and we haven't taken the time to put everything to rights. It will need to be cataloged first but that is work for another day. I noticed Waterford crystal, Fostoria crystal and sets of other crystal. We'll want to be thorough."

Stanley realized there were probably such treasures all over the house. The crystal alone would be worth stealing and selling. He began to wonder about some of the artwork in the house. If they had fine crystal, did they have serving pieces of silver? Maybe an original oil painting that was unknown. He hadn't given it any thought before. Hyacinth was an old woman when he met her as a child. He never thought of her as being a rich old woman. He would have to talk with his father about it. *If Steph were rich, it would be a nice plus to having her as a wife.* Stanley decided he would have to review his opinions about marriage.

*　　*　　*

Hank told George and Jenny during dinner about finding the coal chute. He went on to tell them how Keri's experience led them to the dumbwaiter in the cellar. Jenny was delighted. Hyacinth had told stories about the kitchen being in the basement and when she passed the stories on, it had helped Steph out. She wondered what other treasures were in the house they still didn't know about. It was like having a treasure hunt arranged just for them.

Because of the morning's delay, George needed to go back out to the barn to finish some chores. Even though Hank was tired and just wanted to go to bed, his shower and the meal had revived him a little. He still needed to talk with George and knew this was the best time.

When they got to the barn, George went to the colt's stall to check on him and his mother. "Sure is a beaut! I haven't told Steph about him yet. I hate to think of gelding him. I bet he'll be a good stallion." George stood watching the young horse.

Hank decided now was the best time to tell George about the deputies finding the cameras. He had checked the camera in the barn and Deputy Austin had returned the other camera with a new

SD card. They were hoping to get prints, but everything was wiped clean. As Hank was talking to George, he realized this person might not stop at just doing damage to the Weatherby farm. If he finds out George has Weatherby livestock on his farm, it may put Jenny and the baby at risk.

George was thinking along the same line and mentioned it first. "Hank, do you think we should put up some of those cameras around here? Do you think I need an alarm system? I worry about Jenny. It makes me sick to my stomach when I think what they did to the lawn tractor. I don't want anything happening to my Jenny or the baby."

"I'm going to Lodge's Electronics tomorrow. Deputy Austin gave me directions. I'm going to pick up a few items for both places." Smiling at George, Hank paused. "I care about Jenny and the baby too."

George tried to grin back but just nodded his understanding. He was too choked up to answer. He almost let his frustration and anger get the best of him. Just when he had started to believe that Hank cared more about what happened at the Weatherby Farm than at his farm, Hank threw him a curve by saying he was worried about them too. George couldn't look at his friend, afraid his face would betray what he was thinking.

Hank sighed, "I care about you too. I was thinking; you have a set schedule every day. You leave the house at the same time and you come back at the same time. I need you to make some changes. Leave the house fifteen minutes earlier or later. Check in on Jenny every hour and return early for lunch and dinner. I plan to leave early so I can be there when they open. I'm hoping they have a few other gadgets I can use." Feeling the activity from the day sapping his energy, Hank sat down on the tack box. "Do you need me to help you or are you okay out here?"

George felt sorry for Hank. He knew he was overdoing it, but he was glad to know Hank knew when to quit. "I just came out to check on things and turn off the lights. I'm glad we could talk alone. You go on in, I'll be right behind you." As Hank was heading to the house, George was good on his word. The lights were off and George was soon closing the barn door. George found Hank talking with Jenny when he came in to the house. Hank nodded to George and went to bed, leaving George and Jenny alone.

*   *   *

Steph decided to work on the journals while Stanley worked on the file cabinets. She kept glancing up and was trying to remove the piles off the desk as they grew. She didn't want Stanley to have to keep moving them out of his way to work. She had a large box for the trash, and was carrying the other piles to another table in the conservatory. She would file them or store them as necessary later.

They were finding papers smashed behind each file drawer they removed as Stanley worked. Most of them were old receipts. Steph started a collection of some of the receipts for items she could recognize. Keri suggested making a collage of the receipts to hang as a wall decoration. Steph thought it sounded like more work but decided to indulge Keri. It was amazing what some things cost decades ago. Steph was also amazed at what she found some receipts written on. There was a paper that was part of an old paper bag and it was a receipt for a cow. Another one she thought was just a scrap of fabric but on closer inspection she learned it was a receipt for a bolt of material. Finding it made her even more cautious when she was reading the journals. *What if the document was a page in a journal?*

Steph checked to be sure Stanley had plenty of room on the desk. Then settling herself down she began to read. After a few pages, she stopped, thinking over what she'd just read. *This person is writing about going to a farm with slaves. He writes about how badly they are being treated.* Embarrassed by what she was reading, Steph glanced over at the desk. Stanley was moving through papers quickly. She got up to move the piles out of his way again.

When she returned, she decided to try another page then continued flipping pages. She found it hard to continue reading. Her eyes were clouding up with tears. Determined not to cry, she blinked back the tears. She began talking to herself. *I have to remember this is part of history. I know it was real. I spent weeks this past spring teaching my class at school about the Civil War and the role of the Underground Railroad. At least the writer isn't proud of what he's seeing either. He writes how upset he is with the way his cousin treats his slaves. It must have been hard to live that way. I hope Stanley doesn't know what I'm reading about.*

Steph glanced over at Stanley; he was looking at her with an odd expression on his face. She put down the journal marking the page. "How are you doing?" She realized he finished sorting through a whole filing cabinet. Had she really not been paying attention? She glanced at her watch and saw it was getting late. "You've worked hard tonight. Thank you for coming and doing this."

Stanley was watching her reading. He thought how lovely she was. He couldn't believe this was the same person he met weeks ago. "I think I'll call it quits tonight. One drawer was mostly tax papers and you can burn or shred those, so I went through them quickly. I don't think the government is going to ask about twenty to thirty year old tax returns. I hope the other cabinet is more current. I still don't understand what Keri wants with a collage of old receipts, but I hope she'll enjoy it."

Stanley stood up. "I thought we could sit out on your porch for a little while before I go. It was a nice day and I'll bet it's a pleasant evening." He walked over to the door of the conservatory and waited for her to join him. Looking up through the ceiling, he saw the sky was clear and bright with stars.

They went out to the covered porch. Stanley patted the swing seat beside him. "It's been years since I sat on a porch swing. Come join me and we'll swing together." Steph sat down next to Stanley. He put his arm around her shoulder and drew her over against him. Gently he rocked the swing and Steph began to relax. It had been a long day; she was feeling tired. Sitting next to Stanley was comforting and relaxing. She felt safe and secure. When he leaned over and kissed her, it seemed so natural. He leaned back and smiled. *I'll have to take this slow, or I'll scare her away.* He spoke softly in her ear, "I could get used to this. A beautiful woman relaxed in my arms at the end of a long day. What more could a man want?" With that, he leaned down to kiss her some more.

Keri went to the study to see if Steph or Stanley wanted a drink or snack. It was an excuse to see if they found any more receipts or certificates for her. She found the study empty and went looking for them. She found them on the porch swing. Hoping she wouldn't be caught spying, she slipped back into the house to let them have some privacy.

CHAPTER 16

It's seven a.m. I must be nuts! Hank was driving down the highway toward the neighboring town. *I forgot what morning traffic could be like. I've been spoiled driving around in the country.* Hank took a sip of his coffee and settled back for the rest of the long drive. He knew where he was going thanks to his directions from Deputy Austin.

When Hank finally pulled up in front of Lodge's he was pleasantly surprised. He expected to find a small store in a run-down neighborhood. Here was a large well-lit store placed in a good-sized shopping mall. The large neon sign read: "***Lodge's Electronic****s.*"

An older gentleman in a business suit was unlocking the door as Hank opened the door of his truck. Hank was beginning to feel self-conscious about going into the store. *This is ridiculous.* Hank gave himself a mental shake. *I am not doing anything wrong.* Hank took a deep breath and walked inside the store.

"Wow." Hank didn't realize he'd spoken until the clerk came walking over.

"May I help you?" The man smiled in welcome.

"I was wondering if you sold security systems here. I understand you sell 'Nanny Cams' too. Do you have outdoor cameras I can set up at my farm?" Hank was trying to be discreet as he scanned the merchandise on the shelves.

"We have some fine security systems. Is this for your home or barn?"

The man started to walk away and Hank followed.

"I need one for the house and two for the barns." Hank suddenly felt inspired. "Do you have the cameras I can put up in my barn and watch it in the house so I can check on a mare in foal? I have a friend who has one and he can watch it on his TV."

Hank left the store pleased with himself. He bought a selection of cameras, batteries, SD cards and security systems. He spent the time driving back trying to make a mental list of where and how he was going to set up everything. When he arrived back at Weatherby Farm he knew exactly what he was going to do.

He'd maxed out his credit cards but knew it was for a good cause. Besides, how could you put a price on safety?

*   *   *

Steph had enjoyed herself with Stanley the night before. It was pleasant to sit with him on the porch swing. Smiling, and thinking about the pleasurable kisses, she wandered into the kitchen for breakfast and some coffee. She found Betty and Keri sitting at the kitchen table discussing what they had read in the journals.

"They talk about how horrible it is to have to work so hard when the servant should be doing the work. I think it is a young child from the style of writing. Every other sentence begins 'I hate....' something or other. I think it must be Iris's Journal. She didn't date or sign any of the pages so I'm just guessing." Betty stopped to sip some of her coffee.

Keri shook her head. "It's such a shame for someone to have so much anger."

"I agree. When I first started reading the journal, she was talking about going to parties and buying new dresses. She wrote about her friends who were jealous of this dress or that ribbon. Then she began to complain about having to wear one of her older dresses to the next party. It says she thought her father was trying to punish her by not letting her have a new one made."

"She sounds spoiled, but we don't know the circumstances of the parents. They may have realized they were overindulgent and wanted to stop before she became too spoiled."

Steph quietly joined them at the table. She was enjoying their comments.

"Well, it just gets worse from there. Later in the journal she writes about her father calling him a bad father. He had some financial problems and they had to let the servants go until they just had one. Jenny told us that happened here when Hyacinth was a young girl, so I really think the journal was Iris's." Betty drank more of her coffee. "I made coffee cake to have for breakfast unless you would like something different."

"Coffee cake is great for me, how about you Steph?" Keri rose from her chair and was standing by the coffeepot refilling her cup.

"Sounds good! I'll get it." Steph cut the coffee cake into generous pieces and set them on the table.

"Mmm." Keri was chewing slowly. "This is wonderful." She swallowed before continuing. "In the journal I've got, the writer talks about meeting a man in the neighboring town and how they would sneak around to meet. She mentions she's worried about him learning they have one servant. She is afraid he will think they are too well off. He told her he wants a woman who will work beside him, not one who expects to have servants wait on her." Keri stopped to have another bite of cake. Then she went on. "I wonder if mine is Lily's Journal. It could be possible they left their journals when they left home. It would explain why Lily came back to live here and Iris didn't return."

Steph finished her coffee cake and took her plate to the sink. "It sounds that way to me. We need to see if any of them mention Iris signing any papers. I'm going to sit out on the porch and read for a little while. I probably should be doing something else, but we really need to find that document. Thank you for breakfast. Just leave the dishes and I'll do them later. It's my turn to fix lunch, so I'll do them then." Steph went into the study to collect the journal she was reading.

Steph carried her book and another one to the porch and settled down in a chair to read. After a while Steph stopped reading and glanced around the porch. She thought she heard a noise, but realized she was jumpy and nervous because of what she was reading in the journal. The author is talking again about his experiences with his cousin's slaves. She was interested yet embarrassed at the same time, almost afraid to be caught reading about it. She jumped when Keri came out to check on her.

"Keri, you scared me." Embarrassed, Steph gave her a sheepish grin. "I was just reading in this journal about the way this person's cousin treated their slaves. He talked about their being beaten when they didn't work hard enough. I feel guilty reading about it. The man wrote about his worries and fears. He was there to learn about running a large farm and he was horrified by what he saw being done."

"That's awful." Keri sat down in a chair near Steph. "I was tired of reading and wanted to stretch my legs. My journal was getting boring. Misti was getting restless. I came out to check on you. I wanted to be sure you were doing okay." Keri stretched out and tried to relax. "I don't want to upset Betty but I'm worried. Hank hasn't come over yet. Maybe you should call Jenny and check on him. He's usually here by now."

"He said he had some errands to run. He told me last night he wouldn't be here until later today." Steph was watching Misti chase a butterfly across the porch. "It's so pleasant out here. I wanted to get some air while I read. I'm going to start the other journal I brought out."

"Well, if you're okay, I guess I'll go back inside. Don't forget, it's your turn to fix lunch." Keri rose to leave.

"I won't. Thanks for coming out. I'll keep an eye on Misti. She's enjoying the porch."

"Okay." As Keri left, she noticed Steph was already reading.

* * *

Steph was getting stiff sitting in the chair. She stood up to walk around the porch for a few minutes.

Misti was lying in a patch of sun sound asleep. Steph watched the little dog for a few minutes. She kept reminding herself she was reading real history and she used to teach about slavery in school. She felt a mixture of emotions reading about it in someone's journal, reading what they were actually seeing and feeling. It made it too real. Part of her wanted to pretend it was all made up and not true. After her walk around the porch, she was ready to return to her reading. After all, there was a document to be found. She would use history to change her future. Settling back into the chair, Steph picked up the journal and began reading again.

Steph looked up when she heard a truck coming up the lane. Hank was back. She went into the house to tell Betty and Keri. She found them in the parlor reading.

Keri looked up as Steph entered. "So what's for lunch?"

Steph looked at her. She had forgotten all about lunch. She glanced at the clock on the mantel. It was eleven thirty. Good. She had time to make lunch.

"I'll let you know when I figure it out. I was so caught up in my reading I forgot to watch the time. Hank just pulled in. I was coming to tell you. I'll go get started right now." Steph hurried into the kitchen. She began to search through the cabinets for something she could fix for their lunch.

*   *   *

Hank wanted to take his purchases directly into the house where he would not be seen getting them ready. Since he could monitor the cameras from three hundred feet away, he planned to set up the monitor he bought in the music room.

Hank picked up the first box out of the back of the truck, making sure to keep his back toward the camera on the barn. He was carrying it up the stairway when Steph opened the door to the porch.

"Hi Hank. How was your trip?" Steph was curious about the boxes in the truck. She could look down into the truck bed from her vantage point on the deck and it looked like Hank bought several items.

"It was great! Just let me take this in and I'll tell you about it." Hank walked into the porch while Steph stepped back holding the door. Hank set his box down and turned to greet Keri and Betty who joined them.

"Good morning Ladies. I think I have a solution to one of our problems." Hank opened the box he carried in.

"Why it's another television set! Did we need another television set?"

Perplexed, Keri looked at the others.

"No, it's not a television set, this is a special monitor. I'm going to set up an area in the music room so I can record and watch what is being viewed by the cameras. Let me go get them and I'll be right back." Hank went back to the truck to get another box.

"Let me help." Steph went dashing out behind him. She was feeling guilty Hank made the trip for this equipment on her behalf. He seemed happy about what he bought.

"Which box should I take?" Steph reached the truck soon after Hank, willing to help.

"Here take this one. It's lightweight." Hank handed her the box he had removed from the truck bed. "Go on up, I'll be right behind you." Hank reached for another box and followed closely behind Steph up the stairs.

"My goodness, what all have you bought?" Betty was holding the door open for them to enter the porch. She glanced down and saw a few more boxes in the truck bed.

"I got what was necessary." Hank replied. "I bought some stuff for George and Jenny, including a really neat Teddy Bear with a recording device inside. I thought they could put it in the little guy's room." After putting down his box and checking to be sure Steph could set her own down, he began opening the smaller boxes packed into the larger ones.

From one box he pulled out a birdhouse.

Keri beamed at Hank. "How cute, a birdhouse. We haven't put any up yet."

"This little birdhouse has a tiny motion detector. When the motion detector is activated, it records what it sees. The hole is too small for a bird to fit so birds won't be attracted to it. It will just be a novelty to hang around. I plan to put one on each side of the porch."

Hank put the birdhouse down and reached for another box. "I'm putting these emergency floodlights over the doors of the barn.

They have night vision cameras." He pulled out an emergency flood-light set for them to see. Putting it back, he drew a fake rock from another box. "This rock has a camera inside. I can place them all over and they'll blend right in. I do have cameras that look like cameras and will put them around further out. I'll leave a list by the monitor of where I've put the cameras." He paused, looking at each of them, then, he continued. "Please, please, let me know if you notice any of the cameras moved or if you notice any extra cameras around." Hank showed them a camera similar to the one Deputy Austin had shown him the day before. "Someone has been watching the barn and the barnyard. I don't want to frighten you, but you need to be careful going out at night. I'm doing this to protect you not to scare you. Go about your daily lives, just be careful."

Setting the camera down, he turned to Keri. "Now, I have to get these put up. Keri, will you come with me to the porch and we can start hanging the birdhouses. I want it to look as if you're telling me where to put them." Hank began unpacking the other birdhouses.

Her delight showed on her face. "I'll be glad to help. I always enjoy telling a handsome man what to do. Here let me carry one so it will be even more believable." Keri reached over and picked one up. She led the way to the front of the house. As they started out the door, she started playing her role, carrying her birdhouse as if it was a trophy to be displayed.

Keri turned left once she was on the porch and started looking around, as if trying to decide the best place for the birdhouse. She kept holding it up pretending to picture how it would look hanging. While waiting for Hank to bring the ladder, Keri tapped her foot and looked around. Playing her part, she showed Hank where to hang the birdhouse, shaking her head and arguing with him when she didn't like where he was hanging it. Keri walked back and forth talking as Hank worked.

Steph and Betty were watching them from different windows, laughing at their antics. Steph had to turn away from the window. She was laughing so hard; she had tears running down her face.

"That man is going to need a good lunch to recover from his morning workout. I hope you have something special in mind." Betty was still laughing when she turned to look at Steph.

"Oh no, I forgot about lunch again." Steph rushed into the kitchen and frantically started to search the refrigerator. She quickly took stock of what was available and then searched through cabinets for staples to add to what she found. When Keri and Hank returned from their playacting, she had lunch prepared.

While they were eating, Steph's cell phone rang. She walked into the other room to answer it and not disturb the others. "Hello? Yes, this is Steph Weatherby. Today…? That would be perfect. Thank you… I'll look forward to it… Yes… I'll have a check when they come… Thank you…. That's perfect… No, I appreciate it… I'm looking forward to seeing them. Thanks for calling…'bye."

Steph returned to the kitchen beaming. She didn't try to suppress the joy in her voice. "That was the representative for the chimney sweep I called. They have an opening this afternoon and tomorrow. They're coming out to check our chimneys. My appointment was for two weeks from now. The person on their schedule today canceled because of an emergency. They called to see if someone would be here and we are, so they're coming. Isn't that wonderful?"

Hank sat still, a shocked look on his face.

Keri and Betty looked at each other and then at Steph, averting their eyes from Hank.

"Okay, what is so special about having the chimney sweep come out?" Hank demanded. Deflated and hurt because she was more excited about her chimneys being cleaned than the trouble he was going through to be sure she would be safe, he felt he was due an explanation.

Still grinning, Steph sat back down to finish her lunch. "It's wonderful because it will move our plans along nicely. Jenny and George have an anniversary coming up soon. I wanted to do something special for them, they've both been so kind and helpful. I know they can't afford a fancy restaurant right now, even if we watch the baby, so I had an idea."

Steph looked around the table. "We have all of this beautiful crystal and that lovely dining room. If we moved the long table into the music room, we could set up a smaller, more romantic table in front of the fireplace. Betty can cook an elegant meal, I'll serve it and they can have a romantic evening here."

She turned to Hank and rushed on. "You and the baby can stay overnight so they could have some alone time. I was afraid the chimney sweeps would cancel. It's a great idea!" Pleased with herself, Steph began to take a bite of her sandwich. Looking at the others she noticed their astonished faces. "Don't you like my idea?"

Betty was the first to react. "Was that why you asked me if I could cook prime rib? I think it's a wonderful idea. I'll start planning the rest of the menu right away." Reaching for a tablet lying on the counter, she began to make a list of what she would need.

Keri, who was usually the first to react, slowly appeared to recover. "How are we going to get that big table out of there?" For once, it was she who was overwhelmed.

"I measured the doorway. It will take all of us to move it. I crawled down underneath, it comes apart. There are two large extensions that can be removed to make it shorter. I looked up the table style on the Internet because I didn't think it could've been delivered in one piece. It was delivered in sections and put together on delivery. I could find the pieces, once I knew what to look for."

Steph watched Keri closely.

"Oh well, in that case, yippee! We're going to do something nice for those two young people. How wonderful. Oh!" Keri stopped and looked at Steph. "Are you going to use the silver and the good crystal?"

"Sure, that will make it very special. Why?" Steph was still watching Keri.

"We'll need to get the silver all shined up. When is the anniversary?" Now Keri too was beaming.

Relieved, Steph tried to keep her frustration from her voice. "I don't know exactly." She turned pleading eyes on Hank. "That is something our miracle worker will have to find out. Hank, will you please find out from George exactly when their anniversary is? We'll need to know to be ready."

"Hold it! Why should it be me?" Frustrated, Hank wasn't sure he could ask George without giving it away. Now that he understood the reason for her excitement, he didn't want to ruin it for her.

Steph leaned over and kissed Hank on the cheek. "Because you're the one performing miracles around here. Look at the wonderful things you found and brought today! You bring us luck! Besides, if I try to talk with George, Jenny will want to know why. We're going to need him to bring her here anyway so he'll have to know sooner or later. I just don't want him to know everything we're planning until closer to the day so he won't give it away." Patting him on the arm, Steph rose and began clearing the table.

* * *

While Steph was washing the dishes, Hank asked Keri to walk around outside as if admiring her new decorations. He was in the music room checking the connections and the camera angles. When he was satisfied, he sent Betty to bring Keri back inside. Showing Keri how she looked on the camera took more time than he had planned.

Anxious to get the other cameras up, Hank asked Steph to go outside with him. She was to pretend to show him where to put the exit lights in the barn.

At first Steph was finding it difficult not to laugh, but soon she fell easily into the role.

"How thoughtful you are to do this for me." Steph was holding the ladder for Hank to put a set of emergency lights over the large front doors. Hank explained about the camera in the barn so she was searching for something appropriate to say. "When the horses arrive from the stable, it'll be nice to know we have some security measures in place. Were you able to get a new lock for the tack room? Since you mentioned it needed to be changed, I was hoping it could be done in the next day or so. I'm grateful your employer is letting you come over and help."

Hank was trying to screw in the final screw when Steph started to talk. When she said '*his employer*', his heart skipped a beat. Looking down, he saw her looking up seriously at him. *Okay, so she must have meant George,* he thought. *Maybe it would be best if I were thought to be a laborer. It would explain my coming and going. If my tie to this farm was only employment, then maybe whoever was plaguing Steph wouldn't vandalize George's farm too.* Hank tried not to let his thoughts show on his face. *I'll have to tell her I like her suggestion later, when we're out of earshot of the barn camera.* Hank checked his work then started down. "He said as long as you have work for me and you're willing to pay him for my services, I can help out. I have the lock on order; it'll be in the day after tomorrow. That'll give me time to put these lights up and start cleaning out the other room. When did you say the trainer was to move in?"

Hank turned to face the camera so any surprise on Steph's face wouldn't be picked up.

"The trainer?" Steph stumbled over the word and then tried to recover. "Oh, the horse trainer. He's coming with the horses. He was going to the stable to check the horses and follow the truck from there. They'll all be here by next weekend. We should have this old barn ready by then." Steph was getting caught up in her playacting until she realized if she really had horses in the barn, someone would have to come and take care of them. Having a trainer do it sounded good to her. She started this as role-playing but realized she would have to give some serious thought about what she was going to do with the barn and livestock. To cover up her own misgivings, she gazed up at the emergency lights and patted Hank on the arm. "Good job. That looks great. Shall we move on to the next one?"

Hank was tired from wrestling the long ladder up so he could climb it safely. He hoped to stop and rest before moving it to the other end of the barn. With his '*employer*' standing there, he decided he should try. As he walked over and reached for the ladder, Steph stopped him.

"Someone just drove in. Let's go see who it is."

CHAPTER 17

Hank followed Steph out to the barnyard. A white pickup truck loaded with ladders and an odd assortment of brooms pulled around into the barnyard. A magnetic sign on the door said "***Chimney Sweep.***"

Together they walked toward the truck. As they drew nearer, two men emerged from the cab of the truck.

The first man to step out was tall and thin. He was dressed in white coveralls, a white t-shirt and white shoes. His only concession to color was the red bandana tied around his neck. "Hi, I'm Tad. This is my partner and brother, Brian." Brian, who was six inches shorter, and slightly thicker in the waist, was dressed almost exactly like his brother. The only difference was he was wearing a blue bandana around his neck. Both men had pale blond hair and the same soft blue eyes.

Steph and Hank shook hands with both of the men. "I'm Steph and this is Hank. Thank you so much for coming. I'm so pleased you could fit us in."

Tad grinned. "We're glad you let us come. Most people want more notice nowadays. Of course not many want to see us in the summer. Most of our business is in the fall, just before the weather turns cold. Then we get really busy."

Brian, who stood a few steps away, let Tad do all the talking. He was looking at the house, trying to count the chimneys.

"How many chimneys do you have?" Brian had stopped counting and looked straight at Steph.

She was embarrassed by the attention, finding his stare unsettling. "I don't really know. I've never counted them." Drawing herself up, determined to stand her ground, she looked back at him. "I just know I'll sleep better once you've checked them out. We want to start using them in a few weeks." Steph's voice turned wistful. "I've never had a fireplace. I don't know anything about them, so I called you."

Hank began to say something as he listened to how this stranger was talking to Steph. He had no right to speak with her that way. Hank stopped himself when he noticed the change in the behavior of the other man after she answered him.

"Good thing you called us then." Brian's expression softened. "We'll take good care of you. We'll even teach you how to build a good fire." Sighing he went on, "I love to sit by a good fire in the winter." Suddenly he turned and walked to the back of the truck to unload one of the ladders.

Tad was standing there looking as perplexed as Steph and Hank each felt.

"Please excuse him. He's not much of what you would call a people person. In fact, usually he won't say a word to the homeowner while we're on a job. He says he doesn't like to socialize. He does like to clean chimneys. He's never offered to teach anyone how to build a proper fire before either." Tad reached up and scratched behind his ear. "I just don't know what to make of that."

"I'm honored he made the offer. I was worried I would have to learn by trial and error and I don't always have the patience for it. Please come on in the house, as you need to. I apologize. We're in a mess but let us know if you need anything. We're cleaning and redecorating so we have things scattered in some odd places. I'll let the others know you're here." Steph turned to Hank. "I guess we'd better go in and find Keri and Betty. I'll have to do something about Misti. I don't want her in their way."

When Steph and Hank went into the house, they found Keri in the library holding Misti, trying to calm her down. "She was so excited when they drove up. I heard the truck come around, and saw the sign on the door. I was glad to see you two come out of the barn to talk with them. I thought she might settle down better away from the door. She's not growling, just barking. She doesn't seem worried." Keri looked down at the little wriggling dog.

"She doesn't seem too upset. Maybe we should put her in one of the bedrooms until they're gone." Steph paused to think.

"It would be a shame to lock her up. If you have a leash, I'll watch her for a while. That'll give me an excuse to walk around." Hank didn't want to admit to the weariness that was stealing over him. He knew he didn't have the strength to go back to the barn and move the ladder again. That would have to wait until later. "I'll go cover my stuff in the music room and then come back and get her."

Hank went to check on the monitor and equipment he had started to set up. He put the empty boxes in the cab of his truck. He didn't want to chance having them discovered by the wrong person.

Brian brought in sheets to cover the furnishings in the parlor. Steph introduced him to Keri, Betty and of course to Misti while they waited for Hank. "I usually don't like dogs," he told them; "but she sure is pretty."

Tentatively he reached out and petted her while Steph held her in her arms. "She sure is soft." Grinning, he went back outside to help his brother.

*   *   *

Hank brought in a large basket he found while cleaning in the barn. Steph and Betty found him on the porch putting his rock cameras into the basket. He explained his plan to them when Keri brought out Misti on her leash. He was going to walk Misti around and put the rocks down. His plan was to pretend to be getting rocks for a rock garden.

"Why, Hank! What a wonderful idea! We really could make a rock garden! It would be fun. There's a large pile of stones out behind one of the buildings. I was taking a walk the other day and spotted them. I kept thinking it would be nice to use the larger stones to line a flowerbed. Let me get my gardening gloves and I'll help!" Keri handed Hank the leash and left quickly to get her gloves.

Hank moaned. "I was just going to pretend. Can't a man ever rest around you women?"

Steph and Betty laughed. "Make her walk Misti and just push the wheelbarrow around. She'll probably do most of the work. You can rest between loads." Betty sympathized with Hank. "I'll bring you some refreshments in a few minutes and then you can sit and take a break. You can relax and watch the chimney sweeps at work."

Hank liked the idea of resting while someone else was working. "Okay, tell Keri I'll get the wheelbarrow and meet her at the building with the rocks. Have her bring my basket of rocks and Misti."

Steph agreed to pass on his instructions and took charge of the excited dog.

Hank went on out to the barn. He lowered the tall ladder and laid it down so it wouldn't fall and possibly hurt anyone. Then collecting the wheelbarrow, he went to start loading it with stones.

Keri and Misti found him searching through the rocks. He had several stones already in the barrow. She noticed they were similar in size to the ones in her basket. She carefully exchanged some of the real stones with the fake stones. Afraid the bottom would break in the old basket, she placed it in the wheelbarrow.

Hank kept testing the weight of the stones by picking up the handles of the wheelbarrow to see if it would be too heavy for him to move it. Keri selected one more stone and carried it herself. Hank lifted the handles of the wheelbarrow and they all started back to the house.

Misti was patient while they were loading the wheelbarrow, but she began to get agitated and started pulling on the leash. Keri had to hold the leash with both hands to keep her under control. Keri tried to walk slowly beside Hank, but Misti kept pulling her faster and faster. She finally stopped fighting the little dog and started moving faster behind her. They arrived in the backyard as a deputy sheriff car pulled into the driveway.

Misti stopped fighting the leash when she could see the car. Panting from the effort, Hank drew up alongside Keri. "Does she act like that very often?"

"No." Keri said. "She's usually really good. I've taken her for several walks and she's never pulled me like that. I should have realized she knew someone was coming. She always seems to know when a car drives up the driveway." Keri stood there watching Hank.

Gasping, he grinned at her. "Would you believe one month ago, I wouldn't have been able to move that?" He pointed to the wheelbarrow. "Today I not only moved it, but tried to keep up with a racing dog." He leaned over with his hands on his knees trying to catch his breath.

Deputy Austin spotted Tad and Brian when he drove in and was talking with them when Hank joined them. "Hello," said the deputy. He noticed Hank moving the wheelbarrow and was aware of the other man's labored breathing. Austin had learned from the sheriff about Hank's assault and his recuperation. He decided it was best to chat with Tad and Brian until Hank was recovered enough to talk. Knowing what the other man had been through, Austin was impressed. Many men, he knew would be drinking to forget their pain, feeling sorry for themselves. He admired Hank for wanting to help his friend's neighbor.

Deputy Austin turned to Tad and Brian. "I've kept you boys from your job long enough. Be careful, I'll see you another time."

Hank stepped into stride with Deputy Austin when he turned and walked away. They walked to the stairway at the back of the house. "Is Miss Weatherby home? I have some news for her." Deputy Austin waited to speak until they were walking up the stairs.

"Yeah, Steph's in the house." Hank began wondering what had happened to cause the deputy to drive out to the farm instead of calling.

Keri had gone into the house with Misti to tell Steph the deputy arrived.

*　　*　　*

Keri decided she deserved a quick drink after her marathon with Misti, so she stopped in the kitchen first. "Betty, do you know where Steph is? Deputy Austin, you know, the yummy one, has arrived.

Hank was going over to talk with him but I'm sure Steph'll want to know he's here." Keri placed her empty glass in the sink. "Do you think he's single? Steph needs more choices of men to date, not just lawyer Stanley."

Betty started laughing. Keri's unique perspective always made things interesting. "I think she's in the study. I promised Hank some refreshment after he moved some of your rocks. I hope you didn't wear the poor boy out." Betty went back to organizing a tray of cookies and glasses. "I'll add some more to this and bring it to the study. If you'll go tell Steph, I'll direct Hank and deputy hunk in there too. That should keep them away from the ears of the chimney men." Betty went back to the counter for her container of cookies.

Keri and Misti found Steph in the study as Betty predicted. Steph was reading when they walked in. "Steph, Deputy Austin is here. Hank was going to talk with him and I thought you'd like to know." Keri began clearing the top of the desk. She turned back to Steph.

"Betty's getting some refreshments ready for the men. She'll have Hank bring the deputy in here. We'll watch the men to be sure they won't be listening in."

Keri finished her sentence as Hank walked in with Deputy Austin.

"Who won't be listening in Keri?" Hank always enjoyed teasing Keri and had quietly walked up behind her while she was talking with Steph. He decided, watching her jump, he could tease her more since he was hauling her rocks around for her.

"The chimney men," Keri responded patting her rapidly beating heart. "You rascal! Betty and I will make sure they don't listen in. Since Deputy Austin drove all the way out here, I'm sure it's important." Keri saw Betty coming through the library with her heavy tray. "Betty, let me help you with that. I've made room on the desktop for this to sit."

"I've got it okay. I balanced it out before picking it up. I used to work in a restaurant. I know how it's done." Betty was embarrassed by the gruffness in her voice. Usually Keri's manner didn't bother her. When she set it down, she looked at it one more time and realized the tray with a pitcher of lemonade, glasses and cookies looked heavy. She straightened up, ashamed of herself. "Well, here are some snacks for you. Help yourselves. Come on Keri."

They left the room and headed to the parlor to begin distracting.

Steph rose from her chair and began to pour the lemonade. "Gentlemen, please help yourself to the cookies." When they were all settled with their refreshments, Steph turned to Deputy Austin. "Have you any news for me deputy?" She waited anxiously while he finished eating a cookie.

"I have Miss Weatherby. We were able to get a partial print on the SD card from the camera. It matches a clerk in the local Radio Shack. He is a member of a local electronics club. The club sponsors a kids club at the school and any volunteers must be fingerprinted to work with the kids. That's why he's in our database. The department fingerprinted and ran the background checks for the school."

"I just came from talking with him. When I asked the clerk about the SD card and the camera, he explained to me a customer brought in the camera and asked if he knew how it worked. The customer told him they were going to place it in their garage. The clerk showed him how to work the camera and loaded it for him. The clerk said the man bought some cable, batteries and a few other odd items. He said the man was in a couple of times before; always paying cash. Some of their security footage is in the car. I'm taking it back to the office to view it."

"You didn't come all the way out here to tell us about the Radio Shack clerk. What else is there?" Hank was watching the deputy and realized he was holding something back.

Deputy Austin took a long swallow of his lemonade as if to prepare himself for what he had to say. "There is more. I have a good friend who is a bartender in one of the bars here in town. We were buddies in high school and keep in touch. Anyway, my friend called me this morning. He overheard a conversation between two men in the bar. They were sitting in a booth toward the back of the bar. Business was slow so my friend was giving the server a hand. My friend was clearing up the tables around them. He scooted under the table in the booth behind them to recover a glass from the floor.

214

He was stuck and while he was wiggling his way out, he heard them fighting."

"My friend said at first he didn't understand many of the words being said. They were keeping their voices down. As one of the men became angrier, he became louder. My friend said he clearly heard him say 'when I own the place, it had better be in all one-piece. I forbid you to destroy it. That house and land are mine.' My friend then heard the other man reply 'she didn't take the first hint. I'll have to get clearer. Next time it won't just be a tractor.' At that point the server came over to check their orders. He wiggled out of the booth and went back to the bar. My friend said the bar got busier as the night went on. As he and the server were closing, they talked about the different customers in that night. She told him she heard bits of the conversation the two men were having. She heard one of them mention he had a special surprise for a woman. She had the impression the other man was afraid of him. The server said he didn't appear happy when he heard about the surprise."

Austin continued. "My friend has overheard conversations in the bar before and helped in some of our investigations. He said he didn't know much more, but thought I should know what they overheard. I asked him how they paid the check. They both paid cash, but one dropped a local bank ATM receipt out of his pocket."

"On a hunch, I told the sheriff what my friend heard. We're trying to get a warrant to check the local banks to see if we can get a name from the account the money was withdrawn from. There's a lot of red tape to go through. I wanted to come and warn you to be careful."

Austin took another swallow from his glass before continuing on. "It may not have been you they were talking about. However, no one else has reported destruction of a tractor. Once we get some pictures from the Radio Shack footage, we'll take them to the bar where my friend works. He and the server can tell us if it's the same man. Until then, I'm suggesting off the record for you to take precautions." Deputy Austin slumped against the chair back. He was exhausted from delivering his narration.

Steph was too stunned to think. She felt numb. Why would anyone want to harm her? She looked at Hank wondering if he had any answers. He just sat there.

Disappointed, Steph started thinking, *Maybe, this isn't about me. Maybe it's about someone else. It sounds more like a soap opera on TV than it does about me.* Steph decided she needed to share her thoughts. "I am sure your friend meant well, but it sounds a little to me more like an angry spouse going through a divorce. It could have been someone with their lawyer talking about some divorce tactics. Unless they heard my name mentioned, or the farm, it could be about anyone." Taking courage from her words, she continued. "I want to thank you for coming all the way out here today Deputy Austin. I'm sure when you show your pictures to your friend it will be someone else entirely. I feel sure you'll be getting a report about another tractor in the next few days. Maybe the other woman has not noticed it yet. I do feel bad for her. She'll need to be careful."

Hank was turning events over in his own mind while listening to what Deputy Austin said. He agreed with Deputy Austin the two men were arguing about Steph and the farm. He was surprised by Steph's reaction. He expected her to become fearful, maybe a little hysterical. He didn't know what to say about the way she was rationalizing what she heard. *Maybe she didn't understand. I'll just ask a few questions to make it clear.*

"Deputy, do I understand the bartender heard them say they had a 'surprise for her'?"

Deputy Austin had been dreading telling Steph what his friend heard. He stalled at the office until the sheriff ordered him to leave. He spent longer than necessary at the Radio Shack talking to the clerk. Austin had taken a detour on his way to the farm from the Radio Shack. He was afraid Steph would react with hysteria, not as if he were talking about someone else. He was so astonished by Steph's comments it took him a moment to realize Hank asked a question. "I'm sorry. What did you ask Hank?"

Hank repeated his question and waited patiently for the deputy to answer. Hank understood his confusion. Steph heard the man tell her she was in danger and she acted as if he was telling her about someone else. "I was just asking if your friend actually heard the words 'a surprise for her'. I wondered if he had any idea what the surprise was."

Relieved Hank was taking this seriously; the deputy focused his attention on Hank. "He said those were the words used and it sounded very menacing when it was said. My friend said he later heard something muttered about it was going to get very hot, but he said he didn't hear it very clearly. He's going to call the department if either one of them come back."

"I appreciate the warning. I'm setting out a few cameras of my own and have the security system in place. I'll make sure they are all more careful. I know how it is to have a feeling about something but no tangible proof. We'll keep our eyes open around here." Hank started to rise.

"Hank, I do believe Deputy Austin. It's just it is too much like a bad television show. People talking about me in a bar! It's just too surreal. I refuse to be afraid. So far, the only thing we know is someone has damaged the lawn tractor and put up a few cameras. Now, if he would have overheard them talking about stopping the strip club before it opened or something like that, then I would be worried. Since the land is mine, I cannot believe someone would want me to leave. I just refuse to believe it." Smiling at both men to take the sting out of her words she continued. "It was a good friend who called you and I really am grateful for all you're doing. I'm touched you are working so hard. I do promise to be careful."

Hoping she understood the threat was real, Deputy Austin decided it was time to leave. "I'm glad you understand. I have to get back to check out the footage in the car. I'll let you know what we find." Deputy Austin opened the door to leave the room.

"I'll walk you out. I want to check on a few things." Turning to Steph, Hank continued. "I'll finish putting out the cameras. After the chimney sweeps leave, I want you to move your car to the front of the house with Betty and Keri's. I'll set up a couple of cameras to watch them." Hank followed Deputy Austin out of the house.

Steph carried the tray of dishes back to the kitchen then went looking for Keri and Betty. She wondered if they were still distracting the chimney sweeps.

CHAPTER 18

Steph searched the main floor of the house for the chimney sweeps Tad and Brian. She didn't find them. She also didn't find Keri and Betty, who were supposed to be keeping watch over the two men. Stopping near the fireplace in the parlor, she saw sheets spread out for protection. She noticed a faint black residue over the white fabric. Steph paused wondering how much work was done while she was talking with the deputy and Hank. Steph began to hear the faint noise of a motor. It sounded like it was coming from the fireplace. Realizing someone was in the bedroom above the parlor, she decided to go find out who it was.

When Steph reached the top landing for the main stairway, she could hear the motor more clearly. She followed the sound and found Keri and Betty watching Tad. He was using a machine to collect the dust and debris from within the chimney. Sheets were spread around to protect the furnishings. Keri was holding a funny looking brush, as she stood bent over trying to see inside the fireplace.

Betty stood back, watching Keri. "Keri, get back and let the man work. If I have to tell you one more time, I'm going to go get Steph. She won't appreciate your getting in the way."

Steph was trying to be quiet. She chuckled hearing Betty say she was going to tell on Keri. It was difficult not to laugh. Since they now knew she was there, she thought she should play along. "Okay you two, let the man work." Steph moved further into the room. She had to admit she found what he was doing interesting and fun to watch. Forgetting she came to tell Keri and Betty they didn't need to watch the men anymore; Steph stood for a few minutes and watched as well.

Tad kept on working as if no one was watching him. He called up the chimney and soon there was a different noise.

When Keri realized Tad was backing out of the fireplace, she tried to move quickly out of the way. Keri caught the heel of her shoe, tripped on a sheet and fell on her bottom, raising a small cloud of black dust.

Betty started laughing as she watched her friend fall and become enshrouded by the dust cloud. As the dust settled, the look on Keri's face made her laugh even harder. Trying to speak, she finally managed to get out "I wish I had a camera. This is priceless!"

Keri saw Betty laughing. At first she was embarrassed, but realized the only part that hurt was her bottom. Thinking what it must have looked like, she thought it was funny too and started laughing.

Tad stopped working and turned around to see what was so funny. Then he began laughing too. Reaching over, he helped Keri to her feet. "I never met a woman who wore their dust any better." Tad told her as she stood up. "I hope you're not hurt."

Steph was taking pictures with her cell phone. Deciding it would be a nice to have pictures of the men working, she was taking a picture when Keri started to move. Steph wasn't sure why Keri was moving but she kept capturing pictures as Keri fell. She hoped she had a clear picture of Keri's face. She too was laughing but started laughing even harder after she saw the look on Tad's face.

"No, I'm okay. Thanks for the hand up. I must look a fright." Keri tried to keep a straight face, but began laughing again.

When she could catch her breath, Betty realized if Steph was here with them, they didn't need to distract the chimney sweep any more. "Come on Keri, I'll help you get cleaned up." Betty reached out her hand to help Keri walk across the room. Betty didn't want any ash dust on anything but Keri. They walked down the hall to Keri's room.

Steph worried about what Tad was thinking. She hated giving people the wrong impression. "I'm sorry if they were bothering you. I asked them to check and make sure you didn't need anything. I didn't realize they might get in your way."

"They were a big help and not in any way at all." Tad was still chuckling about seeing Keri covered with dust. "We didn't bring enough clean sheets for such a big job and we wanted to get as much done as possible. They were really nice about getting more sheets."

Tad started to turn back to the chimney, but stopped and turned back to face Steph. "We usually have an audience of some kind. Most people don't like us roaming around their house without someone in the room. Can't say that I blame them; I wouldn't want a bunch of strangers going through my home. We're almost done with this chimney for now. I'll get started setting up in the next room. Miss Betty was nice about putting coverings down ahead so all I have to do is move the equipment. That's a big help." Tad turned back to the chimney and started picking up his brushes.

Steph left the room. She trusted the man but she also knew there was nothing in the rooms except furniture. All the bedrooms were emptied except for the three in use. There was a fireplace in her bedroom, but she'd just hide her jewelry elsewhere while it was being cleaned.

Steph had the feeling it was important for her to finish reading the journal. She had a hunch she was going to find something important. Steph started down the stairway to the main level. When Steph reached the last step, an overwhelming feeling of apprehension settled over her. Since she had no inkling what was wrong, she shrugged it off. She told herself to concentrate on what she could control, not what she couldn't.

*   *   *

Hank walked Deputy Austin out to his car. Once they entered the enclosed back porch area, Deputy Austin stopped walking. He was concerned by Steph's behavior. "Didn't she realize she could be in danger? How could she not believe she was who they were talking about?"

Hank felt the man's bewilderment but didn't want to admit it just yet. "I think she's in denial." Hank paused a moment. "Steph doesn't want to believe someone would hurt her to get the farm. She said she has no other living relatives. I'll check with lawyer Wilbur about what could happen to the farm. It is a great place and has potential if you have the capital." Hank tried to reassure the deputy. "It's good to know you care. I've got to get back to setting up cameras. I'll keep an eye out on the place. I have a few other ideas that may help. I'll keep you and the sheriff informed if anything happens."

Feeling relieved, Deputy Austin moved on outside and down the stairs. "I hated to come and tell you about this. I hope we can get some id from the store footage. If so, we'll at least have something to work with. Meanwhile, it's good to know you're here. It always helps to have someone around who knows what's what." Deputy Austin started to get into his car. "Have you thought of using those driveway lasers that ring a bell inside when someone pulls into the driveway? The sheriff is always telling people to use them and put them far enough up the drive to give you a chance to look out the window. It's just an idea. I'd better get back. So long."

"Good-bye and thanks again." Waving to the deputy, Hank watched as he drove away. "I'd better get back to work." Hank walked over to the barn. Moving the long ladder, he set it up at the other end of the barn. Once it was secure he collected what tools and equipment he needed and started up to fasten the emergency floodlights up with the camera. He intended to finish in the barn before starting Keri's rock garden.

*　　*　　*

Steph returned to the study. She decided to sit at the desk while she read. Picking up the journal, she opened it to the page she had marked and began to read:

Master Hubert has brought the drawings. We are going to tear down the original house and rebuild a new house over the same ground. The original fireplace will be expanded. There will be a part of the hilltop dug out for a base of the house. I have been digging around in the root cellar of the house as it is now. I figure a couple of men with good strong backs should be able to do what I have in mind. Master Hubert has recommended a builder. I will speak with him tomorrow.

"What are you planning? This is getting to be a little mysterious." Steph turned the page to continue reading when her cell phone rang. Steph looked at the Caller ID. Jenny's number appeared on the dial. Steph sighed. She knew Jenny would want to know all about what was happening. Steph answered her cell phone.

"Hi Jenny, how are you doing?"

"Hi, we're doing great. I was calling to see how things were going. Have you found anything yet?"

"No. We're still reading the journals. Yesterday I read about the family being out west. The writer had written several entries about a mare named Honeycomb. He traveled around riding her in races. He met a man in a saloon who went to mining camps and towns. They would bet on races. The man told him a fast horse could make him rich. It must have worked. He left his mother on the ranch in Arizona according to his journal. His father died on the trip out west. He must have had tuberculosis because the journal said the doctor told the father to go west if he wanted to stay alive. They sold their farm and moved west but the father died during the journey. He wrote about riding in a covered wagon and described how bumpy the ride was. The man talks a lot about how upset his mother was to leave her home and family. He said his mother had a sister who lived in Ohio.

Steph paused then went on. "Anyway, according to the journal, Honeycomb won a lot of races and the man returned to his mother a wealthy man."

"Wow, Steph. That sounds interesting. I can't believe you're finding out all this neat stuff about your ancestors."

"I know. It's really great. I was reading today about his buying a farm in Ohio and he was building a house on the side of a hill. Here's some of what he wrote." Steph picked up the journal to read out loud:

"I keep seeing things in my dreams. I see tunnels in the ground going further than I had planned. I know that is what God expects of me.

The hill has been dug out and the house has been framed. I was worried about having servant quarters on the top floor but am less troubled now. It will be okay.

The builder's men have been working hard. The outside of the house is done. It looks good. If I did not know my men and I have been making subtle changes, I would never have noticed. The crawl space along the chimney was not easy to build but unless you stand down below and look up, you would never know it was there. We are doing well digging the tunnel between the barn and the house. Abe and John said they have it planned out. Working from the barn to the house seems to be working out the best. Stu is a wonder with wood. He and Lester expanded the barn with a couple of side rooms. Once the first room was finished, Stu went to work. If I did not know where the trapdoor in the barn was, I would never find it in the side room. It is truly a marvel. John is full of surprises too. Filling old canvas bags with soil to empty at night has worked well. They can dig through the day while the builders work on the house. They are taking turns keeping watch. They are so proud to be a part of the railroad.”

“Why would you put a crawl space along a chimney?” Jenny sounded frustrated over the cell phone. “This is getting to be confusing. If they are going to work for the railroad, why are they working on a house and barn? Steph, do you have any idea what they're talking about?”

“Well, I've been wondering if the railroad they mention may be the Underground Railroad. He talks about using bricks in tunnels. Oh wait, listen to this: *I promised God a room for prayer if all went well. The false room is not visible behind the bricks. The wall covered with shelves built by Stu was a surprise. I had confided to my men I did not know how we would cover the end of the tunnel. While digging, the boys figured it out, a moving wall. It will be very handy. God has truly blessed me with the men I need.*

“A moving wall? How can you have a moving wall?” Jenny interrupted Steph's reading.

“Maybe it's like the pocket doors in the house. Those were made by a skilled craftsman. When my class studied the Civil War and the

Underground Railroad, we learned about the different ways people built tunnels and hidden rooms in their homes."

"Sorry, Steph. This has been fun but I have to go. The baby is waking up. I'll check back with you to see what else you've found."

"Okay. Thanks for calling. I'll let you know if we find anything. Give the baby a squeeze for me." Steph disconnected the call and went back to her reading, eager to learn if her hunch was right.

Misti came running into the study. Steph looked up from her book to see what had excited the little dog. After Misti settled down near the door, Steph began to stare directly at the wall across from the desk. After a few minutes, she put the book down and went over to the wall. She had watched movies with moving walls. The man in the book talked about moving walls and tunnels. What if? Steph moved the chair away from the wall and started to explore. Her cell phone rang again. She checked the Caller ID and saw it was the insurance company calling. Steph forgot about the wall as she turned her mind to finding out how to replace the lawn tractor.

*   *   *

Betty was in the kitchen beginning preparations for dinner. She had offered to take on the responsibility of preparing most of their meals. Steph had protested at first, pointing out that she and Keri were her guests. Betty had worked in the restaurant industry for most of her life as a short order cook and later as a restaurant manager. Betty had argued that she missed cooking for someone other than herself and that she was having a good time. Of course she also admitted she would appreciate their help from time to time, especially with washing the dishes.

Keri enjoyed cooking sometimes but felt her own talents were more along the line of interior decorating, gardening or sewing. Anything that needed an eye for detail and color was what she enjoyed doing. Keri knew if she went into the kitchen now, she would reluctantly volunteer to help and today Betty might accept her help. Trying to find something else to do, she decided to venture outside and study the rock garden. After careful consideration, she decided it would look nice on the opposite side of the house from the large gazebo. Determined to begin right away, Keri went to find Hank.

She found him in the barn up on the ladder. He held a battery operated drill and was putting up emergency lights. Keri decided to do some exploring while waiting on him to come down.

Keri meandered around looking in doorways and corners, hoping to find something she could repurpose and use as a decoration on the enclosed porch. Her wanderings led her into the tack room. Constructed more of brick than wood, the room was built in such a way that it seemed to be a separate building rather than a room attached to the barn. It had a rough wooden floor that was starting to warp in areas from age. A few dusty saddles and bridles hung from the supports on the wall. Keri sighed at the sight of the abandoned relics, leftovers from another time. She walked over to the wall, cringing at the occasional squeak caused by her footsteps. Deciding to look closer at a bridle, she lifted one from its hook. She used her gardening glove to wipe the dust off the silver Concho rosettes. Keri didn't know much about horse bridles, but she knew by the tarnished surfaces it was real silver. Keri smiled as ideas began taking root in her imagination. "Maybe these can be cleaned up and used as part of the western decorations I have in mind." She put the bridle back in its place and looked around at the saddles and the saddle blankets. She was trying to picture using the saddle blankets as throws on the chairs when Hank found her.

*   *   *

Hank heard someone come into the barn. When he glanced down, he saw Keri heading into the tack room. He was just finishing with the last light he intended to put up that day. Emergency lights were now installed over every doorway into the main section of the barn. He had placed motion-activated cameras in a couple of stalls.

Hank took the time to lower the ladder and put it into a stall before he sought out Keri. As he was entering the tack room, he realized with a grin that she didn't hear him approach. Trying not to laugh, which would spoil his delivery, he said, "Doing a little shopping are we, Keri?" As he had hoped, Keri jumped, dropping the horse blanket she was inspecting.

"Hank, you scared me to death!" Holding one hand over her heart, Keri bent over and picked up the blanket. She placed it on top of another blanket then sat down on a large tack box. "I was waiting for you to finish. I need you to bring the wheelbarrow over to the area for the rock garden. I want to put the rocks down and get a feel for the area. Then we'll see what has to be done."

"Just because I scared you, doesn't mean I have to be punished for it." Hank muttered as he followed Keri. Louder, he said, "Exactly where am I moving the rocks to?"

Keri stopped and looked at him as if he were a disobedient child. "I'll go stand in the area I want to put the rocks and you can bring them to me." Seeing the disbelief on Hank's face, she started to laugh. "I'll be over by the chimney sweep truck." Laughing Keri walked off.

Hank shook his head but did as he was told.

When Hank arrived with the load of rocks, he found Keri deep in thought.

"I'm going to take my time with this. Just leave the wheelbarrow. I'll let you know if I need any more."

"Okay, but I want three fake rocks down tonight. I need one to face the house, one to face the driveway and one to face across the lawn in the opposite direction of the house." Hank knelt down. He put three rocks on the grass in the directions he wanted the cameras so Keri would get the general idea. Straightening, he watched her to be sure she understood.

Keri nodded. "I'll set up an outline so I can see what it will look like." She took a few rocks, put them in the basket with a fake rock and started to walk off. Remembering Hank wanted to put a fake rock under the deck, she stopped and turned back to Hank. "Don't forget to put a few over by the deck for me to put in the flower beds."

"Thanks Keri, I'd almost forgotten." Hank shook his head. He was getting tired and his mind was slowing down. Selecting a few other rocks to place with them, Hank carried his armful of rocks toward the back of the house.

As Hank was approaching the house, he noticed Brian looking up and down the chimney of the fireplace for the formal dining room. The chimney and hearth extended out from the exterior wall of the building.

The architect had left an open area between the chimney and the wrap-around, covered porch that ran from the side of the music room, across the front of the house and down the side of the conservatory.

The closer Hank walked, the more perplexed Brian seemed to be acting, pacing between the wrap around porch and the chimney. Hank paused and watched as Brian paced off the outside area of the chimney. Brian spoke into the handset he was holding in his hand then moved quickly in the direction of his truck.

Hank pushed it from his mind. He intended to finish with the cameras before he was interrupted again. He placed his real rocks down in a line around the corner of the flowerbed. Carefully, he set the fake cameras facing the directions he wanted them. Standing, he surveyed the placement. When he was satisfied, he went to check on Brian.

*　　*　　*

"No, I'm telling you the camera is showing a smaller shaft than what was built. Tad, you'll just have to trust me. Something is not right about this chimney." Brian was talking into a handset while looking at a monitor. "I've measured it three times. The shaft should be thirty five inches larger than it is."

Hank was unable to hear the reply but he could see Brian was getting angry and his face was turning red.

"Is something wrong?" Hank asked as he walked over to Brian.

"Yeah, this chimney was built wrong. Tad is feeding our camera down the shaft. The camera measures the shaft while it checks for debris and loose bricks. Tad says I'm reading this wrong. Usually I'm the one on the roof while he's watching the monitor. Since there are so many chimneys here, we decided to switch off. This monitor is showing the shaft to be at least thirty five inches smaller than the bricks on the outside. I went in and measured the hearths. Now if you look up the side of the building, it looks like a normal chimney. You wouldn't know anything was wrong from just looking. Someone built this chimney with a smaller shaft than the bricks on the out-side. I've never seen one like this before. It's almost like they started to build a separate shaft with no hearth attached. I can't figure it out. Tad, he thinks I'm crazy, but look at the measurements."

Brian showed the screen to Hank. "Sometimes in old houses, they would build two shafts side by side for different fireplaces but it's easy to see that in the design. If this is what they had in mind for this chimney, where is the other fireplace? The camera shows both fireplaces on the same shaft. The top is sealed over this odd side."

Hank had never seen the inside of a chimney before. Surprise registered on his face as he watched the screen. It was like looking at something filmed by the nature channel. It felt surreal to watch. "I don't know what to look for," he looked at Brian, unsure what to say and not wanting to upset him any further.

Brian pointed to the bottom of the screen. "See these numbers. They're the width of the shaft. As the camera moves, it measures the size of the shaft. We have a marked rope we use so we know the depth the camera is at. If it shows some damaged bricks, we'll know where they are so they can be repaired. The shaft is pretty secure. It really looks good but its measurements are off." Shaking his head, Brian started talking to Tad with the handset. "Looks good so far. I see the flue. You can haul it up and come on down."

Brian walked away from the chimney looking for Tad.

"Man, I sure am glad I don't have to go up there. That's a long way up." Hank held his hand up to shield his eyes. He watched as Tad came to the edge of the roof and lowered down the end of a rope. Brushes and equipment were attached to the end. "So that's how you got those up there. I wondered." Hank watched as Brian raised his arms to grab the equipment.

"I got it," Brian said into his handset.

"Coming down," was Tad's reply.

Brian stepped back quickly and covered his head. Hank watched as Tad tossed his end of the rope down. Hank was fascinated watching the rope fall, glad it was not Tad falling. Hank looked up and Tad was gone. "Where's he gone to?" Hank asked Brian, who was collecting the rope, gathering it into long loops.

Brian glanced up to the roof and then concentrated on what he was doing. "He's coming down on the other side. Our ladder doesn't fit all the way up to the roof. We don't usually do such tall houses. We put a ladder on the roof of the covered porch. We climb up a ladder to the porch roof and then up another ladder to the roof of the house. That way we're actually only climbing up two stories. It's really high up there, but it's a beautiful view." Brian carried the rope over to the truck and put it into the truck bed. Coming back, he looked at Hank then at the house. "You know, that's one tall house." Brian went back to work as if he didn't know Hank was there.

Hank walked around to watch Tad come down. He found the lower ladder set up on the ground and walked backwards until he could see Tad. Tad was almost at the bottom of the taller ladder set up on the porch roof. Tad shortened the ladder so he could lay it down. He worked it around until it was lying flat on the roof of the porch. Hank was waiting for Tad when he reached the bottom of the ladder on the ground.

Hank watched as Tad worked on shortening the second ladder. Hank waited until Tad had picked up the ladder and was moving toward his truck before joining him.

"Brian was showing me the monitor screen with the camera in the last chimney. He seems to think it was built wrong."

"I'm going to look at the monitor. We record it for every job so we can check it again if a problem develops later or a client complains. We've learned to protect ourselves by using it." Tad carried the ladder to the truck as Hank continued to walk with him.

"Brian doesn't usually watch the monitor, so he may have misread the numbers. I can't say for sure until I look." Tad stopped talking while he secured the ladder to the truck.

When Tad was sure the ladder was secure, he took a deep breath and turned to Hank. "Brian doesn't usually say much, but that chimney sure was perplexing to him. If the numbers he told me are right, there is an area large enough for a person to climb up through." Shrugging his shoulders, Tad went on. "I can't imagine why a person would want to do something like that. We've found some strange things around fireplaces. One fireplace had loose bricks glued together as a large block. They were hollowed out and looked like someone might have used it as a hidey-hole for valuables. Brian likes to find things like that. He thinks he's going to find another hidden doorway someday."

Brian was coming toward the truck carrying a load of folded sheets. Tad glanced at his brother. "Brian's good at finding loose blocks. Instinctively he seems to know when something's not right. He has found hidey-holes for people who didn't know they were there. If he says something's off, I believe him." Tad paused as if thinking. "That is, I usually believe him. Telling me the shaft is short by almost thirty six inches is a little too much even for Brian." Tad shook his head. "He's been different since we got here. I'll take a look at the tape after dinner. I promised the wife, I'd be home on time for dinner."

"I have the sheets from today Tad." Brian came up with his load. "I offered to wash the ladies sheets but they said no. I told them we'd be back in the morning. Betty said she'll have a treat for us when we come." Brian started to walk away. "I like it here," he said over his shoulder as he went to the back of the truck to pack up his load.

Smiling Tad looked at Hank. "I never thought I would ever hear that. What a day." Tad walked to the driver door of the truck cab. "We'll be back tomorrow. See you then."

Hank watched as Brian climbed into the truck and they drove off.

Taking one last look at the chimney Hank headed into the house. He wanted to check and make sure the recorders on the cameras were working so he could get some sleep tonight. "It's been a long day," he said to no one in particular.

Hank was tired when he sat down at the dinner table with George and Jenny. He tried to keep up with their conversation, but finally had to excuse himself to get some sleep. He fell asleep thinking how he was able to move the wheelbarrow full of rocks around the yard. He was glad to know he was finally getting stronger.

*   *   *

"Are you sure there are no other places to look?" Stanley asked Steph. Frustration clouded his voice. He arrived early again to help go through the filing cabinets. He told her to leave them for him, but he was beginning to regret it. "I'm amazed there were two whole drawers in this cabinet of old catalogs and booklets, including old breeding newsletters. Now you'll have plenty of room to file what needs to be kept. Is there a safe or vault anywhere. Father said Hyacinth didn't have a lock box at the bank. There should have been something to put their wills and insurance certificates in."

Steph was getting just as frustrated. *What does he want me to do? I can't conjure one up can I?* "There's still one more box in the library to go through. I'll go get it and then we can call it a night. I can't believe we've been at this for days."

"It's amazing the amount of papers and receipts one can accumulate in a life time." Stanley was feeling the strain of having his efforts thwarted by the other ladies. Just when he thought he and Steph were alone, someone popped up. They were taking their jobs as chaparones too seriously.

"Did I mention the chimney sweeps are coming back to finish up? Keri loves to watch them and tries to help. I meant to show you this." Steph giggled at the memory. Taking out her cell phone, she showed Stanley the picture she had taken. "This was the first day they were here. Keri got so wrapped up in watching, she ended up with ash on her face."

"Keri looks like she was immersed in the job." Stanley chuckled. It helped to lift his spirits. "Since I won't have any excuses to come out after tonight, why don't we celebrate getting all this work done? I'll make you dinner for a change." Stanley smiled, thinking of a romantic dinner at his apartment where they would finally be alone. He had been waiting for the timing to be right so he could invite her. He was delighted this was working out perfectly. Even his father couldn't find fault with a celebratory dinner.

"I couldn't impose on you anymore." Steph felt obligated to Stanley for the time he spent helping her. "It's been nice having you over for dinner. We've enjoyed your company and appreciated your help."

"Nonsense! I find it relaxing to cook now and then. I'm not in the same league with Betty, but I make decent lasagna. Let me do this for you. Let's do it this Friday. My weekends are mine to do with as I please. It would be enjoyable spending time with you without the need to talk about the farm or the office."

Noticing Steph was about to object again, he went on. "I would take it as a personal favor if you would let me do this. Mother has been trying to set me up with someone and this way I can say I have a date. She'll be pleased to know I am not sitting home alone. Will you do that for me?"

Stanley watched Steph closely as the conflicting emotions crossed her face. He noticed her eyes became cloudy and then they brightened.

Steph's mind was running wild with thoughts and fears. *I can't believe he asked me out! It's just to his apartment for dinner. He wants to cook for me! He likes me and wants to spend more time with me. He says he's lonely.* Her thoughts continued to race. *He wants to spend time with me! He says it would be a favor to him. It would be nice to go out! It's not a real date. What's the worse that could happen?* Steph decided she deserved to spend an evening off. She had been working night and day on the house. She needed to do something different.

Steph smiled. "Thank you for the invitation. I'll be glad to have dinner with you Friday night."

"Good. I'll write down the address for you." Stanley found a blank sheet of paper and wrote down his address and a few basic directions. Handing her the paper, "I'll expect you at six p.m. I'm pleased you decided to come."

Blushing, Steph took the paper. She felt as if she was going to regret her promise. Trying to shake the feeling, she decided to change the subject. "I'd better get back to work."

Stan nodded his agreement as he turned back to the pile of papers in front of him.

Steph couldn't help but notice the grin on his face as he worked. Somehow she got through the rest of the evening. She knew she needed to get out and have some fun. She was beginning to wonder if it was proper for her to be dating Stanley while he was her lawyer. She pushed her feelings down and controlled them by reminding herself they were just friends.

After watching Stanley drive away that night, Steph went up to her bedroom. She didn't feel like reading the journal she brought with her. With a sigh, she sat in the small rocking chair near the fireplace, rocking back and forth, letting the motion relax her. Steph stared at the fireplace as if willing it to tell her about the past lives it had seen. She let her mind drift over the events that happened to her and led her to this spot now. Soon the quiet of the house and the motion of the rocker lulled her into a deep sleep.

CHAPTER 19

Betty rose early and was baking fresh cookies when Tad and Brian arrived. She appreciated their quiet, competent ways and wanted to have some special refreshments for them later in the day.

Keri had placed extra sheets on a chair in the library and was outside working on the rock garden when Tad and Brian arrived. She waved as they drove up in their truck.

Steph was restless so she went up to the storage area on the top floor. She decided to open the last of the boxes to see if she could find any other papers or journals. They had moved most of the items down to the conservatory over the last few days. A stack of boxes marked "Christmas" was all that was left. Steph was dragging the boxes over under the light to open them and see what was inside. She was finding it harder to see in the feeble light of the single light bulb. It was flickering and getting dimmer and dimmer. Finally, she moved the last box over, praying the light bulb would last until she was done. When she pried open the box, she realized it was full of ornaments and then the light bulb died. "Thank you for waiting." Steph stood up and looked around. "I guess I'd better get a new bulb." Steph carefully walked around the boxes she'd pushed over by the door and walked out into the hall. This had been the servant's floor and it still amazed her there was only one fireplace on the whole floor. Shaking her head, she started down the backstairs to search for a light bulb.

*   *   *

Steph found Betty talking on her cell phone when she walked into the kitchen.

"Yes, it was a terrible thing... No, no one was hurt... Yes, I'll be careful... No, I don't know when I'll be home. Just forward it to this address and I'll take care of it... No, I'll let you know when I decide. I'm okay. I'll talk to you later. Give my love to the kiddies... I will...love you, good-bye...Okay, 'bye." Betty was sitting at the table. When she hung up, she turned to Steph who was looking under the kitchen sink. "What's the matter, Steph?"

Steph stood holding a package of light bulbs in her hand. "I didn't want to bother you. I had a light bulb go out and wanted to get a new one." She turned slowly toward Betty. She had forgotten her friends put their own lives on hold to come and help her. She walked over and sat down by Betty. Steph put her hand on Betty's searching her face for any signs of stress. "Betty, is there something wrong? I didn't mean to hear your conversation, but is something wrong back home? Do you need to go home?"

Betty was surprised and didn't know what to say. She knew Steph heard part of her conversation but she didn't realize it sounded like there was a problem. After all, Betty didn't have anyone depending on her back in Boston and Steph knew that too. At least, Betty thought she did. "Steph, I'm okay and everything is fine. My sister misread the email I sent out about the lawn tractor. I made a mistake saying anything about it. I was telling my family about how proud I was of you and my sister overreacted. She thinks I've spent enough time visiting you and it was time for me to get back to my own life. She doesn't understand I feel needed here and am having such a good time. If I were home, I wouldn't be in any less danger being a single woman living alone in a big town. Besides I'm also an older woman who lives alone. That makes it more dangerous. I don't intend to go back until I know you are settled and happy. I would just sit around and worry about you and the trouble Keri could be causing. I decided to come and help and I intend to do so. We've done so much and have so much more to do."

"I just don't want you to feel obligated to stay here unless you want to. I appreciate everything you and Keri have done. I wouldn't

236

be this far along without you. I don't want you to be afraid while you are here."

"Child, I am having such a good time cooking for you. I love it! I hated cooking for just myself. Don't forget, I'm going to be cooking a special dinner for Jenny and George's anniversary too! That means a lot to me. I feel younger every day. I used to sit in my apartment and wonder how I got so old that no one needed me anymore. Until you don't need me, I am going to stay, no matter what my sister has to say."

Hugging Betty, Steph tried to keep the tears back that threatened to flow. "I'm so blessed to have such good friends."

"Of course you are but we are blessed too." Betty was finding it hard not to cry herself. Standing up to find something to do, Betty turned away so Steph wouldn't see how relieved she was that Steph wanted her to stay. "I'd better get to work. I have to get a grocery list started. You'd better get that light bulb changed before you forget and someone gets hurt in that room."

*   *   *

After Steph changed the light bulb, she looked around the room one more time. Unable to find any unopened boxes, she walked down the hall. Glancing at the stairs to the enclosed widow's walk, she realized she hadn't been up there since that first day with Deputy Morris. As she climbed up the spiral stairs, she was struck once again with the unique structure of her house. "What was the architect thinking when he added this to the design? Was it added on or built with the original part of the house?" Steph spoke aloud waiting as if to hear an answer to her questions. She walked around the glass-enclosed room, looking out at the view.

Steph walked over to the glass covered area that faced the barnyard and tried to imagine how it must have been when the house was first built. She thought about seeing horses in the field and the men walking around the buildings. She turned and looked over toward the woods. Standing there, she found herself caught up in the view.

After a while, Steph decided she should probably clean the windows. Wondering how they would ever clean the outside, she walked around the room again. Facing the north direction, she carefully looked at the framework and realized there was a door built into the enclosure. Feeling along the wall, she found a latch. Once she found it, she also could clearly see the clever hinges fastened to the door. Opening the door, she stepped out onto the actual widow's walk. She could see even farther when she was standing out on the platform, which surrounded the octagonal glass enclosure. Wrought iron railings were fastened to the platform and stood slightly above her waist. She wiggled the railing to test its stability before moving on around the platform. Satisfied she went back inside.

*   *   *

Steph kept her cleaning supplies downstairs so she headed down the back stairway to get them. She forgot Tad and Brian were there cleaning the chimneys until she heard a voice coming from one of the bedrooms on the second level.

"I told you to leave it alone." Tad was yelling up the shaft at Brian, who was on the roof. "Wait until we're done and we'll check it out one more time. Let's get this one done so we can move to the next one."

Not wanting to startle Tad, Steph cleared her throat before walking into the room. "How's it going? I guess it's Brian's turn to be on the roof, right?" Steph walked over by Tad.

"Yeah, it's his turn. We're almost done with this hearth. You sure have the nicest wooden mantles. Each seems to be made specifically for the room it's in." Tad picked up the few brushes he had put down. He spoke into his walkie-talkie. "I'm moving on down to the study now. I'll let you know when I'm there."

Looking around to make sure he wasn't leaving anything behind. "I'm done in here for now. We'll be moving to the kitchen side later."

"I understand the kitchen used to be in the basement so it should be interesting for you." Steph was not sure what else to say as she walked down the stairs with Tad to the library door.

"Betty told us and we checked it out some. I must admit, that is a large hearth, but the one in the kitchen is partially blocked. We'll have to spend some time on it." Tad walked on into the study and started laying out his brushes. Into his walkie-talkie he spoke, "Okay, I'm here. Let's get to work."

Steph heard the crackled reply and turned to leave. "If you need me, I'm going to be cleaning up the widow's walk. Just come and get me."

*　　*　　*

Steph went into the kitchen and found it empty. As she looked around, she remembered Keri was going to work in the rock garden. Steph wanted to let someone know where she was going to be. She went out the back porch and walked to the end of the deck to try to find her friends. She found them standing near a grouping of stones with Keri motioning and pointing at places. Betty was nodding her head and saying something as if in reply. Steph was too far away to hear them. She wondered where Misti was. Looking around, she realized she hadn't seen the little dog all day. Steph turned to walk down the steps and saw Misti lying in the shade beside the barn. When Steph reached the bottom step, Misti came running over, delighted to see her. Steph stopped and picked up the dog, carrying her with her to check on her friends.

"Thyme and rosemary would look lovely over here and we can mix some other herbs in." Keri was talking when Steph walked up.

"I just think you need a splash of color around the rocks. You said you wanted my opinion and that is it." Betty was shaking her head as she talked.

"This is going to look nice, Keri." Steph noticed the rocks were laid out in a pattern that would allow the plants to grow between them. She wasn't sure what a rock garden was but had envisioned a pile of rocks set up in some odd fashion. Now she understood what Keri and Hank were talking about.

"Let's ask Steph what she thinks." Keri turned to Steph. "Steph, I think we should plant this with a variety of herbs and plants to look like the cascade of a green waterfall."

"She asked for my opinion and I told her I thought it should be bright and colorful. I would like to have the fresh herbs to cook with but something colorful would be nice." Betty stood by Keri, waiting to see what Steph was going to say.

Steph looked at the shape of the rocks and tried to picture what Keri described. "I think a cascade of green would be beautiful if it was offset with color at the bottom. It would look as if the flowers were the splash at the bottom of the waterfall."

"See I told you it needed some color." Betty's voice was heavy with relief. Afraid Keri would go overboard planting herbs they wouldn't be able to use she'd been trying to encourage her to plant more flowers.

"Well, I do like the way you described it." Keri was trying not to be hurt that her friends didn't like the idea of all green herbs. "A few flowers would help keep the bugs away. I can use petite marigolds. That might work. I could put a soft yellow or some white cascading petunias in the middle. That would pull the eye down." Warming up to the idea, Keri began to picture it in her head.

Steph put Misti down and told her friends about the doorway in the octagonal window enclosure. "I'm going to go up and start cleaning now. I didn't find any more papers in the boxes left in the storage area. I want to get it cleaned up and then start in the basement." Steph and Betty walked into the house with Misti following along.

*   *   *

Steph collected her cleaning supplies and stopped by the study to check on Tad before she went up to the widow's walk. "How's it going there, Tad? Find anything interesting?" Steph put her bucket and broom down.

"This was pretty dirty. We're getting it all cleaned up. It must have been used a lot. I noticed this mantel is really thick. I told Brian to come in and look at it when he comes down. It's different from the others so he'll want to see it." Tad continued working as he talked with Steph.

Intrigued, Steph looked at the mantel but she couldn't see anything odd about it. "I'll be up cleaning on the top floor if you need me." Steph picked up her cleaning supplies and walked up the stairs to the widow's walk.

*   *   *

Hank surprised Jenny with the Teddy bear camera he bought for her. He showed her how to watch the baby's room using her computer. She was so delighted she embarrassed him by crying.

He was glad to get out to the barn and set up the cameras. He spent the next few days installing the new alarm system and other cameras on George's property. He didn't have to worry about Steph. The chimney sweeps were there so the women were not alone.

Hank learned alot about babies and mothers as he connected the system for George and Jenny. He learned an infant could scream extremely loud when he tested the alarm and it scared George Henry. He worried Jenny would be too angry to use the alarm system. His knees were weak with relief when she thanked him for installing it as she held the crying baby.

*   *   *

Steph was relieved to be finished with the octagonal widow's walk. She thought she would be able to have it cleaned in one day. Now two days later, she was satisfied with her work. There were several windows and the outside windows were so filthy she was dirty from head to toe when she finished.

She walked down to her bedroom to change out of her dirty clothes when she found Brian standing in her room looking at her fireplace mantel. She was not too surprised since she knew they were working on that chimney. What surprised her was watching him reach out to a circular decoration and turn it. When he turned it, another section moved in a lower portion revealing an opening in the mantel. Steph was so astonished she just stood there watching. She expected him to investigate the contents when he surprised her and spoke into the walkie-talkie. "I've got another one in the bedroom. We'll have to show them what we've found."

She cleared her throat so he would know she was there. "Never mind, Miss Weatherby's here, I'll just show her now." Brian turned around grinning broadly. "I've found some surprises for you." He turned back to the fireplace. "I've found a hidey-hole in this mantel. Here's this one. I think there's another one on the other side. Let's look." Brian reached over and turned the matching circular decoration to reveal another opening. Then he stood and stared at the woodwork above the mantel.

Steph was so fascinated that she walked over and tried to work the mechanisms herself. When Brian spoke it startled her. "Don't forget to check what is in there. It might be something important. I'd check it with a flashlight first for spiders. You never know what you might find."

Steph walked over to her bureau and picked up the small flashlight she kept there. Using it she checked the area for spiders and then removed a long, black box from the first opening. Carefully she wiped the box off using her already dirty shirt. When she opened the box, she found it contained an exquisite diamond and ruby necklace with matching earrings and bracelet. She was so astonished with the find she sat down quickly almost missing the edge of her bed.

"Careful Miss Weatherby, you don't want to hurt yourself."

Steph just looked at Brian. She was so surprised to see him standing there staring at her. "Did you see this?" She asked him, too astonished to believe it was real. "This was really there?" Steph looked back down at the necklace, forgetting about Brian who was watching her.

Brian started to answer then realized she wasn't listening. "Excuse me a minute." Worried about Steph, he went to get Betty and Keri. Finding them in the kitchen, he rushed in. "I think you'd better come upstairs. Miss Weatherby seems to be in a state." Not waiting for them, he hurried back up the stairs to Steph, who was sitting exactly the way he left her.

Keri and Betty rushed up the stairs.

"What's happened? Where are you Brian?" Keri was calling as they were trying to hurry after the upset man. "Brian, Brain, where are you?"

"In here, Miss Keri. I'm in here with Miss Weatherby." Keri and Betty stood at the door to Steph's room, not sure what the emergency was. They saw a grimy Steph sitting on the edge of her bed, holding a black box, looking at it as if it was going to vanish.

"What's happening?" Betty rushed over to Steph to see if she had a fever or was having a seizure.

"What is it Steph? Steph? Stephanotis! What is it?" Gently Betty shook Steph, who had not said a word since they entered the room.

Slowly Steph looked at Betty as if she just realized she was not alone in the room. Expecting the box to vanish, Steph turned and held it up for Betty and then Keri to see.

"Brian found this. He just turned something and found this in the mantle. Isn't it beautiful?"

Betty looked at the jewelry in the box and let out a gasp of surprise. Keri rushed over to look and sat down quickly on the bed.

Brian pulled out his walkie-talkie from his pocket. "You'd better get down here Tad. These women are scaring me. I've never seen anyone act like this." Brian just stood shaking his head.

The women sat on the bed looking at the jewelry and passing it between them. Brian stood outside the door until his brother arrived.

"What's the problem? Why are you just standing here? I thought we were done with this room?" Breathless, Tad had rushed down the ladder and ran up the stairs worried something terrible had happened. He came up the hallway and found Brian standing outside the room with a frightened expression on his face.

"It's the women. They just keep looking at it and there's more. It scared me the way they're acting. You handle the women. I only found the doors."

"Doors? What doors?" Tad looked into Steph's room as he tried to catch his breath. His search took in the openings in the fireplace

243

mantel and the women sitting on the bed, each holding a piece of jewelry.

"Brian, what did you find?" Tad walked into the room. "Miss Weatherby, I hope its okay. I told you Brian finds hidey-holes if there are any there. Are you alright?"

Steph looked up at Tad and then over at the frightened Brian. "Oh, I'm so sorry. I didn't mean to scare you. I was just so surprised at what he found. I walked in and saw him open the door and this was inside. It's so beautiful. I was just overcome." Steph stood on her weak legs and forced herself to walk over to Brian. Putting her hand on his arm, she looked into his face. "Thank you Brian for finding this for me. Are there any others I should know about?"

Brian was embarrassed and stood looking at the floor. Now he looked at Steph and slowly nodded his head. Without a word, he walked over to the mantle and began to clear the few decorations and knickknacks Steph had put there. Once it was cleared, he pushed, and then pulled on different circular parts of the wooden mantle. After a few seconds, a doorway appeared and began to swing open.

The room became eerily silent as they all watched Brian reach up and swing the wooden door further open. A large jewelry box was sitting in the center of the area once hidden behind the secret door.

Tad was just as overwhelmed as the others. It had been years since Brian found such a large hidden area. Brian had found a secret doorway in their grandparent's home when he was a boy. It had been a stopping point on the Underground Railroad and Brian found its secret. He developed a fondness for working with wood and spent many hours learning and perfecting his hobby of making furniture with secret compartments. He was always on the lookout for secret hiding places. Often disappointed, he kept looking and was always surprised if he found one. It had become a source of pride for Tad. If there were one around, Brian would find it. Torn between his astonishment and his pride for his brother, Tad just stood there for a few minutes with the others. Then he walked over and picked up the box setting it down on Steph's dressing table.

Steph, Keri and Betty stood and looked at one another. Finally, hesitantly, Steph walked over and opened the box. It was filled with jewelry, men and women's. There were necklaces, earrings, tiepins, bracelets, and more. Steph just stood and looked at it.

Keri could no longer stand it. She started laughing. "I wish you could all see your faces." She went to Brian and gave him a hug. "Brian, you are a miracle, isn't he Steph?"

Steph turned and looked at all of them. "Is this real? Did anyone take a picture?" She started to laugh, then cry. She handed Keri her cell phone and gestured toward the fireplace, trying to control herself. "No one is ever going to believe this! Oh my!"

Keri started taking pictures and in the flash of the camera phone, she saw other items in the open areas. "Betty, get over here and take these papers out. Let's see what else is here!"

Betty walked to Keri and looked. "I don't see anything."

"Get a flashlight and look inside. There are some papers and another box inside." Steph, flanked by Tad and Brian walked over to see. She picked up her flashlight where she had dropped it on the bed, shining it for Betty. Once Betty removed the other items and papers from all the openings and the large opening had been checked, they carried everything down to the kitchen.

"I think we'll just clean up some and go on home. I want to take my brother and buy him a drink." Tad was folding up the sheets that were spread out in the kitchen. He kept glancing over to the table at the items there. "You need to check that stuff out and put it in a safe place. We'll come back and see you in the morning. Come on Brian, we need to get the ladders laid down and be on our way. I want to take you to celebrate."

"Thanks for everything Brian, Tad. I really am glad you found these. We can't thank you enough. Come and have breakfast with us tomorrow. We'll make a special breakfast just for you!" Steph walked them to the door. After closing it behind them, she moved back to the kitchen table. "Okay, tell me, are these real? I see rubies, emeralds, but are they paste or real?" Sitting down, she started laying out the jewelry on the table.

"There is only one way to find out." Betty left the room.

While she was gone, Keri and Steph sorted through the papers they had found. The most important documents were two birth certificates. Among the other documents were a list of names and addresses and receipts that spanned ten years.

Betty came back carrying a mirror and a magnifying glass. She set her mirror down on the table. Using the magnifying glass, she selected a piece of jewelry with a diamond and reached for the mirror. Then she started laughing.

"You two aren't really going to let me do this are you? I have no idea what I'm doing here. I figured you'd stop me before I got this far."

Keri started laughing with her. "I was impressed. I thought you knew what you were doing."

Steph joined them in their mirth. "I was hoping you had the answers." She mimed Betty looking under the magnifying glass. When she looked up, she had made a decision. "I'll have to take this to a jeweler and have it appraised. For now, where will we be hiding this? I'm really glad Hank has the house security system working. Well, what do you think?"

"It's been all these years in your room. I think it will be fine in the hiding place another night. Will you take it tomorrow or talk with Stanley first?" Betty was looking at a broach while she was talking.

Steph had forgotten about her date with Stanley. Now that Betty reminded her, she felt the familiar stirrings of anxiety in her stomach. She liked Stanley and enjoyed his company. She was just afraid to get too involved until after the legal actions were settled. Steph wondered if her feelings were more gratitude than love. Thinking about her upcoming date, Steph didn't respond to Betty's question.

"Okay, spill it. What's going on? Something's on your mind and it's not the jewelry." Keri noticed Steph seemed withdrawn over the past couple of days. She decided she had been patient and waited long enough for Steph to tell them what was on her mind. "You might as well tell us now. You'll tell us eventually. That's what friends are for. We're here to help and we can't help if you don't tell us what's bothering you."

Steph looked from Betty to Keri. She felt as if she was looking through a fog and they were the lights guiding her way. "Okay, but I don't want either of you to make a big deal out of it. Will you at least promise me that?"

"I promise, if you will hurry up and tell us." Keri wondered if Steph was going to tell them or if she was searching for an excuse to keep her troubles to herself.

"What can we do to help? I promise to do what I can." Betty was concerned Steph had learned something about the person who damaged the lawn tractor.

Taking a deep breath to steady herself, Steph decided to simply tell them and see how they reacted. "I have a date with Stanley tomorrow night." She said it in such a rush that it took Keri and Betty a moment to realize what she had said.

"Why, that's wonderful. You have a date! Well, it's about time you started going out again." Keri was overjoyed. She had been worried Steph would stay homebound and not get out and meet any other younger people. She bounced around in her chair, too excited to sit still.

"Oh Steph, it'll be nice for you to have some fun for a change. Are you going to a movie? I can't see Stanley bowling, but you are going out aren't you?"

"Well... no." Steph paused to gather her thoughts. "Stanley enjoyed so many meals here, he wanted to cook for me for a change. We're having a quiet evening at his apartment." For some reason, Steph found this to be almost embarrassing. Here she was a grown woman embarrassed to tell her friends she was going to a man's apartment for dinner. "It'll be nice to just sit and relax and talk about something other than the house and the lawsuit. I'm really looking forward to it"

Betty realized Steph was trying to convince herself about something. *Maybe it's too soon, or he's not the right one.* She kept her thoughts to herself and decided not to share her opinion. She stood up to hide her thoughts. "I guess I'd better get started getting dinner ready. I need to get a few things ready for the breakfast." Betty walked over to the stove and began to prepare their evening meal.

Steph looked at the jewelry they had spread out on the table. "I'd better get this put away. I'll box it up and take it up to my room.

You're right it'll be safe there for tonight. I guess I'd better check with Stanley in the morning about what to do with it. Maybe he can suggest a jeweler to take it to." She stood up and began packing up the various pieces and put them back into the boxes they had been stored in. When she was satisfied, she picked up the largest box first to carry it up to her room.

"I wonder if any of the journals will mention any of the jewelry we found. Wouldn't it be interesting to know whose it was and if they wore it for any special occasions? Right after dinner, I'm going to get started reading again." Keri, who had been helping pack up the jewelry watched as Steph left the room. Turning away, she shook her head as she went to help Betty with their dinner.

CHAPTER 20

Steph looked at herself in the bathroom mirror as she fixed her hair. Nervous, she decided she needed a pep talk. "Look, a deal's a deal. You called last week and postponed because of nerves. The least you can do is go over tonight for dinner. It's just one meal. What's the worst that can happen? It's just dinner. It's just at his apartment. It's not as if we were going to a fancy expensive restaurant. He said it was just to get away and relax. He seemed understanding about last week. You don't want to disappoint him again."

"Stephanotis, you need some fun. You need to get out and do something besides worry about the jewelry and the house. The jeweler said it could take up to three weeks to clean and appraise the jewelry. It's only been one week. You have to give yourself a break. It'll be just you and Stanley. You say you enjoy his company." Steph lowered her head as she leaned forward, placing her hands on the counter for support.

"I know that's what you're afraid of." Lifting her head she took a good look at herself in the mirror. "You know you owe him for the trouble he's gone to. The least you can do is be nice to him. You don't have to sleep with him; just explain you find him to be a nice man who is attractive and fun, but he's not your type. Gee Steph, what is your type? Was it Fred?"

Turning away from her reflection in the mirror, Steph walked back into her bedroom. She started pacing back and forth across the room, swinging her arms to emphasize her words. "Come on Steph!

You meet a nice man who's interested in you and what do you do? You wish he was someone else. What is the matter with you?"

She walked over to the fireplace and flopped down into the rocking chair. Leaning back, she started to rock back and forth letting the movement calm her down. "Okay, so he's not your idea of a hero, but he likes you and wants to cook dinner for you. The least you can do is show up. You don't have to stay the whole evening. If you get too uncomfortable, you're a big girl, just say so and leave. He should respect you enough to allow you to leave. And if not, well, your lawsuit is screwed." She sighed. "You might as well go and face this. After all, it's just a meal at a friend's house. Yeah. That's the spirit. You're just going to a friend's house for dinner. See, you can do this." Rising from the chair, Steph went back to the bathroom to finish getting ready for the evening.

She kept repeating in her mind: *I'm just going to a friend's house for dinner. I'm just going to a friend's house for dinner.*

*   *   *

Stanley stood in the middle of his apartment surveying the romantic stage he created for the evening. Steph was due any minute and he was ready. In the kitchen the steaks were marinating, waiting to be placed on the grill. The wine bottle was open, allowing the wine to breathe. In the refrigerator staying cold and crisp were cooked, peeled shrimp nestled on a bed of lettuce. With a side of sauce, the appetizer was ready to be enjoyed while the steaks grilled. Vegetable kabobs would complete the meal.

The doorbell rang announcing the arrival of the evening's guest. Not wanting to appear too eager, Stanley walked to the door and opened it slowly. Steph was standing there looking nervous. When Stanley opened the door, Steph took a small, hesitant step backward as if she was subconsciously going to turn and run. As if talking to a small child, Stanley tried a reassuring tone. "Welcome, Steph. Please come in. You smell wonderful." Stanley stepped back to let her enter the apartment.

"Thank you Stanley." Step flashed a nervous smile. "You didn't have to go to all this trouble. We could have gone to a diner for dinner." Steph stepped into Stanley's apartment looking around and realized she was expecting it to look a lot like Fred's. Where Fred had black leather and chrome décor, Stanley had brown leather and antiques. Stanley's apartment was much more inviting and real than Fred's. Relaxing immediately, Steph turned to Stanley and handed him the package she was carrying. "I didn't know which wine to get so I thought it would be better to bring something homemade. Betty made fresh bread today and I brought rolls and a loaf for you. I hope you like homemade bread." Steph waited, not sure what else to do.

"So that's what smells so good. And here, I thought it was you." Stanley chuckled at his own joke. "Why don't I put this in the kitchen for now? Please have a seat and I'll be right back." Stanley took the package and kissed Steph on the cheek before going to the kitchen.

Steph took the time alone to further calm her nerves. *See Steph. And you thought this man was another Fred. Now you can relax and enjoy the rest of your evening.* Steph smiled to herself and sat down on the sofa.

Stanley returned carrying a bottle of wine and glasses. He joined Steph on the sofa, placing the bottle and glasses on the coffee table. "We'll have some wine and then I'll get the appetizers. I thought we'd sit out on the patio while the steaks grill. I hope that's okay with you." Stanley poured the wine and handed her a glass.

"That sounds lovely. It's a beautiful evening and it would be fun to watch you grill. I hope you didn't go to too much trouble." Steph took a sip of her wine. She didn't want to have too much to drink before they ate dinner. She knew it would go straight to her head.

"I like to grill something up now and then. I can handle myself in the kitchen so I don't starve, but I'm still learning to grill. My mother gave me a grill and a cookbook one year for Christmas. It took a while for me to learn to use it, but it works great for steaks and grilled vegetables. I learned using the grill keeps the mess and smell out of the kitchen."

Searching for a change of subject since she didn't know much about grilling, Steph placed her wineglass down on the coffee table and looked around.

"I like your décor. It's warm and inviting." She ran her hand over the brown leather of the sofa. "This is a nice sofa. This coffee table looks like an antique."

"Yeah, it's my mother's. When my ex-girlfriend moved in, I placed most of my stuff in storage and she bought new furniture. I guess it was her way of merging our personalities. She let me keep a few things, but she didn't like the chrome pieces I had. She hated my black leather sofa and we compromised on this brown leather. She liked antiques and we spent weekends looking for pieces. She could spend hours walking through stores. We bought a few pieces I liked. There was a table with a checkerboard painted on it. She called it a game table or something like that. I will admit I didn't pay as much attention to what she called things until I got the bills for them. She bought what she called a sleigh bed but it just looked like a large chunk of wood holding a mattress to me. I didn't care as long as it was comfortable and she was happy."

Stanley stopped to sip his wine before going on. "When she moved out, I went to get my other stuff out of storage and found she cleaned it out too. She took all the furniture but left the paintings and other stuff. I hope she's happy with all that furniture. Meanwhile, I was left with just this sofa. My mother took pity on me and gave me a few of her pieces until I get more. I decided to wait until fall to start buying new furniture. Who knows what could happen by then?" Stanley leaned back and emptied his glass. He leaned forward to refill his glass topping off Steph's and then moved close enough for Steph to smell the wine on his breath. "Do you want to wait a little while to eat or are you hungry now?" Stanley put his arms around Steph and drew her close to him.

After a lingering kiss, Steph put her hand on his chest and leaned back away from Stanley. Steph smiled to take any sting out of her words. "I think I'm hungry now. Do you need any help putting the steaks on the grill?"

Stanley leaned over and picked up his glass of wine. Taking a drink to settle his emotions, he looked at her. Realizing she was serious, he rose and collected the wine bottle. "I'll be okay, but if you'd like to come along, we'll take this out to the patio. I'll show you where it is." Waiting for her to rise, he walked to his kitchen and out the door to his enclosed patio area. "It's not big, but it's nice on a pleasant evening like this and very private."

The area was enclosed with a tall privacy fence. The entire area was covered in concrete. Stanley had added a couple of large planters with blooming and trailing plants that gave the area life and color. A glass topped table with chairs stood off to one side. The large umbrella was placed to shade the table from the evening sun. Toward the back of the area were a couple of chaise lounges and weatherproof chairs. A large stainless steel grill held court on the other side. It was so clean and shiny it was hard for Steph to believe it had ever been used.

Steph wandered over to the table and sat down, placing her wineglass on the tabletop. She selected a chair that would face the grill so she would be able to talk with Stanley as he worked. Stanley came out of the kitchen carrying a tray laden with a covered plastic container and a plate of shrimp for their appetizer. He placed napkins on the table with the plate of shrimp. Then he carried the tray over to the grill. When he opened the grill, Steph could see where there was a mild scorching suggesting he had indeed used the grill previously.

"I'll just put our steaks on and then I'll be right back." Stanley went about his work and then left her to return to the kitchen. Steph began to relax. She was drinking some wine when he walked back out carrying another container. Once he put the contents of the container on the grill, he returned to the kitchen. Steph leaned back and closed her eyes, relishing the quiet atmosphere of the patio area.

"I was hoping you'd like it. I see you haven't touched the shrimp. Don't you like it?" Stanley was helping himself to shrimp and cocktail sauce.

Startled, Steph opened her eyes. "Oh, I was just enjoying being here. This is really nice." She reached over and helped herself. "I love shrimp, thank you. I was just waiting for you to join me. It is so relaxing here. I would have thought you would be able to hear the traffic, but you don't."

"No, I sat out here for twenty minutes before I signed the lease to be sure I wouldn't have to deal with traffic noise. My mother was furious with the location, but I needed a place that was private. It's a great place where my friends can come and relax too."

They ate in companionable silence. Stanley kept an eye on the steaks and vegetables. Once he determined they were ready to eat, he gathered them into new containers and carried them inside.

"We'll be eating in the dining area, away from the evening bugs. If you'll bring the shrimp and plates, I'll get the other bottle of wine."

Steph gathered the dishes and glasses from the table and carried them into the kitchen.

"Just set them anywhere. Leave the glasses too. I have fresh glasses for our dinner wine. I know you'll enjoy this burgundy." Stanley joined her in the kitchen. He reached into the refrigerator and removed an opened bottle of wine. "This wine is from a local winery. They make a fine burgundy I enjoy with a good steak. Everything's ready so we can dine."

Steph followed Stanley through a small doorway into the dining area. It was separated from the living area by an archway, hidden by a paneled room divider. Steph noticed the room divider when she first entered the apartment but only wondered about it briefly. Now she could see what was on the other side. Stanley had lit candles and placed them around the dining room. The sky was getting darker outside, which added to the atmosphere.

"Please have a seat." Stanley held out a chair for Steph. Once she was seated, he moved to sit in the chair to her right.

"I like having the smaller more intimate area for dining. It sets a more romantic mood." Stanley noticed Steph wasn't drinking her wine and relaxing as he hoped she would and so decided to try a different approach. "Besides, it makes it harder to see the bad food I'm serving you." He was rewarded with a laugh.

Steph forced herself to relax again. Subconsciously she tensed up when she saw the romantic dining area where they would be eating their dinner. When he made the comment about the bad food, she couldn't stop herself from laughing. "It smells wonderful and I'm sure it tastes wonderful. I can't wait to taste it. Imagine, a man who can cook. You would make quite a catch for some lucky lady." Steph stopped herself before she said anything more that might ruin their dinner. After all, she was here for dinner and he went to all this trouble, the least she could do was relax and enjoy it.

As they ate, they were both careful not to talk about the lawsuit or the Weatherby farm. When Stanley invited her, he made it clear they both needed a night off. Steph kept eating, complimenting him on the dinner and trying to think of something to say. Finally she remembered something he told her the first day they met.

"How are your plans for the summer going? You told me the first day we met there was a project you wanted to finish this summer. How is that project coming?"

Stanley searched his mind. *When did I tell her that? What is she talking about?* Then he remembered. "Oh, I forgot I told you about that. It's going great. Actually, better than great! My best friend and I were buying a boat together. We picked it out and we were waiting on the financing to come through. It was a smaller boat with one large cabin below decks. Before the deal was finished, we found a larger boat with two cabins, two bathrooms and a slightly larger galley for just a few thousand more. We had to decide if we would use the larger boat. It was a toss-up until we figured out that if we wanted to spend a night or two on board, the double cabins would be better than one large open cabin. The larger boat would be more private and we would be more comfortable. We close on it next week. Would you like to come out next weekend? We're going to have a party and celebrate."

Stanley was animated and excited as he spoke of his plans.

Steph sighed, delighted she found a safe subject to talk with him about.

"Where will you moor your boat? Is there a marina around here to use? Do you do much fishing?" Steph knew Stanley was not a man to fish and it did not sound like a fishing boat was what he had in mind. She smiled at the thought of him holding a wet, slippery fish.

She nearly choked when she imagined him putting a worm on the hook.

Stanley didn't notice Steph's behavior. He was warming up to the subject and getting excited about the fun he was planning to have.

"There's a large reservoir with a marina on it. The City Council purchased property and built the reservoir several years ago. It links with the river through a type of canal. It had many people upset for years. Once the marina was built and people understood the need for the extra water, the property owners settled down." Stanley frowned at the memory. Then he thought of the boat and smiled. "We can take the boat out onto the water or party at the dock. It's going to be great! We're having a party on Labor Day weekend. I plan to stay there the whole time." Leaning back in his chair, Stanley thought for a few moments about the party he was planning.

Steph was relieved he was thinking of the boat and not about her. They finished their meal and he opened a different wine for dessert. If she drank any more, she'd have trouble driving home that night. She only sipped her wine, but during dinner she began to feel the warm glow from the wine. Stanley had chosen excellent wines for each stage of their meal and she felt guilty not to enjoy them. The burgundy had been a delight and she drank more than she planned to. She didn't know he would open the third bottle.

She was feeling guilty about her plan to leave right after dinner. Stanley put time and effort into their meal. Steph was touched and impressed at the same time. He was fun to talk with and she enjoyed his company. She was just not attracted to him sexually and had decided she wasn't going to sleep with him. She learned her lessons with Fred. She would wait until she found a man who loved her as much as she loved him before she slept with him. *Love? Where did that come from? Come on Steph, live a little. Why can't you have an affair with an attractive man? People do it all the time! Why can't you just have sex with this man? Because you don't love him? What does love have to do with it? You find him attractive don't you? You enjoy his kisses and his caresses. You enjoyed the kiss earlier tonight. What is the matter with you?* Steph glanced at Stanley. He had been saying something about the party he was planning. He was talking about introducing her to his friends before the big party. She hoped he didn't notice that she wasn't listening. She was fighting an internal battle of wills. Deciding to stay strong, she stood up and started to gather their plates.

"Stanley, since you went to all of this trouble for me, the least I can do is clean the dishes. It was an excellent meal. I enjoyed myself." She carried the plates into the kitchen planning to return to the table for more dishes. As she turned away from the counter, he was standing there.

Moving closer to her, Stanley didn't care about the dishes. He had a desirable woman in his kitchen and fire in his blood. He leaned in and kissed her. Steph was uncomfortable standing in the kitchen being kissed. It struck her suddenly; this was more intimate than kissing him on the sofa or porch swing at the farm. She instinctively stiffened in his arms. Stanley noticed the change and stepped back. Misunderstanding her body language, he drew her away from the counter thinking he pushed her too hard against the edge. As his kisses and caresses became more demanding and more intimate, Steph became stiffer and more uncomfortable. She moved her hands up his chest and pushed him away.

"Stanley, please let me clear the table and wash the dishes." She broke his hold and moved into the dining area to bring back the other dishes. Using them as a barrier, she carried them back into the kitchen.

Stanley waited until Steph set down the dishes she was carrying and then he took her hands into his. Looking into her face so he would know if she understood his meaning, Stanley watched for her reaction. "Leave the damn dishes; I have other ideas for the rest of our evening."

Ashamed of herself for leading him on, she couldn't meet his eyes.

"Stanley, I came here tonight as your friend and I hope when I leave we can still be friends." Looking up into his face to watch his reaction to her words, she went on. "I admire you and have enjoyed every minute I have spent with you but I don't feel that way about you. I will admit I have enjoyed your attention and should have ended it before it got this far. I was pleased someone like you found me attractive. It was flattering and I am sorry if I've hurt you. I just don't feel comfortable sleeping with you. I'm not attracted to you in that way. After all, you are my lawyer. It just seems wrong. What would your father say? I know he wasn't happy about you coming to the house to help me in the first place."

Stanley looked at her in shock at what she said. "What do you mean you don't feel that way about me? All this time you've been leading me on? What did you think tonight was all about? I was romancing you because I thought that's what you wanted. I thought you and I were going to be something special." He stood and looked at her as if he was remembering the first time they met. He was astonished she didn't find him attractive. What right did she have to take his feelings for her and toss them back at him?

Fearful of having hurt him, Steph tried to explain. "Stanley, you're my lawyer and I hope my friend. I like you an awful lot and it would break my heart if we couldn't be friends. You're a good man and I'm honored to know you. I just don't think we should ruin that by sleeping together."

He looked at her and realized she was right. He wasn't attracted to her as a lover. He was drawn to her because of her money and the possibilities available with her land. On some level, he knew part of the attraction he felt was because his father had not approved. Now it turns out his father was right. He also realized he was willing to compromise his own happiness for money. Deflated, he walked over to the sofa and sat down. Maybe he could salvage something from the evening anyway. He decided to try another approach. "You're right. I shouldn't have pushed you. I am after all your lawyer. You don't have to feel any gratitude for what I've done. I was hoping to take our relationship to another level, but if you don't want to, then you don't."

Steph walked over and stood at the end of the sofa. "It's not that I'm not tempted, but I just feel it would be wrong." Steph turned to go when her cell phone rang.

She turned the phone over to check the Caller Id. *Everyone knows I'm with Stanley. Why would someone be calling me?* The Caller

ID showed it was the sheriff's office. "Hello?" Steph hesitantly answered the phone.

Stanley saw Steph's face go pale and watched as she slowly sank down onto the sofa. Realizing something was wrong, he tried to gather what was troubling her from the conversation she was struggling to have.

"What do you mean someone broke in? I don't understand. Keri and Betty are at the movies." Steph glanced at her watch and saw how late it was. "They should be home any minute. Good. Tell them what happened. I'll be there as soon as I can. . . No, I only told Jenny, Keri and Betty that I would be gone. . . I'll try. I'm leaving right now. . . Okay. Yes, that would be fine. . . No, I'm on my way."

Steph knew she should be running out the door to her car but she couldn't make her legs work. They felt like rubber. She wondered if they would melt if she tried to stand. Sitting still, she stared at her now disconnected phone.

Breaking into her stunned silence, Stanley knew she needed his help.

"Steph, what's the matter? What happened? Who was on the phone?" Steph didn't answer him. She turned and looked at him as if she didn't recognize him. Shaking her slightly to get her attention, Stanley tried again. "Steph! Stephanotis! What happened? Who was on the phone? Talk to me, woman!"

Steph forgot Stanley was there. She realized she hadn't told him about the phone call. Reaching out she grabbed his arm, and then quickly released it after seeing him grimace. She had squeezed it too hard in her grief. "Stanley, someone broke into the house and now Misti is missing."

The impact of what she said hit him like a slap in the face. Someone had broken into her home and taken her dog! Why would someone do that? This was his town and people didn't go around stealing dogs. What would they do with it? Images of the bossy little dog ran through his mind. He wasn't much of a dog person, but it was a cute little dog. He knew it was important to Steph. If he wasn't going to be her lover, he could at least be her friend. After all, he was her lawyer and maybe she would change her mind about him later.

He could wait. Right now he had to get her home and see for himself what had happened.

He stood up and reached down to aid her in standing. "Obviously you're in no condition to drive. I'll drive you home."

Stanley smiled hoping to encourage Steph. "After all, that's what friends are for. Now, let's get your purse and be on our way."

CHAPTER 21

Somehow Stanley managed to get Steph into his car. She was moving like a zombie. She didn't say anything as they were driving. He expected her to cry or babble or something. The stone-cold silence was beginning to play on his imagination. As he drove he imagined they would find anything from a broken window to a ransacked mess.

Steph sat still as Stanley drove. She couldn't trust herself. She was afraid if she said anything, she would break. At first she was sick to her stomach, afraid that she would embarrass herself by losing her dinner in his car. Then the sick feeling turned to a lead weight centered in her stomach pulling it down into the cushions.

Seeing the house in a flood of light surrounded by the flashing lights of the police cars, Steph realized how fragile and precious her happiness was. There was a fleeting moment when she imagined she would never see her dear four-footed friend alive again. Such a brave and fearless little dog! Steph firmly pushed the negative thought aside. She concentrated on remembering when she first saw Misti.

Her dad and mom brought Misti to her apartment on the day they came to tell her about her father's illness. She would never forget her dad's words. *"This little dog is going to be a good friend to you. She'll give you the love and support you'll need."*

Some part of her was hoping this was a sick joke on someone's part. Hoping when they arrived home, they would find a quiet house being guarded by a fearless little dog. Now that she actually saw the blue and white flashing lights, she was sure her world was going to end again. She knew all was lost and once again, someone who loved her was dead. It was too much for one person to bear.

Stanley heard the sobs as they pulled up to the front of the house. He wasn't sure if he preferred the quiet Steph or the sobbing Steph. He was uncomfortable with the quiet Steph but the sobbing Steph was downright frightening. He knew how to handle quiet Steph. What did you do with a sobbing woman? Would she become hysterical? He was relieved to see Betty and Keri come running down the front stairway.

"Steph!" "Steph!" They were both calling her name. She barely heard them. What could she say to them? Steph took a couple of calming breaths and knew that she was about to be assaulted by a new wave of emotion. She knew she needed to see for herself what damage had been done and to make sure that they hadn't overlooked anything. Nagging doubt and worry plagued her mind. Maybe Misti was locked up and no one thought to look for her. Maybe she was out in the barn. Why would anyone want to break into her home? What was wrong with this person? What did they want from her? Steph shored up her fear using anger as the reinforcement. What did she do that made someone want to break into her home? *Nothing! I did nothing to deserve this!*

Steph saw Betty and Keri walk up to the car door. Putting her hand on the door handle to open it, she turned to Stanley. "Thanks for everything Stanley. I'm sorry you were dragged into this but I'm glad you're here." She let herself out of the car, leaving a stunned Stanley in her wake.

Betty and Keri stood nervously waiting for Steph to exit the car. As soon as she was standing, they both threw their arms around her and hugged her. Steph knew she would need to maintain control of her own emotions if she was going to find out what happened here. With her friends support, she knew she would get through the worst of what was to come. She was grateful to her friends but a far off part of her was worried they too would be hurt before this was over.

"Betty, Keri, I appreciate your coming out to the car. I need to talk with the sheriff so please, tell me where he is." She linked arms with them and gently began to steer them back up the stairway they had just come down.

Keri had kept Misti for Steph while she was living with Fred. During that time, she had developed a strong affection for the dog. Unable to speak because of the emotions clogging her throat, she merely hung onto Steph and wept softly as they walked.

Betty also loved the little dog and felt her loss. It pained her to see how distraught her friend was and she was determined to do all she could to help. She too was angry that someone had broken in but was trying to keep her feelings to herself. She knew she could fall apart later when she was alone and could give vent to the fears and anxiety that were waging war within her stomach. She used the anger that she saw on Steph's face to control her own emotions. "The sheriff and Deputy Austin are talking with Hank. They're all on the back porch looking over the damaged door." She paused to catch her breath. "They were here when we arrived."

Stanley followed the women into the house. As Steph's lawyer, he felt obligated to remain and see if his services would be needed. Dealing with frightened, crying women had not been in his plans for the evening. He promised himself he would leave as soon as he talked with the sheriff. His father would expect him to do that much, and would want a full report.

* * *

Steph walked Betty and Keri to the library as if in a dream. "Why don't you both stay here while I go find the sheriff?"

"I'll go with her. Don't worry, I'll watch out for her." Stanley tried to reassure the older women. He was going to stick by Steph until it was time to leave.

Steph walked out onto the enclosed back porch. With all the images she had pictured during the drive, she still wasn't prepared for the damage she saw. The glass on the door was broken and it looked as if a tornado had blown through the room. Chairs were tipped over while the lamps were knocked to the floor. The window coverings were torn, hanging at odd angles from their supports on the wall.

*   *   *

Hank was deep in conversation with the sheriff and Deputy Austin but he knew Steph was in the room before he turned to see her standing there. He hoped to head her off before she saw the damage, but he couldn't leave the sheriff. They found evidence that the brave Shetland sheepdog had bitten the intruder. Drops of blood and pieces of fabric were on the floor in the hallway. The intruder had broken in and damaged the enclosed back porch. The back door was closed and locked. The dog inside the house was the only other obstacle for an intruder.

The alarm had gone off, alerting Hank on his cell phone. He knew Betty and Keri were going to the movies and Steph was going over to Stanley's. Hank and George came as fast as they could, then called the sheriff's department when they saw the broken back door. It wasn't until the deputy arrived that they realized they were not hearing the dog barking. While the deputy called in the break-in, Hank and George searched the house and grounds for the dog.

Hank knew Steph would be upset by the loss of her dog and he was sure this was a deliberate break-in to scare her. Only he, George and Jenny, knew no one was going to be home tonight. Steph's plans had been made over a week ago, but Betty and Keri decided to go to the movies at the last minute. Hank realized whoever was watching the property, had figured out they were all going to be gone. It would be now or never and that meant they had been closer than he expected.

George returned home to be with Jenny and to check his farm to be sure it was secure. George had been worried the intruder would target his farm next and Hank didn't stop him. He felt needed here and knew George could handle things without him.

The deputies collected all the cameras and the recordings to review. Hank was sure they would find the identity of the intruder from one of the cameras. For the time being it didn't help the little dog that either chased the intruder or was forcibly removed from the house. She could be hurt or worse.

Hank turned to sheriff. "If you need me for anything else, I'll be here."

The sheriff turned and saw Steph had arrived and Stanley was with her. "Miss Weatherby, I sure am sorry to be seeing you again under these circumstances. I want you to know the dog must have put up a fight. Deputy Austin here will fill you in. Mr. Wilbur, may I speak with you for a few minutes?" The sheriff looked at Austin and motioned toward Steph with his head.

Deputy Austin moved toward Steph and gestured for her to lead the way.

"Let's go inside where we'll be more comfortable." Hank followed them into the kitchen.

"Miss Weatherby, why don't you sit down and we'll talk." Pointing out a chair for Steph, Deputy Austin walked around the table to sit across from her.

Steph was grateful for the support of the firm chair under her. She didn't realize she was no longer standing on the porch until the coolness of the wooden chair seeped into her skin through the thin cotton of her dress. She was aware of a strong male presence and didn't have to turn her head to know Hank had sat down with them at the end of the table.

Hank positioned himself so he would be able to clearly watch both of their faces. He was there for support and to help Steph if she needed him but he didn't want to interfere.

"Miss Weatherby, I'm awful sorry about this." Deputy Austin drew a small notebook out of his pocket. "I feel really bad about what has happened. I feel bad about the little dog, too. I have to ask you a few questions." He paused, looking at his notebook and flipping the pages until he found a blank page to write on. Looking up at Steph, he took a deep breath and began asking questions.

Steph didn't believe in out of body experiences. She had read stories of people who claimed to have experienced such things. Now she wondered if that was what was happening to her. She felt as if it was not her calmly talking with Deputy Austin. It was someone else, not her, whose home had been violated while her best friend was missing. She knew that competent law enforcement officials were out looking for the intruder and her missing dog. Deputy Austin seemed to be content with her answers. Steph believed someone else was answering the deputy's questions because she was outside calling Misti. It was okay because Misti would be running in the open door any minute and would be happy to see Steph. Until then, she would let the other person sitting in the chair answer questions and her real self would check out the rest of the house.

"Steph, I want you to know we are going to find her." Hank put his hand on her arm, bringing her back to reality. She felt stretched tight like a rubber band and then released to snap back into her body where she was forced to face the truth. Somehow, that simple touch was more reassuring than any words could be. Forcing a weak smile, Steph patted Hank's hand. "I know she'll be okay. I know she'll be found."

"Like I said Miss Weatherby, we need any current photos you may have of the dog so we'll know it's her when we find her." Deputy Austin was glad Hank was sitting there. He hated being the one to talk with Steph and he was concerned by her calm answers to all of his questions.

Rising from the table, Steph stepped away to leave. "I have some shots on the computer in the library. If you'll come along, I'll show them to you and you can tell me which ones you'd like to have. We can print them for you to have tonight. Are you sure you don't want me to go outside and call her? She may be staying in the shadows while everyone is here."

"No, Miss. We may have you do that later, but for now, we're trying to follow the blood drops. The intruder may not realize he's leaving a small trail to be followed. I'll come with you to look at the pictures."

Hank followed them to the library where Betty was sitting with the distraught Keri. When they walked in, Keri was calmer but still upset. "Deputy Austin, would it be alright if I make some tea?" Betty wanted to keep busy.

"I'm sure that would be okay. I'll go along and be right back." Deputy Austin walked with Betty to the kitchen.

Steph walked over to where Keri was sitting. She stooped down beside Keri's chair and took both of Keri's hands into her own. Looking up at Keri's face, she knew she needed to say something to calm the older woman. "Keri, I know it's hard to believe, but I know in my heart Misti is okay. Somehow I know we'll find her. She's going to be okay. She's a smart dog. She'll be found. We have to believe that. Will you believe that for me?"

Keri looked at Steph and slowly nodded her head. Steph released her hands and stood up. "I'm going to print some pictures of Misti for the deputy. Will you be alright?" Steph watched Keri.

"You're right. Misti will be alright." Keri looked at Steph. "Yes, I'll be okay. I just was so shocked and scared for the little dog. It was so brave of her to bite the burglar." Keri gave Steph a weak smile.

Hank walked over and stood beside Steph. He was uncomfortable seeing Keri so upset. He was reassured by Steph's words and her faith. Relief washed over him when he heard Keri's praise of the little dog. He knew they would be okay. "She has a brave heart and a strong set of teeth. It's nice to know she knows how to use them."

Keri laughed at Hank's remark. She realized she needed to calm down and was amazed at how much calmer she felt seeing how brave Steph was behaving. After all, it was her dog, not Keri's. Keri sighed. She loved that little dog.

Steph smiled back at Keri and went to the computer to begin the task of selecting and printing pictures. As she was working, Betty brought in a loaded tea tray.

"I made a pot of tea for all of us. My, Keri, you're looking better." Betty began to set out teacups and saucers. Filling cups, she passed them out so they each had a cup. Hank was helping Steph choose the best pictures for the deputies to use in recognizing the Shetland sheepdog. He pointed out unique characteristics in her fur that would make their job easier.

When Deputy Austin returned to the library, he found a different scene than the one he had left. Betty and Keri were sitting calmly talking and Steph was printing pictures for the deputies who were present.

Hank pulled the photographs from the printer and handed them to Deputy Austin. "Here are the best shots we could find. Steph blew them up to print and we printed several copies for you to use tonight."

"Thanks, I'll get these to the sheriff. They've found tracks leading to the woods but haven't spotted anything else. The sheriff thinks he was parked in the woods so no one would see the car. There's an old gravel drive from the road into the woods that seems to have seen some recent activity. The sheriff wanted to know if you've seen anyone in there."

"No, but it would make a great place to hide." Steph didn't know much about wooded areas. She hadn't walked far into the woods and put off exploring the area while she worked on the house.

Hank shook his head. "I haven't looked in there. I kept thinking about exploring the area but have had a few things come up that kept me away. I'll have to get back to it now."

Hank was thinking how easy it would be to hide in the woods and watch the house.

"Well, I guess we'll be leaving soon. Not much sense in messing up the trail. We'll be back in the morning to search in the daylight. Will you ladies be okay by yourselves?" Deputy Austin was not comfortable leaving but the sheriff was his boss and told him what to do.

"They won't be alone. If you'll wait with them, I'll go get my things and be back. I'm not leaving them alone." Hank saw Deputy Austin nod that he understood why Hank wanted him to stay. Hank left to go get his clothes from George and Jenny's. He intended to move in and keep *"his girls"* safe.

*   *   *

Stanley talked with the sheriff alone. He felt that as Steph's legal representative, he needed to know any information the sheriff had. Stanley wondered to himself if the break-in had anything to do with the discovery of the jewelry the previous week. Since the jeweler still had the jewelry, it may have not been the motive. Stanley also wondered if the dog was kidnapped for ransom. He would wait and see.

Stanley was surprised to see Hank leaving. He didn't think much of the other man, but if he was the good friend that Steph said he was, then why was he leaving? Maybe the sheriff asked him to leave. That would be alright with Stanley. He would make sure they were going to be safe before he left.

"I want to talk with Miss Weatherby one more time before we leave. Do you want to come along Mr. Wilbur?" The sheriff also saw Hank leave and was wondering what was happening. He assumed Hank would be sticking around at least until they all left. Hank had talked as if he was concerned about the welfare of the women.

"Let's go see if we can find her." Not waiting for Stanley to reply, the sheriff went looking for Steph.

Stanley followed the sheriff into the house. They found the women with Deputy Austin in the library. "Austin, I see Hank left. Will he be coming back in the morning?"

"No, he said he's going to get his things and I'm to stay until he comes back. He said he's moving in."

Stanley looked at Steph. She didn't seem upset by this news. "Where's he going to sleep?" Stanley regretted the words as soon as they flew out of his mouth. He saw the look on Steph's face and knew he made a blunder.

"Why, in a bed of course. Lord knows we have plenty of those." Keri stood up from where she sat all evening. "Betty, I guess we'd better make up a room if we are going to have a guest." Keri waited for Betty to join her. "We'll put him in the room next to you so he'll be across the hall from me. It will be nice to have a man in the house don't you think?"

Stanley could hear Keri talking as they walked away. Faintly he heard Betty reply, "What do you think he'll want for breakfast?"

Walking over to Steph, Stanley decided to clarify what he heard. "Are you going to let that stranger move in here with you?"

Steph was exhausted emotionally and physically. She just wanted to have Misti home and live her life in peace. "Hank is not a stranger, he's a friend!" Steph didn't like to be blunt, but she was appalled at Stanley's attitude. Hank hadn't discussed it with her. He just announced he was moving in. She was secretly relieved. She was afraid the intruder would return when the sheriff and deputies were gone. She realized she was suddenly afraid without Misti. She wasn't afraid when she first moved in and was living by herself. She didn't know she relied so heavily on the little dog to warn her of intruders. Now her guard dog was gone and she was afraid. She didn't want Stanley to know of her fears. She was getting tired of how he behaved toward Hank. Hank at least was doing something to help.

Raising her head up to look directly at Stanley, she decided to let him know how she felt. "Hank is worried about our safety. Keri and Betty will sleep better knowing he is here with us and I think I will too." *That should settle it.*

Stanley started to open his mouth to say something and then closed. He realized she was right. He hadn't offered to stay. Maybe if he had, he would be sharing Steph's bed. At least he wasn't being inconvenienced sleeping under the same roof with a bunch of nosey females. He preferred his own apartment. Hank could play the hero if he wanted to. Stanley would be there to pick up the pieces when the hero let them down. "If you think that's wise, I will accept your decision. Just remember I'm only a phone call away." To stake his claim, he walked over and gave her a lingering kiss good-bye. Satisfied he had given the deputy and the sheriff something to think about, he turned and left.

*   *   *

Embarrassed by Stanley's behavior, Steph stood still for a few moments.

"It seems my phone call may have interrupted something. I'm sorry. I wish we wouldn't have had to call you. It always strikes me as wrong when someone decides to steal from someone else. The "Good Book" says not to steal, but there are those who do it any way."

The sheriff was not impressed by Stanley's behavior. He knew when a dog marked its territory and that was what Stanley was doing with his kiss. He wanted to send the message she was his. The sheriff shook his head. *I'd prefer Hank if it were me. He shows genuine care for all of the women and is respectful of Miss Weatherby. He wouldn't treat her like that.* Shaking his head again, he looked at Steph. *I don't think she liked it either. A man shouldn't treat his woman that way in front of other men.*

Steph realized the sheriff was looking at her. She was fighting the urge to follow Stanley and tell him how she felt. She felt her face color with anger but hoped the sheriff and the deputy thought it was with embarrassment. *Better to have them think I'm embarrassed than mad. I may need all of these men before Misti is returned and I don't want to risk losing her.* Keeping her thoughts to herself, Steph looked at the sheriff. "I'd appreciate it if Deputy Austin or someone would stay until Hank comes back. We'll all feel safer."

"Yes, of course. Austin, you stay here. The rest of us will be heading out. We'll be back in the morning to search the grounds again. Meanwhile, lock up and be careful." The sheriff walked out. As he was leaving, he gave directions to the deputies who were still on the scene and they drove off.

*   *   *

A short time later, Hank pulled into the drive. He carried a suit-case and duffel bag. He still couldn't believe someone had broken in. He was relieved to see there was still one police car there. He knew he was doing the right thing by moving in. It had upset Jenny to learn about the break in and she was worried. George agreed someone needed to be with the ladies. He even seemed to be a little relieved Hank was the one to suggest it. Hank walked up the stairway hoping that this was not going to be a big mistake. He prayed he would not embarrass himself by having any nightmares about his assault. He was going to have to risk it to keep his girls safe. Preparing himself mentally to spend the next several hours reassuring the ladies, Hank entered the house.

*   *   *

"Are you sure you don't want another piece of cake, deputy?"

"No, thanks. I've had enough already. I don't want to go back to the office with cake crumbs on my uniform. The others would be jealous. I wouldn't mind another cup of that great coffee though." Deputy Austin was sitting at the kitchen table when Hank walked in. He had an empty plate sitting in front of him.

Keri was standing at the counter pouring coffee into a cup. Betty and Steph were sitting at the table. Steph looked tired and was holding her cup with both hands, staring at it.

Hank was relieved Keri was her cheery self. Her tears and grief had stabbed at his heart. Steph's pain had frozen it solid. He was going to find this man and make him pay for their pain. First, he was going to find the brave little dog whose bravery and sharp teeth gave them a faint trail to follow once it was light.

Hank announced his presence trying not to frighten them. "So this is how it is. I leave you ladies alone for a while and you decide to latch onto another single man."

"Hank!" Keri ran over and gave him a hug. "Steph, Hank's here!" Keri turned to see if Steph was listening. Steph just stared at her coffee cup. Keri leaned toward Hank and whispered. "She's been like that since the sheriff left. I think something else has upset her." Louder she said, "Just put your things down and we'll get you some cake and coffee. I'll show you later to your room. We put you in the bedroom beside Betty, but don't you get any ideas." Linking her arm in his, Keri drew Hank over to an empty chair. "You just sit down here." Keri stood next to Hank as he sat. She was so happy he was moving in. She was never afraid like this before and she didn't like it. She wasn't sure she would feel safe living alone again.

Seated, Hank looked around. Betty had risen and was bringing a slice of cake on a plate to the table. Hank nodded to the deputy. "Thanks for staying deputy. I appreciate your watching out for the ladies."

Betty sat the plate on the table in front of Hank and Keri placed a cup of coffee on the table before sitting back down.

"It's been quiet. Thank you for the cake and coffee. I guess I'd better be going." Deputy Austin began to rise from his chair.

"Sit down, deputy and relax for a couple of minutes. Let me eat this cake and I'll walk you out to your car. I'd like to have it nice and visible for a few more minutes. I don't think the ladies will mind at all. Will you?" Hank glanced at Keri and Betty who were both looking as if they agreed with him. Steph just stared at her cup.

While Hank ate, he tried to decide if Steph was in shock or just still upset. She didn't move the entire time he was there. It was as if she had withdrawn into herself and was just a shell sitting there.

Keri and Betty exchanged worried looks. They didn't know what to do or say to help Steph.

"That was a delicious piece of cake. Thank you. I needed that. If you're ready deputy, I'll walk you to your car and lock up." Hank rose and moved to leave the room.

"Thank you for everything, deputy. I appreciate that you stayed until Hank returned." Steph looked up at the deputy as he rose from his chair. She forced a weak smile. "I'm sorry we've been so much trouble. I'm also sorry I didn't listen to you. Thank you for helping us." Steph sighed. "We'll see you tomorrow." She rose and left the room.

To cover Steph's abrupt withdrawal, Keri blurted out. "Yes, deputy. Thank you for staying with us. I know everything will be better tomorrow." She looked over at Betty hoping for confirmation of what she said.

Betty smiled at Keri. "Yes, it will be better tomorrow." Looking at Deputy Austin, she continued. "Thank you for everything. I am glad you could enjoy some refreshment with us."

"Thanks again, ladies. I'll be coming back sometime tomorrow." Deputy Austin tipped his head to the ladies and followed Hank out of the room.

Hank waited until they were near the patrol car so they would not be overheard. "What time will someone be here in the morning? I want to join the search for the dog. I want to be there when it's found." Hank hoped the deputy did not hear the crack in his voice. He was grateful the darkness covered the tears that were pouring down his face. He was afraid of what they might find and wanted to help find the dog.

"Sheriff plans to begin at six a.m. Some of us are volunteering to work off the clock to come and help search. We're meeting up at the office to gear up and come out. I'll be seeing you in the morning." Deputy Austin got into his car and drove off.

Hank walked back into the house taking his time making sure the inside door was secured. He walked around inside the house checking the doors and windows in the basement and on the main floor.

He placed his suitcase and duffel on the floor near the front stairway. Realizing he was alone on the main floor, he turned off the remaining lights in the kitchen and hall. He left the outside lights on as a security measure. When he returned to the stairway his duffel and suitcase were gone. Climbing the main stairway, he heard voices coming from a room down the hall.

"It's so good to have a man under our roof." Hank smiled. That was Keri's voice. She sounded just like her old self. "We'll just leave his things in here and let him get settled in for himself."

"Did you put out towels and extra blankets for him?" Betty's voice carried out the door.

Hank stopped outside the doorway and watched as the two women fussed over the room so it would be ready for him. His suitcase and duffel were on the bed. "What a nice surprise. Two lovely ladies waiting for me in my bedroom. What more could a man want?" Hank laughed at the surprised looks on both their faces.

Betty looked embarrassed.

Keri was delighted. "We wanted to make you feel welcome. We brought your suitcases up for you." Keri went over and gave the man a hug. She was feeling better and knew everything was going to be alright. She wasn't going to allow herself to think otherwise.

"Can anyone join this party or is it by invitation only." They all three jumped at the sound of Steph's voice. She stood inside the doorway watching them, holding a clock radio in her hand. "Thank you, Betty and Keri for getting Hank's room ready. Thanks, Hank for coming. I hope you'll be comfortable here. If you need anything, please let us know. I brought you an alarm clock in case you needed it. I didn't know what time the sheriff was coming back tomorrow." She walked over and placed it on the stand beside the bed and plugged it. "I'll let you set it."

"We'll say good night now. See you in the morning for breakfast." Betty took Keri by the arm and began walking out of the room. "Oh, the first one up makes the coffee. Good night Steph. Good night Hank. Sleep well."

Keri reluctantly followed Betty out. "Good night, you two. See you in the morning." Keri waved as she left.

Steph stood beside Hank, unsure what to say or do. One minute she just wanted to sit and cry, the next, she wanted to scream with rage over what had happened tonight.

Hank moved to the bed and began unpacking his suitcase. Steph noticed a comfortable chair in the room. Realizing Betty or Keri had brought it in; she made a mental note to thank them tomorrow for their thoughtfulness. Sitting down, Steph watched as Hank unpacked and moved around the room.

Hank sensed Steph's reluctance to leave. He knew she would speak when she was ready. As he carried his toiletries into the bathroom, he wondered if she planned on sitting on that chair all night. He needed to get some sleep so he would be awake when the sheriff arrived in the morning. When he returned to the room, he stowed his suitcase and duffel in the closet and moved to sit on the side of the bed near Steph. Deciding to break the silence, he searched for something to say.

"Well, if this isn't a fine mess. I don't know if I can ever thank you for everything you have done tonight." Steph spoke first, then leaned back in the chair and looked directly at Hank for the first time that evening. "I never thought anything like this would ever happen. When you installed the security system, I thought you were being overly cautious. I didn't think we really needed it." She paused, glanced away from his searching gaze and then looked directly at him again. "Hank, I want to thank you for that. I'm ashamed of myself for not taking the warnings more seriously. I can't imagine what would have happened if Betty and Keri had come home and the intruder would have still been here. I know it looks like Misti ran him off, but I think it was your security alarm. I wouldn't be able to live with myself if someone would have hurt Betty or Keri. They're my dearest friends. You saved them." Steph paused again, fighting down the emotions that were threatening to break loose. "I have the large bedroom down the hall. If you need anything, please let me know." She stood to leave the room.

Hank didn't remember getting off the bed or how it happened. He just realized he had Steph in his arms and she was sobbing against his shoulder. As a cop, he learned comforting someone was part of the job. He never had any trouble saying soothing words then. Now, as a friend, he was at a loss. He just stood there letting her cry.

When she had cried herself out, she pulled away and looked up at his eyes. They were soft and full of warmth. She noticed the worry lines that had developed, adding character to his face. She was concerned she had caused them. She realized she was glad it was Hank who was there and not Stanley. That thought had her glancing away so Hank would not see her thoughts in her eyes.

Embarrassed, she kept her eyes lowered and noticed the wet spot her tears left on his shirt. "I'm sorry I got your shirt all wet." Looking back into his eyes once more, "I want to thank you again for coming to stay and for understanding we need you. I feel more secure knowing you're here." Steph turned to walk away.

Hank reached over and grabbed her. Leaning down, he kissed her softly but gently and then released her. Turning her around, he put his hand on her back and guided her out the door. "I'll see you in the morning." His voice was gruff with emotion. "Get some sleep Steph. You look terrible." Hank quickly shut the door before he changed his mind.

Steph all but floated down the hallway to her room. She enjoyed the warmth and the strength from Hank's kiss. As she passed Betty's room, she was surprised to find Betty still awake reading.

Betty glanced up as Steph paused at the door to her room. "I thought I'd read for a little bit and settle my mind before turning in. Keri was going to take a long soak. You're looking better. Do you want some company for the night? We could make it a real slumber party."

"No, but thanks. I had a talk with Hank and I'm feeling much better. I'm going to turn in now. Good night." Steph walked across the hall to her own bedroom closing the door behind her.

Betty turned back to her book and mumbled to herself, "If we aren't careful, we're going to have another problem on our hands. I'll have to have a talk with that man tomorrow."

CHAPTER 22

Hank was up early. He planned to be the first to rise and get started cleaning up the mess on the porch before the others woke up. Walking down the back stairway, he thought he smelled coffee brewing and something else that had his mouth watering. He walked into the kitchen just as Betty was putting a pan into the oven. Not wanting to scare her, he cleared his throat to let her know she wasn't alone.

"Coffee's on and I just put a breakfast casserole into the oven so breakfast will be ready in about twenty minutes. I've got fresh rolls in the baskets on the counter by the coffee if you can't wait." Betty turned from the stove and smiled at the astonished look on Hank's face. "I couldn't sleep so I got up and made cinnamon rolls for the people coming out this morning. Steph has the coffee going. She makes the best brew. She grinds her own beans, says that's the secret. I think it's the love she uses to make it. Love is always the key." Betty reached for her own mug sitting on the counter, taking a sip.

"Steph's out on the porch cleaning up. Keri hasn't come down yet. We decided to let her rest. Just help yourself since you're one of us now."

Betty busied herself with something on the stove smiling to herself. They surprised Hank. She was tired but it was true she couldn't sleep. She tried reading, which usually helped her. Last night seemed both awfully long and yet too short. She'd get a nap in later if she could. For now, she had work to do. There were people coming who would need food. They needed to keep up their strength to find the little dog.

Hank helped himself to a cup of coffee and a fresh cinnamon roll. The roll he selected was still warm and the icing was sticking to his fingers. Popping the whole roll into his mouth, he reached for another one to take along. Waving his thanks to Betty, he decided to head out to the porch and help Steph.

Hank stopped at the doorway and watched Steph as he chewed. He was surprised at how hard she must have worked. He was relieved to see the calmness on her face. She didn't seem to be upset as she kept working. He finished the other roll and drank most of his coffee while he watched. She had set up the furniture and was sweeping the floor when he finished.

"It's not perfect, but it looks better than it did last night. How are the rolls? Betty was just putting them in when I came outside." Steph looked over at Hank. It was taking all the strength she could muster to keep her voice calm. She had fallen apart when she first came down and saw the mess again. Having something to do like cleaning up had helped calm her down.

He took a moment to swallow the last of his coffee before answering her. Stepping on into the room, he glanced outside at the darkness to see if any patrol cars arrived. "The rolls are delicious. The coffee by the way is great." He waved the empty cup to prove his enjoyment.

"Good, I was afraid it was going to be too strong. I figured we would need the jolt to keep us going today. Betty was going to make a casserole for breakfast. Shall we go see when it'll be ready?" Steph walked past Hank back toward the kitchen. Hank noticed she was taking control. He had to admire her courage. He expected her to still be upset and uncertain. He followed her into the kitchen.

"I'll set the table if you'll get the smaller basket of rolls from the counter."

Steph reached into the cabinet for plates.

Hank walked over and picked up what he hoped was the smallest basket. Turning, he leaned back against the counter and watched Steph efficiently set the places at the table.

She fiddled with the napkins and plates until she was satisfied. "If you find those too heavy to hold, you could set them on the table."

Steph smiled and turned to look at Hank.

He had forgotten he was still holding the basket. He quickly set it down and covered up his embarrassment by pouring himself another cup of coffee.

"Breakfast is ready you two. Go ahead and have a seat." Betty removed the casserole from the oven and carried it to the table.

"Mmm, that smells good." Keri came into the kitchen looking rested and alert. She joined the others at the table.

While they were eating, Betty noticed Hank looking out the window.

"You'd better eat up Hank. I know you want to meet the deputies when they arrive. Let them know we'll have coffee and rolls for them on the porch. That way we'll be out of their way and they can sit and relax."

"Thank you. I'm sure they'll appreciate it." Hank knew some of the deputies getting off the night shift volunteered to help today and they would need the caffeine from the coffee. No longer able to restrain himself, he pushed back his empty plate and stood up. "Thanks for breakfast. I'll go outside and wait. I want to be ready when they arrive." Hank turned to leave the room.

"Let us know what you find no matter what." Keri wanted to know the truth and she wanted Hank to tell her. "If they find anything, I want to know. Promise me, Hank."

Hank turned back and saw the pleading look on her face. He swallowed hard before he answered. "I'll do what I can Keri. I liked the little dog too." Quickly, before one of the women starting crying, Hank left to go outside.

Steph rose to leave as well. "I'm going to see if they need anything. I want to be on the scene." She left the room before the others could protest. She hoped they would understand her need to be out looking for her friend.

When the sheriff and the deputies arrived, they set up a base on the enclosed back porch. The sheriff used a map of the area to send the search parties out in teams. Not wanting to miss any clues, they walked in all directions, moving away from the house to search. There were drops of blood down the stairway, leading off towards the woods. Most of the searchers headed in that direction. In case the intruder backtracked and went a different way, the others searched the barn and the buildings on the property.

Hank joined the deputies searching the wooded area. He was walking along a path when he heard one of the deputies talking. "I don't think you should go in there Miss. I don't think the sheriff would like that."

"Then why don't you stop me?" came the reply. Hank recognized Steph's voice. "I own this property and it's my dog we're looking for. I have the right to search too."

Hank shook his head, deciding it would be best if he helped the deputy. Turning back he walked until he came up to Steph and the deputy. "Its okay, deputy, I'll keep an eye on her." He understood the look of relief the deputy sent his way.

"Okay. The sheriff said to follow any orders you give. If that's an order, it's fine by me." The deputy quickly left the two of them to join the group he was assigned to work with.

Hank saw the determination on Steph's face. He realized if it were his dog, he'd want to be a part of the search. However, he wasn't going to let her take charge.

"I'll let you stay on one condition. You have to walk behind me and do what I say."

Steph looked at Hank. Relieved she wasn't going to have to fight with him too, she sighed. "I thought they only said that in the movies. I never thought I'd hear someone say it in real life."

"You follow me and do as I say or you go back to the house. Do we have a deal?" Hank wanted to make sure Steph understood how serious he was.

Relenting, she nodded as she answered. "Yes. I understand. I follow you and do exactly as directed. So can we get started?"

Rolling his eyes as he turned back to the path, Hank motioned for Steph to follow him.

They walked and looked in the woods for what seemed to Steph like hours. She had no idea how quiet and peaceful it was in there. She kept thinking how romantic it would be if she was not trying to find Misti. Hank told her to call Misti a couple of times but to only do so when told. She was trying to be helpful and followed his directions carefully. He would stop and look over the ground as if he knew what he was looking for. Finally they stopped in a clearing. It was long and narrow, an open area surrounded by thick brush. The grass in the center was trampled and showed signs of activity. Hank knelt down and called the sheriff on his walkie-talkie.

"Sheriff, I'm in a clearing and I found where the car was parked. There's air-conditioner runoff on the ground and a few drops of motor oil. He may be having some car trouble. The plug on the oil pan may have loosened up or he has a pinhole leak. It's not much but it shows a car was parked here recently. We're going to mark it and follow it to the road."

While Hank was busy, Steph wandered around looking for clues. She was doing her best to stay on the edge of the clearing as directed. She noticed some trash in the leaves on the ground and started picking it up. *Someone has left their litter in my woods. I'll have to remember to see what can be done about trespassers. Probably some kids.*

Hank marked the ground where he found the oil stains and looked over to see what Steph was doing. He realized she was picking up pieces of evidence off the ground. He yelled, "Steph, what are you doing?" in a harsh voice.

Startled, she dropped the paper cup she was holding. "Someone has been littering the area and I was just picking it up." She was surprised at the tone in Hank's voice until she realized she was about to pick up some napkins that were red. She thought it was ketchup until Hank called to her. Now as she looked at it again, she realized it was blood. Shocked, she looked over at Hank. "I didn't realize. I just thought it was trash. This is where he was. This is his blood."

"Just stand still. Don't move and don't pick up anything else." Hank rose from where he knelt and stopped to listen. The deputies nearby were coming to collect the evidence. "Just stay there. The deputies will want to know where you found it. Just stand still and show them when they come."

Steph did as she was told, silently scolding herself for not staying back at the house. *I just wanted to help find Misti.* She fought back the tears that threatened to fall. *I couldn't stand staying behind when I'm capable of walking and looking too. What was I thinking? Now I may have messed up everything.* Steph stood where she was trying not to cry. *I don't want to embarrass myself any further by standing here blubbering. I made a mistake, but I did find something.* She held onto the thought as if it were a lifeline. *I found something.* She repeated it over and over while she waited.

Deputy Austin and another deputy walked into the clearing. "Good job, Hank. I appreciate your leaving things alone until we could get here. Show us what you've got." Deputy Austin let the other deputy talk with Hank. He walked over to where Steph was standing.

"Miss Weatherby, have you found something?" Deputy Austin noticed Steph was standing as if frozen to the ground, her face pale and drawn. His quiet question reassured Steph.

Steph was still fighting to keep her emotions in check. She didn't realize how hard it would be to show him what she found. Tears unshed blocked her vision as she raised her hand to show him the paper cup she picked up and the stained napkins at her feet. She couldn't trust herself to speak so she pointed to the other items she had mistaken as obscure trash.

Deputy Austin pulled out an evidence bag from his pocket and held it for Steph to drop the items she was holding into it. He wasn't surprised to see the tears in her eyes, and tried not to dwell on why they were there. He busied himself collecting the other pieces of evidence. Then he went to join the other two men who were collecting soil samples, leaving Steph to remain standing where she was.

Steph remained still and tried to listen to what the men were saying across the clearing. It surprised her at how quiet the area was. She assumed their voices would carry easily, but the dense area of woods around them was muffling the sounds.

After what seemed like an hour to Steph, Hank and the two deputies were satisfied with what they found. They began to walk through the clearing and down a trampled path toward the road. They walked past her without even glancing in her direction. They continued to walk until they were out of site. Unsure about what was expected of her, Steph started to follow them. She tried to listen to their conversation, but was too far away to hear them. When they reached the road, Hank shook hands with the deputies and began to walk across the field toward the house. Steph followed him walking at a slower pace.

Hank knew Steph was following him. He didn't have to see her to know where she was. He was trying to picture what happened in his mind. He was afraid they would find he little dog hurt when he saw Steph picking up the blood soaked napkins. He didn't mean to be harsh with her, but it was important for her to understand she was not to disturb any more of the scene. He was going to have a talk with Steph about staying at the house and not venturing back out. It was not a task he wasn't looking forward to.

*   *   *

Steph walked through the side door from the porch into the conservatory and on into the house. She wasn't ready to talk to the deputies and the sheriff who were based on the back porch and the deck. She noticed tables and chairs set up outside with papers and food stacked on them. She felt ashamed she left Keri and Betty alone to cook for the searchers.

By the time Steph reached the kitchen, Hank was seated at the kitchen table with a sandwich and a cup of coffee. Betty and Keri were hovering nearby. Steph helped herself to some coffee and then sat down across from Hank. Not knowing where to begin, she kept her eyes on her coffee cup while she simply said, "I'm sorry."

Hank was trying to find the right words to tell her to stay in the house. He was prepared for her to come in upset because he was harsh with her. He wasn't prepared for her to apologize. He continued to eat while he searched for the best way to respond.

"Keri, Betty, Hank, I want you to know I am sorry. I should have stayed here and helped with the work instead of going off to help look for Misti. I needed to help find her. I didn't think I could just wait for someone to tell me what was happening. Now I know I had no business being out there. I just got in the way. I'll help with whatever needs to be done here." It took all of Steph's control to keep her voice from cracking. She was trying not to cry. She was torn up inside with guilt, helplessness and fear.

"Why Steph, Keri and I didn't have much to do. The sheriff and deputies have only been drinking some coffee and eating sandwiches so far. They did eat all the rolls though. They were talking about finding a bunch of evidence in a clearing but nothing else has been found. There's not a lot to be done." Betty walked over and put her hands on Steph's shoulders, giving them a squeeze. "We have everything under control. The sheriff said they probably wouldn't be here too much longer unless they find more evidence. They think the man is long gone."

Keri sat down at the table then reached over putting her hand on Steph's. "We're here for you. Don't you worry. They'll find her."

Hank finished eating and then cleared his throat. "The best evidence they have has been found in the clearing we discovered. They'll check it over. Give them a chance. That's what they do." Standing up, Hank carried his plate and cup to the sink. "Thanks for the meal. I'll go talk to the sheriff and see what he plans to do next. It will be ok. We'll find her." Reassured Steph was going to stay at the house, Hank went in search of the sheriff.

*　　*　　*

The man sat in his car trying to decide what to do next. He was living in an apartment where no pets were allowed so he couldn't take the crazy little dog there.

Breaking into the house should've been easy. No one was home. He saw the woman all dressed up and learned earlier in the day from the lawyer's receptionist they had a hot date that night. It was surprising what he could learn by asking the right questions.

285

He saw the two old ladies leave and followed them to the movies. It was a long movie so he would have plenty of time to search the place.

When he checked the layout of the enclosed porch and the house, he didn't see the small tables with plants under the windows. Someone must have put them there recently. His plan was to break in the window quietly with a snack ready to drug the dog. He had it all worked out.

It was unfortunate that when he broke the window and tried to enter, he knocked over the table, the plants and the floor light beside it. Since the neighbors are far away he didn't have to worry about making too much noise. He fell with the furniture and panicked. He didn't like to panic. He planned to open the door and sneak in to drug the dog. Because he fell, he took his revenge out by trashing the room, startling the dog.

He didn't know such a little dog could have so many sharp teeth. When he broke into the main part of the house, the dog was barking and growling like crazy. He was mad and tried to ignore it. He came to get the jewels and money his employer said were in the house. He knew right where they were. All he had to do was find the right mantel and open the hiding place. His employer was going to sell them to fund his land development company. The man didn't care, as long as he got his cut.

He was going to find the money that night no matter what.

Moving down the hallway, the man watched the little dog who was frightened enough to stay away. His mistake was letting the dog get behind him as he began to search one of the rooms. The dog dove at him and bit him on the leg. It sunk its teeth into the back of his leg and then it jumped up and bit his arm. When he reached for it, it bit his hand.

The man didn't find anything worth stealing on the main level of the house while trying to avoid the dog. After searching the first room, he remembered the drugged treat and hoped he hadn't miscalculated the dog's weight. The dog ate the treat but kept trying to bite him. It would stay back just out of reach and then when his back was turned, it would run in, bite and run away.

The man realized he was running out of time so he left by the back door, leaving it open. The little dog followed him and chased him across the area toward the woods. The man was concentrating so hard on his search he didn't realize he was bleeding from the bite on his arm and hands. When he reached his car, he was still bleeding.

He was so angry at the dog. At first he was going to kill it if he could get his hands on it. When it followed him to his car, he realized this was a great opportunity. He wouldn't have to come back and search for the jewelry. He could ransom the dog for it. First though, he'd have to catch the dog. It was beginning to show the signs of being doped with the drug he put into the treat. It would run a few steps and then drop down on its stomach. Maybe if he got behind it, he could pick it up. He tried to pick it up, but the dog twisted around and bit him.

Finally the man remembered he had a small blanket in the back of his car. He took out the blanket and threw it over the top of the dog. Quickly, he scooped the dog up into the blanket and held it tight. There was a box in the trunk. He emptied the box with one hand while holding the dog with the other. Once the box was emptied, he put the dog into the box. The dog was no longer fighting by that time. The drug had taken effect and the dog was sound asleep.

The man got into his car to drive away but then he noticed the blood all over his hands and arm from the dog bites. Using the napkins he collected from various fast-food places, he cleaned his wounds. He kept a small first aid kit in his car and used it to bandage the worst of the bites. He didn't notice the occasional gusts of wind blowing through the open doors of the car. He was hoping for rain to cover any tracks he might have left. The wind picked up the blood soaked napkins and bandage wrappers unseen and tossed them across the clearing.

Now that he had the dog, he needed to decide what to do with it.

The man had rented the small apartment, telling the landlord he would only need it for a few months. He disliked living in hotel rooms where the staff seemed to find it necessary to enter the room daily. He liked to be able to keep his own schedule. He secured a part-time job at the local 24-hour discount store. The story he told his landlord was he was looking into the store for the corporation. If the landlord called the store, he would be told the man was an employee.

The dog was asleep but the man didn't know how long it would stay asleep. He needed to find a place to put it while he worked out the details of the ransom. The man prepared another treat to give the dog if it woke up.

The man left the dog in the box and went to bed. He was on the schedule to work for a few hours the next morning. He needed some sleep. He would have to wear gloves at work so no one would comment about the marks on his hands. He stayed awake into the night thinking of ways he could manufacture an accident to cover the damage from the dog bites.

Before he went to work the next day, the man checked on the dog. It was awake but drowsy. He put another drugged treat into the box and closed the box. He punched a few air holes into the top so the dog would be able to breathe. To make sure his landlord would not hear the dog if it woke up and barked, he put the box into a closet and shut the door.

The man heard the news about the break in when he went to work. He was glad to hear the sheriff was searching the woods. Once they searched, he felt sure they wouldn't go back. He would have to be careful, but he would be able to still use the woods for cover to watch the house.

While at work, he printed the ransom note on the computer. The man stopped at a pet store to buy a muzzle and leash. He planned to muzzle the dog before it woke up. Then he would find a place to stash it until the ransom was delivered.

When he returned to his apartment, the dog was still asleep, making it easy to slip the muzzle on.

He put the box with the dog in it into his car and decided to drive by the farm to see if the police were still there. He was sure he'd be able to outwit a bunch of local cops. As he drove out to the farm, he was thinking of what to do with the dog.

Now that it was muzzled, maybe he could just tie it up somewhere. He couldn't leave it in his closet. The animal was beginning to smell. It must have wet itself in its sleep and he knew his landlord would search for the smell if he happened to come for a surprise check.

Tying it up would keep it out of his way until the ransom was delivered. Then he could tell them where to find it.

If they didn't find it, well that was their problem. He didn't care either way. Now he had to figure out his next step.

Someone returned a remote controlled car today at work. He snuck it to his car. He would need to practice with it to move to the next step of his plans. What he had in mind would be delicate work, but this was the first step.

He told his employer he may have to heat things up a little bit. If she didn't come up with the ransom, well, she'd learn she wasn't dealing with an amateur. He knew how to get results. She had a lesson to learn.

CHAPTER 23

Steph stood at the window feeling useless as she watched Hank talk to the sheriff. She wished she could go out there too but she didn't know what to say. Embarrassed by her earlier behavior, she prayed that it wouldn't cost her Misti's life.

The sheriff was having his deputies pack up everything. They searched the entire wooded area with little result. The only evidence they found other than the blood trail was from the clearing. Their search of the barn and other buildings turned up nothing.

Steph knew they were doing all they could but was sick to her stomach worrying she may have contaminated the evidence. She hoped with all her heart that they would find Misti and bring her home.

Turning away from the window, Steph decided she should find something to do. Betty and Keri were in the kitchen getting dinner ready. The odors from the kitchen only added to her sickness. Steph wanted to be alone for a while and felt drawn to the study. Its masculine atmosphere made her feel safe and secure.

Walking into the study, Steph looked at the mantel, remembering the pipes and tobacco pouch Brian had found. She smiled remembering Brian's excitement in the discovery. The wooden fireplace mantel seemed a fitting place to store the pipes and tobacco. Reverently the items were returned for safe keeping, ready for use if needed.

Steph hoped Brian would find the document signed by Iris, her great-aunt. As of today, they still hadn't located it. Steph was still hoping to find a mention of it in the journals but there was no indication of it in anything they've read so far. She'd set aside the first journal she was reading because the content horrified her. Others she found boring. Today she was hoping to find something interesting to take her mind off Misti.

Picking up an unread journal, she began to read: "*Maw has decided I need a wife. We are having a party. Maw and I have been attending parties at the neighboring farms. She is happy here. I know she wants to be a grand maw. Her sisters are both grand maws and write to her about their grand babies. I just hope I can make it through the night.*"

Steph scanned over the next couple of pages until she read:

"*I met a young woman. Her name is Primrose. She is the niece of our neighbor down the road. She is visiting them for a few months. I never met anyone like her before. She liked our house but said it was not big enough for someone of our status. I did not know women were interested in racing. Honeycomb has won a few local races and Dancer is being trained to run. Having my men bring them from the ranch has given me a good reason for having them come and work. I will send a few mares back with them to breed and train. Miss Primrose is just sure horse racing is going to be a big sport someday. She is from a fine family and Maw is pleased with her. I have only been thinking of getting the house finished and making the farm profitable. I had forgotten how lonely Maw might be. I did not realize how lonely I have become.*"

"Primrose? Primrose! This is my great-great grandfather's journal. Primrose is my great-great grandmother's name! So this is how they met."

Grinning, Steph turned back to her reading, scanning over pages until she read:

"*I have arranged for the architect to oversee remodeling the house while I am on my honeymoon. I have brought Lester, John, Stu and Abe from the ranch back to work with the builders. Primrose is set on having the house remodeled. Maw was pleased I am getting married. She does not seem to be very upset about spending a few months with her sister. She will have a lot to talk with them about. Primrose has a strong mind. I have to be very careful. She has spent many hours with the architect*" *and I had to pay him a bonus for working with a woman. I find myself fatigued by it all. She wants to change the look of the house. The roof is being removed in the middle; an octagon shaped room is being added as another floor. I find it will be a good addition and a look out for the cause. The marshals are prowling the woods and roads more and more looking for runaways. Adding rewards for returned runaways, more bounty hunters have taken up the cause.*

"Master Ward down the road has agreed to oversee the transport of the materials for remodeling the house. He has special wagons with false bottoms to haul the shipments. One wagon will bring them in with the conductor and another wagon will take them out. They will use the barn entrance and because we are going to make several changes, the staff will be staying in town while we are gone. The men from the ranch are staying in the old bunkhouse and will be eating with the other workers in the new main bunkhouse. They will oversee the shipments while I am gone."

Steph laid the book down and searched for something to mark the page she was reading. Carefully she slid a piece of paper into the book then carried it to the kitchen to tell Keri and Betty.

Smiling, Steph walked into the room. "Mmm. Something smells good."

Keri grinned. "You're feeling better."

"I found the journal that tells about the reason for the octagon window cupola and the widow's walk. It was a look out for the marshals." Steph puffed out her chest with pride and sat down at the table. "Who would've thought a member of my family was a part of the Underground Railroad?" Steph laid the book down and leaned back in her chair. "Dad always said this house was special. I never understood what he meant. I wonder if that was what he meant. Imagine! This house was used to help smuggle people to freedom." Shaking her head Steph started to think about her dad and his father. "I wonder if Hyacinth knew. Listen:

"The wedding is in four weeks. Primrose is furious with me. She wanted to add two wings to the side of the house. Because of the tunnel and the way the hill sits, I had the architect design the wings to the front. It gives the house the look of having its arms open in an embrace to wel-

come company. Primrose states that it does not look finished. I will pray for a solution.

"Now listen to this: "*God has inspired the architect. He has learned of a new heating system that uses hot water sent from a boiler into pipes through the house. It will heat the rooms without a fireplace. Primrose was delighted. She has agreed to a covered porch being added around the house to tie the wings together. I like the idea of being able to walk from one side of the house to the other under a covered roof. The architect suggested adding a second covered walkway on the second floor to finish the look of the house. This will give us a look out from three levels of the house. That is truly an inspiration from Heaven.*"

Steph looked up at their faces. Betty and Keri were now both sitting at the table listening to what Steph was reading to them.

"That's so neat to know. I assumed some of the decking was added by different generations, but the majority must have been in place when Primrose was alive. Earlier in the journal it talks about tunnels and being searched." Steph flipped through the journal skimming over the words.

"Oh! Here's more: "*The marshals are getting more insistent. They are checking the wagons as they come into the barnyard. It is good we stopped bringing shipments that way. I have been praying for guidance. I have spent so much time in the prayer room that I found it more expedient to use the tunnels to get to the barn to oversee the workers. The men are finding it stressful to have the marshals around so much. One of the workers said that his wife is pushing for him to quit. They are very afraid. The wedding is just days away. I am praying for patience and help. God will supply.*

I received a letter from Stu. He said I have a few horses that are ready to come to the farm for training. I do not understand but I had asked God for a sign of what I need to do. I wired for them to do as needed."

Steph flipped forward a few pages and back. She looked up puzzled.

"There aren't any pages talking about the wedding or the honeymoon."

"Of course not!" laughed Keri. "Few men pay attention to the details of the wedding. Most only think about after the wedding. Sounds like a typical male to me."

Betty shook her head. "Maybe he has a separate journal for the wedding and honeymoon. We'll have to look for it. I don't think he'd like his wife to find this one. It sounds as if he has some secrets to hide."

"You may be right Betty. If someone found out he was helping runaway slaves, he could be in trouble."

"Steph, you're almost finished. Go ahead and read us the rest of it. I'd like to hear more. Wouldn't you, Betty?" Keri leaned forward eager to listen.

"Sure. I admit I am finding it hard to believe it really happened in this house. It's such a peaceful house." Betty leaned back in her chair to relax while Steph read.

"Okay. Here goes. I'll just keep reading. *'We returned from our honeymoon. Abe, John, Stu and Lester are here. They have been thinking I need a new well. They divined for the water and said that it is over on the side of the house where the forest is. Abe said that is where the kitchen garden needs to be moved. We will find fertile soil there. I have placed the order for the brick. We will start digging the well tomorrow.*

"*I have all the men on the farm take a turn digging the well. We are now fifteen feet down. We have not hit water so we have started widening the well. The marshals have been interested in our digging.*

"*We have reached thirty feet down. Since we have not hit water, I have ordered the men to stop digging.*

"*The tunnel from the well to the house is finally complete. It was a difficulty. Using the canvas bags to fill and haul the dirt out was a marvel. It worked well. The tunnel meets the tunnel to the barn and can be blocked as needed. We have a small room in the well tunnel for the runaways to wait in if the other tunnel is discovered. It was a fine idea the men had. They will return to the ranch tomorrow.*"

Steph paused for breath. "I'll just flip a couple pages here." Then she continued: "*The man wanted to build the gazebo over the well. He wanted to do something to thank me for keeping his woman and him safe through the winter. The babe was born in the small room off the tunnel. It seems like just a few weeks ago when they arrived in the snowstorm. The wind was blowing so hard, the conductor said they were afraid they would miss the well and fall in. They came from the woods into the well. The woman was due soon and having a hard time. The other woman that came with them was worried she would lose the baby if they were forced to move on. I sent the conductor on his way and let them stay. Now, as I watch him work with the other men on the structure that will cover the well, I am grateful to God. The babe is doing well and the woman is recovering. They will put a trapdoor in the floor so we can use it still. Primrose is so happy to have the hole in the yard covered. She thinks I have hired laborers from town to build it. She does not know he lives below. I am looking forward to seeing the structure finished. The man has a knack for turning wood. It will be a wonder to see."*

Steph placed the journal down with a sigh. She was reluctant to leave the journal and return to the present. She looked up and saw tears in Keri's eyes.

"Are you okay?" Steph reached over and placed her hand on Keri's.

Sniff. "It's just so sad to know a baby was born here and most of the people in the house probably didn't even know about it. I'll never be able to look at the gazebo again without thinking of that baby and wondering what happened to it."

"Keri, don't let it depress you. Just think, someone made the gazebo out of gratitude for being free. It makes it something to cherish not mourn." Betty stood up. "I don't know about the two of you, but I'm going to go sit on the back porch for a little while. Dinner won't be ready for another thirty minutes and I want to enjoy some peace for a little while."

"I'll go with you." Keri stood up to join Betty. "Say Betty, don't you think we should decorate Hank's room? We could go into town and get some new curtains and things to make it nice for him."

Steph remained at the table. "I want to take this journal back to the study and see if there are any others we need to read. I'll be out soon."

"Okay Steph." Betty turned to Keri as they left the room. "I'll have to give it some thought. We'd have to pick out colors. Maybe paint it. Let's sit down and talk about it."

*　　*　　*

Steph joined Keri and Betty on the back porch after going through some of the journals still to be read.

"I have to admit, it's nice to sit out here and enjoy the end of the day."

Keri put her feet up on an ottoman. "I always felt as if my apartment was getting too small by the end of the day. I would have the air-conditioner on and it was nice, but I would start to feel confined. When I was first married, we would take long walks in the evening. Then we stopped. I don't remember why, just that we stopped." Keri paused and thought for a few minutes. With a dreamy look on her face, she continued. "I think we found a television program on we liked to watch and it was on at the same time of day we liked to take our walks." Giving herself a mental shake, Keri smiled and looked around. "Oh well, we started to take evening walks again a few months before he died. You might say we walked at the beginning and the end." She shrugged her shoulders. "I guess that was why the apartment seemed so small. I was afraid to walk by myself and I really missed the evening air."

Keri looked over at Steph who had taken a seat while Keri was talking. "Steph, we were just talking about how nice it is here at the end of the day."

"Dinner will be ready in a few minutes. Hank went to take a shower and then we'll eat." Betty glanced at her watch. "My goodness, he's taking a long time in the shower. I wonder if he's okay."

"Maybe you should go check on him."

"Check on who?" Keri jumped when she heard Hank's voice behind her. He had entered the room and snuck behind her chair.

"I was worried because you didn't come back down." Betty started to stand. "I'll get supper on the table."

Hank was still laughing silently about scaring Keri.

Steph enjoyed watching the way his eyes twinkled when he laughed.

Hank walked around Keri's chair, took her hand in his and bowed. "My lady, may I escort you to the dinner table?"

Keri was so delighted she was speechless. She giggled and nodded her head. Standing up, she tried to pull her hand away. Hank moved it to his arm and held it there. In a stage whisper, he said in her ear: "I thought you were going to come up and help me shower. Then I'd have an excuse for being late." Keri tried to look shocked but she was laughing and it spoiled the effect.

Steph followed them in to the kitchen laughing at their antics. She was delighted her friends were there. She knew in her heart everything was going to be okay.

As they sat down to dinner, Stanley called on Steph's cell phone. "I wanted to let you know the jeweler called. He'll have the appraising and cleaning done on the jewelry by next Tuesday. How did it go today? Did they find anything?"

"They found some evidence in the woods but we didn't find Misti. The sheriff was very nice about searching. We haven't heard anything else." Steph walked away from the table to talk with Stanley. She turned away so the others would not see the anger brewing on her face. She struggled to keep her voice light and even. "I wanted to thank you again for dinner. Thank you also for calling about the jewelry. I have to go now. We're just having dinner. I'll talk with you next week. Good-bye." After hanging up the phone, she turned the ringer sound down and walked stiffly back to the table.

"Weren't you being a little hard on him?" Keri was perplexed.

"No, I don't think so. He's starting to act like Fred." Steph resumed her seat across the table from Keri and put her napkin in her lap. Looking up she looked directly at Keri. "I'm not going to let him upset me. He called to tell me the jeweler called him. Why do the people in this town call him instead of me? Just because he recommended them, doesn't mean he's in charge. I intend to let the jeweler know what I think of that on Monday. He said the jeweler would be finished with the jewelry on Tuesday. I can go pick it up then." Steph looked around the table. Pasting a smile on her face, she looked at each one of them. "I can't let things like that get to me. I have all of you to keep me sane, or insane as the case maybe. Now what is this about Keri helping Hank take a shower?"

Keri was drinking iced tea and started to choke. Hank leaned over and started patting Keri on the back.

Betty simply leaned over toward Steph. Smiling she said, "I think we'd better watch those two. I'm not sure which one is the worst."

"I take exception to that!" Hank stopped helping Keri and straightened up. "I would like it to go on record that it's a tie!" Nodding his head, he winked at Steph. "I don't just ask anyone to join me and scrub my back. However, I guess I'll have to keep on asking until one of you decides to join me." Satisfied when he saw Keri blush, he resumed eating.

"You know, Steph, I like this man. I never thought I would meet someone who could keep Keri quiet." Betty looked at her friend and smiled. "It's a rare treat to have a quiet meal."

Steph just shook her head and smiled. She enjoyed the rest of her meal content to be with such good friends.

CHAPTER 24

Keri was working on the covered porch at the front of the house. Watering the pots and hanging baskets of flowers kept her busy for a couple hours each day. She was pleased with how well they were growing and usually found contentment in the work.

After she turned off the water and collected the garden hose, she walked to the area outside the conservatory. Keri paused to admire the riot of color provided by the blooming plants and colorful foliage. Their soft fragrance helped to soothe her troubled spirit and ease her mind.

Steph had splurged on additional chairs, rockers and small tables. She arranged them invitingly in groups around the porch.

Steph painted the older furniture Hyacinth had bequeathed her in bright, bold colors. The eclectic styles created a bright welcome to anyone visiting her home.

Keri added colorful pillows and cushions for a cheerful place to sit and enjoy the evening breeze.

Standing to the side of the porch, Keri decided the furniture was a nice accessory to her plants.

Suddenly feeling very tired, Keri sat down in one of the rocking chairs. Closing her eyes, she let her mind wander over the events of the past few days as she rested. She realized she was not getting much sleep. It was no wonder with everything that happened.

Little Misti disappeared the night someone broke into the house. Then two days later, someone threw a rock through a window of the conservatory. A ransom note for Misti's return was attached to the rock.

Keri remembered how frustrated Hank was. None of them heard anyone in the yard before or after the rock was thrown. Hank said it took a strong man to throw it through the window. He had spent the rest of that night prowling around outside with a deputy.

Keri sighed. She was getting to know the sheriff and his people a little too well.

Rocking back and forth, she enjoyed the peace and quiet, letting it wash over her. The glass technician was there that morning replacing the broken glass on the back door and measuring the conservatory window. Until he replaced it, Hank covered it with an unsightly board. Everything looked different with the board up. Keri longed for things to be as they were before.

Keri didn't know how long she sat there rocking; her thoughts were in turmoil. Hank told her he was working on a project. Steph was going into town later so she and Betty were getting a grocery list ready.

The man who took Misti knew about the jewelry Brian had found. The printed ransom note said she would be returned in exchange for the jewelry. A lock of her fur was taped to the note. The sheriff told Steph not to pay the ransom. He told her they would probably kill the little dog, if they hadn't already, after they got the ransom. A tear slid down Keri's cheek as she thought of Misti being lost to them in this way. It was over a week since the little dog disappeared.

Keri overheard Hank talking to George on his cell phone. He told George the sheriff was right. Keri worried about Steph. She was mad at Hank for telling her he agreed with the sheriff. Steph told Keri and Betty she would have to think about what to do. If it meant getting Misti back, she was willing to give up the jewelry.

Keri didn't know how to help her. Steph had taken the jewelry to have it cleaned and appraised hoping to enjoy it. Because someone else wanted it for themselves, she was forced to decide if she should give it away to save Misti. Keri knew what she would do, but did not want to influence Steph either way. Keri noticed Betty too, refused to give advice as well. Some decisions have to be made on your own. Keri released a soft sigh.

The exchange was last night. Steph was to take the jewelry to a local store parking lot and leave it in a shopping cart at the store. Once the man received the jewelry, he was to contact her about where Misti could be found.

Steph used the costume jewelry the sheriff told her to buy. She put the jewelry in a cart and left it just as ordered.

Keri leaned back in her chair. She and Betty waited with a deputy. It was a long wait until Steph came home. Hank stayed with the sheriff. They explained to Keri and Betty what they were going to do. Once Steph left the jewelry, they would use it to catch the man.

They watched the cart from their cars after Steph left. An employee of the store came out and collected the carts. He pushed them into a line and took them into the store. He left the bag in the cart.

Somehow the bag was exchanged for a different bag when the cart was pushed into the line inside the store. The employee was watched the whole time. The jewelry was lost and now so was Misti. The man still had not called.

It was so quiet and Keri was so relaxed she barely heard the footsteps coming toward her. She opened her eyes to see Hank standing over her grinning.

"I almost got you." He laughed and sat down in a chair beside her. "I caught you napping on the porch." He leaned back and looked out over the lawn toward the gazebo. "I wondered what you were up to. Steph is getting changed to leave for town. I don't like it, but I won't stop her. Betty is looking through some more of the old cookbooks she found. I finished my project for now so decided to see if you needed help." Closing his eyes, he relaxed and put his legs out in front of him, crossing them at the ankle. Folding his hands over his stomach, he sighed, "This is the kind of help I wanted to be."

"Hank, do you think that we'll ever see Misti again?" Keri was afraid to ask the question before. She worried somehow Steph would overhear her.

Hank was silent a few minutes before answering her question. "Yeah, I think we'll be seeing the little dog again. She has a brave heart and too much love to share. I believe God will watch out for her. He knows how much Steph needs her." Hank was afraid to look at Keri to see her reaction so he kept his eyes closed. He wasn't too surprised to hear her quick intake of breath; sure she was going to cry. He was still not comfortable with the women crying around him.

"Hank, is it possible to see something that you really, really want to see happen?" Keri stood up as she talked. She saw some movement in the bushes near the gazebo.

Walking over to the edge of the porch rail, she tried to see more clearly what it was that was moving around over there. It seemed too familiar. She turned slightly to talk with Hank but kept an eye on the animal she saw moving out of the bushes. "Is it possible for a fox to be in the bushes around the gazebo?"

Curious about why Keri would ask such a question, Hank opened his eyes. He saw Keri standing at the rail looking out over the lawn. Rising to stand beside her, he saw a reddish brown animal standing near the shrubbery that encircled the gazebo.

"I've never heard George mention seeing foxes in the daytime. It must be awfully hungry to be this close to the house with the open lawn." As they watched they saw the animal move slowly away from the gazebo and walk slowly toward the house.

The sound of a car engine starting broke through the silence. Both of them were surprised and fascinated at the change-taking place in the animal they were watching. It was moving along as if trying to walk as close to the ground as possible. It had been going slowly as if testing the ground with each step. At the sound of the car engine, instead of running away as they both expected, the animal raised its head and began to move faster toward the sound. It did not run, but it was obvious to both Keri and Hank it tried to increase its speed.

As they continued to watch, the animal came closer and closer. Suddenly Keri started to cry. She reached out and pointed. Between sobs, she finally blurted out, "It's Misti!"

As soon as she said those words, Hank realized she was right! The little dog was coming home.

Hank ran off the porch and headed straight to the scared dog. Misti stopped short when she saw Hank coming. She was heading to the sound of the car at the back of the house. Hank knelt down and spoke softly to her. As if she realized who he was, Misti started to move toward him. Hank tried to stay still until the dog was close enough for him to pick her up. Gently he carried her back to a waiting Keri.

When he reached the porch, Keri put out her hands to take the little dog. Keri was horrified by the condition the Sheltie was in. She was wearing a part of something leather around her head and there was a piece of rope fastened to her neck. It looked as if it was chewed off.

Keri realized it was Steph starting the car they heard. Carrying the dog herself and telling Hank they needed to hurry, they walked around to the front of the house to stop Steph before she left for town. As they arrived at the front of the house, Steph was driving the car toward them. Keri was holding Misti, who saw Steph in the car.

Before Keri realized the dog's intent, Misti jumped from her arms over the edge of the porch and landed on the ground.

*   *   *

Steph noticed Keri and Hank then saw something fly from the porch. She stopped the car to look. As soon as she realized it was Misti, she unfastened her seat belt and fled from the car, running over to the little dog. In her haste, Steph left her car door open and the engine running.

Misti was lying on the ground where she landed. Trying not to upset or frighten the little dog, Steph slowed her steps as she neared. When Steph reached her, she noticed her leg was at an odd angle from her body. Steph saw her beautiful sable fur was tangled with twigs and leaves. As Steph knelt down to touch the little dog, she was aware of an extremely loud sound, a sharp pain and then everything went black.

*   *   *

Keri was so shocked Misti would jump out of her arms; she just stood still for a few seconds. One minute she was holding the dog, trying to comfort herself and it. When she moved toward the porch steps, she felt the little dog gather itself and using her chest as a springboard, the dog propelled itself forward. When Keri realized what happened, she saw the dog laid funny where it landed. She saw Steph jump from her stopped car and run over to the dog.

Just as Keri was about to start down the stairway, the car exploded. The impact knocked Keri down, showering her with mangled bits of metal and car. Keri fell backwards and sideways onto the porch. The roof and railing saved her from some of the hot metal.

*   *   *

Hank started to rush down the stair steps of the porch ahead of Keri so he could stop Steph before she left.

He was almost to the bottom when he heard Keri shriek. He turned in time to see the little dog land. He saw it take a step forward and collapse. He rushed over to help.

Not wanting to move her if she was hurt, he was looking at how the front leg was turned at an unnatural angle away from its body. He knew its leg was broken. He heard Steph running over as he was bending down to check the dog. He started to put out his hand to stop her from moving it when the car exploded and the world shook.

He was knocked down by the force of the explosion. Hank landed on his back a couple of feet from where he was standing.

Hank felt something burning on his chest and pushed himself up. He saw Steph lying on her face bleeding. He didn't stop to think, he just started moving.

*   *   *

Betty was reading a cookbook printed in small print. It was an old book in delicate condition. She was using the printer in the library to enlarge the print on copied pages so she could experiment with a few of the recipes. Steph had shown her how to use it before leaving. Now that she was finished, she decided to go back to the kitchen to see if she had enough ingredients to go ahead and start one of the recipes before Steph returned. There was a cookie recipe she thought would be delicious and she decided to bake them first.

Steph had been distracted before she left. She went out to the car and left her purse on the counter. Betty shook her head remembering. Steph not only forgot her purse, but she forgot her sunglasses. Then she couldn't find her car keys. They searched the counter where Steph always put them down. She had been so upset the night before she wasn't sure where she would have put them. Betty gave Steph her car keys and told her to drive her car. Betty sighed. She was glad she had given the girl a written list for the store. She was not sure Steph would have remembered any of it.

Walking in the hall by the library to the kitchen, Betty heard a loud noise that sounded like an explosion. She turned and hurried to the front door to see what happened. What she saw when she opened the outside front door reminded her of a staged scene in a movie. It couldn't be real.

Betty saw Keri first. She was lying on the porch near the top of the stairs. As Betty came outside, Keri began to sit up. Betty noticed bits of something were scattered all over the porch and steps. As she looked further out, she realized it looked as if her car was on fire. When her conscious mind accepted that was exactly what she was seeing, she ran back into the house for her cell phone. Dialing the emergency number 9-1-1 as she rushed back outside, she told the operator who answered what she heard and saw. When she returned still talking on the phone, she saw Keri had risen and was seated in one of the chairs on the porch. Betty walked over to her.

Keri shook her head weakly as Betty approached talking on her cell phone. Keri was shaken up. Something hurt but she could not focus on the pain. She was frightened for the others. She pointed in the direction where she last saw Hank and Steph, hoping Betty would understand to go and look.

Betty nodded her head at Keri and walked over to see past the porch banister. It took all her strength to hang on to the phone when she looked. After a few failed attempts at trying to find her voice, she told the operator they would need an ambulance. She gripped the phone with both hands to hold it in place as she watched a bloody Hank trying to preform first aid on an unconscious and bleeding Steph. Tears threatened to block her vision. Unable to stop them, she blinked fiercely to clear her vision. After a time she was vaguely aware of hearing sirens in the distance. She was barely aware she still held the cell phone in her hand.

As the sirens became louder, meaning help was getting nearer, she forced herself to turn away from the scene where Hank was fighting for Steph's life. She knew this scene would be what she would see when she closed her eyes for days to come. It was imprinted on her mind. Betty knew she had to turn her back on the scene. There was something she had to do.

Staring at the wall of the porch, she became aware of someone talking in her ear. "Hello? Hello?" The operator was trying to get Betty's attention. Betty had forgotten all about the emergency operator. "I'm so sorry, what did you say?" Betty listened to the operator, nodding her head. Belatedly she remembered the operator could not see her. "Yes, someone's coming... Oh, you want to know who is coming. Well, let me turn and look." Betty turned back toward the front of the house, being sure to avoid looking in Steph's direction. "There's a sheriff's car coming in. Yes, I hear more sirens. Okay, I'm just going to go sit beside my friend." Betty walked over and sat in a chair near Keri.

She looked at Keri who was silently crying. "Keri, are you okay?" Keri nodded her head looking sadly at Betty. Betty reached over and she put her hand on Keri's hand who covered it with her other hand. They drew comfort from each other waiting on someone to come and help.

*   *   *

306

Deputy Austin was in the area when the emergency call came through. As soon as he received the call, he feared for the worst. Calling in his response coordinates, he drove as fast as he could with relative safety on the narrow back roads. He knew it was important he arrive on the scene of the accident and not be an accident himself. Coming down the road, he saw the smoke from the burning car. Hoping it was all that was burning he called in to make sure a fire truck was in route.

As he pulled up closer to the house, he could see the entire scene. To his left was a burning car. In front of him, Hank was kneeling down beside someone lying on the ground. Calling in again, he requested another ambulance; he also verified others were coming. The area was littered with steaming metal and burning debris from the burning car.

Deputy Austin was becoming fond of Steph and the ladies. He felt a healthy respect for Hank and what he had been through. He was not going to find it easy to step back from this and not become emotionally involved. He knew he was good at his job. This was what he did and he would honor them by doing his best. Parking his car over to the side to allow the other emergency vehicles access, he quickly got out of his car.

Opening his trunk, he took out the first aid kit and headed over to Hank and the other person. As he approached, Austin realized it was Stephanotis lying on the ground. He had to look again to recognize the creature licking her face. It was hard to believe the odd looking creature with the matted and tangled fur could possibly be her beautiful sable Shetland sheepdog.

He looked again and realized what made it look odd was the way it was laying, twisted on the ground. Deciding the little dog was hurt, he handed Hank the first aid kit and called in for an emergency veterinarian to come as quickly as possible. Then together they worked on Steph's wounds.

When the ambulance arrived, they had stopped most of the bleeding. Letting the paramedics take over, they stood back and watched.

*   *   *

As she drove down the driveway following an ambulance, Deputy Morris looked over the scene at the house. She saw the ambulance stopped near Deputy Austin. He would continue there so she could be where ever she was needed. Parking the car behind Austin's she removed her first aid kit and headed toward the house. She noticed two people sitting on the porch. As she approached, Deputy Morris saw Keri and Betty sitting together, reassuring each other silently. Seeing Keri's cuts and burns on her face and arms, Deputy Morris moved cautiously toward them. Talking in a quiet and what she hoped was a soothing tone, she began asking questions. She noticed there were no wounds visible on Betty.

Betty was still holding her cell phone and Deputy Morris could hear someone on the line. Gently, Morris placed one hand on Betty's arm to keep her from jerking away. Slowly she reached down and pulled the cell phone out of Betty's hand. Releasing Betty, she stepped back and turned slightly away. Deputy Morris could hear the operator who was trying to get Betty's attention.

"This is Deputy Morris. I am here on the scene with Deputy Austin. We'll take over now. Thanks for the help and staying on with the caller. She's in shock but does not seem hurt. I'm disconnecting the call." Turning off the cell phone, Morris put it back into Betty's hand. Betty instinctively closed her hand over it.

"Keri, Betty. I don't know if you remember me. I'm Deputy Morris. We were just here the other day looking for the little dog." Watching their faces, Morris was relieved to see them reacting to her words.

"Deputy Morris. It's Steph. Is she going to be okay?" Betty was the first to recover. She reached over and patted Keri on the arm. "How silly of me! Of course she'll be okay. Now we have to take care of you, Keri." Betty looked at Deputy Morris for support. "She was lying over by the top of the steps when I came outside. I saw her trying to sit up and I just left her. I knew I had to get help right away." Betty started to cry. "Oh Keri, I should have helped you get up or gotten something for your burns."

Keri, with a distant look on her face, turned and looked at Betty as if seeing her for the first time. "I was okay. I was holding Misti when she jumped from my arms. Steph stopped the car and ran over to her then boom!" Keri just sat and shook her head. Her eyes were seeing something no one else could see.

"Betty, she's in shock. As soon as another ambulance gets here, we'll have them take her too." Deputy Morris turned her head to see the ambulance driving away, hoping Steph was still alive. Turning back, she tried to assess Keri's injuries.

By now the fire truck was on the scene and the fire was being put out. Hearing more sirens arriving, Deputy Morris looked up the drive and back. She was torn between helping Deputy Austin and staying with the women. She didn't see any life threatening injuries on Keri and knew the paramedics would be relieving her.

"Go ahead deputy, I'll stay with Keri until the ambulance people get up here." Betty had noticed the hesitation in the deputy's manner. The paramedics were walking away from Deputy Austin and headed in their direction.

Deputy Morris tried to keep the relief from her voice. "Thank you, Betty. I'll be back in just a jiff. I want to check on Austin. I'll be quick." Deputy Morris turned and headed down to where Austin was standing. Hank sat looking down at the ground, his hand on a furry, dirty creature.

"Austin, how bad is it? Any more injuries? I've got one woman with injuries and the other said she was inside when it happened. Do we need to search for more?"

Deputy Austin heard the other deputy approach. He was watching Hank for any other signs of trauma. Keeping his eyes on Hank, he replied to the other's inquiry. "No, there were just the four of them home according to Hank here. He was playing the hero when I arrived." Shaking his head at the memory, Austin continued. "Stupid idiot! Ripped his shirt into pieces for bandages. He was working on stopping the bleeding on her but bleeding himself when I arrived. Good thing but it cost him." Frowning, he couldn't keep the admiration from his voice. "Idiot probably saved her life." Satisfied Hank was not going to get up again, he looked over at Deputy Morris.

"This guy is refusing treatment of his wounds until the vet comes to take care of the dog. Said the dog's a hero."

Deputy Austin was hoping to get a reaction from Hank as he spoke with the other deputy. Shirtless, the injuries Hank received were visible on his body. It made Austin wince to look at them. He would not force Hank to let the paramedics work on him unless he saw more signs of distress. He would respect his wishes to have the dog tended first. Then he was going to have Hank looked at by the paramedics even if it required handcuffs.

Deputy Morris left the two men and returned to the porch to check the women. She saw Keri being loaded into the ambulance. Betty was standing on the porch watching her friend go. Morris hurried up the steps to Betty. "Betty, she'll be okay. How are you? Can I get you something?"

Betty's cell phone started ringing. She glanced at it but did not answer it. She just kept looking at the ambulance as it drove away.

"Should I call someone for you?" Concern in her voice, Deputy Morris reached out to touch the older woman on the arm.

Betty reacted to the other woman's touch with a slight tremor. Shaking her head, Betty turned to the deputy. "No, thank you. I'll be okay. I guess I'd better get my purse and see about getting to the hospital. Keri wouldn't go until I promised I would find out about Steph and Misti then let her know." Betty walked over to a chair and sat down as if she were suddenly tired.

"Why did this happen? Who would want to hurt Steph? She wouldn't cause harm to anyone." Betty sat there looking at Deputy Morris as if she expected an answer.

"I don't have the answers, but I know we'll find them." Deputy Morris pulled a chair closer to Betty's and sat down. She drew out the notebook she kept handy for taking statements and slowly she flipped it open to a blank page. After jotting down a few notes, she looked up at Betty.

"I'm going to ask you some questions now so we can get started on getting some answers. Is that okay?" Watching Betty nod her head, Deputy Morris prepared herself to begin questioning Betty.

*   *   *

Jenny heard a loud noise but didn't think much of it until George called.

"Jenny, there's black smoke rising over at the Weatherby Farm. I just got a call for volunteer firefighters to stay on alert. They have a truck on the way and will call if more are needed."

"Oh! Give me a few minutes. I want to go along. I'll change the baby quick, grab a bottle and we'll go. Steph may need me."

"I'd rather you'd just stay here. I'll go and let you know what's happening." George tried to keep the anger and fear he was feeling out of his voice. Once again, he had to stop what he was doing and go to the Weatherby Farm and this time someone may be hurt.

"Oh, no you don't! If you're going, I'm going. She's my friend too! If you won't wait, I'll just go myself." Jenny tried to keep her voice from shaking with emotion.

George thought for a moment. He tried to decide if it would be safer for her to go alone or if he took her with him. Quickly he decided. "Okay I'll swing by to get you. I'm on my way. Be out at the car so we can get moving quickly."

"Don't worry. We won't slow you down." Worry and fear gave Jenny the incentive to have the baby changed and the diaper bag packed when George arrived. She knew she had set a new personal record for changing the baby. She was standing beside the car with the doors open to cool it down when George pulled up in his truck.

*   *   *

George and Jenny made their way down the road to the neighboring farm. It was a slow process because of all the extra traffic on the road. People following the sirens were driving by hoping for a look at what was causing all the fuss.

A sheriff's deputy was directing traffic and keeping the cars away from the driveway. Seeing an ambulance drive away, Jenny tried to swallow her tears. She knew someone was hurt. As the traffic moved and they could pull up to the driveway, George rolled his window down to talk with the deputy. Persuading the deputy to check with someone to see if they could come down the drive, they were given permission to enter the property.

*   *   *

"Did you hear the man on the other end of the radio tell the deputy to get us down there? Hank must be okay and causing trouble." George shook his head. He was secretly afraid his friend had been hurt.

Jenny tried to keep herself under control as several horrible images passed through her mind. She didn't trust herself to speak so she merely nodded and gave him a weak smile.

Turning into the drive, they saw a van coming toward them. As the drivers passed each other, George could see clearly who was driving. "Jenny! That was the vet's van leaving. Why would the vet be here?"

"I don't know. Maybe they found Misti." Jenny pushed aside her fears as her curiosity became stronger.

Drawing closer to the house, they saw the fire engine, the water truck and rescue squad. Another ambulance was sitting to one side and deputy sheriff cars were parked haphazardly. George carefully maneuvered around the various vehicles to get to the far side of the house where he could park close but out of the way.

"You go on ahead and I'll bring the baby." Jenny was unstrapping the baby's carrier. "I know you want to check on Hank."

George turned and looked at Jenny, searching her face for any sign she would change her mind. "Are you sure?"

Jenny gave him a weak smile and nodded, hoping he would hurry before he saw she was about to cry. Taking a deep breath, she turned back to her task of gathering up the baby, hoping the flashing lights and noise wouldn't scare him.

George headed straight for an area where he noticed a bunch of deputies were standing with paramedics and volunteer fire fighters. He gambled it would be where he would probably find Hank. As he drew closer he realized he was right.

"I warned you if you didn't go with the paramedics I was going to handcuff you. Are you standing there telling me you don't believe me?" Deputy Austin was in the middle of the group holding out his handcuffs. Hank had a wild look on his face and he was covered with drying blood and cuts.

It was clear to George he arrived just in time.

"I'm not going to the hospital in an ambulance." Hank was trying to find a way out of the crowd. He didn't want to fight Deputy Austin, but he was determined not to get into that ambulance.

George pushed his way through the crowd to stand by Deputy Austin. He looked Hank up and down. "Hank, I should have known. It looks like you've got yourself into a mess again." George shook his head. "Man, you look like hamburger meat. Don't you think you should let these people do their job?"

"It's about time you got here." Deputy Austin heard the radio call and was the one who answered it. "I told them to get you down here as fast as possible. Maybe he'll listen to you."

Hank started to calm down when George arrived. Here was someone who understood, but now it seemed as if his friend was siding against him. "I'm not going to ride in the meat wagon again. I am not going back there."

George started to turn away waving his hand as if saying good-bye.

"Okay, I'll just let the good deputy arrest you and force you to go."

Turning back he looked at Hank to make sure he was listening. "Unless you'll let me take you to the hospital so someone can look at you."

George stood looking Hank in the eye until Hank slowly nodded his head "yes".

"Okay, I'll go get Jenny and the car and we'll take you to the hospital." Hank nodded his head "yes" again and sat down on the ground to wait for George.

Deputy Austin was astonished. "Do you mean you would have gone to the hospital if I would have driven you?"

Hank looked up at him and slowly nodded his head "yes". Hank was feeling the adrenaline rush leaving his body and taking all of his energy with it. He was so worried about Steph and then the brave little dog, that he didn't realize he was hurt. Now the pain was getting stronger. He hated to admit it to even himself but he knew he needed help. He was so dizzy at times he was afraid he was going to pass out. Now he could feel every puncture and tear in his skin. It was getting to be more painful by the minute. Admitting defeat, he knew he would go with George.

*   *   *

George stopped for a moment and talked with the sheriff. He wanted to know what happened and how bad anyone else was. Then he went looking for Jenny.

He found her on the porch with Deputy Morris and Betty. Betty looked as if she had been crying but she was holding the baby and she seemed okay.

"Jenny, we have to take Hank to the hospital. He's been hurt."

Betty saw the last ambulance leave and she assumed Hank was in it. She couldn't keep the panic from her voice. "What do you mean? Didn't he go with the ambulance?" Betty hugged the baby close to her for comfort. She had seen Hank's injuries and knew he needed to be treated. Fear gripped her. She didn't want to be left alone.

Jenny looked from Betty to George and made a decision. "George, you take Hank in his truck and I'll bring Betty and the baby in a few minutes." She saw the panicked look on Betty's face and was not leaving her friend alone.

"Okay, thanks." George left quickly to go bring Hank's truck around from the back of the house.

George didn't want Jenny to know he was relieved she would come later. He would be able to deal with Hank better alone. He had learned from Keri how upset Hank was when Jenny was in the hospital having the baby. George was uncomfortable in a hospital himself. He could only imagine after what Hank had been through, it must be tougher on him.

Bringing the truck to the front of the house, George slowly drove as close as possible to where Hank was sitting. Deputy Austin was standing over him watching him. George was grateful the deputy was close by. It took both of them to help him get to his feet and into the truck. Once they fastened the seat belt on him, Hank just slumped down as if he were exhausted. George drove off, hoping it would not be too late.

*   *   *

Jenny learned what happened from Betty and Deputy Morris. She wanted to get to the hospital as soon as possible but since they left the house so quickly, she wasn't prepared for a long visit away from home. The deputy stayed with Betty and Jenny as they locked up the house.

"Betty, why don't you freshen up and then pack a bag. We'll take your things back to our house. You can stay there with us as long as you'd like. I'll be glad for the company."

"If you're sure it's not a bother. I would feel better not staying here by myself." Betty went up to her room.

Jenny and the deputy stayed in the parlor while Betty changed her clothes.

"Deputy Morris. Thank you for staying with us. What do you think will happen now?" Jenny laid the sleeping baby down in the playpen.

"Well, the sheriff has ordered a deputy to remain at the house tonight. We'll have other cars driving in and out on patrol, checking on the one staying here. It's nice of you to take Mrs. Brown over to your place. That will make things easier on us. We'll keep an eye out."

"I wonder if they'll keep Keri at the hospital. Do you think we should pack a bag for her as well?"

"It wouldn't hurt. I'm no doctor, but she seemed pretty out of it. She had some cuts and burns. They may just keep her overnight for observation, but she may have been hurt when she hit her head and we just didn't know it. She's not as young as she used to be."

Jenny laughed. "Don't let her catch you saying that. She'd probably chase you down just to prove you're wrong." Jenny stood up and looked over at the sleeping baby. "If you'll stay here with the baby, I'll go see if I can help Betty pack some clothes for Keri."

"I'll be glad to. I'll just walk around really quick and check the house again. You can leave whenever you're ready."

Jenny found Betty sitting on her bed in her room. "Are you okay?" Jenny walked in and sat down beside her friend.

Betty looked over at her briefly and then looked down at the floor. "I'm okay. I was just thinking about Steph. That was my car. If I'd been driving it, I would be in the hospital and Steph would be here. She couldn't find her keys so I gave her mine. She was just going to run to the store. Hank said it was okay. She needed to have something to do. Misti didn't just save Steph. She saved me too." Betty looked up at Jenny and grasped Jenny's hands in hers. "Oh, Jenny, what if Misti wouldn't have jumped like that! What if Steph wouldn't have seen her! Steph would have been down the road and would probably be dead!" Betty began squeezing Jenny's hands. "Jenny, why are they doing this? What is the sense of all of this?"

Jenny looked at her friend. At a loss for words, she squeezed her friend's hands in return. "Betty, I don't know what this is all about but I do know that we're going to get through this together. We're going to be here for Steph and we're going to help her get through this." Both women had tears running down their faces.

After a few minutes Betty struggled to pull herself back together. "Then I guess we'd better get going." She hugged Jenny and stood up. "I have a bag packed and I'm ready to go."

Jenny struggled to control her own tears. "I think we need to pack a bag for Keri. She may be at the hospital for a day or two. I'll get a few things for Hank."

"Now why didn't I think of that? She'd never forgive me if we didn't bring her some clean clothes. She'll need a robe and a few things. Let's go get her packed up." Betty started across the hall to Keri's room.

After they packed up the two suitcases, they went down to the parlor.

"Deputy Morris, I want to thank you for everything. It was so reassuring having you here with us. I want to thank you for your help with Keri. You were a comfort to me as well." Betty placed her suitcase by the front door.

"I was glad to help. I just wish we could come here under different circumstances." Deputy Morris watched the older woman.

"I'll remember that. For now, we have to get to the hospital." Betty turned to open the front door then she turned back holding out her hand. "Here's the extra house key I promised the sheriff. I've written down the alarm code too. Tell the deputies to help themselves to anything in the kitchen. I was going to bake some cookies today. We have a cake in the refrigerator that needs to be eaten. Please tell them to eat it."

"We'll stop by my house and get a few supplies for the baby. I left in a hurry and want to be prepared to go to the hospital. It may be a long wait."

Jenny was carrying the baby and her diaper bag. Hank's bag was hanging on her arm. "Betty, are you sure you can manage both suitcases?"

"Yes, I'll be fine. They have wheels." Betty pulled the handles out of the suitcases and headed out onto the porch.

"I'm to wait here until my relief comes. Give my best to Keri and Hank. I'll be thinking about Steph too. I'll give this key to the sheriff myself." Deputy Morris stood at the door and watched as the women carried their loads to the car. She was still standing at the door when the car made its way down the driveway to the road.

Jenny and Betty went to Jenny's house to pack. Jenny intended to be able to stay as long as necessary. She packed anything she thought she might need.

When they were ready to go, Betty laughed at the loaded car. "It looks like we're taking a long trip."

Jenny laughed too hoping that her precautions weren't going to be necessary.

CHAPTER 25

Parking at the hospital, Jenny and Betty went in to find George. Jenny was sure he would know about Keri and Steph.

Betty felt the somber atmosphere of the lobby begin to suffocate her as they walked in. It was unsettling and too quiet. Trying to keep her spirits up, she held herself erect and forced her legs to move step-by-step. The noise from Keri's suitcase as it rolled across the floor seemed to echo from the walls. The closer they drew to the emergency room, the more frightened she became of what they might find.

George was pacing in the ER waiting room when they walked in.

"Finally. What did you do go home and pack the car?" He fought to keep his impatience under control. He had been worried about leaving Jenny alone, afraid something else may have happened.

Jenny shared a secret smile with Betty unaware of what caused George's impatience. "Guilty as charged. You can't just haul a baby around with only one diaper. It could get ugly. How's Hank? What did you find out about Keri and Steph?"

Jenny set the baby carrier down on a chair and sat beside it. Betty sat on the other side. They both looked up at George as if waiting for him to tell a long story.

George just shook his head and pushed a chair over to join them. "Hank is asleep in the ER while they're working on him. He passed out in the truck. I had to get some help to bring him in. He was exhausted. He woke up long enough to tell them his name, where it hurt and that he wasn't going to the hospital. They gave him a shot and he went back to sleep. I had to explain to the doctor about his old injuries. They're trying to get in touch with the doctor who treated him before. Right now they're basically cleaning him up and taking the metal out of him."

George leaned back in his chair. "Keri's going to be admitted and kept overnight. She was in shock and had some bad cuts and burns. They had to dig a couple of pieces of something out of her arm. The nurse is going to let me know when they get her a room so we can go up." George paused and looked at Jenny, hoping she'd sense his discomfort. "She was scared when I saw her and I, um, sort of promised we'd bring the baby to see her." George took a deep breath. He didn't want to be the one to tell them about Steph. Releasing it slowly, he took his time trying to decide the best way to tell them.

"So, what about Steph?" Jenny sensed George's reluctance to tell them and thought she would burst if she had to wait any longer for news of her friend.

"She's in emergency surgery and that's all anyone will tell me since I'm not family." George hung his head in defeat. He tried to explain to the nurse that no, he was not family, but he was close to the family. Yeah he found her frustrating at times, but she was good to Jenny and the baby. He didn't know what to do. He knew Jenny expected him to do something and he failed.

Betty spoke up. "Can I talk with the nurse? Maybe she'll tell me."

Shrugging his shoulders, George pointed to the nurse's station. Betty walked over and talked with the person on duty. She came back slowly shaking her head and sat down.

Betty frowned as she spoke. "She said the sheriff called. They're not to give out Steph's condition to anyone until he gets here. She said he told them he's on his way."

"That doesn't sound good." Jenny fussed with the blanket on the baby. "I hope the air conditioner isn't too cold. I don't want George Henry to get chilled." She sighed. "It's nice to be able to care for someone around here. I feel so helpless just sitting here."

"I'm going to go check on Hank." George rose and walked away, not waiting for an answer. He too felt useless and wanted to be doing. Maybe Hank was awake and needed some company.

George walked into the emergency room assigned to Hank. He found Deputy Austin already in the room. The two men shook hands and both sat down.

"I hope you don't mind, I'm off shift and wanted to check on him."

Nodding his head toward Hank, Deputy Austin went on. "He's quite a guy."

"Yeah, he's a nut." George looked over at his friend trying to keep his thoughts from showing on his face. *That summed Hank up pretty well.*

"Yeah, yeah. Like a Buckeye. Something you have to pick up off the ground, a worthless nut but something you just have to have. Hey, Austin, you don't have to keep me under arrest, I'm already here." Hank was slowly waking up. Because of the pain, he thought at first he was back in the hospital where he was treated for his assault. He worried that the memories of working on the farm were a dream. Then he heard the men talking and remembered what happened.

"So are you awake enough to give a statement?" Deputy Austin couldn't think of anything else to say. He was embarrassed he'd been caught checking on Hank, but he admired him for his courage and his quick action to help Steph.

"Sure, here's my statement. When a guy wakes up and finds that someone's removed his clothes, wouldn't you think it would be some woman he would find in his room, not you two?" Hank hurt like hell, but he wasn't ready to admit it in front of Deputy Austin. He wondered where the nurse was with his pain medication.

George was relieved his friend was trying to be funny. It was a bad attempt, but it was an attempt. Laughing, he stood up. "I think I'll go find a nurse and see if they can give you a shot to shut you up again."

"No!" Hank started to sit up quickly but was too weak and fell back against the pillow. "Err, I mean, sit for a while, I'll be okay."

Hank was embarrassed and shocked at the panic he felt when he thought George was going to leave him. He didn't want to be alone.

George settled back down into the chair. "Okay, but you have to promise not to try to be funny anymore."

Looking at the deputy George winked. "Your joke was a bomb."

"Ugh, that was bad. Maybe I should leave." Deputy Austin wrinkled up his nose in response as if there was a bad smell in the air. He picked up his hat up off his knee where he placed it when he sat down. Waving it in front of his face, he tried hard not to laugh.

"Okay, Okay. I give! We'll leave the jokes for later." Hank put his hands up in surrender.

A nurse walked into the room. "Gentlemen I have to ask you to leave for a few minutes."

"Don't forget to come back." Hank called out to them as they left the room.

George turned and waved good-bye as he left.

Deputy Austin walked with George to where Jenny and Betty waited with the baby.

"Why deputy, what are you doing here?" Jenny saw the men coming and worried something else might have happened.

"Well, I thought I'd come and check on Hank. How's Keri doing?"

Deputy Austin sat down with George and the women.

"Keri has been taken to her room and we're allowed to go visit her in thirty minutes. She'd be delighted to see you if you'd like to wait and go with us deputy." Betty was happy her friend was going to be okay. "She'd like a handsome man to visit."

"Hey, what am I?" George sat up pretending to be insulted.

"You're taken. Keri's looking for a single man." Jenny reached over and swatted George lightly on the arm. Jenny noticed Deputy Austin was blushing.

They talked quietly while waiting to go see Keri. The time flew by quickly. George and Deputy Austin decided to check again on Hank before joining Jenny and Betty in Keri's room.

"Let's stop and get something for her in the gift shop. She may need cheering up." Jenny led the way as they walked into the gift shop.

It was a small shop with mostly baby items in stock. A cheerful man was working as the clerk. After some deliberation, they made a purchase and went up to Keri's room.

Walking onto Keri's floor they were stopped by a nurse. They explained where they were going. She questioned them and then directed them on their way.

Before they arrived at Keri's room, they were stopped three more times.

Knocking at her door, they heard Keri tell them to come in. Jenny and the baby went in first, followed by Betty carrying the gift they had selected.

"Oh, my! Are those for me?" Keri sat up in her bed and laughed. "Oh, it hurts when I laugh.

"We thought you should warn people you were staying over-night." Betty tied the balloons to the end of the bed. "The baby bottle is as close as we could get to a real bottle and the 'new arrival' is so they know you've arrived!"

Jenny set the baby carrier up on a chair for Keri to see the baby.

*   *   *

George and Deputy Austin walked in while the women were still laughing.

"It's nice to hear someone is happy. They sedated Hank before they told him he had to spend the night for observation." George paused remembering Hank's anger when he found out he was going to have to stay. "Austin here offered to handcuff him to the bed. I was able to convince Hank he wouldn't be able to chase the nurses around if he was handcuffed. He settled down when they promised to let him know when Steph was out of surgery." George turned and put a hand on the deputy's shoulder. "The deputy here found out for us. Steph's still in surgery. When she comes out they're going to move her to ICU."

Removing his hand, George went on. "He had the brilliant idea that if they promised to give Hank regular reports on Steph through the night, maybe Hank would settle down. It settled him down alright. That was until he remembered the dog. Then we had to promise to find out about the dog's condition. Since we couldn't tell him, he became so depressed and moody it was nice to have a good reason to leave. We told him we were invited to a party in Keri's room and it was by invitation only."

"I'd better be on my way. I'm ready to get home and get some sleep. I have an early shift tomorrow. I'm so glad you're doing well, Keri. I'll be seeing all of you." Deputy Austin started for the door.

"Thank you for everything deputy." Keri started to cry. "It was so nice of you to care enough to come and see me."

Their thanks and goodbyes followed him out of the room. He went up to the ICU unit to see who was going to stand guard for the night.

CHAPTER 26

Hank was sitting in his room on the medical floor staring at the blank television screen. He was alone with his fears after George and Deputy Austin left him in the ER. Because of the scene he'd made about staying overnight, they sedated him long enough to get him cleaned up and moved. When he woke up, he was in the room he now occupied.

Hank moved the bed up and down trying to find a comfortable position as he let his thoughts wander. It was nice of Jenny and Betty to come with George to check on him before they left. They told him Keri was just down the hall and already asleep.

Hank knew it was wrong to badger George into telling him about Steph. He was grateful the surgery went well. What worried him was her head injury. They didn't know if she would be okay. She was still in recovery and would be moved to the ICU later. It was going to be touch and go but at least he knew where she was and that she was still alive, for now.

George finally heard back from the vet, telling Hank what he learned. Hank was surprised at how extensive Misti's injuries were. Misti had a broken leg and shoulder, was in shock and severely dehydrated. They operated on her leg and shoulder and cleaned her up. They were going to watch her carefully through the night. Her condition was almost as bad as Steph's. The vet was concerned because she didn't react to him when he transported her. He told George it was almost as if she had been drugged.

Hank remembered the strong smell of burned hair. Some of the hot metal had burned her fur in places leaving burns on her skin where it landed. He had been afraid the little dog wasn't going to make it. His heart had wept when he watched her drag herself over so she could lick Steph's face as he tried to help her.

Hank hated being in a hospital again, but he took comfort knowing his previous experiences gave him an intimate knowledge of the routine. Every hospital was the same no matter where he was. The nurses would make their rounds and not be back for a few hours. If he was going to have to be here, he was going to check on Steph himself. He would play the dutiful patient for now.

Hank walked different routes through the hospital when Jenny had the baby. Now he mentally reviewed what he knew about the hospital floor plan as he began to form a plan. Hank tried to wait patiently for the nurse to bring him a pain pill. He hated to admit he was going to need it. The other medications were wearing off and he could feel each welt and cut on his body. He didn't mind the cuts as much as the burns. There would be more scars but these were not the scars of a victim. He was not a victim this time but a bystander. Steph was the victim and Hank was mad. Using the anger to push aside the pain, he tried to concentrate.

He thought back to earlier in the day when he first saw Misti. At the time he wondered why Misti was walking low to the ground, as if she was slinking along. He had been so used to watching her run full out with her head high and her tail wagging. Trying to remember, he realized her posture showed it was difficult for her to walk. Coming out of the bushes, she seemed disoriented. If she had been drugged, as the vet suggested, it would explain the behavior. Hank realized that must have been how she was kept quiet. Hank knew from experience the little dog was quite a barker. She could make a great deal of noise for one little dog.

Thinking about the dog's reaction when they heard Steph start the car, he continued to try to put the pieces together by speaking aloud. "Misti must have recognized the sound of the motor when Steph started the engine. Her behavior was different. She was moving a little faster and headed straight toward the car." Hank moved around in the bed to get more comfortable. He was finding it hard to concentrate so he kept talking. "She let me pick her up but didn't seem to recognize me or Keri. She was relieved but not as happy as she should have been. I hope the sheriff had the Vet run a drug test just to be sure. Man, what if the dog had not taken that dive? Steph would be dead."

Hank was so tired, he felt himself falling into a black pit of emotions. *What would I do without Steph? Why am I thinking this way? It's not as if I love her. Or is it?* Hank was shocked at himself. He spent the next few minutes fighting with himself. He didn't know if he was relieved or angry when his internal struggle was interrupted by the nurse who was bringing him his medicine.

After taking the medicine and wishing the nurse a good night, he pretended to settle down. He knew from experience what each pill was for. He had pushed the sleeping pill into his cheek and swallowed the others. He performed the trick when he was in the hospital for his previous surgeries.

Lying back to wait for the quiet of the night to hide what he intended to do, he explored his feelings of love for Steph. It grieved him because he was an unemployed, broken man. *How could she love someone like me? I knew I was attracted to her, but until tonight, I didn't realize that I love her.* He was determined not to tell anyone. He would be there for her but he wouldn't stand in her way. She could live her life as she wanted and would never have to know he loved her.

Hank felt sure he had nothing to offer her but his love. His body was never going to be the young, strong, healthy body it had once been. He knew it had its limits, but he was getting stronger every day. He was now keenly aware that his body was no longer the unmarked sexy body he had once taken pride in. It was scarred from first the assault and now from the car bomb. He had never thought of himself as vain until now. Now he was ashamed of the scars he had once tried to ignore.

Hank's thoughts kept circling back to the same question. *What woman would want a lover whose body has been mutilated like this?* He gripped the sides of the bed. Feeling the pain in his arm from the IV needle, he forced himself to relax. He needed to appear relaxed and asleep or he wouldn't be able to do what he planned. If the nurse made an unexpected check and he was upset, they would hook him back up to the machines.

Reviewing his plans, he thought of Steph and how she looked the first time he really saw her in the conservatory. *She looked so happy and content. The place was a mess and all she saw was what it had been and what she thought it could be. Maybe someday she'll look at me that way. I'd make her a good husband.* Keeping that thought in his mind and in his heart, he waited patiently until he was ready to carry out his plans.

After he heard the nurse make one more visual check on his room, Hank stood up from the bed. Earlier he practiced how to walk quietly. He had almost forgotten how to walk with an IV stand. It moved silently but was unwieldy to control. There were four drip bags hanging on it, each with a cord that could tangle. He had thought about removing the IV, but he was not sure what would happen. Something told him his body needed the fluids. He knew he had lost enough blood and the doctor was concerned, but it was not enough for him to need plasma. It was just enough to cause him to be light-headed.

Moving out the door and down the hall toward the elevator, he stopped to read a map of the hospital floor plan on the wall. It showed where he was and where the exits were. It also showed the way to ICU. Pleased his memory was accurate he pushed the button for the elevator. Hank stepped over to the side so anyone looking down the hallway would not immediately see him. When the door opened, it caused a slight draft. That reminded him he was going to have to remember to keep the back of his gown closed as he walked. Entering the elevator, he rode up to the ICU floor.

Waiting a moment to gather his courage, he walked off. No one was moving in the hall. There was a sheriff's deputy sitting in a chair by the entrance to the Unit. He hadn't planned on a guard, but was relieved to see him sitting there. Hank stayed near the elevator. He knew there was a guard at the recovery room, why didn't he realize there would be one here too? He tried to shrug it off.

Hank stood still for a moment longer thinking. *I've come this far. I'm not going back until I see Steph for myself.* Drawing on his courage for strength, he started forward quietly. Walking down the hall, he found each step was harder and harder to make. He was getting dizzy, becoming weaker and finding it difficult to stay focused. Using the IV pole as a crutch, he kept walking. Relief washed over him when he realized he knew the deputy sitting there. Hank mentally kicked himself for not recognizing him before. *Whew! I must be more drugged than I thought.*

Deputy Thompson saw Hank coming down the hall. Austin thought he might try to see Steph and warned him. Hank looked almost as bad as he did when he was sitting on the ground back at the house. He was still pale but he was cleaned up and his chest was covered by his hospital gown. Standing up, Thompson walked over to Hank. "Are you supposed to be up walking around?" Reaching out, he stopped Hank from swaying.

"I'm going to see Steph. I heard she was in ICU but they won't tell me anything. I want to see her for myself." Hank pushed away Thompson's hand secretly relieved the other man had steadied him before he fell down. It was embarrassing enough to have to sneak around. Falling flat on his face would have been too much humiliation. Using the IV pole for support, he started moving forward again.

Understanding Hank's determination, Deputy Thompson moved forward. "At least let me help you." Thompson put a steadying arm around Hank. Pausing, he opened the door to the ICU Unit. "She's in the last one on the left."

The ICU was a large semi-circular area. Hank hadn't been on this side of the curtain before. There were glass windowed rooms with beds and most were full of equipment. Some of the equipment hung over the beds, suspended from the ceiling, reminding Hank of a large metal spider. Tubes and wires ran from the instruments to the person on the bed. All of the units were empty but two. There was a man in one unit and Steph was in the other unit.

Hank felt himself sagging as he approached but he moved on, determined to see Steph.

Deputy Thompson waved off the ICU nurse who came rushing over to help. Shaking his head, he put his finger to his lips to signal she needed to be quiet. He helped Hank into Steph's unit. Hank seemed strong enough to stand there on his own, so the deputy went over to explain to the nurse who Hank was. He asked her to get a chair for Hank to sit on.

Hank thought he purged himself of the ghosts that still tried to haunt him, taunting him with the memories of his own experiences. He hoped Steph would not have the same traumatic experiences. He had too many surgeries to try to repair the damage done. Each was painful in itself. He hoped she wouldn't have to endure any more surgeries.

Seeing Steph lying there, machines hooked up to keep her breathing steady and to record her heart beat, Hank felt weak with relief. She was alive. He had been told she was, but a small part of him was afraid she was gone and no one wanted him to know. He worked to control that fear, but as the evening worn on, it had become stronger. It was fear that pushed him to make his plans and gave him the strength to get this far. Now he didn't want to leave. His plan was to check on Steph and then return to his room. He knew now he couldn't leave her.

Reaching out, he took her hand in his. It was cool but still he could feel her lifeblood running through it. He didn't realize he was crying until something wet splashed onto his arm. He was so focused on Steph he didn't understand someone was trying to get him to sit down until a strong hand pushed on his shoulder. An automatic reflex bent his knees and he dropped into the chair, not actually knowing he was doing so.

Hank sat and stared at her face. Unashamed, he allowed the tears to continue to fall until she stirred. Afraid he was causing her discomfort, he released her hand. Steph mumbled something and then said what he took to be his name. She started moving around and the nurse quickly came into the room.

Quietly, glancing down at the man sitting there, the nurse pushed a button, checked a couple of monitors and then left, returning with a syringe. After giving Steph the injection, the nurse left them alone again.

As quietly as possible, she placed a call to the floor she knew Hank should be on. Checking with a supervisor, she received permission to allow Hank to remain in the unit for the night. She, too, sympathized with the man. The deputy had explained about the tragedy that had happened that day and why he was there on guard.

Hank dimly watched the nurse go about her duties and then went back to watching Steph. He wanted to hold her hand again, but was afraid he would disturb her. They had secured the arm on the side of her body where she had been hit in the back by the flying shrapnel from the car. As he gazed upon her face, he relived the memories of that day. He remembered she was struck by a long thin piece of metal. He vividly remembered the fear that overwhelmed him when he saw it.

Hank remembered going over to Misti before the explosion. Steph came from the car to take care of her. Giving them some space, he had stepped away and off to the side, ready to help if Steph called him.

Hank felt the air knocked out of him when he hit the ground, landing on his back by the force of the blast. It took him a couple of minutes to get air into his straining lungs and to breathe. He had gotten up slowly, trying to figure out what had happened. Looking over at Steph, he saw her bleeding with that piece of metal sticking out of her back. She had been knocked forward onto her face.

Hank looked at her face now as she slept. It had been cleaned up and the largest of the cuts had been stitched. He thought about her beautiful hair that was now hidden behind the bandage wrapped around her head.

He tried not to think about the blood that had flowed from the large gash on the back of her head and from the many wounds on her back. He knew he had taken off his shirt and remembered ripping it into bandages. He stopped the bleeding from her head. It was the wound on her shoulder he thought would never stop bleeding. He glanced down at her shoulder and then back at her face.

Hank knew he would never forget the terror he felt when he couldn't get the bleeding to stop. It seemed like he kept pressure on it for hours watching the bright red blood of her life force pool up around the metal. He was afraid to remove it, worried he might cause more damage. He wrapped the remnants of his shirt around it. For a few moments it would stop bleeding and then just as he thought he had won, fresh blood would seep through. He was so relieved when he saw a man's feet walk up and someone handed him a first aid kit. He dug around in it with his free hand until he found gauze, pressing the clean white pads over her wound until they too were red with blood.

Terror gripped him and he fought them off when other hands finally moved in to take over. He was afraid if he let go, he'd lose her. When he understood they were there to help and he finally focused on what Deputy Austin was saying, he no longer had the energy to fight them. Watching them work on Steph and load her onto the gurney, he saw Misti lying very still.

Something inside Hank told him if Steph was going to make it, Misti had to make it too. He crawled over to the dog to reassure her Steph was going to be okay. Looking at the scorched fur, he knew she was in bad shape. Vaguely he remembered fighting off the hands that reached for him, telling them Misti needed help.

That little dog was a hero! Steph didn't know about Misti! Hank straightened up.

"Steph, Misti's going to be okay. I know you can hear me. I want you to know everything is going to be okay. Misti is fine and you are going to be fine too. I love you Steph. I need you. Please don't die on me." Hank found himself crying again but he knew she heard him. He had admitted his love aloud to himself and that was enough for now. He would have to trust for the future. Hank felt the fatigue taking over and he no longer had the strength to fight it.

Hank didn't realize he had fallen asleep sitting beside Steph. He had a vague memory of someone helping him to a bed, telling him he needed to rest and that he would be near Steph. Gratefully, he drifted off into the numbness of sleep.

*　　*　　*

Hank woke up in the ICU unit with a nurse standing over him. He felt panic rise, but it began to subside when he remembered why he was there.

"I have to get you back down to your room. We cleared it for you to only stay last night, so now it's time to get you back down to your floor. Your doctor wants to check you over and make sure you haven't suffered from your adventures."

Hank looked around and was grateful to see someone standing behind a wheelchair. "Thanks for the bed. Is that my ride?" Hank stood up feeling lightheaded. He remembered how exhausting it was for him to walk up here. He wasn't sure he would be able to walk back to his room. The pain meds from last night had worn off. Every movement caused pain. It took all the strength he had to keep it from showing.

The nurse sighed with relief. He wasn't going to fight them. She helped him to the wheelchair and nodded for the orderly to take him away.

Looking up at the nurse, Hank surprised himself when he asked to see Steph one last time. He needed to reassure himself one more time.

Looking in at her, he sighed. He knew she was going to be okay.

"You can take me back to my room now. Thanks for letting me stay."

Hank waved at the nurse as he was wheeled out.

Deputy Thompson was still on duty, looking forward to being relieved. He too, was glad to see Hank going peacefully back to his room.

Hank waved at the deputy as he was pushed by. "Looks like I got caught. At least I've got a ride back."

Deputy Thompson waved back and shook his head. "See you later and I hope in better condition."

"You bet!" Hank relaxed as he was taken back to his room.

When Hank arrived in his room, he found a nurse waiting. After he was examined by the nurse, he was brought breakfast and more pills. He was still eating when Keri walked in.

"I hear you were out causing trouble last night." She was wearing a robe over her hospital gown. She walked over and sat down in the chair by the bed. "So spill it, how is Steph? I can't get anyone to tell me anything. They just say she's in ICU. I heard you went up there and they found you sleeping in one of the beds? Is that true?"

Keri watched Hank waiting on an answer.

Hank knew Keri wouldn't be happy until he told her something, so he decided to tell her the truth. "She's up there and yes, I went up there. Deputy Thompson was on guard so the sheriff is taking precautions. I wouldn't be surprised if he doesn't come and question us today. Steph was resting peacefully when they let me see her this morning. There are several machines hooked up to her. Her face was cut up and she has a few stitches. They cleaned her up pretty well. She had a head wound and they have her head wrapped up in a bandage. One arm is strapped down, I suppose to keep it from irritating her shoulder wound. She looks better this morning than she did last night." Hank sat up and swung his legs over so he could look at Keri better.

"She was awfully pale last night. She had lost too much blood."

Hank paused to get his voice under control so he wouldn't embarrass himself before he went on. "She's strong Keri, she'll be alright. She had a peaceful night. She'll have to take it easy for a while, but she'll be okay." Hank stopped not trusting himself to say any more.

They sat there together in silence, each thinking their own thoughts. It wasn't long before the nurse came looking for Keri. "I saw your note. The doctor is on the floor and he's heading to your room. If you want to go home today, I suggest you be where he can find you."

"Okay." Nodding at the nurse, Keri stood up to leave. "I'll see you later and then we'll go up to see Steph together." Keri patted Hank on the arm and left to go to her room.

Hank stretched back out on the bed and waited for his turn to see the doctor and be released.

*   *   *

George came into the house after feeding the livestock. He found Jenny and Betty sitting at the kitchen table. When he started out that morning, he thought they'd be waiting on him to go to the hospital so he hurried as quickly through the feeding as possible. He needed to shower before they went so he started to walk out toward the stairway.

"I'll only be a few minutes. I just have to shower and change and then we can go." He glanced over his shoulder as he moved to leave the kitchen.

"Don't worry. We're in no hurry," Jenny called back. She didn't even look his way. She just sat with a blank expression on her face.

Sensing something was wrong George turned and moved back into the room. "What's wrong?" Hank had called him asking him to bring clothes. He knew Jenny already had them packed in the car the day before so he readily agreed. Now he wondered if something had happened.

Getting a cup of coffee for himself, George sat down at the table across from Jenny. "What's wrong? Did something happen? Is George Henry okay?"

Betty was staring down at her cup of coffee, not moving or saying a word. She didn't look up when George sat down.

Jenny looked at George and blinked, as if just realizing he was there. "We were talking, trying to understand what happened yesterday. What if Steph had been in the car?" Tears were streaming down Jenny's face. "She'd be dead. It would have been horrible. I called to check on her condition and they said they couldn't give it out. What if something happened and she didn't make it?" Jenny looked at George. "I can't face it. I'm scared. Betty tried to call Keri's room and she didn't get an answer. George, what if Step is dead?"

Relieved Jenny's fears were in vain, George blurted out "Hank called, Steph's still in ICU and Keri is fine. Keri was probably in

334

Hank's room when you called. She went down to check on him. They're both going to be released so they're okay." George gulped down his coffee. Rising from the table to go take his shower, he let his words sink in through the women's grief. "By the way, Hank wants some clean clothes. I hope you packed him some clean underwear. His clothes need to be burned." Grinning at himself, he left the room.

When George came downstairs showered and dressed, Jenny and Betty had the baby ready to go. Relieved Steph was okay, they rushed to get ready.

Once they arrived at the hospital, they went to Hank's room first. Hank was in the shower when they arrived, so leaving George to wait for Hank, Betty and Jenny hurried down to Keri's room.

Knocking on the door, they entered. Betty had brought in Keri's suitcase from the car the night before so she was dressed and waiting.

Betty rushed over to her friend and gave her a hug. "How are you feeling? Did you sleep well?"

Jenny put the baby carrier down and gave Keri a hug too. "Did you have breakfast or do we need to get you something?"

"I'm fine. I had breakfast, and I slept well enough. Hank and I went up to see Steph a little while ago. She's still in ICU and they have a deputy on guard." Keri walked over and ignoring her injuries lifted George Henry out of his carrier. He grinned at her and wiggled around. "My goodness young man, you are getting to be so big." Holding him close, Keri walked back to her chair and sat down. She looked up at Jenny. "He's growing so fast. He's such a happy baby. You're a good mother." Keri played with the baby for a few minutes. "We have to wait for the nurse to bring my discharge papers and then we can go."

The women sat in companionable silence taking comfort in the presence of one another. It wasn't long before they heard a commotion out in the hallway. Walking out, they found Hank arguing with the nurse.

"What do you mean the doctor won't sign the discharge papers? Let me talk to him."

"Hank, keep it down." George was trying to help quiet Hank. He knew the nurse was only doing her job, but he also knew Hank's history and Hank had told him about his adventure the night before. George was glad he was with Hank when the Nurse told him he was not leaving. George had worried that his friend would simply walk out. Instead, Hank had protested, following the nurse out into the hallway trying to get his way.

"I won't keep it down. I want to leave and they say the doctor wants me to stay. What I want to know is why? I'll be fine. I just need to get out of here." Hank was glaring at the nurse.

"My goodness, what is all the noise?" Keri was still holding the baby. As if on cue and sensing trouble, the baby let out a wail.

"There, now you've upset the baby. You need to calm down." George watched as Jenny took the crying infant and walked back into Keri's room. Looking at Hank, he saw Hank struggle to control himself.

"Alright! Please may I talk with the doctor?" Hank sent a pleading look to the nurse, hoping she would at least consent to that.

"If you will let me finish discharging the patients that have been approved for discharge, then I will see what I can do. I need you to return to your room until then." The nurse turned to walk away. She turned back. "And stay there this time!" Then she left.

Hank turned and stomped into his room leaving his friends standing in the hall. George turned toward Betty and Keri. He shrugged his shoulders then followed Hank into his room.

"I guess I'd better be in my room so I can leave." Keri headed back to her room. Betty walked with her, a puzzled look on her face.

They found Jenny sitting on a chair feeding the baby. "So what happened?"

"Hank calmed down and the nurse is going to check with the doctor about getting Hank released." Keri spoke as she walked around making the bed. "If I'm going to have to sit on this again, I want it to be on the outside of the sheets." Laughing she sat on the edge of the bed facing her friends.

Betty moved the other chair in the room over beside Jenny. She too wanted to be comfortable while waiting. They talked about various subjects, carefully avoiding talking about Hank or Steph.

Jenny burped the baby who soon fell asleep. "Why don't you leave the baby here and go on up to see Steph? I can tell you're both worried about her."

"If you want to wait a few more minutes, you can all go." The nurse had walked into the room while they were talking. "I just need to give you these and you can go since we already went over the paperwork. If you'll sign this, we're done."

"What about Hank? Will he be able to go too?" Jenny worried about leaving Hank. She loved him as a brother and was afraid to leave him alone for long.

Sighing, the nurse decided to be honest. "After the stunt he pulled last night, it's no wonder the doctor doesn't want to release him."

Keri hadn't told the other women everything she knew. She had only the details from the night nurse and what Hank was willing to tell her. Biting her tongue to keep quiet, she was hoping one of the others would ask the obvious question.

Jenny was almost afraid to ask but plucked up her courage. "What stunt? What did he do last night?" Jenny remembered the nightmares Hank used to have and worried he started having them again.

Always ready to tell a good story to a willing audience, the nurse told them everything she knew about Hank's adventures. She'd heard different versions from the floor nurse and from the orderly who brought him back. She made sure to tell them she only knew what she heard. She finished her story as she was being buzzed by another patient.

When the nurse left the room, Jenny closed the door. Each of them reacted differently.

Betty was crying remembering how Hank held Steph before they put her in the ambulance.

Jenny was crying touched knowing Hank cared about Steph.

Keri sat there a few minutes watching the other two cry. Giving them time to get control, she walked around the room making sure she was packed and had everything ready to go. Standing by the door she announced, "in case anyone is interested, I'm going to go join the men. They might be planning a jailbreak and I don't want to be left behind this time." Keri walked out laughing.

Betty and Jenny were so astonished they quickly gathered the baby and went to catch up with her.

Keri stopped and waited for them to catch up. Winking at them, she knocked on the door. "Is this the troublemaker's room?" Not waiting for an answer, she walked in. Hank and George were sitting in the chairs. They didn't notice the women, they were both asleep.

Keri turned and looked at the others. "Yep, this is the right room." Their laughter woke up George.

Embarrassed to be caught sleeping, he looked at Jenny. "Why don't you leave the baby with me and go on up to check on Steph? I'll wait here with Hank."

Jenny made sure the sleeping baby was covered to keep out any drafts and placed the carrier on the floor beside George's chair. She leaned over and gave him a kiss good-bye.

Betty had been carrying the diaper bag. She set it beside the carrier. Mimicking Jenny, she leaned over and kissed George on the cheek. "Here's the diaper bag. Thanks"

Keri was feeling left out so she too gave George a kiss on the cheek. "I'll just leave my suitcase over here by the bed."

George was embarrassed by all the attention. "Gee, I feel like a king. Women giving me kisses and placing gifts at my feet."

Jenny laughed. "Well, your Highness remember you're in a hospital; don't snore too loudly."

The women walked out together laughing. Their good humor remained with them until they stepped off the elevator on the ICU floor. The scene that awaited them was not what they expected.

CHAPTER 27

"What do you mean I'm not allowed to see her?" Stanley Wilbur, Jr. was standing in the hall arguing with a deputy sheriff.

"I'm under orders not to allow anyone into the unit. Until the sheriff changes the orders, I am going to follow them." The deputy was holding his ground, standing ready to draw his weapon if necessary.

As the women approached, the nurse opened the door to the main ICU. "Keep it down out here or I'll be calling Security for both of you."

Keri, Jenny and Betty, hurried down the short hall.

"Stanley, it's good of you to come." Keri held out her hand to the young man. Her heart went out to him. He was Steph's lawyer and her friend.

Stanley turned and saw the women standing there. He wanted to check on Steph, but didn't want anyone to know he was there. Stanley didn't want people spreading rumors. He wasn't sure what to say. He'd only phoned once since the break-in after their date. He felt Steph was wrong in letting Hank stay with them. Stanley was embarrassed by his own behavior toward Steph.

Keri took him by the arm and walked toward the deputy. "Deputy, this is Stanley Wilbur, Stephanotis's attorney. I'm Keri, this is Betty and Jenny. We're Steph's friends. I remember meeting you on the Saturday you came to look for little Misti. I'm sorry we have to keep meeting under such unpleasant circumstances. Would it be possible for us to step in and see Steph?"

Keri waited for the stunned deputy to respond.

Thinking it through, he made a decision. "Yes, Mrs. Hall, I remember you and Mrs. Brown from the search that Saturday." Nodding to Jenny, he continued. "I also know Jenny and her husband George. I'm under orders not to let any visitors into the area with the victim until the sheriff clears it."

"Well, that's okay then. We're not visitors, we're friends. We just want to check on her for ourselves and make sure she's okay." Keri was determined to see Steph again. She had been allowed to see her with Hank a few hours before and intended to be allowed in now.

Afraid Keri was about to make a scene, Betty spoke up. "Deputy, would it be alright if you went in with us and we just stood outside the window looking in?" Betty could see through the glass area the floor plan of the unit. They could stand outside her room and look in the window. She wanted to be able to at least see Steph for herself.

Thinking over her suggestion, the deputy relented. "I'll walk in with you to let you see her but only two people at a time. The others are going to have to stay out here until we return."

They agreed to that suggestion. Keri stayed with Jenny while Betty and Stanley went first. He argued he had to get to the office and planned to just pop in to see her.

Keri was curious about Stanley's reasons for coming. She wondered as she waited if he really cared for Steph or if he was just there to check on a client. She hoped it wasn't because he simply found it to be a duty to be performed. A small part of her was pleased when he came back looking a little pale and with a sick expression on his face. Keri had lost respect for the man when he hadn't returned to visit since the break-in.

Betty felt better after seeing Steph. Her last memory of Steph was seeing her covered in blood. Now she was cleaned up and sleeping. She had multiple stitches, besides the obvious injuries, but Betty knew they would heal. Steph was going to be okay.

"Thank you, deputy. Ladies, if you'll excuse me, I must be on my way." Stanley did not wait for a response but headed straight for the elevators clearing his throat as he walked.

"You can all three come in if you promise to be quiet. I hate to leave one of you standing in the hall." The deputy turned and opened the door, holding it for the women to enter.

Keri led the way with Jenny and Betty following close behind her. The deputy stayed with them. After a few minutes he motioned for them to leave.

Once they were out of the unit, they thanked him and walked down the hall. They remained quiet, each contemplating their own thoughts as they waited for the elevator doors to open so they could enter.

When the doors opened, they were surprised to see the sheriff standing in the elevator talking with Hank and George.

Jenny realized there were only the three of them. Watching the men walk off the elevator, she waited until the doors closed and they were all standing together on the same floor. "Aren't you missing someone?"

George looked at Jenny as if he didn't understand what she was talking about.

The blank look on George's face scared Jenny. She grabbed his arm with one hand and shook it. "The baby. Where's my baby?"

"Oh." Bewilderment was evident on George's face. "Deputy Austin is watching him in Hank's room."

"Well, you could've let me know instead of scaring me half to death." Relief and anger mingled in her voice. She released George and took a deep breath shaking her head.

Hank and the sheriff had walked off and were talking with the deputy at the door to the ICU.

George looked in their direction and back at Jenny. "The sheriff said he wanted to talk with all of us somewhere private. He said the doctor called and wants to meet him here. The sheriff knew Hank isn't being discharged. I understand he received a couple of calls about that too." George glanced down the hall again before turning back to Jenny.

"I was going to bring the baby, but Austin was willing to stay with him. He said he'd bring him right up with the bag if he wakes up. Austin sure looked beat. I figured he needed a rest. Now, let's go see what the sheriff wants." George didn't wait for Jenny to respond. He turned and hurried down to join the sheriff and Hank.

When Jenny, Betty and Keri joined them, the deputy led them to the waiting room for the ICU. The deputy returned to his post, closing the door behind him.

"Please sit down. I wanted to talk with all of you together. Over the past few weeks associating with Miss Weatherby, I noticed she considers all of you in high regard. She mentioned once she considers all of you her family. That being said, I talked earlier with Stanley Wilbur, Sr. He said he would accept any decisions you folks make about Miss Weatherby's welfare. He is trying to contact her attorney, Mr. Young, in Boston, who he said is her primary attorney. The doctor called my office and wanted us to call in the next of kin. I figured you folks were it." The sheriff paused and waited for them to absorb what he was saying.

Jenny reached over to George who was sitting next to her and took his hand. George gave it a reassuring squeeze. Betty and Keri reached out to each other. Hank simply sat there watching the others.

"Miss Weatherby has had a few rough times since she moved here." Shaking his head, he went on. "Someone has wanted her to leave since she came. Now they almost killed her. I've asked the state bomb people to step in. I wanted to tell you I've turned it over to them. They have the experience and expertise to handle this case. I want to catch this guy. I don't want him to get away because we didn't handle it right." The sheriff sighed. "I just wanted to tell you folks before someone else did." Looking at each of them, he continued, "It's not that I don't want to handle it, it's that I don't want to mess it up. This is happening on my turf and it shouldn't be. I know my deputies have talked with you and I've read your statements. Is there anything you can think of that might help?" The sheriff paused to give them time to think.

After a few minutes, he turned to Hank. "I know you've been thinking about this. Anything you can come up with will be appreciated. My men think I'm wrong for turning this case over. I figure they can work on the bomb and we'll handle the dog-nabbing. That way we're still part of it and I hope someone will catch this guy." Turning back to the others, he looked at each of them in turn.

There was a knock on the door and the sheriff rose to answer it. He opened it to allow a man dressed in scrubs to enter the room. The sheriff returned with the doctor. Both men took a seat before the sheriff spoke again.

"This is Doctor Andrews. He wanted to talk with us about Steph. It seems there was a slight disturbance here last night and he wants to talk to you about it." The sheriff leaned back and remained quiet, keeping his eye on Hank.

"Thank you for coming to talk with me. I understand Miss Weatherby has no close family. The sheriff has assured me he will abide by any decision you folks make."

Keri could no longer contain herself. "What is it doctor? What's wrong with Steph?"

Hank was having a hard time staying seated. He wanted to get up and pace the room. He wanted to run from it screaming. This must have been how his folks felt when he was in the hospital. As soon as he could, he was going to call and tell them thank you and to apologize for putting them through this. He was scared to hear what the doctor might say. He could no longer meet anyone's eyes, so he stared at his clasped hands resting on the tabletop.

"Well, when Miss Weatherby was first brought in, it was touch and go. She lost a large amount blood and was extremely weak. She had other serious injuries but the metal spike in her shoulder was our worst concern. I was worried going in that she might not make it through the surgery. As you know, she made it and spent a touch and go night in the ICU. I remained in the building last night in case I was needed. She was not responding to our nurses and was fading away. We had called the sheriff here to contact the next of kin when something happened." The doctor paused watching them as his words began to sink in.

"It seems she had a visitor. Someone she did respond to. I don't usually allow guests to remain in the ICU but we made an exception last night. It turned out to be a wise decision. Last night I was prepared to tell you she was dying."

Jenny cried out and leaned into George. Keri and Betty clung to each other. Hank slid further down in the chair.

The doctor cleared his throat. "As I said, I was prepared to tell you that last night. Today it's a different story."

Hank sat up a little straighter so he would be able to hear better. Keri and Betty wiped their eyes and Jenny clung to George.

"Today she's showing signs of improvement. She has a long way to go, but she's going to pull through. We won't know if she has any damage to her brain until we bring her around. The scans all show slight damage. She's going to have a headache for a while. We have to make a decision at this point. This facility is not equipped to handle her medical needs if she has suffered damage to the brain. We are capable of handling her rehabilitation if there's no brain damage. I need a decision from you folks. It may be risky to move her to another facility and I want you to know that going in. However, if she appears to have suffered any trauma we cannot see, we may be endangering her life by not moving her. The choice is this. Do we keep her here at this facility or do we move her to a better-equipped facility? There is a risk either way." Doctor Andrews leaned back in his chair waiting on any questions they may have.

After a few minutes of silence from the others Hank could stand it no longer. "If we say to keep her here, will she stay sedated or will you bring her back?" He remembered the severe pain he had felt when they woke him up after his first surgery. It was unlike any other pain he ever felt.

"If she remains, we'll keep her sedated the next couple of days, then let her come out on her own. If she appears to have a severe reaction to any pain, then we'll sedate her for a longer time, giving her body a chance to heal."

"If you keep her here, will we be able to come and visit her?" Keri wanted to be sure, thinking of the scene with Stanley and the deputy.

"Yes, I'm sure we can arrange that, can't we sheriff? In fact, given the response last night, I would encourage you to come and talk with her." The doctor turned and looked directly at Hank. "Against my better judgment, I am willing to discharge someone, if he will return."

Hank looked at the doctor and slowly nodded his head. Quietly he said "Just don't make me stay here."

"Agreed. The nurses have enough to do and that doesn't include tracking down wayward patients. Now does anyone else have any questions?" The doctor looked around and stood up. "If you have any more questions, I'll be happy to answer them. Otherwise, I need to see to another patient. Let the sheriff know what you decide."

The sheriff rose and walked Doctor Andrews out, giving them time to be alone to talk.

CHAPTER 28

Hank was happy to be out of the hospital. The first thing he did upon returning to the farm was call his parents. His mom cried when he thanked her for staying all those hours at the hospital. He explained about the recent events as gently as he could.

Hank talked to her for a long time, telling her things he wished he had shared before. He told her about Steph and the ladies and let her know why he moved to the Weatherby farm. It was important for her to know he was okay. They talked about the baby and about George and Jenny. He almost told her he was in love with Steph, but he didn't want her burdened with that worry just yet.

Hank made a few other calls. Just when he thought he had something figured out, he ran into a stumbling block. One part of his plan to help Steph was to have a few of his friends bring in their four-legged partners to patrol the farm. If that didn't work out, he knew they were always looking for good homes for the retired police dogs. He wanted to adopt one. It could stay at the farm and protect Steph.

As he made his phone calls he learned there were problems with that idea. The first being, a retired police dog is still a trained police dog. It would not mix well with other pets. He couldn't bring home a dog that might turn aggressive with Misti and possibly hurt her. Not after all she went through to save Steph's life, so Hank discarded that idea.

He tried to have one of his friends come for the weekend and search for any more bombs. Hank discovered they could be fired for coming to his aid and could lose their K-9 partners. Hank reluctantly decided he would have to rely on the state bomb squad. They were better equipped to pursue the bomber.

As he tried to adjust his plan, he found it harder to stay awake. Finally he staggered to bed. Intending only to rest for a few hours, he fell into a deep sleep. He wasn't aware of Keri and Betty taking turns checking on him through the day. He didn't notice the day turned to night.

When he awoke the following day, he was in good spirits. The depression was replaced by optimism. Steph was going to be alright. Hank knew it and he was going to help her get better. First though, he had to spring someone else.

*　　*　　*

Hank pulled up in front of the vet's office. He had called ahead to make an appointment. To understand Misti's condition, he wanted to talk with the veterinarian himself. He needed some specific questions answered in private. Walking in, he noticed an antiseptic fragrance underlying the definite odor of animal. Hank was not looking forward to what he had to do.

Relief flooded through Hank when he saw there was no one in the waiting area. He had no idea why it was so important for him to come see the little dog. Betty and Keri had offered to come along, but he was convinced he needed to come alone. Walking over to the receptionist counter, he told them who he was and the time of his appointment.

The receptionist disappeared and returned with a form for him to sign. He merely glanced down the page before signing.

The receptionist came around the corner and directed him to a room with a wooden bench. Animal prints decorated the walls. Hanging on the back of the door was a sign showing the cost of the various services. Medical instruments were carefully arranged on the cabinet at the back of the room. An examination table was fastened to the wall and there was a door to a hallway at the back of the room.

In through this door walked a man in a white lab coat. He closed the door behind him and stood looking at Hank.

"I'm Dr. Webster. I think we met the day I picked up the Shetland sheepdog. I remember you were in pretty bad shape yourself."

Hank shook hands with the man and grinned. "Yeah, it was a hell of a day. How's Misti?"

Hank was suddenly worried about seeing the little dog. The vet sensed his anxiety.

"I understand you demanded the Sheltie be cared for before you would allow yourself to be looked at. I appreciate your compassion. Not many people would do that. It was a good thing we were called in. The animal was badly injured. I was glad you wanted to talk with me before asking to see the dog. I'll try to answer any questions you have."

Hank began asking the questions that had plagued him. He learned the dog had indeed been drugged. The vet said he was surprised the dog could still walk. The vet described the surgery on the dog's shoulder and leg. He mentioned they cut the fur away to treat the burns and cuts. He explained how much care the dog was going to need over the next few weeks. The vet advised they needed to keep the dog at the clinic so she would receive the necessary care. She would have to be watched and her movements restricted. He told Hank the dog was listless, suffering residual effects from being drugged and in pain.

Listening to what the vet was saying Hank felt sorry for the little dog. He knew how it felt to have to be restricted and isolated from others. He couldn't do a lot for Steph, but he could help her dog.

"I understand what you've been telling me. I also know how it feels to be caged up and not able to go home. I know you're the doctor, but I think she would be better off going with me."

"The dog has to be kept restricted. Taking it home and letting it wander around would be the wrong action to take at this time. Come with me and let me show you. Then you will understand how serious the animal's condition is."

Hank followed the vet through a hallway to a large room. Cages were stacked against two walls. The vet walked across the room to one of the cages. He pointed to the one containing Misti and then he stepped back.

Hank was shocked at the change in the little animal's appearance. The exposed wounds made a sharp contrast to her beautiful sable coat. A cast covered her front leg and shoulder. Fastened to her collar to hold it in place was a large piece of plastic in the shape of a cone. The plastic extended a few inches past the end of her nose, making it hard for Hank to see her. The vet had called it an Elizabethan collar. The widest section of the cone encircled Misti's head preventing her from being able to chew on her cast. The vet had explained the need for the cone but it still shocked Hank to see it. To him she looked like a tiny doll with an oversized lampshade around her head. Trying not to let Misti sense his shock, he walked over to her cage.

The vet watched both the animal and the human closely. He hadn't seen the animal respond to anyone and was surprised to see the little dog recognize Hank. She tried to sit up and turn around in the enclosed area, bumping the cone on the bars of the cage. She wagged her tail and moved her head as if she was happy to see him. Suddenly she barked. During the time she was there, she had simply laid still as if she wanted to die. The vet started to review his reasons for the dog to stay.

Walking over to the enclosed area holding the little dog, Hank put his hand on the wire and started talking softly to her. Misti moved as close to the wire as she could for Hank to touch her. When he turned back to the Vet, he had tears in his eyes.

"If you won't let me take her, may I at least hold her for a little while?"

Seeing the emotions on the other man's face, the vet decided to let him take the little dog home. "I'll bring her back to the examination room for you to hold her. Let me get her out of the cage."

When Hank stepped back to let the vet open the cage, Misti lay down and turned her head as if she'd been abandoned.

Gently the vet lifted the little dog, supporting her leg and head. He followed Hank back to the examination room and placed her on the table. Hank held her there while petting her. When the vet was satisfied the dog was comfortable and secure on the table with Hank, he excused himself.

Hank started talking to Misti as he was petting her. She was wiggling around trying to get to a part of him so she could lick him. He put his hand around her to hold her and then placed the other one palm up so she could lick it. The dog seemed content to just lie there and lick his hand.

After some time, Hank was getting tired of standing. He was still feeling the effects of the previous days. Hank was trying to decide if he should call for the vet when the door opened and a woman came in carrying a box. Behind her came the vet also carrying a box. Confused, Hank struggled to ask what was in the boxes but something told him to remain quiet. The vet placed his box down and then took the box from the technician.

"I've changed my mind. I'm letting you take the dog because she seems genuinely happy to see you. However, you'll have to be sure to care for her. It will not be easy. She'll have to keep the Elizabethan collar on so she won't chew on her cast." Showing Hank the different medicines he had packed for him, he explained the directions and showed him how to mix them and give them to her. He also gave Hank supplements for her food.

Hank was beginning to wonder about taking her home himself if she needed all of this medicine and ointments to take care of her injuries. He stopped wondering when he remembered how the little dog had been hurt. He knew it was the right thing to do but he had to be sure of the vet's decision.

"Why are you letting me take her home? I thought you said it was better for her to stay here?"

"I was certain it would be wrong for you to take her until I saw how she responded to you. All the time she has been here she hasn't responded to anyone. She would just lie still. Animals heal in a way similar to humans. Their state of mind can play an important part in their healing, just like a person's. She was obviously depressed which would slow down any healing, no matter how good the care. She certainly was happy to see you. It was obvious to me you care for her and so I know letting you take her is the right thing to do. However, I want to see her again in three days."

Hank was so relieved his knees began to shake. He was glad he came to get her. Now he just had to get her home.

After leaving Misti with the technician long enough to load the boxes of medicines and supplements into his truck, he carried her out to his truck. He always thought she was light to carry but realized with the collar and the cast, she was a lot heavier. He placed her on the seat and climbed in beside her. He put her as close to him as possible so he could keep her from slipping on the seat. She stayed snuggled against him all the way back to the farm.

Hank called Betty when he was near the farm. He explained the condition Misti was in and asked her to warn Keri. When he pulled up in front of the house, they were waiting on the porch for him. Keri rushed to the door of the truck. She was so happy to see Misti. Carefully, Hank climbed out of the cab of his truck, hoping the dog would not move until he was ready to pick her up.

Keri's gasp of delight at seeing Misti startled the dog and caused her to try to stand up. Hank quickly turned around as soon as his feet were on the ground and reached out to gather her up.

When Misti saw Keri, she was so delighted she started wiggling in Hank's arms. Swinging her head to see better, Misti smacked Hank in the nose with the hard plastic of the cone collar.

Keri and Betty laughed at the sight but Hank had to struggle not to drop Misti as he tried to hold her head.

Trying to walk while carrying the wiggling dog, Hank cautiously took one step at a time up to the porch. Once inside the house, he placed the dog down on the floor in the parlor and plopped into a chair beside her.

Keri gave Misti a treat and sat down talking to her. After she ate the treat, Misti tried to get up and walk to Keri. Hank was watching Misti, who was having a hard time holding up her head with the collar.

"I have to bring in her medicine, food and other stuff the vet gave me. Will you watch her and keep her from moving around. The

Vet said not to let her move on her own too much." Hank stood up as he was talking. He knew Keri would care for the little dog.

"Of course we'll watch her." Keri moved from the chair she was sitting in to sit on the floor beside Misti. She started to tell the little dog about all the events that happened while she was away.

Betty followed Hank out to his truck. "That was a good idea to get Misti. She'll help keep Keri busy for a while. It's time for me to go to the hospital. Can you take me soon?"

Picking up the boxes, Hank followed Betty back into the house. "Let me check something and I'll be ready to go." Hank carried the boxes to the kitchen. Coming back through the house, he disappeared into the library. After a few minutes, he reappeared coming from the conservatory, wearing a large grin on his face. "Let's go, Betty. I don't want to leave Keri alone too long." Hank started to walk out the door. Turning back, he called out "Lock the doors Keri and set the alarm. I have to run a couple of errands so don't expect me back right away." Hank walked with Betty to the truck outside. They walked down the steps in companionable silence, each thinking their own thoughts.

*   *   *

When Hank returned, he had a few surprises for Keri and Misti. Proud of himself for his ingenuity, he carried the first of his parcels inside. He phoned when he was getting near the house so Keri wouldn't be frightened when he drove up.

Hank carried his first surprise into the house and went in search of Keri. He found her in the music room sitting at the sewing machine she had set up in there. Misti was propped up on a pile of fabric. Keri was using some of the old clothes they found to make a quilt and she placed some of them on the floor for Misti to sleep on. Misti tried to get up and move when Hank entered the room.

"It's been harder than I thought to keep her from trying to walk around." Keri stooped over, trying to keep the little dog in one place. She didn't see what Hank was carrying.

"I have a solution for that." Proud of himself, Hank set up the portable playpen he bought. He picked up Misti and put her inside.

Misti seemed to understand this was for her. She moved around and then settled down.

"Why Hank, that was a great idea! It will keep her nearby and safe."

Keri's face lit up. "I'll stitch her up a blanket so she'll have something warm if she gets cool." Keri went to her pile and started selecting fabric to use to make a blanket for Misti.

"I have a few more things to bring in. I'll be right back." Hank left the room and went out to the truck for another surprise he had bought. Carrying it in, he noticed Misti was sound asleep. Hank sighed. He had missed the little dog.

"Keri, I wondered if you would make a thick pad to put in the bottom of this. I think it will make it easier to move her if we wheel her around." Hank set down a child's wagon. It was a red wagon with a deep wooden bed and removable slats on the sides.

"Why, Hank! That's perfect. I'll make a nice soft mattress for it." Keri walked over and inspected the wagon. Lying in the wagon bed, she noticed was something else. Picking it up to examine it, she looked at Hank.

"What's this?"

"That's a sun canopy." He showed her how it fastened to the wagon and spread out.

"Oh! My! That's wonderful! We won't have to worry about her getting too hot if we're outside. That was so thoughtful." Keri gave Hank a hug.

Embarrassed, Hank hugged her back. "I'm going to make a ramp off the porch over the by the conservatory, so we can just wheel her up and down. I'll have to carry her up the stairs at night but we have a place for her to be safe." He walked over and petted the little dog. "I stopped at the pet store and got something for her to wear at night. I'll be back."

Hank brought in a bag of items he had bought at the pet store. "They have these inflatable collars. The vet told me about them. He said he hasn't used them, but we could try it. I got some things to make it easier to give her the medicine she needs. I also got her a couple of soft toys to play with."

Showing Keri all of his purchases, he was feeling pretty pleased with himself.

"You'll make a good father when it's time." Keri looked at Hank. Embarrassed by what she'd blurted out, she quickly looked back at Misti. "Of course, you're still young and have plenty of time for that. Right now I need to get busy." Keri walked over to where Misti slept. She reached down and gave her a pat. "I have to get your mattress and blanket made." Smiling, she got to work.

Hank went to organize Misti's medicines and set up a schedule so he would be sure to give them to her on time. He knew he could ask Keri or Betty to do it, but it gave him pleasure to be responsible for the little dog.

*   *   *

Jenny, Keri and Betty devised a schedule of who would be with Steph. They decided to split the day into three shifts of four hours each.

Jenny and Keri would take turns on the first shift. Betty and Keri would take turns on the second shift. Hank objected to the women being at the hospital in the evening. He argued with them until they agreed to let him and George take turns on the evening shift. The hospital visiting hours were eight to eight and worked well with their plans.

They decided to keep Steph at the same hospital so they could visit her. The doctor wanted someone in the room with her throughout the day. He told them to talk to her so she would hear their voices. He said they could read to her, play recordings of music softly or sing to her. He explained that on some level she would know they were there and she could hear them.

Jenny decided to read a racy romance novel. Keri was going to sew a quilt. Betty would knit sweaters for the baby. They each planned something to do while they were with her. Betty put together snacks and drinks so they wouldn't have to go to the hospital vending machines. Keri made colorful pillows to brighten the room and added a couple of blankets to soften the padded chair. Jenny left the baby with Keri and Betty when it was her shift so she could relax while she was there. Each of them hoped that when they were with her, Steph would wake up.

*　　*　　*

Steph was tired. She knew she should wake up. She was having the strangest dreams. In her reoccurring dream she was in a hospital and people were standing around her talking. She remembered hearing someone crying. She thought it was Hank, but that didn't seem right. It just didn't fit. Why would Hank be crying? It was just a dream. She wanted to go back to sleep but she needed to go into town today. Funny, she couldn't remember why, she just knew it was important. It had something to do with Misti.

As she struggled to become more awake, she was aware of pain slicing through her. It increased every time she inhaled or exhaled. She felt as if she was lying on a sharp knife and every breath drove it deeper and deeper. She struggled to rise off the knife and realized her head felt as if it was four times larger and heavy than she knew it should be. Instinctively, she tried to raise her arm to feel her head. She became frustrated when she couldn't move it. In her frustration she must have moaned because someone was suddenly with her in her bedroom telling her she needed to lay still. She would be able to move soon.

Scared because someone was in her bedroom and she could barely move, Steph started to wiggle to the side of the bed. She had to get up. She was going to fight in any way she could. Suddenly she felt another sharp pain and then she was floating back to sleep again.

Sometimes Steph was vaguely aware of someone talking. She knew the person talking, at least she thought she did, but couldn't remember their name. Their voice was familiar and comforting. They were a comfortable presence in the room. She knew it was someone she trusted. She knew they would not hurt her. She was so tired. Listening to them talk, she decided she was safe. Her arm felt funny, but she was too tired to try to figure out why. Steph decided to go back to sleep. She would figure it out when she was more awake. She was sure someone would tell her. Just before she drifted back to sleep, she felt someone kiss her forehead. She knew it was someone who cared about her. They said they loved her. If only she could remember their name.

Voices and sounds woke her but she couldn't seem to open her eyes. It was too much effort. It was easier to drift on the sounds and just listen. Then she would wonder what was happening around her but she felt as if a weight was holding her down. The hardest time was when she knew she was alone. She longed for the voices that were familiar. Even the gruff male voices were better than nothing but the silence.

CHAPTER 29

The first night was sheer torture for Hank. Driving to the hospital, he was grateful to be alone. He was sweating and nauseous. *I wish I had let Keri or Betty come. I know I'm doing this for Steph but it's harder than I thought it would be.*

His palms were so wet when he reached her room he felt as if he had run them under a faucet and forgot to dry them. He wasn't this nervous visiting Jenny and George Henry. He didn't remember the hospital air being so heavy.

Okay, I've seen her in ICU, what could be worse? Steph had been moved to a private room and the hospital was under orders to keep her condition confidential. When he found the room, he was surprised to see there were flowers there. Someone had sent a basket of flowering plants. *So who sent this if no one is supposed to know about her condition?*

Hank walked over and read the card aloud. "Best Wishes for a speedy recovery, *the Wilbur Law Agency.*" After carefully putting the card back on the forked stick, he walked over to the side of Steph's bed. Looking down at her, he reached out and touched her face. *She never seemed to make up her mind how to wear her hair. Sometimes she'd have it pulled back into a severe knot and other times, she'd let it hang loose and free. I wonder if they had to cut much away to stitch the wound on her head.*

Thinking of how her head had bled before it finally stopped made him nauseous all over again. He found the most comfortable chair and moved it closer to the bed. "This may seem silly, but I'm here to talk to you for the next few hours." Realizing the women expected him to stay for four hours, Hank started to have trouble breathing. "Jenny told me to bring a book to read to you so I won't feel silly sitting here talking." Hank tried to relax. It was hard. He didn't realize how small this room actually was. He picked up the book he'd selected. "I'm not sure what books you like to read, but I'm sure I'm not going to sit here and read a sissy romance book."

"They're not that sissy." Hank jumped.

The male nurse had come in to check on Steph. "I read them all the time. My wife likes me to read to her in bed. She finds them romantic. It's a bonus for me." Shrugging his shoulders, the nurse paused. "It seems to me if women dig it, go for it. Me, I'd rather read a good western." The nurse went about his duties. "If you need me, I put my name up on the board. If she wakes up or shows any signs of waking up, just push the call button. I'll be back later to check on her." The nurse left leaving Hank alone again with Steph.

Hank opened the book to the first page and realized he was shaking. "I guess I'm a little nervous." Taking deep breaths, Hank found he was having trouble breathing. *Is this room getting smaller? Why is my heart beating so fast?* Hank unconsciously put his hand on his chest to feel how fast his heart was racing. He started to worry he was having a heart attack. Then his vision started to blur around the edges. He felt as if he was being pushed and pulled at the same time. He could taste the bile rising in his throat.

Moving as quickly as he could, he went into the adjoining bathroom and threw up. When he could stand up, he splashed cold water on his face. Feeling somewhat better, he returned to the chair.

Hank spent the next couple of hours between the chair and the bathroom, wishing he hadn't promised to come. Every time he returned to the room, he reminded himself why he was there.

Finally, he was so exhausted he fell asleep sitting in the chair. When he woke up, he looked around. *I'm here to be with Steph and look at me, I'm a mess. I hope no one saw me, I'd hate to have Jenny find out I let Steph down.*

Making an effort to salvage what was left of the evening, he dutifully read aloud to Steph. Before he left that night, he leaned over and kissed Steph on her forehead. He told her he loved her and would be back to see her.

She sighed in her sleep. Hearing her respond, he was determined to force himself to come back.

Hank felt better as he drove home. The further away he drove from the hospital, the better he felt. He knew his panic and sickness were real but he felt guilty because he also wanted to be there with Steph. He loved her.

George was to be with Steph the next night since he was going to be in town that afternoon anyway. He was reluctant to promise more of his time. It was getting too close to harvest time and he wanted to make sure his machinery was ready. He had to make plans and preparations to get the most out of this year's harvest. That gave Hank a break of one day before coming back to see Steph.

Hank spent the next two days planning a strategy for his next trip to the hospital. Searching through the boxes of books in the conservatory and the books on the shelves in the library and study, he found some books he knew he would enjoy reading. The book he had taken the first night was just one he had grabbed without thinking. He knew to get past his nerves he would have to be interested in whatever he was reading.

Deciding he would be more relaxed if he was tired, he was determined to spend as much time working outside or on the house as he could. He felt silly talking to a sleeping person. Realizing his discomfort may have increased his anxiety, he decided to practice talking to Misti. Hank told Keri and Betty that Misti needed more fresh air. He put her in her modified wagon and took her with him outside. Misti was shaded by the sun canopy and she wore her inflatable collar.

Slowly, forcing himself to speak, Hank started talking to the little dog as he worked.

*   *   *

Misti was improving in health and Hank was pleased with her progress. When he drove her to the vet for a checkup, Misti rode snuggled up against him.

As Hank entered the waiting area carrying Misti, he noticed a large dog and its owner were waiting to be seen. Hank walked over to the receptionist.

"I'm Hank Dawn bringing Misti back for her checkup."

"Please have a seat and I'll take you back in a few minutes." The receptionist left the area, returning almost immediately.

Hank walked over to an empty chair and sat down. He nodded to the other man sitting in the area. Hank was hoping the other man wouldn't want to talk. He was trying to concentrate on holding Misti. She had been wiggling around since he entered the building.

"Mr. Dawn, you can bring Misti back this way." The vet tech was standing in the doorway.

Hank rose and followed her to an examination room. He placed Misti down on the table, grateful to have something solid for her to rest on.

"Doc will be in shortly. He didn't want you to have Misti sitting out in the waiting area. He has another client and then he'll be in." The vet tech left the room.

"Well girl, it looks like it's you and me again." Hank stood stroking the nervous dog.

"So how is our patient today?" The veterinarian was walking into the room drying his hands on a towel. He stopped and looked at the dog and then at Hank. "I know I treated her, but it's still a shock to look at her. She was in such bad shape. From what I can see now, it looks like I made the right decision letting you take her home." He smiled and walked over to check the dog's progress.

After a physical examination of the dog, the vet looked up and smiled.

"I'm pleased with the way she is healing. She'll need that cast for a while, but her cuts and burns are healing nicely. She'll have some scars, but her hair will eventually grow out again to cover most of them. It'll be a while before she's back to her old self, but I know she's on her way."

Misti wagged her tail at the vet as if to say "Thank you."

"You can take her home. I'd like to see her in a few days. I want to make sure she's not rubbing around the areas of the cast."

"Don't worry, Doc. I'll take good care of her." Hank picked Misti up to leave. "Thanks for everything, Doc. We're glad to have this little lady home."

*   *   *

Hank took Misti with him to work in the barn after returning from the vet's. He found he had to concentrate while talking to her. He learned it was easier to tell her what he was doing than to try to have a conversation.

Hank went to the hospital on his second night so tired he could barely stay awake. He wanted to try out his theory about being less anxious if he were too tired to think.

At the hospital, Hank used what he'd practiced. He told Steph about going to see Misti. He told her about bringing her home. He told her about taking Misti back to the vet's office. He told her about his childhood. He even told her about the dreams he had for his future until his plans were forcibly changed.

*   *   *

As the weeks progressed, Hank found it easier to go to the hospital and be there for the four hours. He also found himself wishing every night this would be the night she would wake up. When he arrived he would kiss Steph on the forehead and tell her he was there. He noticed each time he came that they were slowly disconnecting the machines, allowing her to function more on her own.

He found it relaxing to tell her about what he had done that day. He tried to remember something special and different to tell her about Misti. Before he would leave, he would reward himself by kissing her again. He had changed from kissing her forehead when he left, to kissing her lightly on the lips, keeping it gently and soft. During the drive home, he would imagine what a true kiss would be like.

*   *   *

Hank had finished reading to Steph the dog training manuals he found in the library. Tonight he was going to read a western novel he found at the local bookstore.

When he arrived at the hospital, he greeted Steph in his usual way. He told her she looked peaceful and that he brought a new book to read. Getting comfortable in the chair, Hank began to read.

As he read, he found himself becoming more and more interested in the story. Soon he was no longer reading aloud, having forgotten he was there to read to Steph.

"Why did you stop?"

Hank looked around startled, unsure who had spoken. In fact he wasn't even sure someone had spoken. The sound was a soft, gravely sounding whisper. He looked around thinking a nurse had come in and spoken to him.

Realizing he was alone with Steph, Hank felt his heart begin to race with hope.

Feeling as if the floor was shifting under his feet, he rose and walked over to the bed. Cautiously he leaned down. Steph's eyes were still closed and she was breathing soft and steady. Softly, so he wouldn't embarrass himself if someone came into the room, he whispered. "Did you say something?"

"Yes," she replied softly. "Why did you stop? I enjoyed listening to you. It was relaxing."

Hank was surprised and happy. Steph was awake. Remembering the doctor's instructions, he quickly pushed the button to call the nurse.

"Steph, open your eyes." Hank wanted to see her open them to be sure she was awake and not dreaming. Instinctively he reached out and took her hand in his.

"No"

"Please open your eyes."

Static crackled from the call button. "Can I help you?" The disembodied voice added to the surreal atmosphere. Hank still wasn't sure Steph was awake and not dreaming.

"Go away." Steph's voice was stronger, but it sounded hoarse from lack of use.

"She's awake," was all Hank could manage. He was doing his best to remain calm. He felt as if he was being swept up in a riptide of emotions. He was drowning in panic until Steph squeezed his hand lightly. Hank focused on just holding Steph's hand. He remained quiet, standing there trying to stay afloat.

After what felt like an eternity to Hank, the nurse came in. She saw Hank standing by the bed holding Steph's hand. Looking over at Steph, who was not displaying any signs of being awake, the nurse sighed. She didn't have time for someone who was playing tricks on her. The patient in this room was always asleep during her shift. It took her a few minutes to remember the doctor was to be told the moment the patient started to wake up.

Hank noticed the nurse was just standing in the doorway. Some part of his mind knew this was his lifeline. This was someone who could rescue him from his mental turmoil. As much for himself, as for Steph, he forced himself to turn away from watching Steph. Looking at the nurse he forced out the necessary words. "She's awake."

The rough edge to his words caused the nurse to step closer to the bed as if to be sure the patient was still breathing.

"I said go away." Once more Steph spoke, her voice still gravely, but stronger.

"I'll be right back." Shock caused the nurse to quickly leave the room. She called to her co-worker to contact Doctor Andrews. She returned with the portable blood pressure machine and Steph's chart.

Hank hadn't moved. He continued holding her hand while the nurse examined Steph and documented the time.

Leaning over, she began to ask Steph a few questions. "Do you know who you are? Do you know where you are? Will you open your eyes please? How are you feeling?" The nurse was receiving no response. She began to think the patient was still sleeping.

Steph remained quiet. Hank was so disappointed he began to release her hand.

"Don't go."

"Then answer the nurse and open your eyes."

"It's too bright. It hurts my eyes."

The nurse was so surprised it took her a couple of minutes to move to the light switch and turn the lights down. Nodding at Hank to encourage him, she moved back to stand beside the bed.

"The nurse has turned down the lights so open your eyes."

Slowly, reluctantly, Steph began to open her eyes. Taking her time to allow them to become accustom to the dim light of the room, she finally opened them wide.

"I thought you were a dream. I was afraid you would leave." Steph looked at Hank and smiled.

"I thought I was hearing things. You're awake!" Shocked by how loud he had begun to speak, Hank continued in a softer voice. "Hi. Welcome back." Hank knew he had a foolish grin on his face, but he didn't care. He was so glad to know Steph was going to be okay.

"I heard you but I wasn't sure if it was you. When I opened my eyes to look, it was so bright, it hurt."

"How are you feeling?" The nurse tried to remain patient, but she had to have answers for the doctor when he came. "Are you feeling any pain? Does your head hurt?" Slowly the nurse began to question Steph more.

"I have a headache. I want Hank to go back to reading his book to me. I just want to lie here quietly." Steph tried to lift her arm to push the nurse away. Suddenly realizing she couldn't move it, she burst into tears. "What's wrong with my arm? Why can't I move it? Help me!" She struggled in the bed releasing Hank's hand, trying to jerk open her gown so she could see.

"It's okay. It's strapped to you so your shoulder could heal." Calmly and in a soothing voice the nurse began to explain. "You were injured and to protect your shoulder, your arm is strapped down. Once the doctor arrives, we'll see what we can do to make you more comfortable." The nurse placed her hands on Steph's free hand and gently but firmly moved it back down to her side. Using a more authoritative tone she continued.

"You have to relax and wait. The doctor has been called and he'll be here soon. He'll need to check you out. Please just relax."

The nurse continued to hold Steph's arm down but turned toward Hank. Watching him to be sure he understood, she motioned with her head as she spoke.

"Would you like him to read to you again? I know I would love to have a handsome man sit and read to me. I bet he has a nice voice to listen to."

Hank looked bewildered for a moment and then understanding what the nurse was trying to do, he walked over and picked up the book where he dropped it earlier. "Do you remember where we were? I closed the book and forgot to mark the page."

Steph was beginning to relax. "No, I just remember hearing you talking and then you stopped. Why don't you just start wherever you want? I'll just listen." Steph turned to the nurse. "May I have a drink?"

Quickly, the nurse poured some water into a cup then held it while Steph drank her fill.

Hank pulled the chair as close to the bed as possible and turned pages until he found the page he thought he had last read aloud. Then he began to read to Steph.

Nodding her thanks to Hank, the nurse straightened up and watched for a few minutes. When she was satisfied the patient was calm and the man was going to stay with her, she left the room to make sure the doctor was on his way.

After what felt to be more than an hour, Hank wasn't sure Steph was still listening. She had closed her eyes again and was just lying there. "Steph, do you want me to stop now?"

"No… Yes… No…wait a minute." Cautiously she opened her eyes again to check to be sure the nurse had gone. Looking at him as if to see if he would do as she asked, she paused thinking. Reaching a decision she asked, "Is Misti okay?" Steph started crying. She remembered last seeing her little dog lying on the ground with her leg bent at an odd angle and then nothing. She was afraid the little dog was gone.

"Yeah. She will be, she's a trooper." Relieved he understood why she was crying, Hank reached over and took her hand.

Steph sniffled. "May I have a tissue?" Hank handed her one from the small box of Kleenex from the table across the foot of her bed. Steph blew her nose with one hand and looked at Hank. "Was she badly hurt?"

Choosing his words carefully, Hank explained about the broken leg and shoulder. He told her she was wearing a cast. He explained about the burns and how they were healing. He told her about going to the vet clinic and getting the little dog.

"She's been really good. She has to wear this big collar." Hank stood up and used his hands to demonstrate how it comes from her neck out. "It's a cone shape and fastens to her collar. Of course sometimes she wears a poncho or a smaller, inflatable collar so she can rest." Sitting back down he told her about the playpen and the blanket Keri made for her.

He began to tell Steph how Misti would stay in the child's wagon to be with him outside when he was interrupted by a small group of people including Doctor Andrews coming into the room.

Walking over to Hank, the nurse said softly, "The doctor is here and needs to examine her. If you'll step out for a few minutes, we'll let you know when you can come back in."

Understanding from his own experience, Hank nodded his head to let the nurse know he was willing to leave. "Steph, I'm going to go get a snack, I'll be back in a few minutes."

Steph started to protest, but he was gone before she could form the words she wanted to say.

*   *   *

Hank walked down to the cafeteria. He thought about his parents and all the time they had spent at the hospital with him. Now that he was sitting with Steph, he called them every day. His mother said when the doctor would come to examine him; she knew it would be at least an hour before the nurse would let her return to the room.

Hank glanced at a clock he was passing in the hallway. It wasn't as late as he thought it was. He hadn't thought to check the time when he was in the room. Walking outside, he called George and told him Steph was awake. He told him the doctor was with her now and that he would be going back to the room after a while. Feeling better Hank headed to the cafeteria for a drink and snack.

As Hank approached the cafeteria, he began feeling guilty about not calling Keri and Betty. He knew they'd want to come themselves tonight to see her. Hank felt they should wait until tomorrow. He dialed Betty's number and then Keri's, intending to try to convince them to wait. Frustrated, he gave up when he was only getting busy signals on both their phones. Sending them each a text, he went to the vending machines.

*   *   *

Steph was afraid Hank wasn't coming back. Fear and loneliness settled like a blanket around her. Doctor Andrews told her he was pleased she could answer his questions even though her responses were slow and she kept telling him her head hurt. He explained to her about the injuries she had suffered and the surgery to save her life. She tried to listen patiently but her attention drifted and she had trouble concentrating on what he was saying. She paid more attention when he said she had to undergo minor surgery to remove what he called a feeding port. They showed her the tube going into her chest. He explained it was where they had been feeding her while she slept. He told her they would schedule the surgery tomorrow and she would be on a liquid diet for a few days.

Steph told Doctor Andrews about the pain in her shoulder and that she was uncomfortable. He advised her they would keep her arm strapped down for a few more days and she would be having physical therapy. Vaguely Steph understood it was because of the doctor's skill that she was alive. She tried to force herself to relax and answer his questions. It was so hard for her to think; her throat was parched and dry making it hard to talk. It seemed to take a long time for her mind to think of any questions she wanted to ask. Distracted, she just kept wondering about Hank. It wasn't until after Doctor Andrews had left, that she began to form questions in her mind.

She was tired but not enough to go back to sleep yet. She wanted to be sure Hank would come back. She was afraid if he didn't come back tonight, he would not come back again. She knew it was an irrational fear, but she didn't have enough strength to concentrate on why she was afraid.

*   *   *

Deputy Austin had given Hank his private cell phone number. Austin wanted Hank to let him know if there was anything he could do to help. Hank called the deputy to let him know Steph was awake before he returned to Steph's floor. Calling Austin had cheered Hank up after his disappointment at not being able to talk with Keri or Betty.

Hank was waiting outside the room when the doctor came out. Hank asked the nurse at the desk to let Doctor Andrews know he wanted to speak with him. He forced himself to wait until the doctor approached him.

The two men shook hands. "Doctor, I appreciate this. How is Steph?"

"I only have a couple of minutes." Doctor Andrews stared at Hank for a moment trying to remember where he'd seen him before. He needed to tell the sheriff about the woman's condition before advising any one else. Turning to walk away, he stopped when Hank began to speak again.

"I know you're busy. I just want to make sure she's alright. I want to let the others know if she's going to be okay." Hank stood waiting with a worried expression on his face.

As Hank spoke, Doctor Andrews remembered where he'd met him before. This was the man who had gone to the ICU to see his patient and to whom she had responded. Letting his guard down, Doctor Andrews decided to talk with Hank.

"We'll keep her shoulder secured a few more days. I'm scheduling her to begin physical therapy tomorrow. I want to see how much muscle has been damaged. I can't be sure about any brain damage at this point. There was some confusion during my examination, but that may be some residual shock. She was disoriented. Once she's more alert, we will be able to run some tests."

"Do you have any idea when she can go home?"

"I can't say now. I believe she'll be here for some time. It'll depend on her progress. I have to alert the sheriff's department that she's awake. That's all I can say now." Not wanting to reveal anymore, Doctor Andrews walked away from Hank.

"Thank you Doctor." Hank turned away himself. He started to walk back to Steph's room. Changing his mind, he walked to the elevators.

Hank went to the gift shop and bought Steph a vase filled with flowers. He wanted to cheer her up. Returning with his gift, he found it difficult to enter the room. He stood outside arguing with himself until the nurse walked over.

"Are you okay? Isn't it wonderful? She's still awake and has started asking for you. You'd better go on in." With that, the nurse opened the door for Hank.

Trying his best to look cheerful, Hank entered the room. Steph was sitting up in bed watching the door.

"It's about time. I was beginning to wonder if you'd left. I wouldn't blame you for leaving. I must look a mess from the look on your face."

Hank was ashamed of himself. He was standing there thinking about how beautiful she was with her eyes open. He held up the flowers he had bought so she would be able to see them as he walked over to stand by the bed. "I stopped to get you something to brighten up your room."

"Thank you. They're lovely. I appreciate the flowers, but I'm really glad you're here. I know how hard it must be for you. I remember how you were when Jenny had the baby."

Hank looked down at the floor embarrassed by the memory of being caught raving in the waiting room. Looking up, he let his eyes wander around the room as if seeing it for the first time. "I called George and told him you were awake. I tried to get Keri and Betty on the phone, but their phones were busy. I sent them a text message so they'll know. They've been taking turns coming in the daytime. I know you'll be seeing them tomorrow." Hank heard a noise out in the hall and looked over at the open door.

"Sounds like a party. Don't they know this is a hospital?" Walking over, Hank started to close the door, but at the last minute he looked down the hall. Coming from the elevator were Keri and Betty with Jenny and George. Jenny was carrying the baby, and Betty was carrying the baby carrier. Keri was carrying a basket and George was carrying a box.

Unable to believe what he was seeing, he turned back to Steph. "Brace yourself, you are about to be invaded. The party's coming to see you." Standing out of the way, Hank watched as Keri and Betty raced to the bed. Jenny stood back holding the baby. George set his box down on the floor with a grunt. Scratching sounds were coming from inside the box. Hank quickly closed the door as the nurse headed down the hall toward the room.

Keri and Betty leaned over and they each gave Steph a hug. "Careful, ladies or I'll have to ask you to leave." The nurse entered the room and was making sure the joyous visitors were not getting out of hand.

Stepping back, Keri and Betty started wiping the tears from their eyes.

Jenny walked over to stand beside them. "Welcome back Steph. It's nice to see you awake again." Jenny was now crying too.

George walked over and took the sleeping infant from his wife. "Welcome back Steph. I knew you'd make it."

The nurse seemed satisfied that all was well. She stepped out of the room, closing the door behind her.

*   *   *

Hank was sure he knew the source of the scratching sounds and was worried it would become more than scratching. Walking over to the box, Hank opened the top. As he had suspected, inside with blankets tucked around her was Misti. "Hello girl. So you came to the party too." Carefully he picked up the little dog so he wouldn't bump the cast and cause pain.

Holding Misti, Hank turned to show Steph. "Look, someone else came to the party." Hank walked over beside the bed as Steph reached out her hand.

"Misti, you look so good." Steph started crying as she petted her friend.

Hank looked over at George. They were feeling uncomfortable with the four women crying. "George, I think we should leave the ladies alone for a while." Setting Misti on the bed with Steph, he said to no one in particular. "I need some air. I'll be back in a little while." Heading to the door, Hank only paused long enough to be sure George was going to follow him.

Hank waited in the hall and when George joined him they walked to the elevators.

George had walked out of the room clearing his throat. "Good idea. I could use a drink. If I would've had to spend any more time in there, I think I would've begun to cry myself." As they entered the elevator, George glanced at his friend. "Are you okay?"

"Yeah, I'll be okay. It was getting to be an awfully small room." Hank leaned against the elevator wall. "So why'd you bring Misti?"

George looked at Hank. "To tell you the truth, I didn't know about it. As soon as I told Jenny, she called Keri and Betty. They kept calling back and forth until we got there to pick them up. Keri told Jenny to have me come into the house. They had a few things they wanted to bring. Keri told me to bring the box. I don't like to argue with them. We both know it's easier to just do as they ask. Anyway, I put the box in the back of the car. It wasn't until I was carrying it into the elevator, when the dog shifted and I realized what was in the box. By then it was too late."

Hank and George walked to the cafeteria and bought some sodas. Carrying them back up the elevator, the men were quiet, each deep in thought. When the doors opened, they were both surprised at how quiet it was in the hall.

Quickly they approached Steph's room. "I wonder if they're done crying yet." Hank was hoping they had cried themselves out.

Laughter met them as they opened the door. Jenny was standing beside the bed and Keri and Betty were sitting on the chairs.

With obvious relief on their faces, the men entered the room. "We thought you might be thirsty so we brought some drinks." George handed out the sodas he was carrying, keeping one for himself. Hank did the same.

"So what was so funny?" Hank relaxed now that they weren't crying.

"We were telling Steph about what has happened since she was hurt. We were telling her about the wagon you have for Misti and her playpen." Keri beamed at Hank.

"Oh." Hank cleared his throat to cover his embarrassment. "She needed to be cared for. I was just making it easier to take care of her."

There was a light tap on the door. Someone threw a blanket over Misti who was still on the bed beside Steph. The nurse opened the door. "I hate to cut this party short, but the doctor wants her to have surgery in the morning so I need to begin getting her ready. I'll need you to leave. I'll give you a few minutes to say good-bye then I'll be back."

Murmuring their thanks for the notice, they all turned reluctantly to Steph who merely shrugged as the nurse stepped out.

Jenny put the baby into the carrier and George settled Misti into the box.

"We'll be back in the morning to be with you." Keri leaned over and kissed Steph on the cheek. "I'll see you then." Fighting back tears, she walked over to the door.

They each said good-bye and began leaving the room. Hank waited until the others were out in the hall before he too said good-bye. "I'll stop by sometime tomorrow." He hated being there but now he found himself torn apart leaving her.

"Sleep well." He started to leave the room.

"Don't forget to come back, Hank!" Steph called out. Hank was afraid to turn and look at her. He raised his arm to signal he heard but he kept walking on. It took all of his self-control not to run back to the bed and kiss her good night.

CHAPTER 30

"I can't believe Steph is getting released today." Jenny was sitting at the kitchen table with George having breakfast. "I'm excited to help them bring her home and get her settled." Feeling guilty, Jenny looked over at George. "Are you sure you don't mind going to visit Chris alone?"

George was watching Jenny. He knew she didn't enjoy going to visit Chris with his father as much as he did. They usually spent the whole day talking about old times. He also knew she would go if he asked her to. Sometimes it was hard for him to go, when he had work to get done on the farm, but the man was his father's friend. "No, you stay and take care of Steph. I'm meeting Dad first and we'll go together. Dad wants to take Chris out for lunch as usual so this will work out well. I don't know how long I'll be gone. You know how they are when they get to talking." George chuckled and finished his breakfast.

Chris was a wounded Veteran who lost a leg in the service. He wore a prosthetic leg. Growing up, George thought it was cool for Chris to take his leg off and show it to him.

When George's parents divorced, George's father had no place to live. Chris let him live with him in his apartment for over a year. Once an apartment opened in the building, George's father moved into his own place. George loved Chris like a second father. It had been a kick for him to spend time at "the bachelor pad" as they called it when he went to visit. Chris always had a story to tell. He was a trainer for one of the horse stables in the area before joining the service. After he was wounded, he worked with horses for a while, but couldn't support himself so he went to college and began a new career as an architect. Horse training became a hobby over the years. He still had friends in the business but as he grew older, he lost touch with them.

George loved Chris and enjoyed spending time with him. It was going to the various places he lived over the years that frustrated and embarrassed George.

Chris received a disability pension and was doing well for a while supplementing his income with full-time, then part-time work for an architectural firm. Unfortunately, because of government cutbacks, his pension didn't increase enough to match the rising cost of living. He had invested some money in the stock market, but like many people, he lost it when the recession hit. As Chris became older, he found it hard to keep up with the physically demanding work of being an architect. He had fallen more than once at a job site when he was there to check the progress. Finally the firm could no longer afford the insurance needed to allow him on construction sites. The last firm he worked for laid him off before he could collect his full pension. He was now living off only the disability retirement and a small work pension. Chris was currently in a new place a government social worker found for him and a few other Veterans to live.

Chris always wrote or called George's father to let him know where he was if he moved. Chris looked forward to their visits. George and his father made it a point to visit Chris once a month as often as possible. They would always take Chris out for lunch and spend the afternoon together.

Before she was pregnant, Jenny would join them when she could get the day off from work. George had missed joining his father and Chris for the last two months and was looking forward to seeing his father as well.

*   *   *

George drove down the road hoping this new place was better than the last apartment Chris rented. His old apartment was on the second floor and there was no elevator. Chris had to walk up and down the stairs to go anywhere. George wondered how he was able to carry groceries up the stairs.

George was going to meet his father at a coffee shop south of Columbus and they would go together to see Chris.

As George parked the SUV, he thought about Jenny and how lucky he was. He had driven her SUV as usual for this visit. His father owned a compact car and it was hard for Chris to get in and out. George got out of the car looking up and down the street for his father's car. Not seeing it, he entered the coffee shop to wait and was surprised to see his father sitting at a table.

When George entered, his father looked up and waved. Garth Landsburg was a shorter, slightly smaller version of his son. George walked over and sat down to visit with his father. "Hello Dad. I didn't see your car out front."

"Hi. You're looking good George. I parked in the parking lot out back. They had some room and I thought it'd be safer there. Since we'll be a while, I didn't want to leave it where it would be out on the street. I already talked with the manager, telling him I was leaving it and would be back for it in a couple of hours. He's a good man and said it was okay."

"That's good. Nice to know you're being careful. You're looking pretty good for an old man. How's it goin' Grandpa?" George still found it hard to believe he was a dad and his father was now a grandfather.

Grinning, Garth quickly responded. "So where's my grandbaby? I bet he's growing so fast I won't recognize him."

"Don't worry. Jenny sent a packet with pictures for you to keep. It'd sure make it easier if you had Internet access. You'd get them right away."

"I know, but it's just one more expense that I really can't afford right now. When I get my raise, I'll look into it. I'll have to wait and see. If you're ready to go, we'll need to get going. Chris has moved to a neighborhood I'm not very familiar with. He said it's a boardinghouse run by a woman who's the widow of a Veteran. He said it's different from the last place. He has his own room and there are other Vets living there so he has some company. I have the directions. I wrote him back and told him to expect us around 11:30 a.m. but I'd like to get there earlier."

"Okay, I'm ready whenever you are." George stood up and walked with his father to the SUV. "Better sit up front so you can help me with the directions. Then you can sit in back with Chris."

As they drove down the street, George had a feeling his father was keeping something from him. After they had gone several blocks, George couldn't wait any longer. "What's eating at you, Dad? You seem upset about something."

Garth waited a moment before answering. "It's nothing. I'm okay."

"It must be something since you seem to be upset. What's wrong? Are you sick? What is it?" Concerned, George glanced over at his father looking for any sign of illness he had missed.

"I'm okay. It's Chris who has me worried. Chris's letter had been opened and resealed when I received it. I don't think the post office did it. I asked my mail carrier and he said it has to be stamped if it comes open. They have to stamp that it was damaged. I showed him the envelope and he was sure it wasn't damaged by one of their machines. It was taped shut. I can't imagine why someone would be censoring Chris's mail. That flu knocked me out last month. I've felt guilty about not seeing him before this."

George was surprised. His father wouldn't mention it if he wasn't worried. Maybe something was wrong, George hoped not.

Once they realized they were just a few blocks from the house they were looking for, George slowed down to look around. As he continued driving he saw several of the buildings were boarded up. Graffiti was sprayed on the buildings, fences and sidewalks. Some houses had wooden privacy fences with dogs barking on the other side. There were few cars on the street and many of them were missing parts such as doors, hoods or even tires.

Going even slower, George looked up the street at the building they were approaching. It was in poor condition and one of the lower windows was boarded up. "Dad, is this the place? I can't believe they would let anyone run it as a boardinghouse."

George looked over at his father after he pulled up in front of the building.

"I'm afraid to leave the car, but I'm afraid to let you go in by yourself. Let me go and you stay with the car." As George got out, he turned back. "Lock yourself in and if anyone approaches, honk the horn."

Reluctantly Garth agreed. "I had hoped there wasn't anything to worry about. Now I'm not sure what to think."

With a shrug George stepped out of the car, waiting just long enough to hear the click of the lock before walking toward the house.

George fought down the urge to turn and run as he climbed the broken steps to the front door. Gingerly he tested each board before putting his weight on it. Once he reached the door, he couldn't see a doorbell so he knocked. He continued to knock, hearing someone moving on the other side of the door. It was a heavy metal door with no window or peephole. His knuckles and hands were hardened by physical labor but they were beginning to feel the pain from pounding. He pounded louder and louder. The door opened, a thick chain hung across the opening.

"Who are you and what do you want?" A grimy woman in her late fifty's answered the door. She was wearing a dress that may have once been fashionable and flattering but now it was outdated, wrinkled and stained.

Trying to sound friendly, George smiled at the woman. "My name is George Landsburg. I'm looking for my friend Chris Huckabee. Does he live here?"

"Yes, he lives here, but he can't have any visitors. That's part of the lease. No visitors. I ain't havin' any strangers running around in my home. Go away."

The woman tried to shut the door, but George was not leaving until he saw Chris. His father was right to worry. Now George was worried. Pushing against the door, he heard the chain snap and felt the release of pressure on the door, as it swung free.

The woman scurried away yelling and screaming that she was calling the police. "Go ahead. I'd like them to come." George called behind her.

Pulling his own cell phone out of his pocket, he dialed 911. After explaining the situation to the operator and advising he feared for his friend's life, he asked to have a police car come to the home. George went back to the SUV and told his father what was happening.

When the police didn't show up after ten minutes and there were no sounds of sirens, George went back into the house and started calling for Chris.

Calling out "Chris" and listening for a response, he searched the house, appalled at what he found. The house was filthy. Only one bedroom was clean. It was empty except for a bureau and a bed. The other bedrooms held cots with no sheets or blankets. Many of the rooms had multiple cots lined up in rows; the mixed odor of sweat and urine was overwhelming. George had to keep swallowing hard to prevent the bile from rising in his throat. As he continued to search, he felt his fear crawl up his spine, trying to weigh him down with despair.

Finally, George found Chris on the second floor. He was lying on a cot. His prosthetic leg was missing. He was struggling to sit up; a dazed look in his eyes. His face was covered with a scruffy, gray beard and his gray, coarse hair was long and uncombed. The room smelled of feces and urine. Chris appeared to be drugged. There was an unnatural grey pallor to his skin. He looked at George as if he didn't recognize him at first. Then when he did, the man started to cry.

"Oh, George, I'm so glad you finally came. I tried to let you know where I was. She took my leg and sold it. I've been locked in this room. She's a witch. She cast a spell on me."

The grimy woman had followed George up the stairs. She was standing at the door. "That's a lie. I took the leg away from him to protect him. He tried to run away. Then he tried to hurt one of my boarders with it. I took it away so he couldn't hurt anyone."

They heard the sounds of sirens and the sounds of doors slamming.

"George, George, where are you?" Garth was calling from downstairs.

"Up here. Bring the police with you." George yelled and watched with satisfaction as the woman tried to turn and flee. George reached out and grabbed her before she could go far.

"Let me go! Let me go! Help! Help!" The woman began yelling.

The Police Officer coming up the stairs stopped when he saw George holding onto the arm of the woman.

"Let her go!"

George immediately let her go and put his hands up. "Officer, I want to press charges against that woman. She has abused my friend. We need an ambulance for him."

Chris started moaning and crying. He was so overwhelmed. He was leaving this house.

"Officer my name is George Landsburg. We came to visit Mr. Huckabee and we found him in this state. I demand that you search the property for any other abused men. We were told this is a board-inghouse for Veterans but we found this filthy mess. I wouldn't treat my animals this way."

*   *   *

George and Garth gave statements to the police. They had fol-lowed the ambulance to the hospital. As they sat in the emergency room waiting area they were discussing what they could do to help their friend.

"I'll take him home with me. He'll be able to walk once they get him a leg. He'll enjoy being in the country and I have the horses to take care of."

"You're not being fair to Jenny. She has the baby and you'd be saddling her with more work."

"She'd understand. She wouldn't want him living in a place like that. That woman should be jailed for treating people that way. It's a wonder those men were still alive in the basement. How does she pass government inspections? Why do the social services people let them live like that? It's criminal!"

George was so agitated he began to pace. They had packed what little belongings Chris still owned into a garbage bag and put it in George's SUV.

When they both had calmed down, they went to join Chris in the emergency room. They were pleased to find him alert and waiting.

"Thank you for coming to my rescue. I was sure I was going to die there."

Chris started to cry. "It was as bad as being in combat. She locked me in my room and wouldn't feed me for days. Meals were included in my room and board but I was only allowed to eat if I behaved. What she considered good behavior would change everyday. She took what she could pawn and only left me with memories." He sighed. "At least she couldn't pawn them." He paused as he considered what was to come. "I guess I'll have to find another place to live. There aren't that many places someone like me can live." He sighed again. "I guess that's all I'm good for. To lie in bed and wait to die."

George saw the tears welling up in his father's eyes and knew what he had to do. "No, Chris, you're not going back to that place or any place like it. You're going to come home with me." George turned away before anyone could protest and went looking for the doctor.

When he returned with the doctor, they had reached an agreement.

"Chris, you're going to spend the night here, and I'll come and get you in the morning. You're going to live with Jenny and me on the farm. It's not fancy, but it's clean and you'll have good food to eat."

"I can't do that. You and Jenny are newlyweds and now you have a baby to take care of. You don't need some old war horse like me hanging around getting in your way."

"Okay, look. You have two choices. You can stay in the hospital until the doctor releases you so you can come and live with me. Or you can stay in the hospital tonight and come live with me in the morning. Either way, you're coming home with me. It's up to you."

George had made his decision and he wasn't going to take no for an answer. "The doctor's going to fix you up with a new leg."

"It'll just be temporary until we can get you fitted with a custom leg, but it will be better than crutches. You'll probably need to use a cane for a while, but we'll get you fixed up." The doctor appeared encouraged by George's kindness to the older man.

"I have a friend who works for the VA. I'll give him a call and see if we can get you fixed up by tomorrow." The doctor left to do as he promised.

"At least I was better off than those other guys." Chris leaned back onto the hospital bed. "I could hear them screaming sometimes. I hope you got them out too." He closed his eyes to blot out the memories.

"The police were still searching the place when we left. One of Hank's friends took the call. He was real upset when he saw what was going on in there. He said there's going to be a full investigation. You may have to come back and testify. I told him you'd be at my place so he could contact you there." George paced back and forth. Then he stopped when he realized what time it was. "Are you hungry? Do you want some lunch?"

"I could eat a bite or two."

"Let me check with the doctor, then Dad and I'll go to the cafeteria and bring you up something."

A nurse came into the room. "We have a room open and will be taking Mr. Huckabee up now. If you'd like to give us an hour, we'll have him settled in and cleaned up." She turned to talk to Chris. "Mr. Huckabee, do you have a razor? If not, we can arrange for you to have a shave."

"That would be wonderful. I would love to have a shave. I feel so unclean. Can I have a shower too?"

The nurse smiled. "That can be arranged. We'll take you up and get you cleaned up. Your friends can join you there after we get you settled in. We're moving you to room 412." The nurse began preparing to take Chris up to his room.

As the nurse was working, George decided they should leave. "Dad, why don't we go now and we can bring something up for Chris."

*   *   *

As they walked to the cafeteria, Garth was thoughtful. "George, Chris didn't have many clothes did he? How far away do you think the nearest store is?"

"I saw a mall just down the way when we drove in. What do you have in mind?"

"I think we should go get him a few new things. He should at least have a robe and a razor."

"That's a great idea, Dad! We can grab a bite on the way back. I wasn't looking forward to hospital food."

*   *   *

When George and Garth walked into Chris's room almost two hours later, they found him clean-shaven and showered. He smiled when they walked in.

"Do I smell chicken?" Chris's mouth was already watering.

"Yes. There's also mashed potatoes and gravy, coleslaw and rolls. We brought a variety, not sure what you'd like to eat." George and Garth set the bags of food down on the counter in the corner of the room. They put the other bags they had brought in on the floor for later.

"Let's eat and we'll visit a spell. That's what we planned to do today."

Garth gave Chris a plate loaded with food. Setting it on the rolling table that was over the foot of the bed, he moved the table up so Chris would be able to eat. "Don't eat too fast. We don't want you to be sick."

George helped himself after his father and they sat down in chairs they had moved over by the bed.

The men were quiet as they ate, each absorbed in his own thoughts. When they finished eating, George rose to collect the paper plates.

The men talked awhile about different subjects, none of them ready or willing to discuss the morning's events.

"I might as well tell you things are getting pretty serious with Mrs. Franklin. We've been seeing a lot of each other. I have a date tonight. She's been good for me. I didn't think I would find someone like her. It took a while, but after seeing how happy you and Jenny are, I've decided to rethink getting married." Garth watched to see George's reaction.

George just sat there looking at his father. After a minute or two it seemed to register and George's facial expression changed from one of shock, to surprise then delight. Jumping up, George went over to shake his father's hand and impulsively hugged his father. Embarrassed by his own reaction, George returned to his chair. "Why that's fantastic Dad! She's a nice lady and I like her. Jenny will be pleased to know someone will be looking out for you. She worries about you being alone."

"Don't forget to invite me to the wedding!" Chris too was happy for his friend. It was a good day for him.

George sat back and looked at Chris. He looked more alert. George stood and went to get the other bags they brought in with them. Returning, he placed them on the chair and floor.

"Dad and I went shopping to get you a couple of things. We hope you like them." George began to unpack the shopping bags, laying the purchases on the bed for Chris to inspect.

"We had to guess on some of the sizes and styles, but we can take back whatever doesn't fit." He laid out a robe, slippers, packages of briefs and t-shirts. Reaching into another bag, he laid out some slacks, shirts, socks and pajamas. "We'll have to get you some shoes when we can take you to try them on. Oh, and we got you a razor, deodorant, toothbrush and some other stuff. Dad picked out this neat bag for you to pack it in." George took a duffel bag out of the last bag. "There are a few other things in here we thought you might like." Unzipping it he showed Chris that it contained a package of his favorite candy, a couple of books to read and a pack of playing cards.

Placing the bag beside Chris on the bed, George watched as Chris picked up each item, examining it then placing it beside him; as if afraid it would be taken away.

"We'll do a little more shopping after you leave tomorrow. I'm sure we probably forgot something. Of course, you'll need clothes to wear on the farm. I've got that colt I've been telling you about."

Chris looked up at George with tears in his eyes. "I am so blessed to have friends like you. I won't be any trouble at all, I promise."

"Don't you worry. I know it will all be okay." George leaned over and hugged the older man.

The three men sat and talked for a while longer. George noticed Chris was getting tired. He was yawning and leaning back on the bed; his eyes were half closed.

"Dad, I hate to break this up, but I have to be getting back. Why don't we let Chris relax and get some rest? He can have one of the nurses help him cut the tags off his new duds. I'll come and get him in the morning." George stood up and walked over beside the bed. "Chris, I'll be back in the morning. I don't want to hear any stories about your chasing the nurses down the hall."

As George left the hospital room, his heart was lighter. He was glad they rescued Chris, grateful they hadn't put it off another month.

George took Garth back to the coffee shop to get his car. Then he headed back to the highway and drove south.

CHAPTER 31

As George drove, he tried to think of different ways to tell Jenny about Chris Huckabee. When he thought he had the best wording worked out, he practiced saying it aloud.

As he neared home, doubt began to plague him. Thinking about the conditions they found the man living in, he was determined to help Chris.

George pulled up at the house and sat for a few minutes looking around. Satisfied with what he saw, he allowed himself a sigh of contentment.

Rehearsing his speech once more, George went into the house. He could smell the wonderful aroma of Jenny's cooking as he walked in the back door.

Stopping just inside the door, George said a quiet prayer of thanks. He was grateful he had a job he loved; a wife who returned his love; their precious baby; a home to live in and good food to eat. Giving thanks, he felt at peace, knowing in his heart what he was going to do was right.

*   *   *

Jenny was humming with the music she had playing on the stereo in the next room. She knew George would be home soon and she wanted to have a nice meal ready for him.

She was feeling guilty about not going with George to see Chris. George seemed to understand. She hoped Garth and Chris did.

Jenny had enjoyed going to the hospital with Keri and Betty to get Steph. Betty had made homemade cinnamon rolls for the floor staff. Hank watched the baby and Misti at home letting the women go alone. He seemed relieved to see them when they came home. Jenny smiled at the thought. She was still hoping Hank and Steph would fall in love so Hank would stay on the farm.

Once Steph was settled, Jenny and the baby came home. Jenny had work to do and she wanted to try one of Betty's recipes. Now she had breadsticks in the oven to go with the lasagna she made.

As she turned from the oven after checking the breadsticks, she was startled to see George standing in the doorway.

"Oh George! You scared me." Jenny put her hand over her rapidly beating heart. "I didn't hear you come in." On weak legs she walked over and gave him a welcome home kiss.

"How's your Dad?"

"Fine. He's got a date again tonight. It may be getting serious."

"Good for him." Jenny smiled. "Sit down, dinner's almost ready."

Jenny and George enjoyed their meal. Jenny was happy and content. Steph was home and doing okay. The baby was healthy and happy. George had a nice crop growing in the fields. Everything was as it should be.

As they lingered at the table, George struggled with how to tell Jenny about Chris. He'd been evading her questions about him all through dinner.

"I have to talk with you about Chris." George paused for a moment trying to remember the speech he prepared and practiced on the way home.

"We found him in a bad place. The woman had taken away his leg. She pawned it and most of his stuff. He was weak and filthy when I found him. We called the police and they took him away in an ambulance." George looked at Jenny as he was speaking, hoping she understood what he was saying.

"He'll spend the night in the hospital." George sighed. He looked away from Jenny for a moment to gather his courage and then he looked at her again.

"I can't leave him there. I told him I would come back in the morning and get him. I told him he would be living with us."

George stopped talking, waiting for Jenny's reaction.

Jenny just sat there for a few minutes. Her face was a mask hiding her emotions. She remained still and silent. When she moved, she simply stood up and began to clear off the table, carrying the dishes to the sink. Returning to the table, she didn't sit back down; she simply said "I have to check on the baby" and left the room.

George was confused. He didn't know if he should be relieved or if he should be afraid. Jenny was usually a tolerant person. She had tolerated Hank when he lived there. She had even been glad for the company. But Hank was able to help take care of himself and help with small things. He would drive her places and help with the groceries. Chris would try, but he was slower and he was older.

George didn't know how long he sat at the table waiting for Jenny to come back. He'd been trying to think of different ways he could have handled this. He could spend days trying to find him a place to live, but that would mean time away from the farm. He could just rent an apartment for him, but that would mean spending more money than they had right now.

George knew they had some money in the bank, but he also knew that it had to last them as long as possible. George took a deep breath and decided he'd better go look for Jenny.

He found her in the nursery rocking the sleeping baby. Tears had created streaks in her makeup and her mascara was smeared in the corners of her eyes. She was so intent on looking at the sleeping baby in her arms that George wasn't sure she heard him walk in. He sat down in the other chair in the room and waited.

The only sound in the room was the creak from the wooden rocker as it moved back and forth over the floor of the nursery. Jenny didn't look at George but he couldn't take his eyes off the site of his beloved wife holding their precious child. George wished in his heart the moment would last forever. His heart was full of love and thankfulness.

With the sun setting outside, the room began to grow darker. Before it was too dark to see, Jenny stood and placed the baby back into the crib. She walked past George and patted him on the arm as she left the room.

George rose and followed her back downstairs to the kitchen. Jenny put their dishes into the dishwasher and then sat down at the table across from where George was sitting.

George waited patiently for Jenny to speak. *Right or wrong, what is done is done. I'll have to accept what is to come.*

"George," Jenny hesitated. She wasn't sure what to say but knew she had to say something. "I know you have a good heart. You're a good man and I love you for it. It would have been nice to be a part of this decision. It will mean changes around here. You said he doesn't have both legs. We'll have to move furniture around so he can use a wheelchair. We don't have a downstairs bedroom. I could move my things out of the sewing room, but I was working on clothes for the baby. Where are we going to put him?" Jenny stopped herself before she became more upset.

As Jenny took a few slow calming breaths, George spoke up.

"I know I said he didn't have his leg when we found him. The doctor is getting him a temporary leg while he waits on a new one. The doctor has a friend who works at the VA and they are going to take care of it. He'll be walking around fine. He can have the gues-troom upstairs."

Jenny studied George's face for a few minutes. "What about his things and his furniture? He needs a place to put his things. Will that be enough room?"

"The woman running the place pawned most of it. All he has left is in a garbage bag in the back of the SUV. We had to buy him clothes to have at the hospital. I'll take him shopping before we come home so he'll have more. I have to get him new shoes too."

"Why couldn't your Dad take him? What is he going to do around here?"

"Dad's on a fixed budget himself right now. He's hoping for a raise so he can afford to get luxuries like Internet access. He has enough to do to take care of himself. Chris knows horses. He can help me with them. Maybe Steph or Keri or Betty would have something for him to do. He can go with you over there sometimes. He won't come if he thinks he'll be a burden."

Leaning across the table George reached for Jenny's hand. "Honey, I couldn't leave him. He could wind up in another place like that or worse. He's a good man and he was good to my Dad. I need to do this."

Jenny sniffled. "I know it's just that it's been nice having just you and the baby around. I know it's selfish of me. I understand you feel responsible for Chris. I'll give it a try, but promise me you'll find another place for him if it doesn't work out. Will you do that?"

George would have promised the world to Jenny, but he was a man of his word and he didn't give it freely. "I promise you Jenny that if things don't work out, I'll find a new home for Chris. But I want you to try."

"I'll try to make things work." Rising, Jenny walked over to the counter. "I'll have the room ready when you get home tomorrow."

*   *   *

George woke up early the next day. Hank was coming over to help with the chores. George wanted to leave as soon as possible so he would be at the hospital when Chris was released.

Jenny's reluctance to have Chris move in nagged at George's conscience as he drove to the hospital. He knew Jenny would have more work to do but Chris needed a place to live. George had put off talking to Steph about the colt. He knew it had great confirmation. If Chris could train him as a show horse, George knew Jenny would understand Chris was needed.

When George arrived at the hospital he found his father already waiting with Chris.

"I thought I'd bring Chris breakfast while we waited for you. Would you like a doughnut?" Garth pointed to the counter across the room.

George eyed the box of doughnuts sitting on the counter and the discards in the trash container of a fast-food breakfast. "No thanks, maybe later." He turned to look at Chris. Something was different. "So how are you feeling today?"

"I'm doing great. They measured me for a new leg and look," Chris threw aside the blanket that was across his legs. "I have a great replacement."

"It looks just like your old one. How did they get one so fast?"

Garth tried not to laugh as he watched the by play between the two men.

"That's because it's mine. The police found it in a closet when they searched the house. A police officer brought it for me to iden-tify. He took my statement and said they'd let me know if they find any of my other stuff. I had to give him a list of what was taken. My mind is not what it used to be. It was hard to remember everything she took."

"So when will you be released?" George was getting eager to go. He still had to take Chris shopping. George preferred to go when the stores first opened so they wouldn't be crowded.

"I don't know. The nurse said she was going to get the paper-work started."

"When Jenny and the baby were supposed to be released, it took two hours for just the paperwork. I hope this place doesn't take that long."

Chris pulled out the deck of cards they had given him. He waved his hand so the others could see what he was holding. With a twinkle in his eye, he asked, "How about a game of cards while we wait?"

George looked over at his father. It had been a long time since the three of them had played cards together. Grinning he turned back to Chris. "You're on!"

When the nurse came in with the wheelchair to tell Chris he was ready to go, she found the three men immersed in a lively game of poker. It took a few minutes for her to get their attention.

*   *   *

It was late afternoon when George and Chris arrived home. Chris had never been to the farm and didn't know what to expect.

As they drove up the road to turn into the driveway, George became nervous and edgy. He was worried his friend would be disappointed in the farm. His fears vanished when he turned and looked at the home he was bringing Chris to.

Jenny's flowers were in bloom and Hank must have mowed the lawn. Everything looked neat and tidy. George felt a small thrill of pride as he saw the home he and Jenny had made.

"What a lovely home." Chris couldn't keep the envy from his voice. "Are you sure it's okay with Jenny for me to come and live here?" Chris blinked back tears, turning his face away so George wouldn't notice.

"Of course, it's okay." George glanced over at Chris as he parked the SUV at the back of the house. They both sat for a moment after the engine was turned off. "Listen, Chris, I know I practically forced you to come but I want you to know that you're not just a guest. You're part of the family and this is your new home. Since you're family, if you don't like living here with us, you just say so and we'll find you somewhere else to live. I just want you to be happy and safe."

George climbed out of the SUV and went to the back to get Chris's bags and packages.

Chris climbed out slowly. He was stiff from the ride and apprehensive about his future.

"Help me get these things and we'll get you settled in. Then I'll show you around some." George left a few lighter bags for Chris to carry.

"I'll have to show you how to work our security system too. Remember I told you we had Hank install one in the house and I have a camera set up in the barn." George walked to the back door of the house. "We'll go in and I'll take your things on upstairs."

The aroma of bread baking and fresh baked apple-pie greeted them as they entered the house. The golden brown, lattice crusted pie was cooling on the table in the kitchen. Walking into the kitchen, both men inhaled deeply.

Chris sighed. "I haven't smelled anything like that in years. It's enough to make a man think he's died and gone to heaven."

"Jenny's a great cook! She'll have some meat on your skinny bones in no time." George didn't bother to hide the pride in his voice.

"Welcome home!" Jenny came into the kitchen carrying the baby.

"Look someone woke up in time for you to come home." Jenny held out the baby for Chris to see him.

"My goodness, he's getting to be a handsome lad."

Jenny was pleased with the compliment. Kissing Chris on the cheek, she moved over to kiss George. "If I'd have known you were doing some shopping, I would've given you my list."

George laughed. Jenny knew he hated to go shopping for clothes. "I'll take these things up to Chris's room. Can you show him around so he can find his way? I want to take him out to the barn and show him the horses later."

Jenny laughed back. She had a surprise for George. "Sure I'll show him around and then we'll be up. Come on Chris, I'll give you a tour."

George carried the bags up to the spare room that would now be Chris's room. When he left in the morning, he had assumed Jenny would wash the bed sheets and clean up the bathroom. Opening the door, he was surprised at the transformation.

The beige walls looked fresh and clean. There were new curtains on the window, new throw rugs and a matching bedspread and sheets. The bathroom had new towels and a new shower curtain. A wing back chair was grouped with a small table near the window. A floor lamp stood next to the chair within easy reach. Checking to see what else she had done, he opened the closet. It had new hangers just waiting for clothes to be hung and a full-length mirror had been attached to the closet door.

Jenny was excited to see how the men liked the room. She stood near the doorway as Chris went into the room.

Chris turned back to Jenny. "Are you sure this is my room? This must be your room. It's too nice."

"I had some friends come and help me. We got you some new things too. I wanted to make it special for you so you'd feel at home. I had Hank put a mirror on the closet door for you. Hank even installed a couple of grab bars and a new showerhead in the bath."

Jenny giggled before continuing. "I left the baby with Betty while Keri and I went shopping. Hank surprised me by mowing the lawn. We had such a good time fixing the room up, I hope you like the colors." Jenny had selected blue as the main color, using different shades and hues in the bedroom and the adjoining bathroom.

"There are more towels in the bathroom cabinet and extra blankets in the bottom drawer of the bureau. If you need anything else just ask." She walked over and gave Chris a hug. "Welcome to our home, Chris. It's your home now so just relax. I have to go get the bread out of the oven. It's probably ready. I'll have dinner ready in half an hour so take your time. The baby and I will be in the kitchen." Jenny had heard the oven timer going off and she headed to the kitchen to check the bread.

George was uncomfortable just leaving Chris there so he tried to think of what he could do to make the other man feel more comfortable. "Do you need help putting your things away? If you need anything washed, just speak up. Jenny usually does a load or two of wash every day. She says that between my clothes and the baby's, she always has dirty clothes."

"I think I can handle it. I may need something to remove the tags. Could you spare a pair of scissors?"

"I'll go get them. I left your other bag in the car. I'll go get it and have Jenny wash your things. You'll want them washed after being in the other house."

George left the room and returned with a pair of scissors. Then he left to go get the other bag of items.

Going through the kitchen, George stopped once more to inhale deeply the wonderful aromas.

"Jenny, you didn't have to go to all this trouble. Fixing up the room was more than enough. You're a wonder."

Jenny was sitting in the corner of the room feeding George Henry. Looking up with mirth in her eyes, she started laughing. "I'm not that good or that much of a saint. Hank told Steph, Keri and Betty about Chris coming after you called him last night. Keri got all excited about getting the room ready. She's been dying to redecorate over at Steph's and had great ideas for the room. She and Betty came over soon after you left and they scrubbed the room down. Keri and I went shopping while Hank mowed the lawn. We had a good time going to different stores, picking out what we needed. Betty made the pie and the bread so all I had to do was bake them."

Jenny paused to get her breath. "Oh, George! It was like being caught up in a whirlwind. It was so much fun." Jenny laughed at the memory.

Shaking her head, she laughed again. "Keri and Betty both said the best way to welcome a man home was to have a fresh made pie and a clean bed. I hope it worked."

George grinned back. "It worked for me. I really appreciate everything you've done. I've got a bag of things out in the SUV yet to bring in. It's the stuff that was left at the other place. It's probably all going to need cleaned up. I'll just put it in the laundry room."

"As soon as the baby is done, I'll get the rest of the meal ready so we can eat. Then you can take Chris out to the barn and show him the horses." Jenny leaned back into the chair, smiling with pleasure knowing George was pleased.

CHAPTER 32

Hank walked into the barn on George's farm, knowing he would find his friend somewhere around there working. It was after dinner and George would check the barn to be sure the horses were secure. He liked to brush Sun Dancer or the colt at night. He told Hank he found it soothing.

Walking through the barn, Hank looked into the stalls until he saw a pair of human legs clad in denim. Stopping at the stall door, he leaned against the door.

"Evening, George. I see you made it back okay. I need to talk with you."

George saw Hank walk into the barn and quietly followed him inside.

"Okay, what's up?"

Hank jumped. He hadn't expected to hear George's voice behind him.

"What's the matter with you?" George laughed at his friend's behavior. "Spooked you, didn't I?"

Chris came from behind the horse to see who was there.

Hank looked from Chris to George. "I thought you were in the stall. Hi, Chris. It's been a long time. Remember me?" Hank held out his hand and the two men shook hands.

"You're Hank, the friend of George's who used to come by once in and while."

"I see he's already putting you to work." Hank turned to watch George as he kept talking. "It's not as if he doesn't have enough slave labor around already."

George looked uncomfortable. Seeing George's reaction, Hank began to laugh. "I tell you Chris, when I first arrived, I was a mess." Hank walked over to stand beside George. He put his arm around his friend's shoulder. "I don't know how he and Jenny put up with me." Dropping his arm he moved away as he continued. "Look at me now. I'm getting better and soon I'll be all grown up."

"Nope, you'll never grow up." George almost regretted the words as soon as they were spoken.

Hank just laughed. "Sounds good to me! I'll leave being grown up to George here. See Chris, George lives with one lady. Don't get me wrong, Jenny's wonderful. But me, I'm living with three lovely ladies. They can't seem to get enough of me. They feed me, they clean my clothes and they even find things for me to do."

Hank decided it was time to talk about why he was there so he turned and walked over to the nearest tack box settling down on top of it.

"Even tonight they found something for me to do. I don't know why they couldn't call Jenny. They talk on the phone all the time. But no, they had to send me. I had to come down here and do this in person."

George pulled up a couple of battered stools for Chris and himself. Sitting down, he decided Hank was going to take all night if he didn't hurry him along. "Do what?"

"This." Hank paused trying to create a more dramatic effect. "Tomorrow night, you, Chris, Jenny and the baby are invited over for dinner. I'm supposed to ask if you'll need my help so you can come. They were afraid you'll say you don't have time."

Hank let the invitation sink in before he continued. Hank looked Chris up and down. "You see, my ladies are single and they heard another stud was in the area. They want to meet you." Hank winked at Chris.

"Jenny said it was okay with her, but she wasn't sure about you two. She told Keri she would have to ask you and let them know.

Keri didn't want to wait so she pestered me until I promised to come and ask. I figured it was the safest thing to do."

Hank started to get up then sat back down. "Two more things before I go. Betty wants to know what Chris would like for dessert and Steph wants to know what he thinks of Sun Dancer and the other horses."

Hank looked expectantly at Chris who was standing in the stall doorway.

"I'm not fussy about dessert. I'll be happy with anything. Jenny had the best apple pie for us tonight. She said it was made from scratch. I don't think I've ever tasted better." Chris was overwhelmed; emotions clogged his throat, stopping him from saying more.

"Not good enough. Do you like homemade ice cream? Cake? Pie? You have to be partial to something. I have to tell her something." Hank looked at George for support.

"Hank's right." George turned to look at Chris. "They'll want to make you something special. These ladies can cook anything. You say you like it and they make it. Do you still like pineapple upside down cake?"

"Oh. I haven't had that in years." Chris leaned on the stool next to George. "I'd forgotten all about old Mrs. Street. She'd bake pineapple upside down cake for her grandson when he would come to visit and she'd bring some over for us bachelors. She said she never learned to make a small one and would have too much leftover. He'd come once a month and spend the day. She passed away while you were in college, George."

"Pineapple upside down cake it is. I'll tell Betty. She'll be pleased. Now for Steph, what do you think of the big guy?" Hank looked over at Sun Dancer's stall.

Chris turned to look in the same direction. "Sun Dancer is a right smart horse. He's sired some beauties. I like the looks of the colt. I think he'd be a good show horse. He has great confirmation. He might shape up to be a real champion. Of course it's been a long time since I've worked with a horse, but I'd sure like to try."

"Okay, I've found out what I was sent to find out. Now maybe I can get some peace." Hank started to stand up then flopped back down. "Oh, I almost forgot. Keri wants to know how you like the room. She has some other ideas if you don't like it. I told her it was fine, but you know how women are. I have to work hard to keep up with them." Hank grinned.

"It's almost too pretty for an old saddle bum like me. I haven't slept in such a nice room in an awful long time." Chris wiped a tear away as he stood and turned back to finish brushing the mare.

Hank rose to leave. "I'll see you tomorrow. I have to go check out the grounds before I turn in."

*   *   *

When Hank returned to the Weatherby farm, he sat in his truck for a few minutes. He thought he saw movement by the shed as the truck lights flashed over it when he drove up. Watching, he noticed something moving in the weeds. Realizing it was too small for a person, he decided to check it out. Taking a flashlight from his toolbox behind the seat, he climbed out of the cab.

As he walked toward the shed, he shined the light towards the weeds. He had worked on trimming the weeds around the barn a few days before, planning to work on the other buildings another day.

When he was a couple of yards from the building, a cat darted out of the weeds. For a moment he thought it might be a skunk since he hadn't seen any cats around before. He watched it for a few moments. The tawny cat was marked by a white patch around one eye and a white sock. The cat stopped and looked at him before running off toward the field.

Relieved it was just a feral cat, Hank returned his flashlight to his truck and then went on up to the house.

*   *   *

Keri was tidying up the enclosed back porch when Hank returned. She was eager to know how Chris liked his room. When she learned Chris was coming, she wanted to help. She was happy to be busy helping Jenny. It was fun to go shopping and get the room ready.

Keri saw Hank pull up and watched him walk over to the shed. She waited patiently for him to come in to the house.

Steph was tired and had already turned in for the night. She was still weak and needed time to recover. Keri was pleased to have Steph home but she still worried about her. Betty was in the music room watching a television show. Keri often watched it with her, but she was too eager to sit and watch television. She wanted to be doing something so she decided to begin arranging and hanging the pictures and livestock certificates she had framed.

Hank saw Keri working through the windows on the porch. Entering the porch, he began walking around drawing shades over the windows. "Keri, if you're going to work out here, please pull the covers over the windows so you're not being watched. I think you need to quit for tonight and come inside now. It's getting late and I don't want you out here."

To take the sting out of his words, Hank walked over and put his hand on Keri's arm. "I worry about all of you. The bastard hasn't been caught yet and until he is, I am taking no chances. So please, let's go inside and lock up."

Hank lifted the hammer from Keri's hand and went to lock the back door. "I'll lock up, you go on in."

Keri went into the house but stood inside the door waiting for Hank.

Hank walked into the house, locked the door behind him then went on into the kitchen. He laid the hammer on the end of the counter then sat down at the table.

Keri followed and sat down across from Hank. "Okay, so what did you find out?"

"I don't know what you're talking about." Hank kept his expression bland. He was hoping to be bribed with another piece of pie.

"Didn't you just come back from talking to George?" Keri was becoming frustrated with Hank. Usually he was more cooperative.

"He's waiting on a piece of pie to loosen his tongue." Betty joined them in the kitchen. She walked over to the refrigerator and removed the pie. Cutting a piece for each of them, she brought the plates to the table.

"How kind of you to feed a starving man, Betty." Hank smiled and immediately began to eat.

"Okay, you've been bribed so spill it." Keri was trying to control her urge to rise from her chair and shake the man.

"No, thanks, but I will talk." Hank laughed at the look on Keri's face.

"You'd better start talking or I think she's going to get violent." Betty too was enjoying watching Keri's frustration.

"Okay. Okay. Chris said he liked the room. He said it was comfortable. George liked it too, so good job ladies." Hank took another bite of pie and chewed it slowly savoring the flavor.

"Keri, I think we'll have to ration this man's food unless he learns to talk and then eat." Betty was feeling a little of Keri's frustration. She had worked hard on the bread and the pie. She was concerned about what to cook for the following night.

"Oh, yeah! They loved the pie. Chris said it was the best pie he'd ever had. I got the impression he thinks Jenny made it. I know she'll set him right. He likes pineapple upside down cake. Some neighbor he had years ago used to make it for him before she died. He hasn't had any since. George said he loved it."

Hank saw the thoughtful expression on Betty's face. "Is that a problem?"

"What? Oh no." Betty sounded distant. "I was just trying to revise my menu. I had something else in mind, but it's no problem. I have everything to make it but the maraschino cherries. I can run to the store in the morning." Betty finished her pie silently as she began thinking about the next day.

"I sure hope Steph's up for company. She was awfully tired tonight. I know she's only been home one day, but she seems to become exhausted easily." Keri looked at Hank.

"It takes a while to build up your strength. She's been through a lot but she'll get stronger." Hank tried to sound encouraging. He remembered it was a number of weeks before he could go through a whole day without taking more than one nap.

"It's hard to adjust. Doing simple things like getting dressed can wear you out."

Keri sighed, reassured. She finished her pie and gathered the dishes from the table. Coming back to join the others, they sat there for a few minutes in companionable silence.

"Where's Misti? I should take her out one more time before turning in." Hank didn't let the ladies walk the little dog in the dark.

"She's still in the music room. She was sound asleep so I left her." Betty felt bad she forgot to bring the little dog. She started to rise. Hank waved her back down.

"I'll go get her and take her outside. I can take her out the side door off the music room to the porch." Hank rose to leave the room. "I'll turn the alarm on when I lock up. Don't stay up too late ladies. You have a single man coming to dinner tomorrow night." Hank laughed to himself as he left the room.

Misti was still wearing her cast. Hank would be taking her to the vet's in a few days to have it removed. He was glad it would soon be off. She was healing well. The vet was pleased at her last checkup.

Hank found Misti awake in her playpen. "Ready to go outside, girl? We're going out the side door tonight." He went over and unlocked the door before going to pick up the dog. He learned quickly how difficult to it was to open doors while carrying the little dog.

Hank carried Misti outside and placed her on the ground. It had taken only days for the dog to learn to walk with the cast. She developed a hop style of walking and Hank felt she was now well adapted to the cast.

Keeping an eye on Misti, Hank walked around in the yard. He enjoyed the evening air and appreciated the open expanse of the night sky.

Breathing in the clean air, he wondered if he would feel this way once he was back on the force. Would he miss the quiet, broken only by the sounds of the evening insects? Pushing those thoughts aside, he gathered Misti and returned to the house.

Misti slept in a playpen upstairs in Hank's room. It was easier for him to take her up when he went to bed and to bring her down right away in the morning. He quickly adapted to the early morning routine of the house and was learning to make passable coffee. He was looking forward to Steph brewing it again. No one could make it as delicious as she did.

"Let's lock up and go to bed." Hank was now in the habit of talking to Misti and he often did so without thinking. He placed her down on the floor in the hallway and went around checking all the doors and windows. When he was finished, he picked her up and carried her upstairs.

When he reached the second floor, he lingered for a moment outside Steph's door. Shaking his head, he moved on to his room.

Once inside his own room, he placed Misti in her playpen and closed the door. "You know girl, its nice having Steph home. I don't know about you, but I missed her." Hank sat on the edge of his bed for a while thinking before getting ready for sleep.

CHAPTER 33

"I can't believe this!" Betty stood in front of an oven that was still cold. She had a cake to bake and the oven wasn't working. She went over to the table and sat down to regroup.

Betty baked pies and fresh bread the day before. She tried to remember if she noticed anything wrong with the oven then. As she was sitting there going over her options, Hank wandered into the kitchen.

He noticed Betty sitting at the table as he went to the refrigerator for a cold drink. He had been cutting weeds and needed to take a break. Going over to the table, he sat down at the opposite end so he wouldn't disturb her.

The noise of Hank's chair scraping on the wooden floor caught Betty's attention. With a defeated look she asked, "I don't suppose you know how to fix a stove do you?"

"I've never tried. What's wrong?"

"The oven's not working. It won't heat up. I turned it on to preheat and it's not getting hot. The top element gets hot on broil, but the bottom element for baking won't heat up."

Rising, Hank went to take a look. Opening the oven door, he removed the racks for a closer look. "It looks like it's cracked." Returning to the table, he finished his drink. "Can you get a new part? I can take it out from the looks of it, but it'll have to be replaced."

"I guess I'll have to. I don't need it except to bake the cake and I can do that on the top of the stove. I wasn't planning on baking it that way but this cake I can."

Betty began preparing to bake the cake on the top of the stove, placing the rings of pineapple flat in the bottom of a large pan. Hank watched as she worked.

"How does it bake in a flat skillet?" Hank marveled at Betty's ingenuity.

"This is the only cake I know of you can bake this way. I've never tried it with any other kind. I had to bake one on a camp stove once when the electric went off. We were going to a party and I was supposed to bring the cake. It was my husband's idea and it worked out great."

Betty put her cake on to bake then sat down again. "Do you have the grill cleaned? I don't want you cooking those steaks and burgers on a dirty grill."

Steph bought a propane grill during a weak moment earlier in the summer. She was thinking of having a party and serving grilled hamburgers and hot dogs. She never owned one before and she was excited about it, going on her own to pick it out. They were surprised when it was delivered. Betty smiled at the memory. Steph bought the biggest grill the store had in stock. Betty estimated it was large enough to cook twenty five hamburgers at one time. Steph was reluctant to return it, hoping some day to have a party where she would need a large grill. Enjoying the warm weather, they'd used it a few times and Hank was getting to be pretty good at using it.

"Yep, it's all set and ready to go. I even checked the jet fuel. I'm already drooling just thinking about those beauties."

"I have corn on the cob to grill, too. Everything is marinating and soaking, ready to go. I haven't decided what to have for drinks, but I thought we'd figure it out later. Right now, I have to get the oven part ordered."

"I'm going to go check on Misti. It's been a while since she's been out. Who's with her?"

"She and Keri are sewing. Steph was in there too reading." Betty answered absently as she picked up the phone book from the counter where it was kept. "I'll call around and see if there's a store that carries the part. If not, I'll have to order one."

"Okay, let me know if you find one. I want to get a couple things and can run to town and can pick it up if that will help."

"I'll let you know." Betty sat down at the table, looking through the telephone book.

Hank put his glass in the sink and went to find Misti.

"We'll have to finish the quilting on this and then we can bind it. It's turned out lovely, hasn't it?" Keri's voice carried out the open door as Hank walked through the parlor.

Hank walked into the music room and found Keri showing Steph the quilt she was working on.

"It looks warm and inviting." Steph was seated looking at the quilt as Keri held it up.

Hank was impressed. The last time he saw Keri's latest project, it was only stacked piles of material. "Wow, Keri, that's a big blanket."

Keri was holding the quilt with her arms high in the air and didn't see him enter the room. Lowering the quilt, she smiled at Hank.

"Hi. It's not a blanket. It's a quilt. This is a rail fence pattern. It's easy to do and I can do what's called stitch-in-the-ditch quilting. It's easier and faster to do on this sewing machine." Keri began folding up the quilt. She laid it on the sewing machine. "It makes me wish I had my own machine sometimes. But, we'll make do with this one."

"I came to get Misti and take her outside. It's been a while since she's been out." Hank walked over and picked up the dog from her playpen. He carried her outside and placed her on the lawn.

"I still haven't gotten used to seeing her in that cast." Steph followed Hank outside. "It'll be nice when she gets it off. I miss seeing her run around." Steph sat down on the porch steps.

Hank walked over and sat beside her. "I miss that, too. She was so entertaining when she was running around. I can't wait to see her when she finds the cat that's been roaming around. I bet she'll go crazy."

"We have a cat? I don't remember having a cat." Steph thought for a while.

"I think it's a stray that's moved in. I don't remember seeing it before last night." Hank understood Steph was still having trouble remembering everything that happened just before the explosion. He had a similar experience after his first hospital stay.

Misti settled down in the grass. "I guess she's done. I'll take her back in. The bottom element on the stove is cracked. Betty's trying to find a store that carries them. I need to go check to see if she was able to find one or if she has to order the part." Hank collected Misti and went inside.

Hank was finding it harder and harder to be in the same room with Steph for long. He longed to kiss her and tell her he loved her. He berated himself for falling in love. He was a broken man and had nothing to offer. He made a list one night sitting at the hospital of the reasons he was wrong for her. He memorized it and would review each reason when he found himself yearning for her. The first and most important reason was he didn't currently have a job. He didn't know when he would be able to return to the force.

Thinking about Steph, Hank walked back into the kitchen. He nearly collided with Betty as she was leaving the room.

"I'm sorry. I guess my mind was elsewhere." Guilt clouded Hank's face. He had been thinking about kissing Steph. There were times when he felt useless, unable to do anything right, as if he was just taking up space. Then he would remind himself the ladies needed him, Steph needed him and he could function again.

"It's alright." Betty noticed there were days when Hank was moody and withdrawn. She understood this was one of them. So far she hadn't been able to discover the cause and promised herself she would find out soon. Right now she had to check with Steph about the dinner for tonight.

"Did you find a store that carried the part?"

"Yes, but they didn't have one in stock so they're going to order one. It's going to be two to three weeks before it comes in. They have to special order it because this is such an old oven. They're going to call when it comes in. At least the rest of the stove is working." Betty moved on down the hall toward the music room.

Hank went outside to work on the weeds again. He wanted to trim another area before working in the shed.

*   *   *

Steph was up in her room when Jenny, George, Chris and the baby arrived. Sitting in the rocking chair, she was contemplating on the up coming dinner, hoping her earlier nap would bolster her energy level.

Hearing a knock on the door, Steph answered. "Come on in." Unwilling to rise yet, she continued to rock slowly back and forth.

Jenny came into the room. "Hi, how are you feeling? I was worried when you weren't downstairs."

"I thought I'd just relax for a few minutes. Everything's under control thanks to Hank and Betty. I didn't want to be in the way. Sit down and let's talk for a few minutes." Steph tried to keep her frustration from her voice. "It's hard not to be working but Betty chased me upstairs earlier. They keep telling me I have to rest."

Jenny sat down on the edge of Steph's bed. "Well, you looked so tired yesterday."

Steph tried not to frown. "I know. It was more tiring coming home than I thought it would be. But let's talk about you. So tell me, how are things working out?"

"Do you mean how is it working with Chris being here?" Jenny sat on her hands and swung her legs out as she looked down at her feet. Putting her feet down, she looked up at Steph. "I think it's going to work out okay. He's trying to be helpful and he spends time out in the barn with the horses. I've shown him how to use the computer and the Internet. He spent a couple of hours today doing some research. He's a smart man and knows a lot of things."

Jenny stood up. "I think we'd better get downstairs if you're okay. The men are going to grill dinner and I'd like to see that. Betty said the bottom oven element went out. She was telling Chris how she baked the cake on the top of the stove. She's amazing." Jenny stood still for a moment. "Sorry, I know I'm talking a lot but I got so used to telling you everything when you were asleep. It's harder than I thought it would be to stop."

Steph grinned at her friend. "It's okay. I appreciate it. Sometimes I feel as if I've missed so much. Betty and Keri try hard but they've been tiptoeing around so much today, I was beginning to wonder if anything would get back to normal."

Jenny giggled. "I can't say it was ever normal, but that would be a good start."

Laughing, Steph followed Jenny as they went down the stairs. They heard laughter as they entered the kitchen.

*　　*　　*

"I don't believe it." Betty was standing at the window watching Hank, Chris and George from her vantage point.

"Now what's going on?" Steph was not ready for more bad news. It surprised her how depressed she became over the element breaking in the stove.

Betty turned from the window laughing. "Those men are standing around trying to figure out how to grill the steaks and the corn on the cob. Hank put the corn down on the same level as the steaks. I told him to put them on the top level. One of the corn husks caught fire and they all tried to put it out." Betty shook her head and sighed.

"Where's Keri?" Steph noticed Keri was missing all the fun.

"She went out to show them how it was done and they refused to let her near the grill. Hank grabbed her and danced her back to the steps. He told her it was a man's job work to run the grill." Betty sat down at the kitchen table.

"If they burn my meal, I'm going to make them eat it anyway. I can't watch anymore." Betty sighed. "I just hope they remember to turn it off when they're done."

Steph and Jenny looked out the window for a few minutes and then Jenny went to collect the baby from the playpen. The baby was asleep when they checked on him before coming into the kitchen. Jenny heard him stirring on the monitor and didn't want to leave him alone for too long.

"I guess that grill is getting a real workout. Hank sure has taken over using it. He seems to be more confident now." Steph was thinking about how quiet Hank was when she first met him.

"Oh, yeah. He's getting more and more like his old self every day. You ladies have been good for him." Jenny returned holding George Henry. She was sure it was being at the Weatherby farm that was helping Hank to heal. He was being fed well and he was getting stronger. Secretly she was glad no one could read her thoughts. She couldn't help thinking how nice it would be if Hank and Steph would fall in love.

They sat at the table for a few minutes watching the baby giggle and make faces when they heard a commotion at the back door.

"I'll get it." Keri's voice drifted into the room.

"No, this is man's work and I'll get it." Frustration could be heard in the male voice.

Keri and Chris came into the kitchen together. Steph watched as they entered the room.

"This must be Chris. Hello, I'm Stephanotis, Steph. We're so glad you came for dinner."

"It's nice to meet you." Chris shook her hand. "You've got yourself some good horses. I'll want to talk with you about that later. Right now, I've got to deal with this filly."

Keri walked over to the counter and picked up two platters intending to take them outside. "I said I would get them."

"Hank told me to come and get them since the men were in charge of the meal. I'll take them now." Chris held out his hands.

"You're a guest so you don't have to do that." Keri turned sideways, holding the platters just out of his reach.

"Jenny says I'm family and family helps out." Chris's frustration was clear in his face.

Steph stood up and walked over in between Keri and Chris. Reaching out, she gently took the platters out of Keri's hands while Keri was arguing with Chris.

Quietly she left the room, carrying the platters outside.

Hank hailed her when he saw her coming down the stair steps. "What happened to Chris?"

Walking up to him, she looked at his expression and started to laugh. Keri and Chris were coming down the stairs still arguing.

"You knew what would happen when you sent that poor man after these." Steph held out the platters. "You set him up. Was Keri hovering too much?"

"Nah," Hank took one of the platters and handed it to George. He began to load it with steaks. "I knew we were making Keri nervous when she offered to call the fire department. She said she has Deputy Austin on speed dial."

"Hold this for a moment." Hank started loading Steph's platter with the grilled corn on the cob.

After Hank loaded both platters, he carefully turned off the grill and double-checked it. "I'll come back and put this away later when it's cooled down. Here let me take that." Hank reached for the platter Steph was holding.

They all marched up the stairs with Keri and Chris in the lead. Steph followed, slowly bringing up the rear.

*   *   *

They ate in the formal dining room spread out down the long table.

George Henry giggled and kicked while reclining in a bounce chair. Jenny sat on one side of the table and George sat on the other. The baby's chair was placed on the table between them.

Misti laid in her wagon at the end of the table near Steph.

To keep peace, Hank sat beside Keri with Betty beside Chris.

"I am so happy to be home." Steph raised her glass in a toast as she started to get misty-eyed. "I'll make this brief. Thanks for everything."

The others raised their glasses and drank but remained silent at the table, each with their own thoughts. Jenny looked at George, then the baby and smiled.

Hank was not having his hard work and good food cried over. "Chris, you'll have to get Steph to take you on a tour of the house. As an architect, you may find it interesting."

Chris turned to Steph. "I would like that. I was impressed by the widow's walk. Any idea why it was built up there?"

"Steph found a journal written by the man who built the house. He put it there as a look out. This house was once part of the Underground Railroad." Keri spoke up before Steph could answer.

Chris looked a Keri with suspicion on his face. "Are you sure?"

Steph could see an argument brewing. "Yes, we still have to go to the local historical society and confirm it, but according to the journals we found it was."

"Have you found the place where the slaves would hide?" Chris felt his interest rising.

"Not yet, but we have found some clever hidden areas in the mantels. I'll be glad to take you on that tour after we eat."

Betty passed Chris a dish of salad. "Don't forget to leave room for dessert. I have pineapple upside down cake just waiting to be served."

Chris looked at Betty as if considering his options before speaking. "Mrs. Brown, will you marry me?"

Betty choked on her food. When she was in control again, she looked at Keri laughing. "We have a live one on our hands."

The meal progressed with laughter and talk of the house, the farms and the horses.

As everyone finished eating, Betty and Keri began to clear the dishes. Steph rose to help.

"Sit down, Steph. You'll need your strength to take Chris around. We'll get this." Betty turned to Hank. "While George is here, don't forget to put the grill in the basement. Keri and I don't want to have to be out there helping you in the dark again."

"Oh yeah, George, we need to get the grill back to the basement. It's too big for me to move alone." Hank rose to leave. "We'll go work some of this meal off and come back for more dessert. That is if there's any left." He grinned as he left the room.

"I don't know where that boy puts his food. Sometimes he eats like a bird and other times it's like he can't get full." Betty shook her head.

"Yes, but you love it! Come on Betty; let's get this table cleared off so we can play with the baby." Keri turned to Steph. "Leave

Misti with us, we'll take care of her. I want to show Jenny the quilt I finished."

"Well, Chris, shall we start that tour? You've already seen some of the house let me show you the rest."

Chris followed Steph around as she showed him each room. He was fascinated by the secret areas in the fireplace mantels. Taking the stairs carefully, he stood in wonder at the size of the cupola. Steph showed him the door to the widow's walk, before they began to slowly walk back down to the main level.

"You're welcome to come as often as you like." Steph liked Chris and hoped he knew he was welcome in her home.

"Your home is a wonder. Thank you for showing me around. I would like to come back and study it. I must admit I'm a little tired. This is a big house to walk around and see everything. It's been a pleasure to be here tonight."

"You're family now Chris, so don't be a stranger." Steph winked at him.

"I'll admit I'm tired too. Let's go join the others. I'd like to talk to you about the horses, but if you don't mind, I'd rather not talk about them tonight."

Chris nodded his head, silently agreeing. When they joined the others in the parlor, Jenny saw the weariness on both their faces.

"George, I hope you and Chris don't mind, but I'm awfully tired. I think it's time for us to say good night." She rose and walked over to Steph, giving her a hug. "Thanks for the party. It's been wonderful. Get some rest."

After their guests left, Steph looked at Keri and Betty. "I hate to say this, but it's going to take any energy I have left to get to my bed. I'll say good night."

"I need to get something from upstairs, I'll walk with you." Keri noticed Steph was turning pale. She took her arm in a companionable way. "I'll be back in a few minutes, Betty."

Keri helped Steph to her room and made sure she was settled in before returning to the kitchen to help finish the clean up.

When Keri returned, she was happy to report Steph was sleeping.

CHAPTER 34

Everyone had something important to do, except Steph. Betty was working in the library, Keri was finishing another quilt and Hank was working on a tractor he found locked up in a shed.

Steph was feeling better every day. The first week she spent much of the time sleeping and resting between trips to the hospital for her physical therapy. She was happy to sleep in her own bed. She had finished reading the journals and she was ready for something else to do. They still needed to find the document Iris signed. Steph was beginning to give up hope of ever finding it. The court date was only a few weeks away. She was going to have to fight for her right to the property.

Steph wandered into the study to think for a while. She was bored, restricted from a lot of activity while her shoulder healed. She went to physical therapy and thought she was getting stronger. The physical therapist would make her promise before she left each session to not strain her shoulder and just do the exercises she was given.

For the past two weeks she and Betty scanned the pictures they found into the computer. Steph wanted to have a party and invite local people who could tell her about the people in the pictures. Betty didn't think it was wise to have a party yet. The oven element was on back order and she wouldn't be able to make any cakes or pies.

Steph knew it was an excuse. They still hadn't caught the man responsible for taking Misti or for blowing up Betty's car. Steph was beginning to hope it was over and he had left town.

Steph sat at the desk staring at the wall across the room. Slowly she turned and looked at the wall from one corner to the other. This wall always bothered her. *Why leave a large area uncovered? No pictures were hung there. No shelves or decorations were on that area of the wall.* She walked over to inspect the wall. Steph had seen several movies with secret doors in spooky houses. She went back over to the desk and sat down again to ponder the problem.

Steph let her mind wander. She remembered watching a movie where they used a candle to find the secret passage. In another movie they used a cigar. In a different movie, it was the temperature difference that showed them where a door was. She wondered if any of those tricks really worked.

Steph left the room in search of a candle and matches. Returning, she placed her hand on different areas of the wall. It seemed cooler in some areas than others. Lighting the candle, she began moving the candle around. As she worked, she hoped no one would come looking for her. It would be embarrassing to explain what she was doing.

Suddenly, the candle began to flicker. Steph watched the smoke from the flame. It looked easier on television. She needed more smoke. Blowing out the candle she sat down for a few minutes to think.

Incense created smoke. They had found some old sticks of incense in the kitchen. She just had to remember what she did with it. She tried to force the thoughts to come. She found it frustrating to have to work so hard to remember the information she wanted. She knew it was there, but her mind was playing tricks, hiding the information, or keeping it just out of reach like a game. Only it wasn't a game.

Her therapist had her doing exercises to strengthen the pathways to her memory. It was getting better, but some days she felt as if she would always be a stranger to herself. She practiced the exercises she was given, knowing the information would come to the front of her mind eventually and she'd be able to latch onto it.

After a while, she remembered they had put it with larger candles and brass candle holders in a box. She went to the conservatory and brought the incense back to use.

Carefully she lit the incense and held it near the wall where the candle had flickered. As the incense smoked, she watched where it was drawn in. Once she had the outline of the doorway determined, she began trying to find the best way to open it. As she was pushing on the wall, she started to lean and the wall moved as if it was a pocket door. Now that she had a small opening, it was a simple matter to finish pushing the section of the wall or door until it was open. There standing in a closet sized area was an old safe. Steph was so surprised she just stood there looking at it. She was afraid if she moved, it would disappear. She almost closed the door and walked away afraid it would just yield more disappointment. Stepping back, she fought to control the internal struggle that threatened to overwhelm her. Calling Betty in from the library, she knew this was the first step in taking back her life.

Betty heard Steph calling her from the study. She had smelled Steph burning incense and was starting to get curious about what she was doing. When Betty entered the study, Steph was standing in an opening Betty had not seen before. Walking over, she peered inside.

"Why it's a safe! How wonderful! Maybe it contains the document you need." Delighted, Betty grabbed Steph and gave her a hug. "Have you tried to open it?"

"No, I called you before I touched anything. I wanted to be sure I wasn't just seeing things." Steph sat down. She no longer trusted her legs. If that safe contained the document, her troubles would be over. "I can't believe it's been there all the time. It may be locked, I just don't know."

"Well, let's try it and see. Look at all this stuff stuck in this closet." Betty was looking for a light switch. "I wonder if there's any light available."

Seeing a cord hanging down, she pulled on it. A single light bulb hanging on a cloth covered cord switched on.

The light revealed trophies on a shelf set high up on the wall. Along the side of the safe was a set of shelves that went from the floor to the ceiling. Some were empty while others held plaques or large leather-bound journals. A layer of dust gave evidence to how long the area had remained undisturbed.

Steph walked over and looked into the weakly lit area. Reaching out a tentative hand, she tried to pull open the safe door.

"I think you have to turn the lever." Betty was watching with her fingers crossed.

Steph gave the safe handle a couple of pulls and the safe door began to open. Years of dust and moisture had corroded the hinges of the safe. "This is harder to open than it looks. Can you give me a hand?"

Between them, Betty and Steph pulled open the safe door. Inside were two shelves holding papers and a drawer that could be locked using a separate key.

"Let's get a box and clean it out so we can sort these papers." Steph was overwhelmed with curiosity about what could be in the safe.

"Do you think we need to call Stanley and tell him about the safe?" Betty was curious too, but did not want her friend to forget what the lawyer had told them.

Steph looked over at Betty, a strained look on her face. Steph had mixed feelings about seeing Stanley again. "I think we'll have a look for ourselves and then I can take these papers to his office for him to see if we don't find it. He's a busy man and I don't want to bother him to come out if I don't have to."

They cleaned out the safe and began sorting the documents. They found birth certificates, marriage certificates and a few contracts. Reading each piece of paper carefully, they did not find what they were hoping for. Disheartened, they began removing the trophies, plaques and journals from the shelves. The journals contained old household records, farm tax records and breeding records.

They spent the afternoon cleaning the trophies and dusting the shelves.

After dinner, they showed Hank and Keri what they found.

*   *   *

As Hank inspected the doorway, he had a thoughtful look on his face. Steph mentioned reading in a journal about a secret passageway. He began to wonder about the wall in the basement. He would have to look into it another day. For now he marveled at Steph's find.

"Did you find the document Iris signed?" Keri was torn between being upset with her friends for not calling her to help explore and with being grateful the work was already done.

"No. We found some marriage and birth certificates though. There were some fancy contracts and receipts but nothing signed by Iris. I'm not giving up. We'll find it." Steph had promised herself as she lay in the hospital bed that she would do whatever it took to keep the farm.

Keri picked up one of the trophies. "These are beautiful! I wonder why they were hidden away. Look at the date on this one! 1925! Wow!" Keri's voice was filled with delight. "I wonder if we could use them in some way to decorate a room." She stood looking at them with a thoughtful expression on her face.

"I don't know. I think I'm going to turn in." Steph was trying to hide her disappointment. She was frustrated worrying about the upcoming court case and right now she was tired.

Steph went up to get ready for bed. She sat down in the rocking chair for a while. Getting into bed, she laid there for a long time before falling asleep.

$$* \quad * \quad *$$

Hank rose early as usual the next morning. He stayed awake late in the night thinking about the hidden closet Steph found. It was too small in his mind to be called a hidden room.

It was raining outside and he stood looking out the kitchen window glad for the excuse to stay near the house. He was able to get the engine started on the old Massey-Ferguson tractor he found in the padlocked shed. For now he had the engine running smoothly. He was still waiting on the new tires he ordered.

Hank smiled. *It's going to be fun to drive the tractor around once it's done.*

"You look deep in thought." Betty had come in and was helping herself to some fresh coffee. "It would be a good day for baking if I had an oven. I hope the part I ordered comes in soon."

Hank turned from the window. "I don't feel like going out in the rain today. I think I'll see what I can find around the house that needs to be done. Maybe I'll check out the boiler in the basement." Hank sat at the table and drank the coffee he had poured for himself earlier.

"That's a good idea. Steph'll need to heat the house for the winter. It's hard to believe summer is over." Betty sat at the table opposite Hank. "It's been fun to be here, but I need to be thinking about getting back to Boston before winter. I hate to leave, but I have my apartment there. I have the insurance check for my car and I need to figure out if I'm going to get one now or later. I guess I'll have to start making some decisions soon." Betty rose, put her cup in the sink and left the room.

Hank sat for a few minutes deep in thought. He had forgotten Betty and Keri had homes elsewhere but were here to help Steph. He had grown to love them and would miss them when they left. Standing up, he decided to head down to the basement. Betty was right. Steph was going to need the boiler to be in good shape to heat the house when winter came.

As he walked down into the basement, he surveyed the room. It was an open area, bigger than the kitchen above but not as large as the main floor.

Steph said a passageway was built behind a wall of shelves. The journal didn't say it was in this house. Hank was trying to stay open to the possibility that maybe it was.

Going into the boiler room and coming out, he carefully inspected all of the walls. Steph used incense to find the opening upstairs, so Hank brought candles and incense with him to use too.

Moving and pushing on sections of the wall, Hank tried to figure out which area would have an opening. Using the incense, he found a slight draft.

Pushing the wall of shelves backwards did not move the shelves. Leaning on the shelves, pulling and tugging did not accomplish opening a doorway. Taking his flashlight and carefully inspecting the construction, Hank was able see the shelves were built as a solid unit.

Hank began looking for a handle to move the unit. What he found was an indentation in the wood. Using that as a handle, he pulled on the unit. The shelves opened, pivoting on the opposite side.

Hank felt his heart pounding with excitement. He found the hidden passageway mentioned in the journal! Not wanting to alert the women until he inspected it, he went out to his truck to get his large beamed flashlight.

When he returned, Hank carefully entered the passageway. Trying to stay oriented with the upper structure of the house, Hank explored the small room he found himself standing in. Shining his flashlight around, he found a ladder placed in an opening surrounded by brick.

Hank looked around carefully before realizing this was the missing shaft the chimney sweep had been unable to discover. Hank became more and more curious. Why would anyone build a passage up in a chimney?

Determined to find the answer, Hank went out to his truck for rope. The ladder looked sturdy, but it was definitely old. He planned to climb up and see where it led. He would trust the ladder going up, but would secure the rope as he went so he would not have any problems coming back down.

Hank had a flashlight that was fastened to a headband in his truck and he brought it in with the rope. It was not as bright as he would have liked, but it would be bright enough to allow him to have his hands free to climb.

When Hank began his climb up the ladder, he was excited and a little nervous. His heart was pounding with the adrenaline rush. He felt alive, determined not to be afraid. As he climbed, he tried to estimate out how far he had gone and where in the house he would currently be.

Hank never thought of himself as claustrophobic. When he had climbed up to what he estimated to be the second floor, he began to wonder about the safety of what he was doing. He felt as if the air was getting heavier and the shaft was pushing in on him.

He put his foot on the next rung to move on up and it broke under his weight. *Get a grip Hank! Sometimes you can be a fool. You should have learned your lesson. You're going to have to finish this, there's no going back now. If you fall, it'll be hours before they look for you. They may not even find you. Then where will you be? This has to go some-where, just take it one rung at a time and you'll get there.*

Calming down, he looked up. *It looks like an opening of some kind. It has to go somewhere, I just have to get to it.*

Forcing himself to continue on, he climbed to the top of the ladder and crawled to safety. Lying on the solid floor, he rested for a few minutes before exploring the area of the house he was now in.

It was a long narrow room with no windows or light. The air was stuffy and heavy. At each end, the roof angled low toward the floor. Hank had to duck down to keep from hitting his head when he examined the corners. Discarded candles and other debris littered the floor.

Searching along the inside wall, he found a three foot high doorway disguised in the wall. Crawling through it, he found himself in the storage area on the top floor. He had worked in this room and had not noticed a doorway.

Carefully marking the doorway, he closed it. The storage area was an unfinished room. The wooden wall slats were exposed on all four walls. This helped to camouflage the small door.

Well, no wonder I didn't see this before. Oh well. At least I don't have to go back down that ladder. Now, to see where the passage ways go. After one more look around, he headed down the stairway.

Hank stopped in the kitchen for a drink on his way back down to the basement. He decided he deserved a treat and was helping himself to some cookies when Steph came in.

"My goodness, Hank, what have you been doing?" Hank had dirt smeared on his face and cobwebs and dirt on his clothes.

"I'm working downstairs. I was checking out the boiler." Hank wasn't ready to share his discovery with Steph. He wanted to go back and explore some more. If Steph knew about his find, she would insist on coming with him. He wasn't sure it was safe for her yet.

"Okay, but be careful. I'll have someone come and look at it if I need to." Steph turned away so she wouldn't give away her fears. *I need to be careful. I don't want to become dependent on Hank. I need to learn to take care of myself again. When this is over and he's gone, I don't want to go through all that pain again. It hurts too much. Just thinking about it hurts.*

"Don't worry. If I can't figure it out, I'll be sure to stop so you can call someone." Hank finished his snack and headed down the stairs.

Steph stood with a worried look on her face as she watched Hank go.

* * *

Hank hated deceiving Steph but he was determined to search by himself. Returning to the room he had discovered, he lit some of the candles scattered on the floor. Placing one in each corner, he sketched it out on a note pad he brought from the kitchen.

He drew in the area for the ladder and documented the room he had found at the top. It was challenging balancing the flashlight as he drew.

The room he was standing in had a narrow opening in the far side of wall. Another opening was next to the hidden doorway. Deciding to leave the smaller passageway for later, he moved into the larger passageway, realizing it was the size of a small doorway. Hank was forced to walk slightly stooped over between the short ceiling and sloping floor.

A few yards into the passageway, wooden barrels and crates were stacked along one side. He notated their whereabouts and the markings on them. Hank decided to leave them for later. Steph and the ladies would want to see what's inside them. Walking sideways to avoid the barrels and crates, Hank moved on.

He had gone about twenty five feet before he could stand up between the ceiling braces. There was enough room to walk a few steps before he had to bend down to pass under the support beams. *Whew, it's widening out.*

Hank reached his arms out but couldn't touch the sides. *I wonder why they made this so much wider. It looks as if they hurried to finish it.*

As he walked, using the flashlight beam, Hank checked the ceiling supports. He noticed the wooden support beams holding the wide wooden ceiling planks began to change to bricks. Deeper into the passage, columns of bricks supported the ceiling planks. The depth of the rafters was different enough that he found himself misjudging how low to bend. He tried to pace the distance as he walked but stopped counting after hitting his head a few times.

He came to a junction where the passageway split with one passageway moving off at a ninety degree angle. Deciding to stay in what he now considered the main passageway, Hank moved cautiously on.

Occasionally drops of water from the rain outside made their way into the passageway. Hank at first found it disconcerting, but tried to ignore it. He realized he was coming near the end when the ground began sloping upward under his feet and he was forced to bend over more as he walked. At the end of the passage area was a small room with a wooden ceiling.

Short crude steps led up to the ceiling. *This must be somewhere near the barn.*

Walking up and opening the trapdoor in the ceiling-floor, he stepped out into the tack room. The trapdoor had been cleverly disguised in the design of the floor. Now that he knew what to look for, he could see the notched area of the door handle. Hank noticed it when sweeping the floor, but assumed it was a gouge caused by something heavy being dropped on the floor.

Hank stretched and inhaled deeply. The damp earth smell of the tunnel had been overwhelming. Hank walked out of the tack room into the barn. *I wonder what other surprises this place holds.*

Sitting on an old bale of straw, he looked around the barn. Something was different. Something felt wrong. He hadn't been in the barn for a few days. He was focused on fixing the tractor and spent the daylight hours working on it or exploring and clearing the other buildings. Hank stood up and walked around. Walking toward the main doors of the barn, he began looking around. Looking up, he saw a terrible sight.

The dead body of a cat was balanced on the beam above the barn door. Hank could see the rope was rigged to swing free and drop the cat down when the big door opened. He recognized it as the tawny cat living in the weeds.

He shuddered to think of the horrifying effect it would have when someone opened the door and the dead animal would fall down into their face.

This bastard had to be stopped. Hank cut the animal down, hiding it so he could give it to Deputy Austin later. Collecting the cards from the cameras in the barn, he decided to return to the house the same way he came.

Stopping at the junction, he was torn between going back to the house and investigating the other passageway. His curiosity overcame his concern about the person in the barn. He was afraid he would not have the opportunity to explore alone once he told the others about the passageway. He also wanted to be sure no one else was using it. The main passageway had not shown any signs of recent use but Hank wanted to be sure.

Hank noticed how much smaller the adjoining passageway was. He had to stoop again to walk. The walls were much closer together. There was only enough room for two people to walk abreast. Not far down the second passage, he came upon a small room to his right.

It held the remnants of a wooden framed bed. Bits of a decayed straw mattress hung limply from rope supports. It had a low ceiling, a few inches lower than the passageway. Hank saw an old kerosene lantern on the floor beside the bed. A three-legged milking stool sat in the corner of the room. Further down the passage was another room on his left. This one was larger than the other room. The bed in this room was lying broken on the floor. Across the room was a crude table made by placing wide planks over stacked crates. Four wooden barrels near the table suggested to Hank they had been used as chairs. Near the table was an empty crate lined with rags.

Hank could only wonder at what would cause someone to live in such conditions. He was appalled and yet marveled at the strong spirit of the people who did. Continuing his journey, he came to a brick wall. There was a wooden door set in the center of the bricks. The door had a metal bolt fastening it shut. When Hank opened it, he found himself in a large brick shaft. Looking down, he saw the wooden floor of the shaft was about three feet down. It was covered with disintegrating leaves and other debris. Looking up, he saw a wooden ceiling over the top of the shaft. A ladder stood against the wall reaching up to the wooden ceiling. Realizing there was another trapdoor at the top Hank climbed the ladder, testing each rung as he went. Hank carefully opened the trapdoor and found himself in the gazebo.

This was where Keri saw Misti coming from. Hank looked carefully for signs of recent use. Relieved he didn't find any he carefully closed the trapdoor. Moving back along the passageway, he had a lot to think about.

CHAPTER 35

Steph had been in the basement and looked at the boiler before her accident. There were a few cobwebs and some dirt but she wondered what Hank was doing to get so dirty.

Thinking about Hank, Steph almost forgot why she was in the kitchen. She found herself thinking about him more and more. She realized when she woke up in the hospital that she loved him. She was overwhelmed by all he had done for Misti. When she tried to thank him and explain how much it meant to her, he walked away.

Steph stood for a moment thinking over Hank's behavior since she'd come home. He was in and out of the house, never staying very long when she came in the room. Sometimes she had the impression he'd rather not be around her. Maybe he was just keeping busy as he said. She had noticed he was cleaning up around the buildings outside and Keri had said he was fixing a tractor he found in one of the locked buildings. Shrugging Steph returned to the study feeling depressed and restless. Assuming her mood was just reflecting the day outside, she knew she needed something to occupy her mind.

Steph decided to search the study again. She took her time looking around in the safe closet and wondered if it held any more secrets. She measured the walls in the library and the walls in the study.

Something was nagging at her. Steph lit the incense and followed the flow with her flashlight. Stepping further into the small area, she moved to stand beside the safe and realized there was enough room for two people to stand there side by side. Carefully searching, she found a doorway in the wall behind the safe. There was a wooden sliding bolt mounted low on the door, keeping it shut. The door opened more like a regular door, pivoting away over what appeared to be an opening in the floor.

Steph stood looking at the open doorway. She was both terrified and thrilled. Finding the safe closet hadn't been this exciting. She knew what she needed was down there. Carefully shining her flashlight, she found a spiral shaped stairway made of iron and wood that lead down into the dark.

Steph was afraid the loud beating of her heart would bring Keri and Betty running to see what frightened her. Her pride was fighting with her sense of survival. Her mind was a whirl of thoughts, her excitement mounting. *I don't want to share my new secret about my wonderful house just yet. I'd like to be the first to see any treasures I can find.*

Steph remained still. *If only I could remember better. Did I read something in one of the journals about a staircase and a room? No one else mentioned reading about one. I think I only read one that mentioned a set of shelves that moved. This is my discovery without any hints or leads. Why shouldn't I see what's down there? Because there might be mice or worse down there! Steph you scaredy cat, you won't know what's there until you look!*

Steph didn't know how long she stood there looking down. *It can't hurt to go down and take a peek. After all, this is my house. Why shouldn't I go down there?* Feeling like a kid doing something she might get into trouble for later, she stepped forward determined to explore this new gift.

Gingerly taking one step at a time and holding firmly to the rail, Steph started down. Moving cautiously, she continued. With each step she found herself moving more and more into total darkness. A slightly damp, musty smell confirmed she was somewhere no one else had been for a long time.

She was almost to the last step when she realized she was in a large room. Searching with the beam of her flashlight, she discovered a bare light bulb hanging from the ceiling. Turning on the weak light, she released the breath she didn't realized she'd been holding.

Reassured she hadn't discovered any rodents so far, she stopped and looked around.

This looks like an underground version of the study. A large desk sat in the middle of the room. Moving toward it, she switched on the desk lamp. Rewarded with more light, she decided to first search for more lights. Crudely rigged bare bulbs hung widely spaced from the ceiling. Turning them all on Steph allowed herself to marvel at her discovery.

She stopped beside the desk, slowly turning and looking about her. The ceiling had been finished off with rough, wide planking. The walls were slanted wood panels that had been smoothed and polished. It reminded her of the box stalls in the barn. A large braided rug under the desk was the only cover on the rough cement floor.

No photos or decorations graced the walls except for a simple wooden cross hanging on one wall. Underneath it was a small table with a cloth draped over it. Steph walked over to the table. A closed Bible rested on the cloth. Thick dust had settled over the Bible and cloth. Two burnt down remnants of candles in wooden holders were the only other objects on the table.

Steph moved back to the desk. Several documents were scattered over the top of the desk. An open book was lying beside the papers. Steph glanced over it before moving on.

Steph found a potbellied, wood-burning stove under what she assumed to be the fireplace above in the study. She sat in the chair at the desk and studied her discovery.

This is clearly a man's room. I wonder why it's down here. I feel welcome here. I could stay down here if it wasn't so cold. Obviously this is underground as cold as it is.

She sat for a few minutes reveling in her discovery, trying to picture what the room would be used for.

Looking around again, she spied a doorway. Expecting to find another room, she opened the door. To her dismay, it opened into a passageway. Packed dirt was used to form one wall and the floor. Wooden slats enclosed the opposite wall. Steph noticed the ceiling was supported by heavy wooden beams and planking similar to the ceiling in the room she was standing in.

Shining her light around, she was able to see a bend in the passageway. Leaving the door open in case she needed to make a quick return, she walked slowly down the passage, keeping an eye out for rodents and spiders.

Coming to the bend, she peeked around the corner and saw flickering lights. Steph stepped around the bend. Moving as quietly as possible, she stepped out into the room.

Candles were burning in each corner giving off the flickering light. Steph stood there wondering why they were there when she heard a noise coming from the opposite passageway.

There was a scuffling sound and an oath. It sounded very male and very nearby. Steph hurried into her passageway and stepped into the bend. Peeking around to see whoever it was that was coming, she was shocked.

Walking into the small room as if he owned the place was Hank! He was rubbing his head as if he'd just bumped it. Instead of feeling sympathy, Steph was furious. He found this secret area but hadn't told her about it. She began to wonder what else he had found and if it was his guilt about keeping the secrets that cause him to behave the way he did toward her.

Deciding to wait and see how long it would take for him to reveal his secrets, Steph returned to what she thought of as her secret room and headed up the spiral stairs as quickly as possible.

Not realizing she, too, had dirt smudges and cobwebs clinging to her, Steph walked into the kitchen planning to catch Hank and force him to tell her about what he had been doing.

"My goodness, Steph! I sure hope you're planning on cleaning up before lunch." Betty was working in the kitchen.

Looking down at her shirt, Steph realized she was almost as dirty as Hank. "I'll go right up and get cleaned up." Steph hurried up the backstairs to her room.

Steph was shocked when she looked at herself in her bathroom mirror. Dirty cobwebs were hanging from her hair and she had streaks of dirt on her face.

Steph jumped into the shower, annoyed her wanderings had already been discovered. She would have to tell all at lunch or Keri and Betty would wheedle it out of her.

*   *   *

When Steph returned to the kitchen, she found Keri and Betty talking in the kitchen. "Where's Hank?" Steph tried to hide her annoyance.

"Right behind you! Did you miss me?" Hank was so pleased with his discovery of the passage and so excited to tell them, he grabbed Steph and gave her a quick kiss on the lips. Releasing her, he was immediately sorry. He had to fight the urge to not grab her again and make it a longer kiss, something he had wanted to do since she woke up in the hospital.

Flustered, Steph grabbed the back of a chair for support. She knew he affected her as no one else could. She longed for him to kiss her as a lover, not just a friend. He was the man who haunted her dreams at night.

Keri watched her friends, saddened that they would not allow themselves to love each other. "Come on children, it's time for lunch."

As they were eating, Steph tried to think of a way to enter her discoveries into the conversation. She was going to give Hank enough rope to hang himself.

Bracing herself, Steph decided to simply share her surprise. "I found the hidden room." Steph watched the others as her bombshell announcement landed.

"Why Steph, that's wonderful. We'll have to check it out right after lunch. I hope you didn't go doing anything strenuous or dangerous." Betty had wondered about Steph's earlier appearance.

"No, nothing strenuous. It took me a while to figure out how to open it. I'll show everyone after lunch and we can explore. It's down in the basement." Satisfied with the flow of the conversation, Steph kept her eyes glued to Hank's face.

Noticing a slight redness creeping into his face and that he was averting his eyes, Steph decided to continue her advantage. "I went down a spiral stairway and found a room that opens onto a passageway." Noticing she now had Hank's attention, she went on. "I checked out the room. It's set up like a study. The passageway leads to another room and another passageway."

"I found something like that when I was working downstairs this morning. Maybe they're connected." Hank decided it would be best to play along. "We'll check them both out."

Keri looked at Betty. "How exciting! An adventure right here in our own house!"

As soon as they finished eating, they all trouped into the study. Steph showed them how she opened the door. She went first, turning on lights as she moved through the room.

"Oh, my!" Keri wandered around exploring.

"This has been here all this time?" Betty shook her head in wonder.

Steph was feeling proud of her discovery. She saw Hank's face and realized he didn't know about this room. While the others looked around, she walked over to the desk and began to look through the papers. There was an unlined paper that seemed different from the others. She noticed it was written in an unusual style, almost like a legal document.

Holding it up to the light, she saw the clear signature 'Iris Weatherby.'

"I think I found the document." Steph showed the others. They all agreed this was the document they had been looking for.

"I'll have to show Stanley, but that will keep." Steph felt a little let down now that she found the document. She carefully laid it back down planning to recover it later.

"Keri, what do you suppose this was used for?" Steph walked over to the small table holding the Bible.

"That's an altar for prayer. Some families would have a room in their homes for worship. This was obviously a very private room. Hyacinth's father must have come here to pray. He probably used this room for other things as well." Keri walked over to the desk. "It's a nice room with lots of possibilities."

Hank noticed the door. "Is this your passageway?" Walking over, he didn't wait for an answer but simply opened the door.

They had each carried a flashlight. Turning his own on, Hank led the way down the passage. Coming to the bend, he moved confidently into the next room. "This is the room I found this morning." Hank walked around lighting the candles in the corners for the women to see.

"I found these candles discarded on the floor. Steph, do you remember how upset the chimney sweep was about the extra shaft in the dining room chimney?"

"You mean, Brian? Yes, I remember now. He was so frustrated by it. He said there was a shaft running up beside the chimney. Why?"

Hank walked over to stand beside the ladder shaded in the dark. Shining his flashlight up, he showed them the shaft. "I climbed up that shaft this morning."

As each of the women walked over and looked up, Hank went on. "It goes straight up to the top floor. There's a narrow room the width of the house. It must have been a place to hide slaves. There is a small, and I mean small, door." Hank used his hand to show how short the door was, coming up to his knee. "I crawled out of it and it opens into the storage area on the top floor."

"It must have been hidden or we would have noticed it." Steph was sure she would have seen a door. She had spent hours in that room.

"It was flush with the walls and hidden very well. As short as it is, you probably wouldn't think it was a door."

"So how did you get in here?" Keri was sure she hadn't seen a door in the basement. She had checked it out for other storage areas when they were cleaning up.

"I used Steph's idea of the incense and watched the smoke." Walking over to the door that was clearly a door on this side, he gave it a pull. "Watch, the whole shelf unit swings. Once I realized how it was built, I figured out how to open it."

The women took turns walking over to the door and looking into the main part of the basement.

Steph still wasn't sure she believed Hank found this room today. She pointed down the passageway. "So where does this go to?"

"It goes to the barn and there's a branch that goes to the gazebo. I'll show you some time but not today. The rain is dripping in places and I'd rather not risk a cave in. However, if you'll promise to wait here, I have a surprise for you."

Hank went into the passageway and brought back a crate for them to see. "There are crates and barrels blocking the passageway. I thought you'd like to be the ones to open them."

"Bring it into the basement where we'll have room." Keri was delighted with the condition of the crate. "I wonder what's inside."

"It's nailed shut. I may have to use a crowbar to open it." Looking around for something to use to pry the crate open with, Hank found an old metal screwdriver.

"This is so much fun! This place is always full of surprises." Keri was beaming. "I feel like a kid at Christmas."

Steph laughed at Keri. "What if it's empty?" She had forgiven Hank. Now she believed him. He seemed genuinely happy to have something to show them.

"Who cares? I love the crate, don't break it. I can use it for so many things!" Keri was trying hard not to help Hank as he slowly pried the lid off.

"Humph! I hope they're not all nailed this tight shut." Hank had managed to pry open a corner.

"It should go easier now that you've got one side loose." Betty stood to the side trying to stay out of the way.

"Crack!"

"You did it Hank! Now open it!" Keri was so excited she was almost jumping up and down.

Steph stood back and watched her friends.

Keri was tired of waiting for Hank. As soon as he had the lid off, she pushed him aside and began to carefully remove the packing. The crate contained crude crockery bowls nestled in straw packing. The straw had deteriorated around the bowls leaving them unharmed.

Carefully Keri removed a couple of bowls and held them out for the others to see. "Steph, these are beautiful!"

Steph was surprised Keri was so delighted. "They're okay, I guess. I mean, I'm sure you'll have ideas on how to use them." Steph didn't want to hurt her friend's feelings but they were thick and heavy.

"How many crates did you find Hank?" Betty didn't want to spend the afternoon watching Keri have all the fun.

"There are about seven crates and four barrels in the passageway. I can bring them all in here and we can open them all at once if you'd like." Hank was not looking forward to opening them if they were all as difficult to open as the first one. He would like to get that part over with.

"Yes. Let's get them all in here and we'll help open them. I'll go upstairs and get the big hammer and crowbar." Betty had seen the look of despair on Hank's face.

"I'll let you open these. I'd like to start emptying the desk in the other room." Steph went up the stairway to get a box. She wasn't going to travel down the other passageway if she could use the stairs.

Keri and Betty spent the rest of the afternoon unpacking the crates and barrels while Steph discovered what surprises might be hidden in the study.

CHAPTER 36

Hank had arranged to meet with Deputy Austin the day after his grizzly discovery.

Since he was going into town, Hank offered to take the document to the attorney's office for Steph. He planned to drop it off on his way to his meeting. It would give him a chance to talk with the lawyer himself.

When Hank walked into the law office he paused for a moment to become acquainted with the office layout. Steph had talked about the office so he had a general idea what to expect. Pasting on a friendly smile, he walked over to the receptionist. "Is Stan Wilbur in?"

The receptionist smiled at Hank. He noticed she sat up straighter and pushed out her breasts a little more.

In a breathy voice she asked "Junior or Senior?"

Hank was amazed he was not willing to be drawn into her game. He used to find such blatant flirtation amusing, often intriguing. Today he didn't have the time.

Still smiling, he leaned forward just a little and asked, "Which one is available?"

The receptionist jumped up and went immediately to check. She returned with an older gentleman.

"I'm Stanley Wilbur, Senior. How may I be of assistance?" The two men shook hands.

"I'm Henry Dawn and I'm here for Stephanotis Weatherby."

"Please come to my office." Hank followed the older man down a short hallway and into his office.

*   *   *

When both men were seated, Hank began, "Steph found a document yesterday we believe is the document you're looking for." He handed Stanley Sr. the manila envelope Steph had given him to deliver.

"Steph wrote you a note to explain how it was found. I just wanted to be sure you or Stan received it directly from me. I want to tell Steph you have personally received it."

"I thought I'd find you in here." Stan Jr. was standing in the doorway. "My receptionist said a dangerous looking man was with my father. I assumed it was you."

Hank rose and shook Stanley Jr.'s hand. "I brought something from Steph. It's the document you have been looking for."

Hank sat back down and looked at Stanley Sr. "If you'll check it before I leave, I'd appreciate it."

Hank carefully watched Stanley Sr. as he opened the envelope and removed the contents. Steph's letter was on top of the other document. Stanley Sr. set Steph's letter aside and read the document.

Smiling, Stanley Sr. handed it to Stan Jr. to read. After he finished reading it, he nodded and handed it back to his father.

"This will go a long way in getting this case resolved. Thank you for bringing it in." Stan Jr. was relieved to have the document found. He now had something to work with. He rose as if to signal the end of the conversation.

Hank understood Stanley Jr. was dismissing him, but he had something else to say to these two men and he planned to say it.

"Steph's been through a lot over this farm. I want you to end this ownership business quickly. The person harassing her may start up again. I found evidence he's been back. I need you to get out the news as quickly as possible that this is now a done deal and she is the rightful owner." Having said what he wanted, Hank rose to leave.

"Now, just one minute young man!" Stanley Sr.'s face was red with fury, a muscle twitched over his left eye. He stood up and looked at the other man across his desk. "It has not been proven the activities at the farm have been about the property. It may just be someone from Stephanotis's past trying to get even with her."

Hank barely controlled his rage. "I'm telling you! No one who knows that lady is going to do the terrible things this person has done. They destroyed the lawn tractor; they broke into her house; they kidnapped her dog; they blew up a car and almost killed her. Yesterday, they killed a stray cat and hung it in her barn. You're not going to tell me that nice lady has made someone that angry on purpose. There has to be a reason."

Hank took a deep calming breath before going on. "The strongest motive I can think of is that farm and what's on it. The land would be enough of a motive for someone to want to scare her off. You need to do your job and get this ownership settled once and for all." Hank realized he had said more than he meant to. He moved toward the door for a quick exit before someone else challenged him. His anger had erupted unbidden and it had rocked him to his core. He was usually slow to anger but knowing Steph may still be in danger kept it bubbling near the surface.

"Don't worry Hank. We'll do our job. I'll tell the correct parties right away to get the ball rolling and get the word out." Stan Jr. realized he underestimated Hank. Hank would be a formidable opponent. Stan Jr. was glad he was an ally if but a tentative one.

* * *

Hank's stomach was churning when he left the attorney's office. He mulled over the conversation while he drove to the sheriff's office.

Deputy Austin was waiting for him when he arrived. They went into a smaller office and sat down. Hank realized he was more comfortable here than he had been in the attorney's office. Looking around the shabby office, he saw stacks of papers to be filed and empty coffee cups that needed to be thrown out. He relaxed and let go of some of his anger. This was a workingman's environment.

"Let's see what you brought me. I've got the equipment set up to view the cards." Deputy Austin laid out the memory cards Hank had given him. "Which one is from the camera you think may have the best pictures?"

"I think the camera in the emergency lights. They're near the rafter where they hung the rope for the cat and would have the best light. The motion sensor should have noticed the movement." Hank pointed to the correct card.

Deputy Austin put the card into the computer reader and put the images up on the screen. "I've been practicing with this so it shouldn't take us long to see something. I'll just fast-forward it until we see something and then I can... Oh, look! Here's an image."

They both watched as something moved into range on the camera. It was blurry but Austin tapped a few keys on the computer keyboard and the image became a little sharper. As they watched, the image of a man wearing a baseball cap began to appear. As it focused, they were able to see he was carrying the ladder Hank used in the barn.

They continued to watch as the man moved across the floor. He was carrying something in a bag. For a few minutes the man disappeared from the screen. The man was careful to keep his face averted from the stall cameras.

"It's as if he knows they're there. Look, he has his collar up and the hat down. He knows something." Hank moved to the front of his chair and perched there precariously as he watched.

When the man returned, he set the ladder up near the camera to reach the rafter.

"Come on, show us your face." Deputy Austin was as entranced as Hank. If they could just get a look at his face!

The automatic focus on the camera had focused in on the ladder nearby and they had lost the image of the man for a few minutes. Both men sat back in their chairs disappointed with the results so far.

Still watching, they saw the ladder move, as if someone was climbing up. "Why doesn't the camera focus move back?" Deputy Austin's frustration was clear in his voice.

"The motion detector is part of the automatic focus. As long as the ladder near it is moving, it'll focus on that. Look!" The camera image had begun to pick up the top of the navy blue baseball hat. The man's head was getting near the camera.

Both men held their breath as the man's head moved into view. All at once the screen showed a perfect shot of a man's face turned toward the camera as he was reaching up to swing the rope over the rafter.

"Yes, Yes!"

"Hooray!" The two men looked at each other, each wearing a silly grin on their face. After a brief pause, they did a 'high five'.

The shouts of the happy men drew those working at their desks into the small office. Congratulating each other, Hank and Deputy Austin now knew what the man looked like. They accepted the congratulations of the other deputies and the office staff.

*   *   *

Drawn out of his office by all the noise, the sheriff himself came to see what was happening. He too offered his congratulations. He'd been on the phone with the insurance company. They weren't pleased with the slow progress of the case. The aggressiveness of the person on the telephone had shaken him up. He began questioning the ability of his department to handle this investigation when he was distracted by the noise.

"It's a pleasure to see how well you two are working together on this case. I must admit I was beginning to wonder if we'd ever get a break. Now, once you figure out who this fellow is, maybe we can make an arrest and end this once and for all." The sheriff beamed at Hank and Deputy Austin.

"I'll get right on it." Austin was still excited about having the evidence. "I'll need to review the other evidence as well."

"I left the cat back in the barn. I didn't want Steph to see me bring it in. Keri has been putting out food for it so I don't want them to know what happened to it. They've been upset enough over all of this." Hank was pleased with the evidence they'd uncovered. It made all his work worthwhile. He was feeling more like a policeman again and he had some ideas he wanted to share.

"I need to talk with you and Austin in private a moment if I can sheriff. Then I need to get back to the house. I don't like being gone very long. I have a funny feeling it's not over."

"Sure, let's go into my office." The sheriff led the way to his office and closed the door behind them. "Have a seat." Once they were all seated, he looked at Hank. He wasn't sure if this meant good news or more bad news.

"Sheriff, I think you and Deputy Austin should know that we've located the document signed by Iris Weatherby. Until the court agrees Steph is the only legal heir, I think they are going to step up their harassing."

"You've given this a lot of thought haven't you?" The sheriff watched Hank for a reaction.

Hank sighed. "I have. If I were after some property like that farm, I wouldn't stop until I was absolutely sure there was no other way to get it. I called one of my friends in Columbus. He does research for the state housing development. He looked into a few things for me. I asked him to check into the most profitable use for the land. He advised me that if it was used for agriculture, it would take some money to make it profitable again, depending upon the crops being planted, the livestock raised and the market."

"Now, if someone were to be enterprising enough to use it for a business venture such as a golf course then sell the land in lots for houses, they could make at least a million dollars in profit over time. He said it would take some serious capital to start, but it would be possible."

Hank paused to let them mull over what he said. "I don't know about you, but I can picture the place with a golf course, using the house as a clubhouse. I haven't told Steph about this yet. If it were me, I'd find that to be enough incentive to try to get her to leave."

The sheriff was leaning forward, listening eagerly when Hank began talking. Now he leaned back in his chair looking tired and deflated. "You paint a really pretty picture. I can see what you're thinking. Someone wants to make themselves some serious money." Moving forward again the sheriff searched Hank for any signs of a reaction. "Have you been thinking of trying to get your hand in that kind of pie?"

Something in the sheriff's tone alerted Hank. He smiled ruefully. Hank knew what the sheriff was thinking. Steph was single and he was now living at her house. "I'm glad to see you are checking all the angles, but if I were you sheriff, I'd get my mind out of the gutter. Steph's a great lady and I care about her a lot. I also care about Keri and Betty. I'm not sleeping with any of them. It's Steph's property and she needs to be the one to decide what to do about it." Satisfied with the shocked look on the sheriff's face, Hank leaned back in his chair waiting for the sheriff to make up his mind.

"Yeah, I checked you out." The sheriff relaxed again. "Your superiors all told me you were on the level and they had a lot of respect for you. I must admit, you've been straight with me so far."

"Good. That's settled. I'm just worried the violence and harassment is going to escalate until. . ." Hank broke off with the violent knocking on the sheriff's door.

"What!" The sheriff yelled across the room.

Deputy Thompson opened the door. "We just got a 911 call from the Weatherby farm. One of the buildings is on fire."

Hank jumped up and was out the door before the sheriff and Deputy Austin registered what was being said. He plowed his way through the gathering deputies and was headed for his truck before Austin could get his attention.

Breathing heavy from the exertion, Austin caught up with Hank. "We'll take my car. I'll get you there faster." Austin pointed to a car parked off to the side of the building.

Hank swung around, motioning for Austin to hurry along. Both men piled into the car. As Austin started the engine, he risked a glance over at Hank. "I would have hated to be forced to give you a ticket for speeding."

Hank stared at Austin. "Just shut up and show me what this thing can do."

Austin nodded his head and turned on his lights and siren before peeling away from the building.

Hank was relieved Austin was driving. He didn't trust himself. He heard the word fire and he was terrified. It had rained the day before, but was it enough to keep it from spreading? Steph was in the house, or at least he hoped she was. Was it the house that was on fire? Hank's mind raced, dwelling on the worst he could possibly imagine.

When they pulled onto the road leading to the farm, he could see smoke billowing in the distance. He saw, rather than heard other flashing lights as emergency vehicles raced to the scene. When Austin turned onto the driveway, Hank saw more than one shed was burning.

Austin called into the dispatcher for an update. The dispatcher reported that after the first call came in, they received a second call advising another shed was burning.

Hank was relieved to see Steph, Keri and Betty, standing out on the porch of the house, out of the way when they pulled up. Austin parked the car directly in front of the house, beside the other two cars.

Hank raced up the steps followed by Austin.

"Hank! Oh Hank! It's just awful." Keri was standing there, pale and shivering.

Betty and Steph were watching the fire burn. They were so intent in watching as the firefighters were trying to get to the fire, they didn't realize Hank and Austin were there.

"It's okay, Keri, we're here. Is everyone alright?" Hank put his arm around Keri and gave her a reassuring hug. Realizing she was trembling, Hank gently aided her in sitting down in a chair. "Sit here, Keri. You'll be okay."

Hank approached Steph and Betty. When he touched Betty on the shoulder, she jumped bumping into Steph. "I'm sorry I didn't mean to startle you. Are you both alright?" Hank knew his voice sounded gruff but he was too relieved to care.

When Steph turned to look at Hank, he saw the tears streaming down her face. She struggled to speak, then gave up and merely nodded to let him know she was okay.

"We're alright. I was frightened at first, but we're not hurt and it looks as if they should be able to get it under control." Betty walked over and sat down by Keri. She took her friend's hand into hers and patted it reassuringly. "Keri, it's alright. We're safe and the men are working to put out the fire. Everything's going to be alright."

Hank walked over and put his arm around Steph, not knowing what else to do.

Clearing her throat, she found her voice. "This makes me so mad I could scream! When will this stop?" Steph kept watching the fire not expecting a reply. Steph felt the anger moving from her stomach up into her throat. "I don't know why this is happening but I'm not giving up. This isn't going to chase me away. This is my home and they can't have it. I won't be chased away. I belong here no matter what anyone does or says." Feeling herself begin to shake, Steph moved away from Hank, not wanting him to know how close she was to falling apart.

Hank let his arm drop as he stepped away saying a prayer of thanks Steph was okay.

Deputy Austin left the porch to join the other deputies who arrived. When he returned with the sheriff, he motioned for Hank to join them.

Hank was reluctant to go, but knew Steph would be alright. Anger was better than fear.

As he walked over to join the other men, Hank looked once again over at the scene of the fire. The burning sheds were the farthest sheds away from the barn. The sheds were built close together and they were the closest buildings to the woods. He knew they were empty having emptied them himself. The buildings were made of old wood and as he looked, he began to wonder why the fire wasn't being extinguished at either shed.

"What's actually happening?" Hank looked at Austin and then the sheriff.

Steph had quietly joined the men and stood behind Hank waiting for the answer. She was still too upset to say anything aloud, not trusting her own voice.

"There seems to be a problem. The sheds must have been drenched with gasoline from the smell. The wood is old and wet. It should have been hard to start burning like that. Is there anything flammable in either shed?"

"Both sheds were empty. There were pieces of farm machinery scattered around, but I moved them to the big shed with the tractor so I could fiddle with them. I go through all the buildings every couple of days. With the rain, I figured it would keep until tomorrow." Hank was finding it hard to take his eyes off the blaze.

As the men were talking, they were joined by one of the volunteer firefighters. "I came to see what you've found out. We've got some kind of liquid running from the buildings into the field and need to know what it is."

"As far as I know, both sheds were empty two days ago. I cut the weeds around them last week and there was no sign of any liquid being stored in the sheds."

"I'll give the men the okay to move closer then. We try to stay back as far as possible until we know what's inside. If something flammable is being stored, we don't want to be near it when it goes."

The firefighter turned to leave when one of the sheds exploded. The men were shaken by the blast. Sparing just a moment to glare at Hank, the firefighter ran to help those who were nearest the sheds.

"Shit! What was that?" The sheriff was shaking his head.

"Damned if I know!" Hank too was shaking his head to stop his ears from ringing. They were standing over five hundred feet from the blast. He could only imagine how the men closer to the blast were feeling.

Hank looked at Steph who had turned very pale. "Are you okay?"

Steph wrenched her eyes away from the burning buildings to look at Hank. "I'm okay, I just feel helpless. I wish I could do something to help."

Hank glanced over at Betty and Keri then back at Steph. "Maybe you could get some drinks lined up for the men. They're going to be at this a while."

Realizing Hank was giving her an excuse to stop watching, Steph gave him a weak smile. "I guess it would be good to get Keri inside. We'll get something put together."

As Steph walked away, Hank and the sheriff both turned in time to see a small ball of fire begin to move as if it was a living creature across the ground. Some of the firefighters had noticed the flames and were now spraying it with water. They watched the flames spread faster as if running away from the force of the water.

"I guess we know what the liquid was." The sheriff shook his head in disgust. "It's headed right for that field of wheat. There'll be no stopping it if it gets there."

Hank realized the sheriff was right. George was counting on that wheat crop. "Will they be able to stop it?"

"There's no telling. If it's gas or kerosene, they're just spreading it with the water and it looks like it's just making it worse. If they had the foam truck or a bulldozer, they could bury it and put it out."

"Of course!" Hank took off running to the big shed that housed the tractor. He had made a copy of Steph's key and was pulling out his key chain as he ran. Fumbling with the lock, he slammed the doors open.

Hank started up the tractor. He had never driven it but thought it should work like George's tractor. He'd have to figure it out as he drove.

At first it moved along jerking and stopping. Once he learned how the gears worked, he was moving forward. He coaxed it along on the flat tires, heedless of the damage being done to the rims.

*   *   *

Unknown to Hank, George was one of the volunteer firefighters helping to battle the blaze. He was trying to help keep it contained when he heard someone yell it was spreading. The noise of the blaze was making it hard to understand what was happening. Concentrating on keeping the hose focused on his assigned area, George didn't know the blaze was making its way to his precious crop of wheat. It wasn't until he noticed the firefighter closest to him was trying to spray the ground that he realized it was spreading into the weeds.

George watched as the water sent the blaze scattering. He grabbed the other man's hose and shouted at him trying to be heard above the roar. "Stop, you're making it worse. Don't you know better than to pour water on a burning gas fire? It won't put it out, just spread it, look!"

Horrified, George watched as it began to gather momentum and head straight for his wheat field. George handed his hose to the man behind him and ran to his truck for a shovel. If he could smother it enough to stop it before it got to the wheat, it would be okay.

Running back with the shovel, George saw Hank heading across the field on the tractor. George began shoveling dirt onto the blaze. Instead of putting it out, it seemed to ignite it further. George was determined to save his wheat. Putting his back into it, he kept shoveling, watching as each shovelful did less and less to stop the blaze.

In disgust and frustration, George threw down his shovel and ran to join Hank.

*   *   *

Hank saw someone running toward him. With immense relief he saw it was George. As the tractor began to slowly pass him, George ran up, grabbed the back of the seat and jumped up behind Hank. "Put her in gear and get her moving. You've got to put that out before it gets to the wheat."

"I'm trying. I can't seem to get it going any faster." Hank realized his best wasn't going to be good enough.

"Move over, I'll take it." George was desperate. Hank moved off the seat and George slid in. After some shifting and moving, Hank was now standing behind George.

"Do you know how to drive this?"

"Yeah. I had to borrow it the first year I was here. It wasn't working very well then, but I figure you must've worked on it." George felt the gears grind as he pushed the gearshift around to get more speed. Anger fueled George's efforts. "I've got to save my wheat."

George lowered the front-end loader with the tractor moving fast. For a moment it seemed as if the tractor was going to flip over. Then he raised it and the grass tore loose, leaving a large hole. Spinning the steering wheel, he bypassed the hole he had created and shifted gears again. Coming to the section of the blaze that was licking at the leading edge of the wheat field, he dropped his load on the wheat and fire. Backing up, he continued to dig up loads of soil and drop it on the fire stream.

George worked at a steady pace until he was near the sheds. Then he backed up the tractor out of the way and surveyed his work. Hank slapped him on the shoulder and praised him for his work. "I never thought this old beast would work that well. You sure know how to drive it."

Hank jumped down and turned to look at the blaze.

George came down more slowly. He was still wearing his fire suit. He'd removed his mask as he ran to jump onto the tractor, but the suit was cumbersome and not built for getting off old tractors. "It's all thanks to you. Only you could have gotten it to work again." George nodded his thanks to his friend. "I'd better go see if I'm needed elsewhere." George stalked off, trying not to let himself think about what this disaster could have cost him. Once again, the events at the Weatherby Farm were costing him and his family. Pushing those thoughts away, he went to check in and find out where he was needed next.

Hank remained standing by the tractor. He watched as the firefighters began to douse the grass around the buildings.

"They're going to let the buildings burn themselves down. We're hoping for no more surprises." The sheriff walked over to join Hank. Slapping him on the back, he started to laugh. "You were sure a sight driving this old thing across the field. It doesn't even have tires anymore. Talk about peeling rubber." The older man pointed back the way Hank had come. "You really did a number on those tires, now all you have are rims." The sheriff stood laughing for a few minutes.

Hank looked at the pieces of disintegrated tires that were scattered in his wake. Then he looked at the dents in the rims and winced.

The sheriff sobered up. "You did what was right. It was a good thing though that old George knew how to work this baby. I thought you two were going to flip when he dug that crater back there. I never saw anyone try that sort of stunt. It sure made my stomach flip." The sheriff shook his head at the memory. "When he pulled loose and moved on, it was sure a sight to see." The sheriff turned and patted the tractor. "I haven't seen one of these for years. They don't make tractors like this anymore. They're all fancy with actual tires and everything. What model is this?"

Hank couldn't help replying, "It's a workhorse!" He and the sheriff both laughed.

Jenny and Steph came running over to Hank and the sheriff. They had been watching from the porch. Jenny reached Hank first and gave him a big hug. Then she pushed him away punching him in the chest. "You idiot!" She yelled. "You could have been hurt. Where's George? Wait till I get my hands on that man! I got here just in time to see you two fools." Jenny was looking around and spied George talking with the Fire Chief by one of the fire trucks. She ran over and grabbed George.

Hank was still reeling from Jenny's assault when Steph reached him. She had seen him driving the tractor over the field and wondered why. Then watching George jump onto the moving tractor, she realized where they were headed. When George had dug into the ground while the tractor was moving and it looked as if they were going to flip, Steph thought she was going to faint.

As Steph saw Jenny run up to Hank and grab him in a hug, Steph felt a stab of fierce jealousy. This was her man and if anyone was going to be angry at him, it was she! When she reached Hank, she stood for a minute looking at him. Then she reached up and pulled his head down to hers. Kissing him roughly, she released him. Reeling from the emotions in her kiss, she punched him in the chest. "Don't you ever scare me like that again! You're an idiot! What were you thinking?" Steph felt her heart still pounding as she turned to walk away.

Hank instinctively reached out, grabbing her arm to stop her from walking away. Pulling her to him, he kissed her back with all the emotion he felt for her.

Clearing his throat, the sheriff decided it best to leave them alone. "I think I'll go see how the Fire Chief's doing." The sheriff hurried away.

When Hank broke the kiss, he was surprised to see Steph smiling at him. Not trusting his voice, he merely stood there looking at her. At some point during the kiss she had wrapped her arms around his neck.

They were so wrapped up in each other they didn't hear anyone come up.

"Well, it's about time." Jenny and George were standing there watching. "I was beginning to wonder what it was going to take for you two to figure this out. Come on, George. Let's go check on the others at the house." A grinning Jenny led George away by the hand. George had a surprised look on his face.

Laughing, Hank kept his arm around Steph to hold her close as they followed their friends.

CHAPTER 37

"Are you sure you can do this for me?" Steph was sitting at the kitchen table with Chris. "I just know this place is going to be a wonderful Bed and Breakfast. It's going to be worth all this work." Over the past few weeks she had been making phone calls, setting up appointments, filling out forms and setting her plans into motion.

"I'm a little rusty, but I think I can work up a reasonable layout. How much time do I have?" Chris tried to keep the anxiety from his voice.

"I was hoping to get started in three weeks. I have all the paperwork filled out for the permits but they said I have to have an architect draw up the plans for them to approve. In addition, I need to have the place inspected. Usually it takes weeks to get an appointment with the building inspector. I'm beginning to think providence is on my side. The clerk called this morning and the inspector is coming tomorrow. He'd like to see a rough draft of my building plans." Biting her lip, she knew it was a lot to ask. If Chris would just work up the rough draft, she could try to get another architect to draw up the final plans. When the architect she talked with two weeks ago had called to tell her they were too busy to work with her, she almost gave up. She would have to wait another month for them to even begin, which would put her months behind on her plans.

"I guess I could have the rough draft done by tomorrow. What time?" Chris was nervous. He owed George a lot and these were his friends. He would at least try.

Steph's face glowed with delight as she jumped up and gave Chris a hug.

"What's this? Someone's moving in on my girl?" Hank walked in just as Steph was hugging Chris. He was still slightly uncomfortable admitting his feelings for Steph but he could never resist the urge to tease her.

Steph walked over and kissed Hank. Pulling him over with her to the table, she waved to the papers spread out. "Chris has agreed to work up a rough draft for the inspector's visit tomorrow. Isn't that wonderful?"

Hank grinned. "Wow, Chris. Do you know what you're getting into?"

Betty brought a plate of freshly baked cookies to the table. "Sure he does. All the cookies he can eat!" She laughed and joined the others at the table.

"Steph, if you're going to turn this into a B & B are you going to remodel the kitchen?" Betty had been giving it some serious thought but would not offer her suggestions unless Steph asked her to.

Steph motioned for Hank to sit down. "I'll be right back." Steph left the room and returned carrying some books. She also brought Keri with her.

After they were all seated, Steph began talking. "I've given this a lot of thought. I realize this is a small kitchen and works well for just us, but I wondered what all of you thought about remodeling the basement for the kitchen?" Steph looked at each of their faces for a hint of their reactions. Since they were still quiet, she decided to go on with another idea. "I also thought of remodeling the top floor into a private suite. That would give the guests the complete run of the second floor and main level. We could have the family rooms on the top level. There's plenty of room up there for bedrooms, a kitchen and a living room."

Keri shook her head. "Steph, you'd wear yourself out running up and down the stairs. Don't you have to have handicap accessible rooms as well to pass the inspection?"

"They make hydraulic elevators for homes that don't need a machine room now. Everything is self-contained. You could have one or more depending on the location. I would recommend running one from the main level to the second floor on one side of the house. On the other side of the house you could run one from the top floor to the basement. A security system can be installed to keep guests from going up to the top floor." Chris was warming up to the idea as he talked.

"You could put in a new more fuel-efficient boiler that would be smaller. It would give you more space for commercial washers and dryers." Chris reached for a blank piece of paper and began sketching.

"That's a good idea. I was thinking we could knock out the shelves in the basement along the wall and open it up to the hidden study. The finished room could be the office. It wouldn't take much to cover the cement floor and it already has the wood stove for winter." Steph opened one of the books she had brought with her. "This is called a radiant floor. It's used for additional warmth in the winter. I wondered about having something like that put in for the basement." She passed the book around.

Steph looked over at Hank. "You're being very quiet. What were you thinking about?"

He seemed startled to have been asked. "I was just thinking how nice a hot tub would be in the cupola." Embarrassed by their laughter, he looked down at the table.

"That's a great idea. A little extra support in the floor and you could do that. I was trying to think of something special for that area. It's a remarkable example of construction. I wasn't being as creative as you Hank. Some of my ideas sound lame compared with that." Chris winked at Hank.

They spent the next two hours going over ideas for the new kitchen and the upper floor. There were several suggestions made for the use of the current kitchen.

"I'd like to walk around a little and take some measurements before I go. Hank can you help me?" Chris gathered up papers as he stood up. He was going to have a lot of work to do that night.

"Sure." Hank followed Chris out of the room.

The two men walked around the different floors and ended in the cupola. As they were measuring it, Hank noticed a car drive slowly up the road. The woods obstructed part of the road and the car drove into the obscured area. Hank could not explain why, but he had the urge to watch and see if the car would be appearing on the other side of the woods. He stood and waited. After several minutes had passed, the car did not reappear. Hank realized the only explanation was the car had been driven off the road into the woods. He searched but couldn't see the car.

Hank pulled his cell phone out of his pocket and immediately called Deputy Austin.

"I just saw a car come down the road and I have good reason to believe it may be our intruder. He drove past the house but hasn't reappeared on the road yet. Can you get someone out here? . . . What? Oh, I'm standing in the cupola on the top of the house. . . No, I still don't see them. . . Yeah, Chris and I'll keep watching."

Hank disconnected the call. Without taking his eyes off the road, he explained his idea to Chris. "We'll stay and keep watch. You take that half and I'll watch this half. Let me know if you see anything move or if you see anything suspicious."

The two men stood quietly, focused on their assignment. After what seemed like an eternity to Hank, he saw a deputy sheriff's car drive slowly down the road. Looking in the other direction he saw another deputy's car coming.

"Good, boys, you've got his escape blocked, now don't lose him." Hank didn't realize he was talking aloud.

"I think I see something moving." Chris was worried his eyesight might let him down. He was getting tired of standing there but he was excited to be helping Hank.

Hank moved closer. Looking in the direction Chris pointed, he could see someone moving along the edge of the woods. "Good eyesight." Hank called Deputy Austin on his phone.

"We see your cruisers. There's a man walking along the edge of the woods. He's back in the area near the burned sheds."

Hank and Chris watched as the man seemed to be searching for something. They tried to see what he was looking for. Sparing a glance towards the road, Hank saw a third cruiser coming down the driveway. He hoped the man in the woods didn't see it.

Suddenly, the man stopped what he was doing and moved quickly back into the woods. After a few moments there was a blast of a siren and then a bang. The cruiser in the driveway turned around in the grass and sped off toward the road and the woods.

Hank was frustrated. His view of the action was blocked by the trees. After a few minutes, his cell phone rang. It was Deputy Austin.

Hank was grinning when he hung up the phone. "Chris, let's go tell the ladies. We just helped catch the bad man. You're a hero, Chris, old boy! There'll be celebrating tonight."

They finished their measurements and drafting before leaving the cupola. As they walked down the stairs, Hank called George and told him what happened.

When they reached the main floor, Deputy Austin was in the kitchen talking with Steph, and the ladies. Seeing Hank and Chris walk in, Austin walked over and shook their hands. "We got him. It's a wonder. We couldn't see anything in the woods where his car was. If he hadn't panicked and pulled out, I don't think we'd have found him. He had a big camouflage canvas on his backseat. He used it to cover the car.

"What made you think of staking out the cupola? That was an excellent idea. I don't know why we didn't think of that before?" Deputy Austin looked at Hank.

"Actually we sort of stumbled into it. Chris and I were up there measuring it for a hot tub." Hank was slightly embarrassed but he started laughing. "I still think that would be the perfect place for it."

Steph walked over and kissed him. "My hero." Then she walked over and kissed Chris on the cheek. "My other hero. Thanks, to both of you."

"I think this call's for a party! Let's call George and Jenny!" Keri reached for her cell phone.

"I hate to spoil your fun, but I was wondering if Hank would like to come and listen in on the interrogation. Since he's been a major part of this I asked the sheriff if it was okay. He said to bring you on in."

Hank was quiet for a minute. This was not something he had counted on. He was glad the man was caught but something in

Austin's manor indicated it wasn't over yet. "I'd like that. I'll meet you there in a few minutes. I have something I need to do first."

Hank went into the music room and collected his laptop. Returning, he asked Steph to walk him to his truck.

"I want you to hold off having your party for tonight. Chris has to do those drawings for you. We'll have the party another night and invite Deputy Austin and the sheriff if that's okay. I think they need to celebrate too. Have George come and get Chris, then lock up the house. Turn on the alarm after Chris leaves. Will you promise me you'll do that?" Hank kissed Steph good-bye after she reluctantly agreed to do as he asked. When he got in the truck, he rolled down his window. "I'll call you later to let you know what's happening."

Steph stood in the driveway and watched Hank drive off. Turning to return to the house, she thought about his change of behavior and wondered why he seemed to be afraid.

*   *   *

Steph was sitting at the table the next morning thinking about the night before when Keri walked into the kitchen.

Seeing the look on her friend's face, Keri helped herself to a cup of coffee. She sat down at the table to wait for Steph to tell her what was wrong. Hank had not returned last night when she and Betty went to bed.

Betty wandered in a few minutes after Keri and mirrored Keri's movements.

They were sitting there quietly drinking their coffee when Steph finally spoke. "I don't know what to do about Hank. He called last night just as he said he would, but it was really late when I heard Misti bark as he came in." She looked down at her feet where her faithful friend laid. "She's recovering so well."

Keri reached across the table and laid her hand on Steph's arm. "What do you mean you don't know what to do about Hank?"

"I feel as if he's keeping something from me and I don't like that feeling." Steph looked down into her coffee cup. "I love him. He hasn't said anything, so I don't know how he really feels. I just worry that when this is all over, he'll leave. There won't be any reason for him to stay." Steph looked up at Keri and then Betty.

"I wish I knew what happened at the sheriff's office. I want to know why that man has been doing these terrible things." Steph realized she was getting angry and loud. Calming herself down, she continued. "I have the building inspector coming today. He'll be here at ten a.m. I keep thinking about Chris's rough draft. I know it will be okay, I guess I'm just getting nervous." Steph forced a weak laugh.

"It's going to be alright." Betty stood up. "I'll get breakfast started. You get yourself together for the inspector."

"I was looking at some of the kitchen appliances available on the Internet." Steph opened up the notebook she had with her. "We're going to need a new range, counters and a refrigerator. If we stay small and just serve breakfast, we won't need a lot of equipment. However, if we do other meals or any catering, we're going to need more stuff. It's all so expensive." Closing her notebook, Steph sighed. "I have an appointment with the loan officer at the bank this afternoon. If the inspector approves the plans, they're willing to talk about a loan. I just don't know how big of a loan I'm going to need."

Keri was concerned about her friend. "Okay, let's think about this. You can start out just serving breakfast and then get the other equipment as you need it."

"I thought of that. Chris and I talked about it. He said it might be more expensive to buy it as we grow. It might mean remodeling the kitchen again. He also thought it might make it more difficult to pass inspection. I need to show the inspector I mean business."

Betty came over and stood by them. "It makes sense. If you're going to have parties catered or weddings, you'll need a place for the caterer to work. If the kitchen is well equipped, you'll find the caterer will be easier to work with and they'll recommend you for their events."

Steph reluctantly reopened her notebook to a blank page. "Help me make a list of possible events and maybe that will help me figure this out." She put a heading on her page and looked across the table at Keri.

Keri thought for a moment before speaking. "Fall is almost here. How about hosting Halloween parties? They could go on a hayride and then later they could have a hot dog roast. How about evening barbecues? You could have square dances in the barn."

"Weddings. You could host small weddings in the music room or conservatory." Betty brought platters of bacon and eggs to the table. Returning with plates and flatware, she joined them at the table. By the end of the meal, they had filled the page of the notebook with ideas.

"All of this tells me I might as well do this right and set up a complete kitchen."

"That was what I thought." Chris came into the room carrying a large sheaf of papers. "Hank dropped me off on his way to the sheriff's office. Jenny said to tell you she'll be over later." Chris's eyes wandered around the room, stopping at the almost full coffee pot. "Coffee!" Chris put down his bundle on the counter and helped himself to a cup of coffee.

After drinking deeply from his cup, he walked over to the table and joined the women.

"I was having trouble thinking this out. I apologize for the crudeness of some of the drawings but it's been awhile." He motioned to the papers he had left on the counter. "I hope you like some of it."

Curious, Steph rose and walked over to the counter. Opening the bundle, she began flipping through the pages. Her gasps of excitement and delight brought Keri and Betty over to look as well.

Turning back to the table, Steph was greeted by the smile on Chris's face. "Chris, these are wonderful. I can't believe this is possible." Picking up the papers, she carried them to the table where they all gathered around.

"I had to practice so the first ideas are really rough." He showed them the pages containing a basic sketch of the basement and the third floor.

Pulling out a different sheet, he showed them the design he had finally settled on. It showed a walk in refrigerator with a separate freezer unit. He began pointing out the features he added. "I put in a wine cooler here, near the door to the office. If you don't like it, you can build in cabinets for storage."

"I like the idea of an alcove for the range. That will keep the heat condensed more in one location and make it easier for the vents to pull the heat out." Betty was studying the floor plan looking for any suggestions she could add.

"I must say, I'm impressed." Steph just sat looking at the drawing in amazement.

"I took the liberty of sketching in an area for the elevator by the stairway. I widened out the stairway and gave it a slightly different angle. I also kept the dumbwaiter where it is. It can be modernized with a new car and electricity."

"I thought if we remodel the entire stairway going down, then this room." He indicated the current kitchen they were in, "Can be refurbished for another use. I had a look in the butler's pantry and it could use a little modernization. I have sketches for those as well." Chris passed around the other sketches he made.

"I drew up a couple of different floor plans for the top level. I spent most of the night working on the kitchen so I just sketched them out. You can show them to the inspector and tell him it's still in the planning stage."

CHAPTER 38

They were still in the kitchen when the building inspector arrived.

Steph answered the door expecting to find an older gentleman, close to retirement age. Standing there was a short, thin man in his late forties. "Hello, I'm Wade Law, Building Inspector."

"Please come in." Steph held the door open wide. "I'm not sure about the protocol for being inspected so please tell me how it's supposed to be done."

"Of course. If you'll show me around I'll check things out. Then we'll take a look at your ideas." The man looked around the house as he entered. "Nice place. If it's structurally sound we'll see what we can do."

Steph took Wade first to the kitchen and introduced him to the others. She picked up the sketch of the kitchen to take with them to the basement.

Misti started to growl and moved away from the stranger.

Keri picked her up. "I'll just hang onto her while you show the Inspector around.

Steph nodded her thanks and wondered why the dog reacted that way.

*   *   *

"I brought you downstairs to show you the area I plan to remodel into a kitchen. I intend to put in radiant floor heating, and of course, we'll put in a new ceiling. To make more room, we'll

458

remove the shelves along one wall. . ." While Steph talked, Wade walked around making notations in his notebook, checking the floor, walls and ceiling.

When looking at the plans Steph was holding, Wade would stand as close to her as possible, making her nervous. She hated the way her hands shook as she held the pages.

"I see you plan to put in an elevator. May I ask why?" Wade looked expectantly up at Steph.

"We have a total of four floors if you go from the basement up to the top floor. That's a lot of walking."

A thoughtful expression crossed his face before Wade made another notation in his notebook. "May I see outside where the elevator would go?"

"Yes, we can go out this door." Opening the basement door, Steph led the way outside and showed him where the elevators would be placed. "Right now we're toying with the idea of just having one elevator go from the main floor to the guest rooms and the other elevator going from the basement to the top floor."

Wade's answer was a slight nod as he made notes. Then it was Steph's turn to follow Wade as he walked around the outside of the building looking at the foundation and lower exterior walls.

As they went back into the house through the music room, Steph tried to draw the inspector's attention to the details of the room. "The music room has French doors that open onto the porch. I hope to rent it out for wedding receptions and parties." Steph watched for any reactions from the inspector but he merely made another note in his book.

As they passed from the music room to the parlor, Steph was surprised when the inspector closed his notebook, marking his place with a finger. "This is an awfully big house for one person."

Steph smiled. "It may seem that way right now, but as a Bed and Breakfast it'll be just the right size." Steph showed him the other rooms on the main floor of the house.

"So far, I've been impressed with the construction and foundation. Everything seems structurally sound but you never know. I'll need to see all of it."

Wade kept walking close to Steph. As they began to climb the main stairway up, he began reaching out and touching her on her arm. Steph tried to control the chills his touch caused. She was repulsed by the man but tried to hide it. He was becoming too familiar. She kept reminding herself she needed him to okay her permits for the remodeling to begin. If she could just get the okay, everything would work out.

Steph walked him down the hall on the second level and showed him where they would build a hallway for the elevator over the music room. She remained in the hall as he walked in and looked around each bedroom, opening closet doors and checking under the bathroom sinks.

Steph opened the long windows that swung out onto the roof of the porch at the back of the house. Gingerly, he stepped out, testing the planks as he walked. Satisfied it would hold him, Wade walked around checking the supports and railings. Returning to the top of the stairs, she showed him where the larger elevator would be placed. All through the process, Steph kept reminding herself he was a professional and there at her request.

Wade stopped for a few minutes to write in his notebook. With his attention diverted, Steph began to relax hoping the inspection was almost over.

Snapping his notebook shut, Wade looked at Steph. "Now, where is the other floor that will be remodeled?" Steph led the way and began to walk up the back stairway to the next level.

Wade walked further behind Steph and it wasn't until she reached the top of the stairs that she realized he must have been watching her walk up. Moving quickly away from the stairs, she stepped into the middle of the servant's hall. "This is the top floor. I plan to tear down the walls, redo the ceiling and build a private suite up here." Steph stood with her arms across her body as if she were cold.

Wade looked around at the various rooms, checking the roof line and exterior walls, stopping long enough to make more notations in his notebook.

Steph was beginning to worry about what he was writing when suddenly he stopped and began to move toward the circular stairway to the cupola.

"What's up here?"

"That's the cupola." Steph tried to keep her voice level. There was something unnerving about the way the man was looking at the stairway.

"Please show it to me. I must see all of the building if I am to make a complete report."

Tentatively, Steph walked over to the bottom of the stairway. She tried to reassure herself she was not in any danger. This was her home. She walked up the spiral staircase with Wade close behind. When they reached the top, Steph walked across the cupola to the section containing the door.

Entranced by the view, Wade began to walk around slowly, finally ending beside Steph.

"You know, you have a very nice piece of property here and with the right management, you could make a fortune." Wade moved a step closer to Steph, still looking out over the farm. Without Steph noticing, he had positioned himself between her and the stairway.

"What do you mean management? I don't understand." Fear gripped Steph as she began to wonder if this was the person who had been terrorizing her.

"I have been approached about zoning this area to include a few luxury properties. I don't think you realize it but I can help you get the most out of your property." Slowly, Wade began to move toward Steph, getting close enough to put an arm around her.

Dazed by his words, Steph stood still.

Encouraged by her lack of response, Wade smiled. "Careful, Miss Weatherby, I don't want you to feel dizzy at this height. I'm sure I could help you get the right kind of permits to turn this into a nice resort area with executive housing. This house would remain, but you'd have to tear down the other buildings and the barn. With that wooded area, it would be a terrific business venture."

Steph had felt his arm go around her and something inside her shifted. Anger began to melt the fear. While he was across the room, she had unlocked the outside door thinking to show him the widows walk. Now as she shifted slightly away from him, she decided to play his game her own way.

"How large of a return are we talking about?" She turned and smiled at him.

"Of course, it depends on the type of management you have. With a shrewd partner, you could easily make a one to two million dollars. Everything would be depending, of course, on the layout and the housing market. I could help you get the permits and set you up with the right contractors to get things going right away. All you need to do is show me how appreciative you would be." He pulled her to him and tried to kiss her.

Steph turned her face in time for his kiss to land on her cheek. "It would be more exciting to show you my gratitude out on the landing. Have you ever been kissed up in the air?" Steph tried not to tremble with anger as she pretended to flirt with this man.

"You mean outside this thing?" Wade relaxed his grip enough for Steph to wiggle free.

Opening the door, she laughed and pretended to encourage him. "Come on, let's go outside." Waiting for him to follow her, she walked around the cupola backwards. "Look how high we are, isn't this exciting?" As soon as he looked down, she rushed to the door and closed it, locking the man outside.

Not knowing what else to do, Steph started running down the stairs as fast as she could. As she neared the main floor, she started yelling for Chris. Shocked at herself, she wasn't sure what to do next.

*   *   *

Steph didn't know Hank had returned and it was he who came running in response to her calls.

Finding her shaking, he grabbed her and held her while the others came. Steph clung to him while trying to catch her breath. "Are you okay?"

Steph managed to nod, not knowing whether to laugh or cry.

"Steph, what's the matter?" Keri came running followed by Betty and Chris.

"What's going on? Why were you calling for Chris?"

"I need his help." Steph was still panting.

Betty looked around and realized that she didn't see the building inspector. "Steph, where is the building inspector? Has something happened to him?"

"He's... he's outside the cupola."

"What do you mean he's outside the cupola?" Worried, Keri started up the stairway to the top floor followed by the others.

As they neared the upper floor, they could hear someone pounding on the glass and their frantic calls for help.

Hank looked at Steph and started laughing. "Steph, where is he?"

Steph smiled weakly at Hank. "He's out on the widow's walk. I wasn't letting him in until he cooled off and I didn't trust myself not to push him off." As Steph continued talking, her anger began to show in her voice. "He kept touching me and telling me he could help me if I'd be nice to him." Steph looked at her friends to be sure they understood she was angry.

During his career, Chris had found most inspectors to be honest and competent. His surprise on this man's behavior registered on his face.

"You don't have to worry Hank. Our Steph's always been able to handle herself around raging hormones. She taught middle school for years!" Keri's eyes twinkled with laughter. "That funny little man is stuck out on the roof!" Keri's laughter became contagious and soon they were all laughing.

Betty collected herself first. "You'd better let him in."

"Not by myself. He's fast for a little guy." Steph started up the stairway looking back to make sure someone was following her.

"Don't look at me." Hank held up his arms in surrender. "I might end up decking the guy."

Chris shook his head and chuckled. "I guess it falls to me to be the defender of the lady's honor."

Chris slowly followed Steph up the stairs.

Steph went over and opened the door where Wade fell inside gasping for breath. He looked up at her with accusation written all over his face.

Chris walked over and looked down at the man. Stamping his prosthetic foot Chris watched the man. "What do you think? Good strong foundation right? I've known a few building inspectors to crawl under the foundation but I never met one who checked out the roof." Chris reached out his hand. "Need some help getting up?"

Wade crawled over to the top of the spiral stairway and looked down. He held onto the railing with an iron grip as he stood up and walked down the steps.

Keri and Betty met him at the bottom of the steps.

"Oh my, what a terrible experience! And so devoted to his job. Why don't we take him to the kitchen, Betty, and get him a nice glass of lemonade and some cookies. He can sign the papers for Steph as he rests." Keri reached for the man's arm nodding at Betty to do the same. Slowly they led him off to the kitchen.

When Steph followed Chris down the stairs, she noticed Hank was missing.

"Hank must've decided to make himself scarce." Chris winked at Steph.

"At least you were here to help me." Steph took Chris by the arm and they began to follow Betty and Keri. When they reached the main floor, they found Hank waiting for them.

"I was angry until I saw how shook up he was. Remind me not to make you mad." Grinning, Hank joined them as they made their way to the kitchen.

When Steph walked into the kitchen, she found Keri and Betty sitting at the table showing Wade the sketches Chris made.

He looked up slowly when they entered the kitchen. "I owe you an apology. I came here under a false impression. I heard you were looking for a way to make some easy money, willing to do anything and I tried to take advantage of that. The experience on the roof and the information I have learned from these ladies has taught me that I was totally wrong. I'll be glad to submit my report for your permits to be accepted for the remodeling of the building."

"Thank you, Mr. Law. I appreciate your honesty. I'm sorry I had to lock you outside, but you left me no choice." Steph still didn't trust the man, but he looked shaken from his experience. "When you were telling me someone approached you with plans for this place, who was it?"

Hank had been leaning against the counter eating a cookie, but he became alert when Steph asked her question.

"I don't remember his name. He came into the office a few weeks ago and has been back only a few times since. He wanted to know about the zoning and the permits needed. Said he'd make it worth my while to help him. I just assumed he was someone you knew."

"I don't know why anyone would want to put a development here. It's beautiful the way it is." Steph frowned thinking that it may have been Rodchester Wilgood. She looked at Hank. Now things were beginning to make more sense.

"Hank, I think we need to talk." Steph left the room and headed for the study. She didn't turn around expecting Hank to follow her.

When he was in the room she closed both doors then turned to face him. "I want to know what is going on. Has all this been happening so I would give up the farm? Just so Rodchester can develop the land?" Steph watched as Hank squirmed under her gaze.

Finally he sat down at the desk and looked at her. "It seems to be that way. The man we caught yesterday was a local man. He claimed to have been approached in a bar. Someone, who we have yet to identify, paid him to come out and walk around. He was supposed to look for poacher traps. The man thought he was protecting the wildlife."

Hank put his face in his hands. "We thought this was over. We have a picture of the man who has been harassing you. Unfortunately, the man we caught doesn't recognize him. They're making a composite of the man he met in the bar." Hank pulled his phone out of his pocket. "I'll call Austin and tell him about your Mr. Wade. Maybe he'll recognize one of them. Austin said he was coming out this way to check on a few things some time today."

Feeling as if Hank was still hiding something Steph stayed quiet while he called Deputy Austin. When Hank ended the call, Steph decided to try another way.

"I need to know for my own sanity what you're not telling me. Are you going to leave when this is all over?"

"Do you want me to leave?" Hank was surprised by Steph's question. He tried not to show his dismay as he searched her face for answers.

"No, I just want answers. I haven't told you, but I love you. I want to know if you love me."

Hank stood up and walked over to Steph. He kissed her gently and with love. Taking her chin into his hand, he looked into her eyes. "Yes, Steph, I love you, too. I don't deserve you, but I love you."

Exasperated Steph turned her face away. "You say you love me, but you're keeping things from me. I know there's something else you are not telling me. I want to know what's going on!"

Hank tried to keep his expression neutral as his mind raced for something to say. He didn't want to jeopardize Steph's trust, but he didn't want to worry her more.

Ding-Dong.

"That was fast." Relieved Hank walked over to open the door. Steph grabbed his arm. "Keri or Betty will get it. I want an answer."

"I can't tell you. Until we know more there is nothing to tell." Hank tried to keep his voice even. He didn't want to let his own frustration show.

There was a knock on the door. Keri walked in with Deputy Austin following her. "I know I'm interrupting something but Deputy Austin said Hank called him a few minutes ago. I thought it might be important."

"Yes, come on in deputy, I wasn't getting anywhere with Hank. You can have him." Steph stood and started to leave the room.

"Steph." Hank felt a stabbing pain in his heart knowing he hurt her.

"It's okay. You need to do what you have to do. I'll be back in a few minutes." Steph left to spend some time alone and calm down.

"Keri, would you bring Mr. Law in? Deputy Austin and I want to talk with him." Hank watched Keri leave on her errand.

Keri returned a few minutes later with a slightly revived Wade Law.

"Deputy Austin, Hank, this is Wade Law, Building Inspector." Keri had to swallow a chuckle when she saw the panic on Wade's face as he realized he was being left alone with the two men.

Hank closed the door. "Please have a seat Mr. Law. I hope you're better after your experience." He pointed to a wooden chair by the front of the desk.

Hank had told Austin about Steph locking the other man out on the widows walk. Keeping a straight face, Hank turned and winked at Austin. "I was telling the deputy about your devotion to your job and how you were even inspecting the roof for Miss Weatherby."

Deputy Austin cleared his throat. "Mr. Law, I understand someone has been in your office asking you about zoning and permits for this particular property." Deputy Austin moved over toward Wade holding the composite picture and the blown up copy of the picture of the man on the top of the ladder. "Was that person either one of these people?"

Wade Law looked up at Deputy Austin and then down at the two pictures.

"Take your time. This is important." Austin stood as still as possible waiting for the answer.

"It was this man." Wade pointed at the picture of the man on the ladder. "He came in a few times asking questions as if he owned the property. He said he was going to own it soon and wanted to know about renovations. He said the current resident was his relative and they didn't know the value of the place. He said it was rightfully his. I didn't do anything wrong. You can't arrest me for talking to someone in my office." Suddenly Wade began to turn pale. "Is this the farm I've been reading about in the paper? The place where they had the fire a few days ago? The paper said it was arson."

"Yes and I'm not going to arrest you unless you did something I should arrest you for. You're being helpful in a police investigation. Now, I have a few more questions and then we'll go down to the office so you can file a statement." Austin walked over to the desk and laid down the pictures. Turning around, he looked at Law. "Do you happen to know the name of the man?"

"I had him fill out a preliminary form. I have the information at the office." Law checked his watch. "I can go to the office and bring the information to you."

Austin glanced at Hank and nodded. Looking at the frightened man in front of him, Austin made a decision. "I'll tell you what. Why don't I take you to the office and then we'll go to the sheriff's department to file that statement. I've never been to your office and I'd like to see how you handle such an important job. Why don't we give Hank here the keys to your car and he'll bring it to the department for you?" Austin held out his hand waiting for the man's car key.

"Oh, I'll be glad to show you the office." Law took out his car keys and handed them to Austin. Turning to look at Hank, he watched as Austin handed the other man his keys. "Be careful with it please. It's a county car. I wouldn't need you to drive it but I understand I have to go with the deputy."

As the men walked down the hall, Steph walked up behind them. "Mr. Law, I wanted to thank you for coming out today. I know it hasn't turned out the way either one of us expected it to, but I hope this will not affect my getting the permits."

"Miss Weatherby, I have already signed the permits and they are on your kitchen table. I apologize for the bad impression I may have made."

Steph smiled down at the man. "Mr. Law, thank you for helping me."

Steph didn't know what else to say so she stepped back out of their way, a defeated look on her face.

"I'll be back later." Hank walked away leaving Steph standing by herself. It hurt but he had work to do. He knew it was up to him to protect her.

Steph followed them out and stood watching the men drive away. With a heavy heart she turned and walked back into the house. She wondered how much this day was going to change her life. She told Hank she loved him and learned that he loved her. She still didn't know if that was enough to keep him there, or if she wanted him there. She knew she was on the right path for her future but did that include Hank? If she was going to have to do this alone, then she knew she would.

Steph knew she had made a good beginning. Now she had to set the rest of her plans in motion. Going back into the house, Steph shoved Hank from her thoughts as she began thinking about her upcoming meeting with the bank loan officer. One way or another she had to succeed. Her own future, with or without Hank hung on the outcome of this meeting.

CHAPTER 39

"Thanks for coming over to help me. I've been making so many decisions I feel as if my head is going to bust. I've been trying to visualize how it will all look finished but I need someone else's opinion once in a while."

Steph was sitting with Jenny and Chris in the study where they could talk. The construction crew was hard at work in different areas of the house.

"How do you stand all the noise?" Jenny shouted to make herself heard over the noise from the floor above.

"You get used to it I guess. It's so loud all day that when they leave, it's almost too quiet. They've only been at it for a few months now but it seems like years." She glanced at her watch. "They'll be finishing up and leaving before long. You'll notice the quiet then too."

"How are Keri and Betty doing? I haven't seen them on line lately."

Steph smiled. "They're glad to be away from the noise. Keri's back to volunteering and Betty's working on some secret project. She said she's spending a lot of time at the library doing research. They keep busy but I do miss their company." Steph's sigh was drowned out by the noise coming from above.

Steph put a box on the desk and removed two carpet samples to show the others. "I have to choose a different color of carpet for the second floor hallway. I had planned the décor around the carpet I'd chosen but now it's out of stock. This is what I have selected but I also like this. My problem is I'm not sure about either one, my original choice would have been perfect."

Chris shrugged. "They look alike to me."

Steph shook her head. "That's what Hank said before he disappeared for the day. He can find more places to hide during the day. He appears at night like a spook. I think he's working on a project somewhere. He appears after the workers leave and doesn't say where he's been or what he's been doing. He just goes around locking up and then goes to his room until dinner. After that I don't see or hear anything until the next morning."

Jenny felt sorry for her friend. She sat and studied the carpet samples. She knew what Hank was doing, but she was sworn to secrecy. She hoped he would tell Steph soon. Keeping the secret wasn't easy for her. The man was working every odd job he could get and it was taking its toll on him. She pushed those thoughts away and looked at the samples Steph showed her. "I like this one the best."

Satisfied, Steph moved on to the next decision to be made. "I couldn't believe so many items I've ordered have been back ordered or are no longer available. The contractor said he'll give me a good deal for changing, but it was hard to make the decisions the first time. Now picking out something different seems to be harder."

As they chose bathroom faucets and more carpet, the house started getting quieter. When she knew the construction crew would be gone for the day, Steph decided to reward them with a tour. "Chris, I know you've been over during most of the major construction, but I'd like to show you some of the finished work. Your suggestion for the placement of this elevator was an inspiration. I can't imagine having it anywhere else." Steph led the way to the main elevator.

When the elevator doors opened on the basement floor, Jenny was impressed. The stainless steel counters gleamed and the floor was spotless.

Walking out of the elevator, Steph too was pleased with what she saw.

"We're waiting on a few more pieces of equipment but most of it's here now." She walked over to where her new bake oven stood.

"This just arrived today." She opened the doors and looked inside. "It bakes cookies, cakes and even pizzas."

"The radiant floor is wonderful in the mornings." Steph crossed the room to the new door where the boiler room used to be. "I want to show you my new laundry area."

Jenny and Chris looked inside while Steph walked around pointing as she talked. "I had these counters installed so it will be easier for folding the laundry in here. We have racks for hangers and these nice little carts to carry the laundry. The commercial washers and dryers will go along this wall. I have a regular washer and dryer over there for small loads and our clothes. I had to special order the commercial sets and needed something to use. I gave the old washer and dryer to the local animal shelter. I decided I should have everything new."

Steph laughed at her own extravagance. She walked over to the wall and opened a door in the wall near the floor. "Here's the laundry chute they installed." She closed the door and turned back to the others. "Of course it doesn't work from the top floor, but at least we won't need to bring the laundry carts up and down in the elevators."

Jenny's eyes twinkled with mischief. "I still think you should have used my idea and lined the crawl space by the fireplace to use for a laundry chute. That way you would have access from the top floor."

Chris shook his head, a patient look on his face. "As I've explained before, they would have to tear out part of the fireplace on the second floor and destroy that wonderful mantle. It would be criminal to destroy such craftsmanship."

"I know I was just teasing." Jenny grinned.

Steph sighed. "I can't believe everything is almost done down here. I'm glad we decided to start with this area first." Steph turned off the light and closed the door on the small room as she walked out.

Jenny spotted the old kitchen table and chairs in the corner. "Oh, you've kept the table." She ran her hand over the smooth wood of the table.

Steph walked over beside her. "I couldn't part with it. I may move it upstairs, but for now, we need a place to sit and eat. I'll need to figure something out about an area for the staff to take breaks too. Come and see my office." She led the way to the glass door that served as her office door. She sighed as she opened the door. "I just love it." The potbellied stove was scrubbed and cleaned; the metal glistened under the new fluorescent lighting. The wood paneling and ceiling gleamed. "I kept the old desk that was down here. I've ordered another desk and some office equipment. I plan to hire a manager once the B & B is up and running.

Jenny walked around looking at the room. When she was at the bottom of the spiral stairway, she sat down on the steps. "It's sure hard to remember how this room was before with its weak light. It's so warm and inviting. Do you think this is what they had in mind when they built this room?"

Steph shrugged. "I think they'll be happy to know its being used and appreciated. Oh, Jenny, you should have seen the look on Brian's face when he and Tad came out to check the pipes for the stove. He was surprised he missed the opening into the chimney. Of course Hank showed him the ladder beside the dining room chimney. Tad had to hold on to him to keep him from climbing up the ladder himself." Steph laughed.

"It's lovely. I know you'll enjoy using it." Jenny stood up. "How's it coming upstairs on the other floors?"

"I haven't been up there since this morning. They said they would have the bathrooms almost done today except for the faucets. Let's go look at the top floor. It still looks pretty rough, but each day they get more done."

Chris led the way to the elevator, holding it open for the ladies.

"Oh, my! I'd forgotten how big this is." Jenny's words echoed as she stepped out onto the third floor. She looked at the open beams and roughed in walls.

"Chris's design opened it up. I just love having the living area here and the kitchen over there. Let's go check out the master suite. They were installing the whirlpool tub and the separate stand up shower." Carefully stepping around discarded tools and lumber, Steph hurried forward to the area designated for the master bath.

"It's beautiful. I'm so jealous." Jenny leaned over the tub and looked up at the skylight overhead.

Steph moved around moving boards and checking on the changes being made.

"There's going to be a propane fireplace in the master bedroom and we'll keep the wood burning fireplace at the other end. We have four bedrooms and an office area marked out. There was so much room it's like having a house on the top of the house. We added insulation between the floors for a sound barrier between. " Steph walked over to the wall that faced the back of the house.

"Building up the walls to raise the roof on each side of the house was a great idea." She opened a set of doors that led to an outdoor patio. "I'm so glad we could build this patio out here. It'll be nice to have a place to sit outside and relax." Stepping back inside, Steph looked at Chris. "You're really talented. I'm so grateful you were able to design this for me." Steph fought back tears.

Chris was pleased with her praise but embarrassed at the same time. He looked away for a few minutes not wanting the women to see he was getting choked up. He cleared his voice before speaking. "I was worried it wouldn't work out. A lot of the credit goes to your contractor for knowing his job and following the plans. I see he took a few liberties of his own."

Steph laughed. "Yeah, he wanted to make a few minor changes, but he was delighted with the plans you drew up. Of course, he wasn't so happy in the beginning. I had to talk him into taking the job."

Jenny laughed too. "George was so frustrated when the man Stanley recommended told you it couldn't be done. He knew if Chris could draw it, someone could build it. It was just a matter of finding the right man.

"I love what they've done so far. I know you want to see how everything else is progressing so I'll let you look around on your own. I want to check out a few things."

Jenny ventured up into the cupola area. "Steph, you put a hot tub up here!"

Smiling, Steph joined Jenny. "Yeah, it was Hank's idea and I thought it would be fun. It makes it special. We've added recessed lights and tint on the windows. There are lights outside to show off the widow's walk. There's plenty of room for seating and I plan to put some live plants in here too."

Steph sat on the edge of the hot tub. "When you're ready, we can go down to the guest floor and look around."

"Ok, let's get Chris and go. I can't wait to see what's been done." Jenny headed down the stairway looking for Chris.

They took their time wandering around the guest floor. Steph too was curious about what had been done during the day.

When their curiosity was satisfied, they took the elevator down to the main level. Before the doors to the elevator opened, Misti, who was riding with them, began to growl.

When the doors opened, they saw a man standing in the doorway to the hall. Steph knew the workers were gone for the day but she assumed it might be one of the many salespeople who often stopped by to see the contractor. Dressed in boots, jeans and a brown jacket, he had a black baseball cap pulled low over his face.

Stepping out of the elevator, she began to walk toward the man. "I'm sorry sir but we're not open for business." Misti dashed past her, growling and barking at the man. Without thinking, Steph tried to pick up the angry little dog. It took her two attempts to pick the dog up.

"Call off the mutt or I'll quiet it for good." The man waved a gun at Steph. "You thought you'd stop me? I won't be stopped."

"I don't know what you're talking about. I don't know who you are and I don't appreciate you're bringing a gun into my house." Steph spoke in a loud voice. She hoped her friends hadn't followed her out of the elevator.

"You don't need to shout lady. No one can hear us. It's just you, the other woman and the cripple." He looked toward the elevator and spoke louder. "Come on out here slow and easy like. I'll shoot her if you don't."

Slowly, Chris and Jenny stepped from the elevator. Jenny said a prayer of thanks that she left the baby with George before coming over today.

"Put your hands up. All of you! I mean it." The man waved his gun to emphasize his point.

Steph was holding on tight to the struggling dog. "I can't raise my hands or she'll get loose."

"Put it down, I'll solve your problem lady. I'm here for the jewels. You owe me at least that much."

"What jewels?" Steph was thinking quickly. She'd put all of her own jewelry along with her mother's jewelry into a safe deposit box at the bank while the construction was going on. Then she remembered the jewelry found here in the house. Those pieces were in the bank vault also. The man who broke in and took Misti had known about the jewelry.

"Are you talking about the estate jewelry? It's not here. It's in the vault at the bank. How do you know about the jewelry we found?" Steph began to wonder if this was the burglar the police were looking for.

"Don't get smart with me, lady. I know you have a safe here and the jewelry's in the safe. I came through with the construction crew a couple of times and found the safe. It's locked and you're going to open it." Motioning with the gun, the man pointed the direction he wanted them to go.

* * *

When Hank came into the house he heard Misti growl and bark. He knew the construction workers all left at the same time every day and he made it a point to be home from work by then. He didn't recognize the voice of the man he heard talking. He knew Chris and Jenny were coming over to help Steph so he hadn't hurried home. Jenny's SUV was still outside. That meant some stranger was here with them and it was someone Misti didn't like.

Moving slowly and deliberately Hank backed away, trying to see though the doorway. Straining his ears to hear over the sound of his racing heart, he tried to listen to what was happening. What did he want? Why was he here? How could they get out safely? Steph and Jenny were young and in good shape. The problem was Chris couldn't move very fast. Hank listened long enough to learn the man was after something he thought to be in the safe.

476

Hank realized Chris had noticed he was there. He mimed for Chris to stall and hoped the other man understood. Moving as silently as possible, Hank rushed out.

As he ran down the back steps, Hank placed a call to Deputy Austin. When Austin answered the phone, Hank was racing through the kitchen trying not to bump into anything that would alert the intruder. He stammered out, "Man with gun in house" and disconnected hoping Austin would understand. Hank paused at the bottom of the spiral stairway. He had to go slowly and cautiously at this point to get up the stairs without revealing his presence. His plan was to be at the door when they opened the safe. He had no other weapon but the advantage of surprise.

*   *   *

Chris was wracking his brain trying to come up with an idea. He understood he needed to stall and give Hank enough time to get help. It was up to him now. With the cooler weather outside, Chris was feeling his age but he saw the murderous look in the man's eye and knew he had to do his part to protect the women. He knew they would not be allowed to live. If this was the man who took Misti, this man was dangerous and he had to play his part.

When the man told them to head for the study and the safe, Chris stayed back waiting on the girls to walk past him. He had been standing sideways to hide his efforts. Wiggling his leg, he tried to loosen his prosthetic. When he felt it start to give, he stepped forward and fell between the man and the girls.

When Chris fell, the man jumped back and yelled for Steph and Jenny to come and help him. Chris struggled for a few moments, trying to fix his leg before allowing Jenny to help him up.

Steph was trying hard to hold onto her enraged dog.

Once he was up, Chris had no other choice but to do as the man said and to move through the library toward the study. Chris felt light-headed from his fall and was hoping he'd given Hank enough time.

As they entered the study, Misti began to whine. Somehow Steph knew Hank was nearby. Holding onto the dog, Steph noticed Chris was watching the hidden door to the safe. Steph suddenly realized Hank was behind the door. She had to do something to help.

"May Chris sit down? He could hold Misti for me so I can open the safe." Steph watched as the man looked around the room and then motioned with his gun toward the wing-backed chair. "Have him sit there where I can keep an eye on him."

Chris sat down and when Steph bent over to give him Misti. She smiled and winked at him hoping he understood her signal. Standing back up, Steph slowly turned toward the man who was now standing with his back toward the hidden door.

Distract him. Distract him. Steph heard the words running circles in her mind as she tried to think of a way to distract him. Then she remembered the hidden panel in the fireplace.

Moving slowly toward it, she was almost there when the man realized she wasn't moving toward the safe.

"Where are you going? Get over here and open that safe. If you don't, I'm going to shoot that dog and then your friends. I should've killed that miserable mutt when I had the chance."

At the threatening tones in the man's voice, Misti starting fighting to get away from Chris. She thrashed and twisted. It took all of Chris's strength and attention to hold her. When she began to bite him, he had to grab her muzzle and hold it shut. He was talking to her in a quiet and soothing voice, but the dog was so focused on the man, she was not responding.

Jenny had been standing beside Chris and she found herself sitting on the arm of the chair shaking with fear. She reached out and tried to help Chris but Misti snarled and snapped at the air. Jenny watched in horror as the scene played out before her eyes.

Steph began to tremble with anger. *This should not be happening. This is the man who took Misti and tried to kill me!* Taking deep breaths and trying to keep her thoughts from showing on her face, she turned toward the mantle. Steph knew their only chance was on the other side of that door but he needed to be able to open the door.

Calm down Steph. Get a grip. You can do this. You can do this. Steph took a step forward and pointed at the fireplace.

"There's a secret lever here that opens the door there. I just have to push it." She opened the hidden doorway in the fireplace where she had left the tobacco pouches and pipes on the day it was discovered. "Oops. Wrong one." Trying to act surprised as if she didn't know the pouches were there, she reached in and pulled the cloth one out. Holding it up for the man to see, she went on. "Look. I found a jewelry pouch." Slowly she opened it to see what was inside. "Oh, it's just some tobacco see?" She showed the man and he moved closer to examine the find. As Steph reached into the hidden door to pull out another pouch, Hank slid the door to the safe's closet open.

Jenny saw Hank and started to squeal but Chris grabbed her arm to give her a shake and stop her. In doing so, he loosened his grip on Misti. Misti jumped from Chris's lap and ran for the man with the gun.

The man was watching Steph and didn't see Misti running toward him until she was almost on him. He turned to shoot her as she jumped against him.

Steph watched as the man tried to shoot her dog. Anger overcame caution. She searched for a weapon and found the fireplace poker. She swung it wildly at the man, causing him to move backward away from the angry woman, stumbling over the snapping dog.

Hank saw Misti get loose and he raced toward the man from behind as Steph swung the poker. Hank grabbed the man's arm trying to get the gun away. As Hank wrestled with the man for the gun, Misti was biting his legs. Suddenly both men went down, tripping over the dog. The gunman lost his grip and dropped the gun while trying to fight off both the man and the dog.

Steph stood watching not knowing what to do.

"The gun, get the gun." Chris was unable to get up with his loose prosthetic leg and with Jenny still sitting on the arm of the chair.

Looking around, Steph saw the gun lying on the floor beside the two struggling men. She kicked it aside toward Chris.

"Misti, Misti! Get back! Let Hank take care of him." Steph was trying to get her dog. She dropped the poker and grabbed the dog as it was biting both men on the floor. Misti stopped struggling when Steph picked her up and almost threw her at Chris and Jenny. "Here, hang on to her." Steph leaned over and picked up the gun. "I've got the gun and I'll shoot. Both of you stop! Do you hear me! That's enough!"

The men continued to struggle, one trying to knock the other out.

Bang!

The men stopped struggling, both of them stared at the angry woman holding the gun.

Steph stood with the gun now pointed at them. "I said that's enough!" Her anger was clear in her voice.

"Okay, I give up." The man leaned back on the floor and put his hands over his head in a sign of surrender.

Slowly Hank stood up and moved toward Steph to get the gun. Hank had to pry the gun from her grip while he kept his eyes focused on the man lying on the floor.

When Hank trusted his voice to work, he glanced over at Steph. "Are you okay?"

Steph was struggling between anger and relief. Steph looked over at Chris. "I think we're okay now."

"I can't believe you did that!" Jenny stared in horror at the scattered bits of glass from the broken window.

"I had to do something!" Steph glared at her friend.

"Can you get some rope or something to tie him up with until Austin and his troops decide to arrive?" Hank knew his voice sounded harsh, but he was tired and needed to sit down. He could feel the adrenaline rush draining away.

When Steph returned with a length of rope, she handed it to Hank and watched as he tied the man up.

Jenny and Chris had moved to the sofa in the library and were sitting together quietly talking. Misti was lying calmly between them.

Steph was about to join them when she heard the sound of a siren coming down her driveway. Going to the front door, she opened it in time to wave to the deputy getting out of the cruiser.

Steph didn't wait for the deputy but turned and started moving back into the house. She walked slowly down the hall as the deputy raced in. Motioning for the deputy to go on in ahead of her, she followed him hoping it had been a dream.

She stood at the doorway and watched them cut the rope then handcuff the man.

Hank waited for the deputy to take the bleeding man out to the cruiser before walking over to Steph. Reaching for her he pulled her close and kissed her.

"Don't mind us. We'll just be on our way." Jenny had recovered enough to realize she wanted to get home and hold her baby. Jenny motioned to Chris to get up so they could leave.

"Don't go too far just yet." Deputy Austin came into the room. "We're going to need some statements so we can put this guy away. I hope the little dog had its shots. It looks like it got a few good bites in. The man is bleeding in some pretty strange places." He looked over at Hank and winked, "unless it was Hank who did the biting."

Steph started laughing. The others joined in.

Hank gave Steph a squeeze before releasing her. "I don't think I'd have knocked him down if Misti wouldn't have started it. She was one mad little dog." Hank lifted up his own arm. "I think a couple of times she missed him and got me." He gave Steph a weak smile. "It's okay. Sometimes it's hard to tell the bad guys from the good guys. I've been through worse."

"So who broke the window? Is that how he came in?"

It was Hank's turn to laugh as Steph blushed. "No, it was Steph. She took his gun and shot out the window. I think she was trying to get our attention."

Glaring at him, Steph choked out "well, it worked!" before she joined the others in laughing.

Austin shook his head grinning. "Better be careful there Hank. Next time she might try aiming it at you."

CHAPTER 40

Hank reluctantly went with Deputy Austin to the Emergency Room. From there they went to the sheriff's office. It took most of the night to interrogate the man but Hank was satisfied with the results. The sheriff had a good solid case against him. He gave them the name of the man who hired him and why.

Hank returned to the house and slipped into his bed exhausted. He had one more thing he had to do tomorrow and then he would have to sit Steph down and talk to her.

It had begun to rain in the night and Hank woke up to a typically cold, wet winter day. He made his way downstairs and found Steph fixing breakfast in the new kitchen.

"Good morning. I heard you come in late and didn't want to disturb you. I was hoping you'd let me fix you breakfast this morning. Usually you're up and gone by the time I get downstairs."

Steph was trying her best not to bother Hank with any questions before he had breakfast. She had gone to a lot of trouble and knew he would just get up and walk out if she pressured him. That was a lesson she learned the day after Keri and Betty left. She had eaten breakfast alone since then.

Hank sat down at the table and allowed Steph to serve him. She sat down at the table across from him and patiently waited while they ate.

When he was finished, Hank stood and carried his dishes to the sink. "Thanks for breakfast. I enjoyed it." Reluctantly he returned and sat down trying to find the right words to use. "You'll be needed at the sheriff's office to file charges. They have a lead on the person behind all of this. They'll call once they've made the arrest."

"Will you be there too?" Once again Steph had the feeling Hank was getting ready to say good-bye. Love was tugging at her heart, telling her not to let him go.

"I'll be around. I want to talk with Austin." Hank swiftly rose and left the room, leaving a worried Steph in his wake.

*　　*　　*

It was still raining that afternoon when Steph arrived at the sheriff's office. The weather echoed her mood. Stepping cautiously inside, she remained by the door searching for a familiar face.

"Please come this way Miss Weatherby." Austin had been waiting for her to arrive.

"Hello, Deputy Austin." Steph tried to keep her voice steady. She was getting nervous about being in the office, knowing they had the suspect in custody.

Austin led her into an empty room and closed the door. "Please sit down. I know you're probably anxious to know about the case. We've arrested the man we believe to be responsible for all the trouble, a Mr. Rodchester Wilgood. We're still questioning him but the sheriff wanted you to know."

There was a commotion in the outer office. Steph followed Austin out to see what was happening. A woman with two children was talking with the dispatcher.

"I'm here to see my husband, Rodchester Wilgood. You've arrested him and I have the right to see him."

Austin stood by the doorway assessing the situation before going to the aid of the dispatcher. "Mrs. Wilgood, we're still questioning your husband. It will be some time before you can see him."

Steph watched as the woman deflated before her eyes.

Mrs. Wilgood looked at the floor. "What'll happen to us? Now that he's been arrested, what'll we do?" As she spoke, her voice became softer and softer.

Austin had to strain to hear what the woman was saying.

The dispatcher gave the woman a kind look. "Is there someone you can call?"

Mrs. Wilgood shook her head.

Austin looked at the dispatcher. "Let's settle them in the conference room while we wait for the sheriff to get back." He turned to the woman. "Come with me. We'll get you a cup of coffee and some hot chocolate for the kids. Miss Weatherby, I'll be back in a minute." Austin took the woman by the arm and led the way to the conference room.

After a few minutes he returned and motioned for Steph to join him in the room they had occupied a few minutes before.

"Please, Miss Weatherby, won't you sit down again. I'm sorry for the interruption. That was the family of the man we've arrested. We've gathered sufficient evidence to prove he was trying to scare you off the farm."

Steph stared out the office window at the conference room across the hall. She was having a hard time accepting that the wet mousey looking woman would have had anything to do with trying to harm her. As she watched, an officer walked by the window leading a medium height, overweight man in handcuffs. The man stopped when he saw the family through the large glass window of the conference room.

"Let me see them. That's my family! I have the right to see them!" The handcuffed man tried to pull away from the restraining arm of the deputy. "Let go. I haven't been charged yet. I have the right to see my family while I wait for my attorney. Let go!"

Reluctantly, the deputy opened the conference room door and let him in.

"So that's Rodchester Wilgood." Steph watched in horror as the man walked over and glared at his wife.

"Yes, that's him." Austin too had been watching.

Steph stood up. "I want to know why he's been doing this to me. I want to ask him myself." Not waiting for an answer, she left the room and walked into the conference room.

"What are you doing here? Why did you come? Take the brats and go back to the hotel. Did you call the attorney like I told you to?" Rodchester was shouting at his wife.

"That's enough!" Austin had followed Steph. "Everyone sit down." The authority in his tone had even Rodchester grudgingly move to sit down.

Austin nodded to the other deputy who moved to stand behind Rodchester before sitting down himself. "Miss Weatherby, this is Rodchester Wilgood, the man behind the damage to you and your farm."

"Her farm! It's my farm. My grandfather was cheated out of his inheritance and he left it to me to get it back." Rodchester's anger surged as he tried to stand. "You have no right to arrest me like this. You have no proof I did any of the things you say I did. Besides, she's the one who's squatting on my land. I demand you arrest her!"

"Sit down and be quiet!" The deputy pushed Rodchester back into his chair.

Austin glared at Rodchester before speaking to Steph. "As I was saying, we have sufficient evidence including a picture of him taken in your barn hanging a dead cat from your rafter."

"That was my cat. I killed it." The boy stood up with enough force to cause his chair to slam backward into the wall making a loud bang. "Pa said if I could catch it I could keep it but it scratched me, so I killed it."

Mrs. Wilgood had been startled by the boy's outburst but recovered enough to sit the chair back in place for the boy to sit down. "Sit." She turned pleading eyes toward Deputy Austin. "Please, he's not a bad boy he's just been misled to do bad things."

"We'll deal with him later." Austin stared at the boy making sure he returned to his seat.

Steph was horrified. "He hung a dead cat in the barn?"

"There were other things, but Hank felt it would upset you to know all that was going on. This man paid a man named Homer Brewster to scare you off. When Brewster got out of hand, he fired him and started doing the scaring himself." Austin paused for a moment.

"Out of hand?" Steph thought the lawn tractor was out of hand but the car bombing was deliberate intent to commit murder.

Rodchester leaned forward. He glanced at Austin before speaking. "I told him to scare you off so I could get the land. I had a plan. I'm willing to split the money. I got it all figured out."

"Quiet!" Austin had risen from his seat with his hand on his gun.

Obediently Rodchester leaned back and tried to look humbled. Austin waited a minute before continuing. "Rodchester states he told Brewster about the hidden jewels. It was Brewster who we arrested last night."

"Iris," Rodchester looked at Austin, who nodded slightly, before going on. "Iris told my granddad about the jewels her mother used to keep in the fireplace mantel. Iris said they were worth a fortune. I told Brewster if he stole them, he could have twenty five percent. She also said there was always cash somewhere in the study." Rodchester glared at Steph.

Steph looked from Rodchester to Austin who nodded before speaking. "That's who broke into your house that night. Brewster told us after he was arrested yesterday that he was attacked by Misti, 'the vicious little animal' as he put it. He said he went out the door and she chased him all the way to his car. He caught her, drugged her then kept her drugged, tying her out in the woods. We talked to the man's landlord. He makes surprise checks to be sure his tenants don't break his rule of no pets. He said there was an animal smell in one of the closets. He was keeping an eye out trying to catch him." Austin paused as he sat back down.

"Misti made it difficult for him. She put up a fight." Austin allowed himself to smile at the thought. Sobering up he went on. "It was Brewster who put up the cameras around the property and he recognized some Hank put up. Wilgood here didn't realize when he looked at the camera that it was a camera. It was a pretty good picture too. It helped us run him down."

"It was that small man of a building inspector who led you to us. I know it was." This time it was the woman who interrupted.

"Well, he gave us your name and local address, but it was the picture that proves he was responsible." Austin turned from Mrs. Wilgood back to Steph.

"We now know from Rodchester here that it was Brewster who put the bomb in Betty's car. He figured if someone died, you would no longer want to live there. When he found out it was you, he thought if you were dead then Wilgood would inherit. Everything would still be okay. He hadn't counted on your survival. He was watching and told us he used a remote control toy car to put the bomb on the first car going out that day. He told us how he used glue to fasten it to the car. When we caught Wilgood here, we learned he had fired Brewster after the bombing. He couldn't stomach being a part of that."

"Killing cats is one thing, killing people will get you jail time. I told him not to destroy any of the property and he goes and starts a fire. I saw that on the news too. He could have burned the whole place down. What good would that do me?"

"Shut up Wilgood." Deputy Austin nodded at the other deputy who put a restraining hand on Rodchester's shoulder.

"As I was saying, Brewster was acting as a free agent, trying to get the jewels. He said since Wilgood welched on his payment, someone had to pay for his expenses. He's being charged with attempted murder."

"That's right. That was all him. I had nothing to do with that. I just wanted you out of there. You don't want to live there. Let me have the place and I'll split the profits with you. Of course, I'll need the jewels to get some start up money, but we could make a nice bit of change on all of it." Rodchester tried to move toward Steph.

The deputy once again placed his hand on the man's shoulder. "Settle down!"

Steph stood up. "I've heard enough. I'm ready to talk with you privately Deputy Austin."

Austin opened the door for Steph to enter the small office one last time. Steph walked to the far wall and then turned slowly around. Spotting a chair near by, she sat down. Relief warred with anger causing her stomach to churn. Trying not to let her emotional turmoil show on her face, she looked at Austin who had taken a chair nearby.

"What happens now?"

"Well, we've arrested both men. They'll each get their day in court. Things should settle down at your place. At least you'll be safe now."

Steph tried to appear more cheerful. "Let's hope so." She felt let down and disappointed. Not knowing why, she looked once again across at the conference room. "What happens to his family?"

"We'll handle that. Social services will handle investigating the situation with the kids. It's not going to be easy, but I'd say she's better off without him. For the boy it could go either way. It's going to be up to the Judge." Austin stood up. "We'll let you know if there's anything more. I hated having you come in but Hank thought you'd want to see they'd been arrested for yourself."

Steph sighed and then stood up. "Yes, I do feel better knowing they're both behind bars. I just wish this was all over and I could put it behind me."

"For you it is. We'll finish the job here and see to it that they get the punishment they deserve." Austin opened the door. "Let me walk you out."

Steph looked around the office as they walked through to the front door. When they reached the outside she stopped and touched Austin on the arm. "Thanks for everything deputy. Please tell the sheriff that I appreciate all that you have done." She tried to stop the tears that threatened to fall. "I don't know what I would have done without you." Quickly she left, letting the rain mingle with the tears that fell down her cheeks.

*   *   *

"Well Misti, it looks like we're alone again. Hank will soon be leaving and George is mad at me right now. I didn't realize that I should have talked to him before hiring someone to install a fence around the property. He thinks I didn't have the right gates installed on purpose so he couldn't get his farm machinery into the fields. It was stupid of me to forget about that. I can't blame any of them, I'm not sure I'd want to be my friend right now."

Steph petted Misti who laid beside her on the loveseat in the Parlor. The only light in the room was from the fire in the fireplace.

"Daddy was right. Life can be sunny or stormy. It's been quite a storm that's blown through our lives. It brought rain, thunder and the way I feel, there must have been some hail mixed in." Steph sighed. "Daddy always said rain is not only good for plants. But it's good for people too because it clears the air and lets you see things for what they are. Rain can be a drizzle or it can become a major storm, upsetting lives and forcing changes. At the time we wonder, fuss and worry. Daddy would call this a large storm. Changes have been made in our lives Misti. Daddy always said that with the help of God, our family and our friends, we would always make it through the storm. Then we start again with the air cleared and the sun shining bright to show us the way. We weathered the storm when daddy died and then mother. Now we've just survived another one." Steph pulled the little dog to her in a hug.

"Hank was swept away from us in this storm. He'll be leaving soon and going back to the police force. I'm happy for him even though I'll miss him but he'll be doing what he loves. At least we have this place." Steph settled Misti beside her then stretched to turn on the lamp. Absently Steph stroked the dog as she looked around the room and rallied her spirits.

"This is going to be a wonderful Bed and Breakfast. You wait and see Misti. We've got a lot of work to do. The seeds we've planted have been watered by the rain. Now we need to watch them grow."

"I thought I'd find you in here. Mind if I join you?"

Hank didn't wait for an answer. He sat down on the other side of Misti and began petting her too. "Austin said I'd just missed you at the sheriff's office. He said they arrested Wilgood and you ran into him and his wife. He said Wilgood tried to persuade you to share this place with him."

Steph nodded as she continued to pet the quiet dog.

Hank had worried about Steph after Austin told him Steph left crying. At a loss for words, he remained quiet hoping she'd give him a clue as to how she felt.

Softly and quietly Steph began talking. "When I came here to live in this house I had no friends, I was a stranger in a strange town. I didn't know what I was going to do or how to proceed but I knew what I left behind me was not what I wanted. I was alone and miserable. Some of the people I had trusted had hurt me; I was anxious and insecure. I didn't know what to do but I had a place to go so I came. Then I met Stanley, Jenny, George and you. I've learned to trust people again. I've learned to fight for what's mine and to work hard to keep it."

Steph's voice grew stronger and clearer as she talked. "I never thought I'd have good friends I could trust other than Keri and Betty but I have Jenny now and George." She reached over Misti and put her hand on Hank's, her eyes seeking Hank's. "I have you too now. I've learned what I had before was not love. I was insecure and accepted something that was less than what I wanted. Now I know love works two ways. I can accept that." She released his hand and turned away.

"I want to thank you for everything you've done. You've saved my life and my soul." Steph fought the tears that threatened to choke her. She'd promised herself she would let Hank go if he wanted to leave. She loved him, but if he didn't love her enough to stay, she would try to understand.

Steph steeled herself to look at him as she finished speaking. "I couldn't have made it through this without you. You're a wonderful man and I just want you to know that I hope I'll always be your friend. I know you want to go back to Columbus and be a part of the police force. I won't stand in the way of your dreams."

Hank just sat beside her for a moment. Then he slipped down on one knee. From his pocket he removed a small box. "Steph, I can't offer you riches. I can't offer you the world. All I can offer is myself. I know I'm not much but I'll do my best to take care of you. If you'll have me, I'd like you to marry me and be my wife."

Hank slowly opened the box and showed her the ring he had bought for her.

Steph didn't know what to say. Frustrated she looked at him then stood up and started pacing. "I know you want to go back to being a police officer. If you stay, you'd be giving that up. Why would you want to tie yourself down like that?"

She walked back and looked down at him. "You've spent the last few months acting as if we were strangers living together. You'd come and go, barely speaking to me. I've spent hours wondering what I'd done to upset you. I finally decide you needed to be free, not tangled in a relationship. I've come to terms with letting you go. And what do you do? You go and do something like this!" Steph started pacing again.

Hank stood up and moved to stop her. Gently he drew her into his arms and looked deep into her eyes. "Believe it or not, I love you! I want to be with you. I want to grow old with you. I've been working any odd job I could get so I could buy you a ring to show you how much I love you. Look at me Steph. When you met me I was a broken man, both in body and in spirit."

Hank paused watching her face. "Loving you has given me the courage to begin the journey back. I'm closer to being the person I once was because of you. I'm stronger physically and mentally. I know with you beside me, I can do anything. Yes, I want to go back to being a police officer. I loved my job Steph. It's who I am, but I also love you. Think about all that we've been through together. We've already been through more in our short time together than most people go through in their lives. We can do anything together. I believe in you Steph. I need you to believe in me." Hank paused, waiting for her to absorb what he was saying. "Steph I love you. I can't live without you. Will you please marry me?"

Steph's throat was choked with tears. She had been prepared to live the rest of her life alone. She thought Hank was moving on and leaving her behind. He wanted to marry her. He wanted to be with her. She tried to smile, but tears began to fall. "Yes. Yes! I'll marry you! I love you too!" was all she could say. Tentatively at first, she drew him to her looking him deeply in his eyes. Seeing the love reflected there, her kisses said all that was in her heart.

ABOUT THE AUTHOR

KJ Ten Eyck was born and raised in Ohio and will always be a "Buckeye" at heart. She graduated from Ohio State University with a BS in Education. Growing up, she heard local stories about the Underground Railroad and was especially intrigued by stories of houses with secret passages and hidden rooms. She is currently residing in Texas with her husband and daughter, along with their multiple canine companions.

CPSIA information can be obtained
at www.ICGtesting.com
Printed in the USA
LVOW12s1040090517

533851LV00001B/74/P